Bound By His Vow

MELANIE MILBURNE
MICHELLE SMART
MAYA BLAKE

First Published in Great Britain 2016
By Mills & Boon, an imprint of HarperCollins*Publishers*
1 London Bridge Street, London, SE1 9GF

His Final Bargain, *The Rings That Bind* and *Marriage Made Of Secrets* were first published in Great Britain by Harlequin (UK) Limited.

ISBN: 978-0-263-92083-3

05-1016

Our policy is to use papers that are natural, renewable and recyclable products and made from wood grown in sustainable forests.The logging and manufacturing processes conform to the legal environmental regulations of the country of origin.

Printed and bound in Spain
by CPI, Barcelona

HIS FINAL BARGAIN

BY
MELANIE MILBURNE

From as soon as **Melanie Milburne** could pick up a pen she knew she wanted to write. It was when she picked up her first Mills & Boon at seventeen that she realised she wanted to write romance. After being distracted for a few years by meeting and marrying her own handsome hero, surgeon husband Steve, and having two boys, plus completing a Masters of Education and becoming a nationally ranked athlete (masters swimming), she decided to write. Five submissions later she sold her first book and is now a multi-published, bestselling and award-winning *USA TODAY* author. In 2008 she won the Australian Readers' Association most popular category/series romance, and in 2011 she won the prestigious Romance Writers of Australia R*BY award.

Melanie loves to hear from her readers via her website, www.melaniemilburne.com.au or on Facebook: www.facebook.com/pages/Melanie-Milburne/351594482609.

With special thanks to
Rose at The Royal Guide Dogs of Tasmania
for her time in helping me research this novel.
Also special thanks to Josie Caporetto and Serena Tatti
for their help with Italian phrases.
Thanks to you all!

CHAPTER ONE

IT WAS THE meeting Eliza had been anticipating with agonising dread for weeks. She took her place with the four other teachers in the staffroom and prepared herself for the announcement from the headmistress.

'We're closing.'

The words fell into the room like the drop of a guillotine. The silence that followed echoed with a collective sense of disappointment, despair and panic. Eliza thought of her little primary school pupils with their sad and neglected backgrounds so similar to her own. She had worked so hard to get them to where they were now. What would happen to them if their small community-based school was shut down? They already had so much going against them, coming from such underprivileged backgrounds. They would never survive in the overcrowded mainstream school system. They would slip between the cracks, just like their parents and grandparents had done.

Like she had almost done.

The heartbreaking cycle of poverty and neglect would continue. Their lives—those little lives that had so much potential—would be stymied, ruined, and possibly even destroyed by delinquency and crime.

'Is there nothing we can do to keep things going for

a little while at least?' Georgie Brant, the Year Three teacher asked. 'What about another bake sale or a fair?'

The headmistress, Marcia Gordon, shook her head sadly. 'I'm afraid no amount of cakes and cookies are going to keep us afloat at this stage. We need a large injection of funds and we need it before the end of term.'

'But that's only a week away!' Eliza said.

Marcia sighed. 'I know. I'm sorry but that's just the way it is. We've always tried to keep our overheads low, but with the economy the way it is just now it's made it so much harder. We have no other choice but to close before we amass any more debt.'

'What if some of us take a pay cut or even work without pay?' Eliza suggested. 'I could go without pay for a month or two.' Any longer than that and things would get pretty dire. But she couldn't bear to stand back and do nothing. Surely there was something they could do? Surely there was someone they could appeal to for help…a charity or a government grant.

Something—*anything.*

Before Eliza could form the words Georgie had leaned forward in her chair and spoke them for her. 'What if we appeal for public support? Remember all the attention we got when Lizzie was given that teaching award last year? Maybe we could do another press article showing what we offer here for disadvantaged kids. Maybe some filthy-rich philanthropist will step out of the woodwork and offer to keep us going.' She rolled her eyes and slumped back in her seat dejectedly. 'Of course, it would help if one of us actually knew someone filthy-rich.'

Eliza sat very still in her seat. The hairs on the back of her neck each stood up one by one and began tingling at the roots. A fine shiver moved over her skin like the rush of a cool breeze. Every time she thought of Leo Valente her body reacted as if he was in the room with her. Her heart picked up its pace as she brought those darkly handsome features to mind…

'Do *you* know anyone, Lizzie?' Georgie asked, turning towards her.

'Um…no,' Eliza said. 'I don't mix in those sorts of circles.' *Any more.*

Marcia clicked her pen on and off a couple of times, her expression thoughtful. 'I suppose it wouldn't hurt to try. I'll make a brief statement to the press. Even if we could stay open until Christmas it would be something.' She stood up and gathered her papers off the table. 'I'm sending the letter to the parents in tomorrow's post.' She sighed again. 'For those of you who believe in miracles, now is a good time to pray for one.'

Eliza saw the car as soon as she turned the corner into her street. It was prowling slowly like a black panther on the hunt, its halogen headlights beaming like searching eyes. It was too dark inside the car to see the driver in any detail, but she immediately sensed it was a man and that it was her he was looking for. A telltale shiver passed over her like the hand of a ghost as the driver expertly guided the showroom-perfect Mercedes into the only available car space outside her flat.

Her breath stalled in her throat as a tall, dark-haired, well dressed figure got out from behind the wheel. Her heart jolted against her ribcage and her pulse quickened. Seeing Leo Valente face to face for the first time in four years created a shockwave through her body that left her feeling disoriented and dizzy. Even her legs felt shaky as if the ground beneath her had suddenly turned to jelly.

Why was he here? What did he want? How had he found her?

She strove for a steady composure as he came to stand in front of her on the pavement, but inside her stomach was fluttering like a moth trapped in a jam jar. 'Leo,' she said, surprised her voice came out at all with her throat so tightly constricted with emotion.

He inclined his darkly handsome head in a formal greeting. 'Eliza.'

She quickly disguised a swallow. His voice, with its sexy Italian accent, had always made her go weak at the knees. His looks were just as lethally attractive—tall and lean and arrestingly handsome, with eyes so dark a brown they looked almost black. The landscape of his face hinted at a man who was used to getting his own way. It was there in the chiselled line of his jaw and the uncompromising set to his mouth. He looked a little older than when she had last seen him. His jet-black hair had a trace of silver at the temples, and there were fine lines grooved either side of his mouth and around his eyes, which somehow she didn't think smiling or laughter had caused.

'Hi…' she said and then wished she had gone for something a little more formal. It wasn't as if they had parted as friends—far from it.

'I would like to speak to you in private.' He nodded towards her ground-floor flat, the look in his eyes determined, intractable and diamond-hard. 'Shall we go inside?'

She took an uneven breath that rattled against her throat. 'Um…I'm kind of busy right now…'

His eyes hardened even further as if he knew it for the lie it was. 'I won't take any more than five or ten minutes of your time.'

Eliza endured the silent tug-of-war between his gaze and hers for as long as she could, but in the end she was the first to look away. 'All right.' She blew out a little gust of a breath. 'Five minutes.'

She was aware of him walking behind her up the cracked and uneven pathway to her front door. She tried not to fumble with her keys but the way they rattled and jingled in her fingers betrayed her nervousness lamentably. Finally she got the door open and stepped through, inwardly cringing when she thought of how humble her little flat was compared to his villa in Positano. She could only imagine what he was thinking: *How could she have settled for this instead of what I offered her?*

Eliza turned to face him as he came in. He had to stoop to enter, his broad shoulders almost spanning the narrow hallway. He glanced around with a critical eye. Was he wondering if the ceiling was going to come tumbling down on him? She watched as his top lip developed a slight curl as he turned back to face her. 'How long have you lived here?'

Pride brought her chin up half an inch. 'Four years.'

'You're renting?'

Eliza silently ground her teeth. Was he doing it deliberately? Reminding her of all she had thrown away by rejecting his proposal of marriage? He must know she could never afford to buy in this part of London. She couldn't afford to buy in *any* part of London. And now with her job hanging in the balance she might not even be able to afford to pay her rent. 'I'm saving up for a place of my own,' she said as she placed her bag on the little hall table.

'I might be able to help you with that.'

She searched his expression but it was hard to know what was going on behind the dark screen of his eyes.

She quickly moistened her lips, trying to act nonchalant in spite of that little butterfly in her stomach, which had suddenly developed razor blades for wings. 'I'm not sure what you're suggesting,' she said. 'But just for the record—thanks but no thanks.'

His eyes tussled with hers again. 'Is there somewhere we can talk other than out here in the hall?'

Eliza hesitated as she did a quick mental survey of her tiny sitting room. She had been sorting through a stack of magazines one of the local newsagents had given her for craftwork with her primary school class yesterday. Had she closed that gossip magazine she had been reading? Leo had been photographed at some charity function in Rome. The magazine was a couple of weeks old but it was the only time she had seen anything of him in the press. He had always fiercely guarded his private life. Seeing his photo so soon after the staff meeting had unsettled her deeply. She had stared and stared at his image, wondering if it was just a coincidence that he had appeared like that, seemingly from out of nowhere. 'Um…sure,' she said. 'Come this way.'

If Leo had made the hallway seem small, he made the sitting room look like something out of a Lilliputian house. She grimaced as his head bumped the cheap lantern light fitting. 'You'd better sit down,' she said, surreptitiously closing the magazine and putting it beneath the others in the stack. 'You have the sofa.'

'Where are you going to sit?' he asked with a crook of one dark brow.

'Um…I'll get a chair from the kitchen…'

'I'll get it,' he said. 'You take the sofa.'

Eliza would have argued over it except for the fact that her legs weren't feeling too stable right at that moment. She sat on the sofa and placed her hands flat on her thighs to stop them from trembling. He placed the chair in what little space was left in front of the sofa and sat down in a classically dominant pose with his hands resting casually on his widely set apart strongly muscled thighs.

She waited for him to speak. The silence seemed endless as he sat there quietly surveying her with that dark inscrutable gaze.

'You're not wearing a wedding ring,' he said.

'No…' She clasped her hands together in her lap, her cheeks feeling as if she had been sitting too close to a fire.

'But you're still engaged.'

Eliza sought the awkward bump of the solitaire diamond with her fingers. 'Yes…yes, I am…'

His eyes burned as they held hers, with resentment, with hatred. 'Rather a long betrothal, is it not?' he said. 'I'm surprised your fiancé is so patient.'

She thought of poor broken Ewan, strapped in that chair with his vacant stare, day after day, year after year, dependent on others for everything. Yes, patient was exactly what Ewan was now. 'He seems content with the arrangement as it stands,' she said.

A tiny muscle flickered beneath his skin in the lower quadrant of his jaw. 'And what about you?' he asked with a pointed look that seemed to burn right through to her backbone. 'Are *you* content?'

Eliza forced herself to hold his penetrating gaze. Would he be able to see how lonely and miserable she was? How *trapped* she was? 'I'm perfectly happy,' she said, keeping her expression under rigidly tight control.

'Does he live here with you?'

'No, he has his own place.'

'Then why don't you share it with him?'

Eliza shifted her gaze to look down at her clasped hands. She noticed she had blue poster paint under one of her fingernails and a smear of yellow on the back of one knuckle. She absently rubbed at the smear with the pad of her thumb. 'It's a bit far for me to travel each day to school,' she said. 'We spend the weekends together whenever we can.'

The silence was long and brooding—*angry.*

She looked up when she heard the rustle of his clothes as he got to his feet. He prowled about the room like a tiger shark in a goldfish bowl. His hands were tightly clenched, but every now and again he would open them and loosen his fingers before fisting them again.

He suddenly stopped pacing and nailed her with his hard, embittered gaze. 'Why?'

Eliza affected a coolly composed stance. 'Why… what?'

His eyes blazed with hatred. 'Why did you choose him over me?'

'I met him first and he loves me.' She had often wondered how different her life would have been if she hadn't met Ewan. Would it have been better or worse? It was hard to say. There had been so many good times before the accident.

His brows slammed together. 'You think I didn't?'

Eliza let out a little breath of scorn. 'You didn't love me, Leo. You were in love with the idea of settling down because you'd just lost your father. I was the first one who came along who fitted your checklist—young, biddable and beddable.'

'I could've given you anything money can buy,' he said through tight lips. 'And yet you choose to live like a pauper while tied to a man who doesn't even have the desire to live with you full-time. How do you know he's not cheating on you while you're here?'

'I can assure you he's not cheating on me,' Eliza said with sad irony. She knew exactly where Ewan was and who he was with twenty-four hours a day, seven days a week.

'Do you cheat on him?' he asked with a cynical look.

She pressed her lips together without answering.

His expression was dark with anger. 'Why didn't you tell me right from the start? You should have told me you were engaged the first time we met. Why wait until I proposed to you to tell me you were promised to another man?'

Eliza thought back to those three blissful weeks in Italy four years ago. It had been her first holiday since Ewan's accident eighteen months before. His mother Samantha had insisted she get away for a break.

Eliza had gone without her engagement ring; one of the claws had needed repairing so she had left it with the jeweller while she was away. For those few short weeks she had tried to be just like any other single girl, knowing that when she got back the prison doors would close on her for good.

Meeting Leo Valente had been so bittersweet. She had known all along their fling couldn't go anywhere, but she had lived each day as if it could and would. She had been swept up in the romantic excitement of it, pretending to herself that it wasn't doing anyone any harm if she had those few precious weeks pretending she was free. She had not intended to fall in love with him. But she had seriously underestimated Leo Valente. He wasn't just charming, but ruthlessly, stubbornly and irresistibly determined with it. She had found herself enraptured by his intellectually stimulating company and by his intensely passionate lovemaking.

As each day passed she had fallen more and more in love with him. The clock had been ticking on their time together but she hadn't been able to stop herself from seeing him. She had been like a starving person encountering their first feast. She had gobbled up every moment she could with him and to hell with the consequences.

'In hindsight I agree with you,' Eliza said. 'I probably should've said something. But I thought it was just a holiday fling. I didn't expect to ever see you again. I certainly didn't expect you to propose to me. We'd only known each other less than a month.'

His expression pulsed again with bitterness. 'Did you have a good laugh about it with your friends when you came home? Is that why you let me make a fool of myself, just so you could dine out on it ever since?'

Eliza got to her feet and wrapped her arms around her body as if she were cold, even though the flat was stuffy from being closed up all day. She went over to the window and looked at the solitary rose bush in the front garden. It had a single bloom on it but the rain and the wind had assaulted its velvet petals until only three were left clinging precariously to the craggy, thorny stem. 'I didn't tell anyone about it,' she said. 'When I came back home it felt like it had all been a dream.'

'Did you tell your fiancé about us?'

'No.'

'Why not?'

She grasped her elbows a bit tighter and turned to face him. 'He wouldn't have understood.'

'I bet he wouldn't.' He gave a little sound of disdain. 'His fiancée opens her legs for the first man she meets in a bar while on holiday. Yes, I would imagine he would find that rather hard to understand.'

Eliza gave him a glacial look. 'I think it might be time for you to leave. Your five minutes is up.'

He closed the distance between them in one stride. He towered over her, making her breath stall again in her chest. She saw his nostrils flare as if he was taking in her scent. She could smell his: a complex mix of wood and citrus and spice that tantalised her senses and stirred up a host of memories she had tried for so long to suppress. She felt her blood start to thunder through the network of her veins. She felt her skin tighten and tingle with awareness. She felt her insides coil and flex with a powerful stirring of lust. Her body recognised the intimate chemistry of his. It was as if she was finely tuned to his radar. No other man made her so aware of her body, so acutely aware of her primal reaction to him.

'I have another proposal for you,' he said.

Eliza swallowed tightly and hoped he hadn't seen it. 'Not marriage, I hope.'

He laughed but it wasn't a nice sound. 'Not marriage, no,' he said. 'A business proposal—a very lucrative one.'

Eliza tried to read his expression. There was something in his dark brown eyes that was slightly menacing. Her heart beat a little bit faster as fear climbed up her spine with icy-cold fingers. 'I don't want or need your money,' she said with a flash of stubborn pride.

His top lip gave a sardonic curl. 'Perhaps not, but your cash-strapped community school does.'

She desperately tried to conceal her shock. How on earth did he know? The press article hadn't even gone to press. The journalist and photographer had only just left the school a couple of hours ago. How had he found out about it so quickly? Had he done his *own* research? What else had he uncovered about her? She gave him a wary look. 'What are you offering?'

'Five hundred thousand pounds.'

Her eyes widened. 'On what condition?'

His eyes glinted dangerously. 'On the condition you spend the next month with me in Italy.'

Eliza felt her heart drop like an anchor. She moistened her lips, struggling to maintain her outwardly calm composure when everything inside her was in a frenzied turmoil. 'In…in what capacity?'

'I need a nanny.'

A pain sliced through the middle of her heart like the slash of a scimitar. 'You're…*married?*'

His eyes remained cold and hard, his mouth a grim flat line. 'Widowed,' he said. 'I have a daughter. She's three.'

Eliza mentally did the sums. He must have met his wife not long after she left Italy. For some reason that hurt much more than if his marriage had been a more recent thing. He had moved on with his life so quickly. No long, lonely months of pining for her, of not eating and not sleeping. No. He had forgotten all about her, while she had never forgotten him, not even for a day. But there had been nothing in the press about him marrying or even about his wife dying. Who was she? What had happened to her? Should she ask?

Eliza glanced at his left hand. 'You're not wearing a wedding ring.'

'No.'

'What…um—happened?'

His eyes continued to brutalise hers with their dark brooding intensity. 'To my wife?'

Eliza nodded. She felt sick with anguish hearing him

say those words. *My wife.* Those words had been meant for *her*, not someone else. She couldn't bear to think of him with someone else, making love with someone else, *loving* someone else. She had taught herself *not* to think about it. It was too painful to imagine the life she might have had with him if things had been different.

If she had been free…

'Giulia killed herself.' He said the words without any trace of emotion. He might have been reading the evening news, so indifferent was his tone. And yet something about his expression—that flicker of pain that came and went in his eyes—hinted that his wife's death had been a shattering blow to him.

'I'm very sorry,' Eliza said. 'How devastating that must have been…must still be…'

'It has been very difficult for my daughter,' he said. 'She doesn't understand why her mother is no longer around.'

Eliza understood all too well the utter despair little children felt when a parent died or deserted them. She had been just seven years old when her mother had left her with distant relatives to go on a drugs and drinking binge that had ended in her death. But it had been months and months before her great-aunt had told her that her mother wasn't coming back to collect her. She hadn't even been taken to the graveside to say a proper goodbye. 'Have you explained to your daughter that her mother has passed away?' she asked.

'Alessandra is only three years old.'

'That doesn't mean she won't be able to understand what's happened,' she said. 'It's important to be truthful with her, not harshly or insensitively, but compassionately. Little children understand much more than we give them credit for.'

He moved to the other side of the room, standing with his back to her as he looked at the street outside. It seemed a long time before he spoke. 'Alessandra is not like other little children.'

Eliza moistened her parchment-dry lips. 'Look—I'm not sure if I'm the right person to help you. I work full-time as a primary school teacher. I have commitments and responsibilities to see to. I can't just up and leave the country for four weeks.'

He turned back around and pinned her with his gaze. 'Without my help you won't even have a job. Your school is about to be shut down.'

She frowned at him. 'How do you know that? How can you possibly know that? There's been nothing in the press so far.'

'I have my contacts.'

He had definitely done his research, Eliza thought. Who had he been talking to? She knew he was a powerful man, but it made her uneasy to think he had found out so much about her situation. What else had he found out?

'The summer holidays begin this weekend,' he said. 'You have six weeks to do what you like.'

'I've made other plans for the holidays. I don't want to change them at the last minute.'

He hooked one dark brow upwards. 'Not even for half a million pounds?'

Eliza pictured the money, great big piles of it. More money than she had ever seen. Money that would give her little primary school children the educational boost they so desperately needed to get out of the cycle of poverty they had been born into. But a month was a long time to spend with a man who was little more than a stranger to her now. What did he want from her? What would he want her to do? Was this some sort of payback or revenge attempt? How could she know what was behind his offer? He said he wanted a nanny, but what if he wanted more?

What if he wanted *her*?

'Why me?'

His inscrutable eyes gave nothing away. 'You have the qualifications I require for the post.'

It was Eliza's turn to arch an eyebrow. 'I just bet I do. Young and female with a pulse, correct?'

A glint of something dark and mocking entered his gaze as it held hers. 'You misunderstand me, Eliza. I am not offering you a rerun at being my mistress. You will be employed as my daughter's nanny. That is all that will be required of you.'

Why was she feeling as if he had just insulted her? What right did she have to bristle at his words? He needed a nanny. He didn't want her in any other capacity.

He didn't want her.

The realisation pained Eliza much more than she wanted it to. What foolish part of her had clung to the idea that even after all this time he would come back for her because he had never found anyone who filled the gaping hole she had left in his life? 'I can assure you that if you were offering me anything else I wouldn't accept it,' she said with a little hitch of her chin.

His gaze held hers in an assessing manner. It was unnerving to be subjected to such an intensely probing look, especially as she wasn't entirely confident she was keeping her reaction to him concealed. 'I wonder if that is strictly true,' he mused. 'Clearly your fiancé isn't satisfying you. You still have that hungry look about you.'

'You're mistaken,' she said with prickly defensiveness. 'You're seeing what you want to see, not what is.' *You're seeing what I'm trying so hard to hide!*

His dark brown eyes continued to impale hers. 'Will you accept the post?'

Eliza caught at her lower lip for a brief moment. She had at her fingertips the way to keep the school open. All of her children could continue with their education. The parenting and counselling programme for single mums she had dreamt of offering could very well become a reality if there were more funds available—a programme that might have saved her mother if it had been available at the time.

'Will another five hundred thousand pounds in cash help you come to a decision a little sooner?'

Eliza gaped at him. Was he really offering her a million pounds in cash? Did people *do* that? Were there really people out there who *could* do that?

She had grown up with next to nothing, shunted from place to place while her mother continued on a wretched cycle of drug and alcohol abuse that was her way of self-medicating far deeper emotional issues that had their origin in childhood. Eliza wasn't used to having enough money for the necessities, let alone the luxuries. As a child she had dreamt of having enough money to get her mother the help she so desperately needed, but there hadn't been enough for food and rent at times, let alone therapy.

She knew she came from a very different background from Leo, but he had never flaunted his wealth in the past. She had thought him surprisingly modest about it considering he was a self-made man. Thirty years ago his father had lost everything in a business deal gone sour. Leo had worked long and hard to rebuild the family engineering company from scratch. And he had done it and done it well. The Valente Engineering Company was responsible for some of the biggest projects across the globe. She had admired him for turning things around. So many people would have given up or adopted a victim mentality but he had not.

But for all the wealth Leo Valente had, it certainly hadn't bought him happiness. Eliza could see the lines of strain on his face and the shadows in his eyes that hadn't been there four years ago. She sent her tongue out over her lips again. 'Cash?'

He gave a businesslike nod. 'Cash. But only if you sign up right here and now.'

She frowned. 'You want me to sign something?'

He took out a folded sheet of paper from the inside of his jacket without once breaking his gaze lock with hers. 'A confidentiality agreement. No press interviews before, during or once your appointment is over.'

Eliza took the document and glanced over it. It was reasonably straightforward. She was forbidden to speak to the press, otherwise she would have to repay the amount he was giving her with twenty per cent interest. She looked up at him again. 'You certainly put a very high price on your privacy.'

'I have seen lives and reputations destroyed by idle speculation in the press,' he said. 'I will not tolerate any scurrilous rumour mongering. If you don't think you can abide by the rules set out in that document, then I will leave now and let you get on with your life. There will be no need for any further contact between us.'

Eliza couldn't help wondering why he wanted contact with her now. Why her? He could afford to employ the most highly qualified nanny in the world.

They hadn't parted on the best of terms. Every time she thought of that final scene between them she felt sick to her stomach. He had been livid to find out she was already engaged to another man. His anger had been palpable. She had felt bruised by it even though he had only touched her with his gaze. Oh, those hard, bitter eyes! How they had stabbed and burned her with their hatred and loathing. He hadn't even given her time to explain. He had stormed out of the restaurant and out of her life. He had cut all contact with her.

She could so easily have defended herself back then and in the weeks and months and years since. At any one point she could have called him and told him. She could have explained it all, but guilt had kept her silent.

It still kept her silent.

Dare she go with him? For a million pounds how could she not? Strictly speaking, the money wasn't for her. That made it more palatable, or at least slightly. She would be doing it for the children and their poor disadvantaged mothers. It was only for a month. That wasn't a long time by anyone's standards. It would be over in a flash. Besides, England's summer was turning out to be a non-event. A month's break looking after a little girl in sun-drenched Positano would be a piece of cake.

How hard could it be?

Eliza straightened her spine and looked him in the eye as she held out her hand. 'Do you have a pen?'

CHAPTER TWO

LEO WATCHED AS Eliza scratched her signature across the paper. She had a neat hand, loopy and very feminine. He had loved those soft little hands on his body. His flesh had sung with delight every time she had touched him…

He jerked his thoughts back like a rider tugging the reins on a bolting horse. He would *not* allow himself to think of her that way. He needed a nanny. This was strictly a business arrangement. There was nothing else he wanted from her.

Four years on he was still furious with her for what she had done. He was even more furious with himself for falling for her when she had only been using him. How had he been so beguiled by her? She had reeled him in like a dumb fish on a line. She had dangled the bait and he had gobbled it up without thinking of what he was doing. He had acted like a lovesick swain by proposing to her so quickly. He had offered her the world—his world, the one he had worked such back-breaking hours to make up from scratch.

She had captivated him from the moment she had taken the seat beside him in the bar where he had been sitting brooding into his drink on the night of his father's funeral. There was a restless sort of energy about her that he had recognised and responded to instantly.

He had felt his body start to sizzle as soon as her arm brushed against his. She had been upfront and brazen with him, but in an edgy, exhilarating way. Their first night together had been monumentally explosive. He had never felt such a maelstrom of lust. He had been totally consumed by it. He had taken what he could with her, how he could, relishing that she seemed to want to do the same. He had loved that about her, that her need for him was as lusty and racy as his for her.

Their one-night stand had morphed into a passionate three-week affair that had him issuing a romantic proposal because he couldn't bear the thought of never seeing her again. But all that time she had been harbouring a secret—she was already engaged to a man back home in England.

Leo looked at her left hand. Her engagement ring glinted at him, taunting him like an evil eye.

Anger was like a red mist in front of him. He had been nothing more to her than a holiday fling, a diversion—a shallow little hook-up to laugh about with her friends once she got home.

He *hated* her for it.

He hated her for how his life had turned out since.

The life he'd planned for himself had been derailed by her betrayal. It had had a domino effect on every part of his life since. If it hadn't been for her perfidy he would not have met poor, sad, lonely Giulia. The guilt he felt about Giulia's death was like a clamp around his heart. He had been the wrong person for her. She had been the wrong person for him. But in their mutual despair over being let down by the ones they had loved, they had formed a wretched sort of alliance that was always going to end in tragedy. From the first moment Giulia had set eyes on their dark-haired baby girl she had rejected her. She had seemed repulsed by her own child. The doctors talked about post-natal depression and other failure to bond issues, given that the baby had been premature and had special needs, but deep inside Leo already knew what the problem had been.

Giulia hadn't wanted *his* child; she had wanted her ex's.

He had been a very poor substitute husband for her, but he was determined to be the best possible father he could be to his little daughter.

Bringing Eliza back into his life to help with Alessandra would be a way of putting things in order once and for all. Revenge was an ugly word. He didn't want to think along those lines. This was more of a way of drawing a line under that part of his life.

This time *he* would be in the driving seat. Once the month was up she could pack her bags and leave. It was a business arrangement, just like any other.

No feelings were involved.

Eliza handed him back his pen. 'I can't start until school finishes at the end of the week.'

Leo pocketed the pen, trying to ignore the warmth it had taken from her fingers. Trying to ignore the hot wave of lust that rumbled beneath his skin like a wild beast waking up after a long hibernation.

He *had* to ignore it.

He *would* ignore it.

'I understand that,' he said. 'I will send a car to take you to the airport on Friday. The flight has already been booked.'

Her blue-green eyes widened in surprise or affront, he couldn't be quite sure which. 'You're very certain of yourself, aren't you?'

'I'm used to getting what I want. I don't allow minor obstacles to get in my way.'

Her chin came up a notch and her eyes took on a glittering, challenging sheen. 'I don't think I've ever been described as a "minor obstacle" before. What if I turn out to be a much bigger challenge than you bargained for?'

Leo had already factored in the danger element. It was dangerous to have her back in his life. He knew that. But in a perverse sort of way he *wanted* that. He was sick of his pallid life. She represented all that he had lost—the colour, the vibrancy and the passion.

The energy.

He could feel it now, zinging along his veins like an electric pulse. *She* did that to him. She made him feel alive again. She had done that to him four years ago. He was aware of her in a way he had never felt with any other woman. She spoke to him on a visceral level. He felt the communication in his flesh, in *every* pore of his skin. He could feel it now, how his body stood to attention when she was near: the blood pulsing through his veins, the urgent need already thickening beneath his clothes.

Did she feel the same need too?

She was acting all cool and composed on the surface, but now and again he caught her tugging at her lower lip with her teeth and her gaze would fall away from his. Was she remembering how wanton she had been in his arms? How he had made her scream and thrash about as she came time and time again? His flesh tingled at the memory of her hot little body clutching at him so tightly. He had felt every rippling contraction of her orgasms. Was that how she responded to her fiancé? His gut roiled at the thought of her with that nameless, faceless man she had chosen over him. 'I think it's pretty safe to say I can handle whatever you dish up,' he said. 'I'm used to women like you. I know the games you like to play.'

The defiant gleam in her eyes made them seem more green than blue. 'If you find my company so distasteful then why are you employing me to look after your daughter?'

'You have a good reputation with handling small children,' Leo said. 'I was sitting in an airport gate lounge about a year ago when I happened to read an article in one of the papers about the work you do with unprivileged children. You were given an award for teaching excellence. I recognised your name. I thought there couldn't be two Eliza Lincolns working as primary school teachers in London. I assumed—quite rightly as it turns out—that it was you.'

Her look was more guarded now than defiant. 'I still don't understand why you want me to work for you, especially considering how things ended between us.'

'Alessandra's usual nanny has a family emergency to attend to,' he said. 'It's left me in a bit of a fix. I only need someone for the summer break. Kathleen will return at the end of August. You'll be back well in time for the resumption of school.'

'That still doesn't answer my question as to why me.'

Leo had only recently come to realise he was never going to be satisfied until he had drawn a line under his relationship with her. She'd had all the power the last time. This time he would take control and he would not relinquish it until he was satisfied that he could live the rest of his life without flinching whenever he thought of her. He didn't want another disastrous relationship—like the one he'd had with Giulia—because of the baggage he was carrying around. He wanted his life in order and the only way to do that was to deal with the past and put it to rest—*permanently.* 'At least I know what I'm getting with you,' he said. 'There will be no nasty surprises, *sì*?'

She arched a neatly groomed eyebrow. 'The devil you know?'

'Indeed.'

She hugged her arms around her body once more, her eyes moving out of the range of his. 'What are the arrangements as to my accommodation?'

'You will stay with us at my villa in Positano. I have a couple of developments I'm working on which may involve a trip abroad, either back here to London or Paris.'

Her gaze flicked back to his. 'Where is your daughter now? Is she here in London with you?'

Leo shook his head. 'No, she's with a fill-in girl from an agency. I'm keen to get back to make sure she's all right. She gets anxious around people she doesn't know.' He handed her his business card. 'Here are my contact details. I'll send a driver to collect you from the airport in Naples. I'll send half of the cash with an armoured guard in the next twenty-four hours. The rest I will deposit in your bank account if you give me your details.'

A little frown puckered her forehead. 'I don't think it's a good idea to bring that amount of money here. I'd rather you gave it straight to the school's bursar to deposit safely. I'll give you his contact details.'

'As you wish.' He pushed his sleeve back to check his watch. 'I have to go. I have one last meeting in the city before I fly back tonight. I'll see you when you get to my villa on Friday.'

She followed him to the door. 'What's your daughter's favourite colour?'

Leo's hand froze on the doorknob. He slowly turned and looked at her with a frown pulling at his brow. 'Why do you ask?'

'I thought I'd make her a toy. I knit them for the kids at school. They appreciate it being made for them specially. I make them in their favourite colour. Would she like a puppy or a teddy or a rabbit, do you think?'

Leo thought of his little daughter in her nursery at home, surrounded by hundreds of toys of every shape and size and colour. 'You choose.' He blew out a breath he hadn't realised he'd been holding. 'She's not fussy.'

Eliza watched as he strode back down the pathway to his car. He didn't look back at her before he drove off. It was as if he had dismissed her as soon as he walked out of her flat.

She looked at his business card in her hand. He had changed it since she had been with him four years ago. It was smoother, harder, more sophisticated.

Just like the man himself.

Why did he want her back in his life, even for a short time? It seemed a strange sort of request to ask an ex-lover to play nanny to his child by another woman. Was he doing it as an act of revenge? He couldn't possibly know how deeply painful she would find it.

She hadn't told him she loved him in the past. She had told him very little about herself. Their passionate time together had left little room for heart to heart outpourings. She had preferred it that way. The physicality of their relationship had been so different from anything else she had experienced before. Not that her experience was all that extensive given that she had been with Ewan since she was sixteen. She hadn't known any different until Leo had opened up a sensual paradise to her. He had made her body hum and tingle for hours. He had been able to do it just by looking at her.

He could still do it.

She took an unsteady breath as she thought about that dark gaze holding hers so forcefully. Had he seen how much he still affected her? He hadn't touched her. She had carefully avoided his fingers when he had handed her the paper and the pen and his card. But she had felt the warmth of where his fingers had been and her body had remembered every pulse-racing touch, as if he had flicked a switch to replay each and every erotic encounter in her brain. He had been a demanding lover, right from the word go, but then, so had she.

She had met him the evening of the day he had buried his father. He had been sitting in the bar of her hotel in Rome, taking an extraordinarily long time to drink a couple of fingers of whisky. She had been sitting in one of the leather chairs further back in the room, taking much less time working her way through a frightfully expensive cocktail she had ordered on impulse. She had felt in a reckless mood. It was her first night of freedom in so long. She was in a foreign country where no one knew who she was. That glimpse of freedom had been as heady and intoxicating as the drink she had bought. She had never in her life approached a man in a bar.

But that night was different.

Eliza had felt inexplicably drawn to him, like an iron filing being pulled into a powerful magnet's range. He fascinated her. Why was he sitting alone? Why was he taking forever to have one drink? He didn't look the type to be sitting by himself. He was far too good-looking for that. He was too well dressed. She wasn't one for being able to pick designer-wear off pat, but she was pretty sure his dark suit hadn't come off any department store rack in a marked down sale.

Eliza had walked over to him and slipped onto the bar stool right next to him. The skin of her bare arm had brushed against the fine cotton of his designer shirt. She could still remember the way her body had jolted as if she had touched a live source of power.

He had turned his head and locked gazes with her. It had sent another jolt through her body as that dark gaze meshed with hers. She had brazenly looked at his mouth, noting the sculptured definition of his top lip and the fuller, sinfully sensual contour of his lower one. He'd had a day's worth of stubble on his jaw. It had given him an aggressively masculine look that had made her blood simmer in her veins. She had looked down at his hand resting on the bar next to hers. His was so tanned and sprinkled with coarse masculine hair, the span of his fingers broad—man's hands, capable hands—clever hands. Her hand was so light and creamy, and her fingers so slim and feminine and small in comparison.

To this day she couldn't remember whose hand had touched whose first…

Thinking about that night in his hotel room still gave her shivers of delight. Her body had responded to his like bone-dry tinder did to a naked flame. She had erupted in his arms time and time again. It had been the most exciting, thrilling night of her life. She hadn't wanted it to end. She had thought that would be it—her first and only one-night stand. It would be something she would file away and occasionally revisit in her mind once she got back to her ordinary life. She had thought she would never see him again but she hadn't factored in his charm and determination. One night had turned into a three-week affair that had left her senses spinning and reeling. She knew it had been wrong not to tell him her tragic circumstances, but as each day passed it became harder and harder to say anything. She hadn't wanted to risk what little time she had left with him. So she had pushed it from her mind. Her life back in England was someone else's life. Another girl was engaged to poor broken Ewan—it wasn't her.

The day before she was meant to leave, Leo had taken her to a fabulous restaurant they had eaten in previously. He had booked a private room and had dozens of red roses delivered. Candles lit the room from every corner. Champagne was waiting in a beribboned silver ice bucket. A romantic ballad was playing in the background…

Eliza hastily backtracked out of her time travel. She hated thinking about that night; how she had foolishly deluded herself into thinking he'd been simply giving her a grand send-off to remember him by. Of course he had been doing no such thing. Halfway through the delicious meal he had presented her with a priceless-looking diamond. She had sat there staring at it for a long speechless moment.

And then she had looked into his eyes and said no.

'Have you heard the exciting news?' Georgie said as soon as Eliza got to school the following day. 'We're not closing. A rich benefactor has been found at the last minute. Can you believe it?'

Eliza put her bag in the drawer of her desk in the staffroom. 'That's wonderful.'

'You don't sound very surprised.'

'I am,' Eliza said, painting on a smile. 'I'm delighted. It's a miracle. It truly is.'

Georgie perched on the edge of the desk and swung her legs back and forth as if she was one of the seven-year-olds she taught. 'Marcia can't or won't say who it is. She said the donation was made anonymously. But who on earth hands over a million pounds like loose change?'

'Someone who has a lot of money, obviously.'

'Or an agenda.' Georgie tapped against her lips with a fingertip. 'I wonder who he is. It's got to be a he, hasn't it?'

'There are female billionaires in the world, you know.'

Georgie stopped swinging her legs and gave Eliza a pointed look. 'Do *you* know who it is?'

Eliza had spent most of her childhood masking her feelings. It was a skill she was rather grateful for now. 'How could I if the donation was made anonymously?'

'I guess you're right.' Georgie slipped off the desk as the bell rang. 'Are you heading down to Suffolk for the summer break?'

'Um…not this time. I've made other plans.'

Georgie's brows lifted. 'Where are you going?'

'Abroad.'

'Can you narrow that down a bit?'

'Italy.'

'Alone?'

'Yes and no,' Eliza said. 'It's kind of a busman's holiday. I'm filling in for a nanny who needs to take some leave.'

'It'll be good for you,' Georgie said. 'And it's not as if Ewan will mind either way, is it?'

'No…' Eliza let out a heavy sigh. 'He won't mind at all.'

CHAPTER THREE

WHEN ELIZA LANDED in Naples on Friday it wasn't a uniformed driver waiting to collect her but Leo himself. He greeted her formally as if she were indeed a newly hired nanny and not the woman he had once planned to spend the rest of his life with.

'How was your flight?' he asked as he picked up her suitcase.

'Fine, thank you.' She glanced around him. 'Is your daughter not with you?'

His expression became even more shuttered. 'She doesn't enjoy car travel. I thought it best to leave her with the agency girl. She'll be in bed by the time we get home. You can meet her properly tomorrow.'

Eliza followed him to where his car was parked. The warm air outside was like being enveloped in a thick, hot blanket. It had been dismally cold and rainy in London when she left, which had made her feel a little better about leaving, but not much.

She had phoned Ewan's mother about her change of plans. Samantha had been bitterly disappointed at first. She always looked forward to Eliza's visits. Eliza was aware of how Samantha looked upon her as a surrogate child now that Ewan was no longer able to fulfil her dreams as her son. But then, their relationship had always been friendly and companionable. She had found in Samantha Brockman the model of the mother she had always dreamed of having—someone who loved unconditionally, who wanted only the best for her child no matter how much it cost her, emotionally, physically or financially.

That was what had made it so terribly hard when she had decided to end things with Ewan. She knew it would be the end of any further contact with Samantha. She could hardly expect a mother to choose friendship over blood.

But then fate had made the choice for both of them.

Samantha still didn't know Eliza had broken her engagement to her son the night of his accident. How could she tell her that it was *her* fault Ewan had left her flat in such a state? The police said it was 'driver distraction' that caused the accident. The guilt Eliza felt was an ever-present weight inside her chest. Every time she thought of Ewan's shattered body and mind she felt her lungs constrict, as if the space for them was slowly but surely being minimised. Every time she saw Samantha she felt like a traitor, a fraud, a Judas.

She was responsible for the devastation of Ewan's life.

Eliza twirled the ring on her hand. It was too loose for her now. It had been Samantha's engagement ring, given to her by Ewan's father, Geoff, who had died when Ewan was only five. Samantha had devoted her life to bringing up their son. She had never remarried; she had never even dated anyone else. She had once told Eliza that her few short happy years with Geoff were worth spending the rest of her life alone for. Eliza admired her loyalty and devotion. Few people experienced a love so strong it carried them throughout their entire life.

The traffic was congested getting out of Naples. It seemed as if no one knew the rules, or if they did they were blatantly ignoring them to get where they wanted to go. Tourist buses, taxis, cyclists and people on whining scooters all jostled for position with the occasional death-defying pedestrian thrown into the mix.

Eliza gasped as a scooter cut in on a taxi right in front of them. 'That was ridiculously close!'

Leo gave an indifferent shrug and neatly manoeuvred the car into another lane. 'You get used to it after a while. The tourist season is a little crazy. It's a lot quieter in the off season.'

A long silence ticked past.

'Is your mother still alive?' Eliza asked.

'Yes.'

'Do you ever see her?'

'Not often.'

'So you're not close to her?'

'No.'

There was a wealth of information in that one clipped word, Eliza thought. But then he wasn't the sort of man who got close to anyone. Even when she had met him four years ago he hadn't revealed much about himself. He had told her his parents had divorced when he was a young child and that his mother lived in the US. She hadn't been able to draw him out on the dynamics of his relationship with either parent. He had seemed to her to be a very self-sufficient man who didn't need or want anyone's approval. She had been drawn to that facet of his personality. She had craved acceptance and approval all of her life.

Eliza knew the parent-child relationship was not always rosy. She wasn't exactly the poster girl for happy familial relations. She had made the mistake of tracking down her father a few years ago. Her search had led her to a maximum-security prison. Ron Grady—thank God her mother had never married him—had not been at all interested in her as a daughter, or even as a person. What he had been interested in was turning her into a drug courier. She had walked out and never gone back. 'I'm sorry,' she said. 'It's very painful when you can't relate to a parent.'

'I have no interest in relating to her. She left me when I was barely more than a toddler to run off with her new lover. What sort of mother does that to a little child?'

Troubled mothers, wounded mothers, abused mothers, drug-addicted mothers, under-mothered mothers, Eliza thought sadly. Her own mother had been one of them. She had met them all at one time or the other. She taught their children. She loved their children because they weren't always capable of loving them themselves. 'I don't think it's ever easy being a mother. I think it's harder for some women than others.'

'What about you?' He flicked a quick glance her way. 'Do you plan to have children with your fiancé?'

Eliza looked down at her hands. The diamond of her engagement ring glinted at her in silent conspiracy. 'Ewan is unable to have children.'

The silence hummed for a long moment. She felt it pushing against her ears like two hard hands.

'That must be very hard for someone like you,' he said. 'You obviously love children.'

'I do, but it's not meant to be.'

'What about IVF?'

'It's not an option.'

'Why are you still tied to him if he can't give you what you want?'

'There's such a thing as commitment.' She clenched her hands so hard the diamond of her ring bit into the flesh of her finger. 'I can't just walk away because things aren't going according to plan. Life doesn't always go according to plan. You have to learn to make the best of things—to cope.'

He glanced at her again. 'It seems to me you're not coping as well as you'd like.'

'What makes you say that? You don't know me. We're practically strangers.'

'I know you're not in love.'

Eliza threw him a defensive look. 'Were you in love with your wife?'

A knot of tension pulsed near the corner of his mouth and she couldn't help noticing his hands had tightened slightly on the steering wheel. 'No. But then, she wasn't in love with me, either.'

'Then why did you get married?'

'Giulia got pregnant.'

'That was very noble of you,' Eliza said. 'Not many men show up at the altar because of an unplanned pregnancy these days.'

His knuckles whitened and then darkened as if he was forcing himself to relax his grip on the steering wheel. 'I've always used protection but it failed on the one occasion we slept together. I assumed it was an accident but later she told me she'd done it deliberately. I did the right thing by her and gave her and our daughter my name.'

'It must have made for a tricky relationship.'

He gave her a brief hard glance. 'I love my daughter.

I'm not happy that I was tricked into fatherhood but that doesn't make me love her any less.'

'I wasn't suggesting—'

'I had decided to marry Giulia even if Alessandra wasn't mine.'

'But why?' she asked. 'You said you weren't in love with her.'

'We were both at a crossroads. The man she had expected to marry had jilted her.' His lip curled without humour. 'You could say we had significant common ground.'

Eliza frowned at his little dig at her. 'So it was a pity pick-up for both of you?'

His eyes met hers in a flinty little lock before he returned to concentrating on the traffic. 'Marriage can work just as well, if not better, when love isn't part of the arrangement. And it might have worked for us except Giulia struggled with her mood once Alessandra was born. It was a difficult delivery. She didn't bond with the baby.'

Eliza had met a number of mothers who had struggled with bonding with their babies. The pressure on young mothers to be automatically brilliant at mothering was particularly distressing for those who didn't feel that surge of maternal warmth right at the start. 'I'm very sorry… It must have been very difficult for you, trying to support her through that.'

Lines of bitterness were etched around his mouth. 'Yes. It was.'

He didn't speak much after that. Eliza sat back and looked at the spectacular scenery as they drove along the Amalfi coast towards Positano. But her mind kept going back to his loveless marriage, the reasons for it, the difficulties during it and the tragic way it had ended.

He was left with a small child to rear on his own. Would he look for another wife to help him raise his little girl? Would it be another loveless arrangement or would he seek a more fulfilling relationship this time? She wondered what sort of woman he would settle for. With the sort of wealth he had he could have anyone he wanted. But somehow she couldn't see him settling for looks alone. He would want someone on the same wavelength as him, someone who understood him on a much deeper and meaningful level. He was a complex man who had a lot more going on under the surface than he let on. She had caught a glimpse of that brooding complexity in that bar in Rome four years ago. That dark shuttered gaze, the proud and aloof bearing, and the mantle of loneliness that he took great pains to keep hidden.

Was that why she had connected with him so instantly? They were both lonely souls disappointed by experiences in childhood, doing their best to conceal their innermost pain, reluctant to show any sign of vulnerability in case someone exploited them.

Eliza hadn't realised she had drifted off to sleep until the car came to a stop. She blinked her eyes open and sat up straighter in her seat. The car was in the forecourt of a huge, brightly lit villa that was perched on the edge of a precipitous cliff that overlooked the ocean. 'This isn't the same place you had before,' she said. 'It's much bigger. It must be three times the size.'

Leo opened her door for her. 'I felt like I needed a change.'

She wondered if there had been too many memories of their time together in his old place. They had made love in just about every room and even in the swimming pool. Had he found it impossible to live there once she had left? She had often thought of his quaint little sun-drenched villa tucked into the hillside, how secluded it had been, how they had been mostly left alone, apart from a housekeeper who had come in once a week.

A place this size would need an army of servants to keep it running smoothly. As they walked to the front door Eliza caught a glimpse of a huge swimming pool surrounded by lush gardens out the back. Scarlet bougainvillea clung to the stone wall that created a secluded corner from the sea breeze and the scent of lemon blossom and sun-warmed rosemary was sharp in the air. Tubs of colourful flowers dotted the cobblestone courtyard and a wrought iron trellis of wisteria created a scented canopy that led to a massive marble fountain.

A housekeeper opened the front door even before they got there and greeted them in Italian. 'Signor Valente, *signorina*, *benvenuto*—'

'English please, Marella,' Leo said. 'Miss Lincoln doesn't speak Italian.'

'Actually, I know a little,' Eliza said. 'I had a little boy in my class a couple of years ago who was Italian. I got to know his mother quite well and we gave each other language lessons.'

'I would prefer you to speak English with my daughter,' he said. 'It will help her become more fluent. Marella will show you to your room. I will see you later at dinner.'

Eliza frowned as he strode across the foyer to the grand staircase that swept up in two arms to the floors above. He had dismissed her again as if she was an encumbrance that had been thrust upon him.

'He is under a lot of strain,' Marella said, shaking her head in a despairing manner. 'Working too hard, worrying about the *bambina*; he never stops. His wife…'

She threw her hands in the air. 'Don't get me started about that one. I should not speak ill of the dead, no?'

'It must have been a very difficult time,' Eliza said.

'That child needs a mother,' Marella said. 'But Signor Valente will never marry again, not after the last time.'

'I'm sure if he finds the right person he would be—'

Marella shook her head again. 'What is that saying? Once bitten, twice shy? And who would take on his little girl? Too much trouble for most women.'

'I'm sure Alessandra is a delightful child who just needs some time to adjust to the loss of her mother,' Eliza said. 'It's a huge blow for a young child, but I'm sure with careful handling she'll come through it.'

'Poor little *bambina*.' Marella's eyes watered and she lifted a corner of her apron to wipe at them. 'Come, I will show you to your room. Giuseppe will bring up your bag.'

As Eliza followed the housekeeper upstairs she noticed all the priceless works of art on the walls and in the main gallery on the second level. The amount of wealth it took to have such masters in one's collection was astonishing. And not just paintings—there were marble statues and other objets d'art placed on each landing of the four-storey villa. Plush Persian rugs lay over the polished marble floors and sunlight streamed in long columns from the windows on every landing. It was a rich man's paradise and yet it didn't feel anything like a home.

'Your suite is this one,' Marella said. 'Would you like me to unpack for you?'

'No, thank you, I'll be fine.'

'I'll leave you to settle in,' Marella said. 'Dinner will be at eight-thirty.'

'Where does Alessandra sleep?' Eliza asked.

Marella pointed down the corridor. 'In the nursery; it's the second door from the bathroom on this level. She will be asleep now, otherwise I would take you to her. The agency girl will be on duty until tomorrow so you can relax until then.'

'Wouldn't it be better for me to move into the room closest to the nursery once the agency girl leaves?' Eliza asked.

'Signor Valente told me to put you in this room,' Marella said. 'But I will go and ask him, *sì*?'

'No, don't worry about it right now. I'll talk to him later. I suppose I can't move in while the other girl is there anyway.'

'*Sì, signorina.*'

Eliza stepped inside the beautifully appointed room once the housekeeper had left, the thick rug almost swallowing her feet as she moved across the floor. Crystal chandeliers dangled from the impossibly high ceiling and there were matching sconces on the walls. The suite was painted in a delicate shade of duck egg blue with a gold trim. The furniture was antique; some pieces looked as if they were older than the villa itself. The huge bed with its rich velvet bedhead was made up in snowy white linen with a collection of blue and gold cushions against the pillows in the same shade as the walls. Dark blue velvet curtains were draped either side of the large windows, which overlooked the gardens and the lemon and olive groves in the distance.

Once Eliza had showered and changed she still had half an hour to spare before dinner. She made her way along the wide corridor to the nursery Marella had pointed out. She thought it was probably polite to at least meet the girl from the agency so she could become familiar with Alessandra's routine. But when she got to the door of the nursery it was ajar, although she could hear a shower running in the main bathroom on the other side of the corridor. She considered waiting for the girl to return but curiosity got the better of her. She found herself drawn towards the cot that was against the wall in the nursery.

Eliza looked down at the sleeping child, a dark-haired angel with alabaster skin, her tiny starfish hands splayed either side of her head as she slept. Sooty-black eyelashes fanned her little cheeks, her rosebud mouth slightly open as her breath came in and then out. She looked small for her age, petite, almost fragile. Eliza reached over the side of the cot and gently brushed a dark curl back off the tiny forehead, a tight fist of maternal longing clutching at her insides.

This could have been our child.

The thought of never having a child of her own was something that grieved and haunted her. All of her life she had craved a family of her own. Becoming engaged to Ewan when she was only nineteen had been part of her plan to create a solid family base. She hadn't wanted to wait until she was older. She had planned to get married and have children while she was young, to build the secure base she had missed out on.

But life had a habit of messing with one's carefully laid out plans.

There was a part cry, part murmur from the cot. '*Mamma?*'

Eliza felt a hand grasp at her heart at that plaintive sound. 'It's all right, Alessandra,' she said as she stroked the little girl's silky head again. 'Shh, now, go back to sleep.'

The child's little hand found hers and she curled her

fingers around two of hers although she didn't appear to be fully awake. Her eyes were still closed, those thick lashes resting against her pale cheeks like miniature fans. After a while her breathing evened out and her little body relaxed on a sigh that tugged again at Eliza's heartstrings.

She looked at the tiny fingers that were clinging to hers. How tragic that one so young had lost her mother. Who would she turn to as she grew through her childhood into her teens and then as a young woman—nannies and carers and a host of lovers that came and went in Leo's life? What sort of upbringing would that be? Eliza knew what it was like to be handed back and forth like a parcel nobody wanted. All her life she had tried to heal the wound the death of her mother had left. Of feeling that it was *her* fault her mother had died. Would it be the same for little Alessandra? Feeling guilty that she was somehow the cause of her mother giving up on life? Of constantly seeking to fill the aching void in her soul?

There was a sound from the door and Eliza turned and saw Leo standing there watching her with an unreadable expression on his face. 'Where's Laura, the agency girl?' he asked.

'I think she's having a shower. I was just going past and I—'

'You're not on duty until the morning.'

Eliza didn't care for being reprimanded for doing something that came as naturally to her as breathing. Sleeping children needed checking on. Distressed children needed comforting. She raised her chin at him. 'Your daughter seemed restless. She called out to her mother. I comforted her back to sleep.'

Something moved through his eyes, a rapid flash of

pain that was painful to witness. 'Marella is waiting to dish up dinner.' He held open the door for her in a pointed fashion. 'I'll see you downstairs.'

'She looks like you.' The words were out before Eliza could stop them.

It was a moment or two before he spoke. 'Yes…' His expression remained inscrutable but she sensed an inner tension that he seemed at great pains to keep hidden.

She swallowed against the tide of regret that rose in her throat. If things had been different they would both be leaning over that cot as the proud, devoted parents of that gorgeous little girl. They might have even had another baby on the way by now. The family she had longed for, the family she had dreamed about for most of her life could have been hers but for that one fateful night that had changed the entire course of her life.

'*Mamma*?'

Eliza swung her gaze to the cot where Alessandra had now pulled herself upright, her little dimpled hands clinging to the rail. She rubbed at one of her eyes with a little fisted hand. 'I want *Mamma*,' she whimpered as her chin started to wobble.

Eliza went over to the cot and picked up the little toddler and cuddled her close. 'I'm not your mummy but I've come to take care of you for a little while,' she said as she stroked the child's back in a soothing and rhythmic manner.

Alessandra tried to wriggle away. 'I want Kathleen.'

'Kathleen had to go and see her family,' Eliza said, rocking her gently from side to side. 'She'll be back before you know it.'

'Where's *Papà*?' Alessandra asked.

'I'm here, *mia piccolo*.' Leo's voice was gentle as he placed his hand on his daughter's raven-black head.

The base of Eliza's spine quivered at his closeness. She could smell his citrus-based aftershave; she could even smell the fabric softener that clung to the fibres of his shirt. Her senses were instantly on high alert. Her left shoulder was within touching distance of his chest. She could feel the solid wall of him just behind her. She was so tempted to lean against the shelter of his body. It had been so long since she had felt someone put their arms around her and hold her close.

'I wetted the bed,' Alessandra said sheepishly.

Eliza could feel the dampness against her arm where the little tot's bottom was resting. She glanced up at Leo, who gave her a don't-blame-me look. 'She refuses to wear a nappy to bed,' he said.

'I'm too big for nappies,' Alessandra announced with a cute little pout of her rosebud mouth, although her deep-set eyes were still half closed. 'I'm a big girl now.'

'I'm sure you are,' Eliza said. 'But even big girls need a bit of help now and again, especially at night. Maybe you could wear pull-ups for a while. They're much more grown-up. I've seen some really cool ones with little pink kittens on them. I can get some for you if you like.'

Alessandra plugged a thumb in her mouth by way of answer. It seemed this was one little Munchkin who was rather practised in getting her own way.

'Let's get you changed, shall we?' Eliza said as she carried the little girl to the changing table in the corner of the nursery. 'Do you want the pink pyjamas or the blue ones?'

'I don't know my colours,' Alessandra said from around her thumb.

'Well, maybe I can teach you while I'm here,' Eliza said.

'You'd be wasting your time,' Leo said.

Eliza glanced at him with a reproving frown. Little children should not be exposed to negative messages about their capacity to learn. It could set up a lifelong pattern of failure. 'Pardon?' she said.

'My daughter will never learn her colours.'

'That's ridiculous,' she said. 'Why ever not?'

He gave her a grim look. 'Because she is blind.'

CHAPTER FOUR

ELIZA BLINKED AT him in shock.

Blind?

Her heart clanged against her ribcage like a pendulum struck by a sledgehammer.

Alessandra was blind?

Her emotions went into a downward spiral. How cruel! How impossibly cruel that this little child was not only motherless but blind as well. It was so tragic, so unbearable to think that Leo's little girl couldn't see the world around her, not even the faces of the people she loved.

How devastating for him as a father. How gut-wrenching to think of all the obstacles that little mite would face over her lifetime. All the things she would miss out on or not be able to enjoy as others enjoyed them. The beauty of the world she would never see. It was so sad, so tragic it made Eliza's heart ache for Leo. It made her ache for the little toddler who lived in a world of blackness. 'I'm sorry…I didn't realise…'

'Will you tell me a story?' Alessandra piped up from the changing table.

'Of course,' Eliza said. 'But after that you have to go back to sleep.' Oh, dear God, how did the little babe even know it was night? Anguish squeezed the breath out of her chest. She felt as if she was being suffocated by it. How had Leo coped with such a tragic blow? Was that why his wife had ended her life? Had it been too much for her to cope with a child who was blind?

The agency girl, Laura, came in at that point. 'Oh, sorry,' she said. 'Is she awake? I thought she'd settled for the night.'

'My daughter's bed needs changing,' Leo said curtly.

'I'll see to it,' Laura said and rushed over to the cot.

Eliza had finished the business end of things with Alessandra and gathered her up in her arms again. 'I have just the story for you,' she said and carried her back to the freshly made up cot. 'Do you like dogs?'

'Yes, but Papà won't let me have a puppy,' Alessandra said in a baleful tone. 'He said I have to wait until I'm older. I don't want to wait until I'm older. I want one now.'

'I'm sure he knows what's best for you,' Eliza said. 'Now, let's get you settled in bed before I start my story.'

'Where's Kathleen?' Alessandra asked. 'Why isn't she here? I want Kathleen. I want her now!' Those little heels began to drum against the mattress of the cot.

'I told you she had a family emergency to see to,' Leo said.

'But I want her here with me!' Alessandra said, starting to wail again.

Eliza could see that Alessandra was a very bright child who was used to pushing against the boundaries. It was common after the death of a parent for the remaining parent or other carers to overcompensate for their loss. It was just as common for a child with a disability to be treated the same way. The little girl was used to being the centre of attention and used every opportunity she could to grasp at power.

'Kathleen is going to be away for the next month,' she said. 'But I think it might be nice if Papà gets her to call you on the phone while she's away.'

'Does she miss me?'

'I'm sure she does,' Eliza said. 'Now, let's get those feet of yours still and relaxed, otherwise my story won't come out to play.'

'How long are you staying?' Alessandra asked.

Eliza glanced at Leo but his expression was as blank as a mask. 'Let's not worry about that just now,' she said. 'The important thing is that you get back to sleep. Now, let's see how this goes. Once upon a time there was a little dog who loved to chase…'

'Asleep?' Leo asked as Eliza joined him downstairs a few minutes later.

'Yes.' She came over to where he was standing and looked up at him with a frown. 'Why on earth didn't you tell me?'

'I did tell you.'

'I meant right from the start.'

'Touché and all that.' He gave an indifferent shrug of one broad shoulder before he took a sip from the drink he was holding.

Eliza gave him a cross look. 'You should've told me at the beginning.'

'Would it have influenced your decision in taking up the post?'

'No, but I would've liked to know what I'm dealing with. I could've prepared myself better.' *I could have got all this confusing emotion out of the way so I could think straight.*

'Yes, well, life doesn't always give one the chance to prepare for what it has in store.'

Tell me about it, Eliza thought. 'She's a lovely child but clearly a little headstrong.'

His look was brittle. 'Are you saying I'm a bad parent?'

'Of course not,' she said. 'It's very clear you love her as any good parent should. It's just that it seems she's in control of everyone who has anything to do with her. That's very stressful for young children. She needs to know who is in charge. It's especially important for a child with special needs. How long has she—?'

'She's been blind from birth.'

Eliza felt her heart tighten all over again. It was a cramped ache deep in her chest. 'That must have been a huge blow to you and your wife.' How she hated having to say those words—*your wife.*

'It was. Giulia never quite got her head around it. She blamed herself.'

'It seems to me every mother blames herself no matter what the circumstances.'

'Perhaps, but in Giulia's case it was particularly difficult. She thought she was being punished for setting me up.'

'Did *you* blame her?' Eliza asked.

His brows came together over his dark eyes. 'Of course not. It was no one's fault. Alessandra was premature. She has retrolental hyperplasia. It was previously thought to be caused by an excess of oxygen in perinatal care but there's divided opinion between specialists on that now. It's also called ROP. Retinopathy of Prematurity.'

'Can nothing be done?' Eliza asked. 'There are advances happening in medicine all the time. Surely there's something that can be done for her?'

'There is nothing anyone can do. Alessandra can

only distinguish light from dark. She is legally and permanently blind.'

Eliza could hear the pain in his voice but it was even more notable in his expression. No wonder those grey hairs had formed at his temples, and no wonder his eyes and mouth were etched with those lines. What parent could receive such news about their child without it tearing them apart both physically and emotionally?

'I'm so very sorry. I can't imagine how tough this has been for you and will no doubt continue to be.'

'I want the best for my daughter.' His expression was taut with determination. 'There is nothing I won't do to make sure she has a happy and fulfilled life.'

Eliza wasn't quite sure what role she was meant to play in order to give Alessandra the best possible chance in life. The child had suffered enough disruption already without a fly-in, fly-out nanny to confuse her further. What Alessandra needed was a predictable and secure routine. She needed stability and a nurturing environment.

She needed her mother.

The aching sadness of it struck Eliza anew. How devastating for a little toddler to have lost the most important person in her life. How terrifying it must be for little Alessandra when she woke during the night and wanted the comfort of her mother's arms, only to find a series of paid nannies to see to her needs. No wonder she was difficult. Even a sighted child would be hard to manage after suffering the loss of her mother.

'What do you hope to gain for her from my period as her nanny?' she asked.

'You're an excellent teacher. You understand small children.'

'I've never worked with a vision impaired child before, only a profoundly deaf one,' Eliza said.

'I'm sure you'll find a way to make the most of your time with her,' he said. 'After all, I'm paying you top dollar.'

She frowned. 'It's not about the money.'

A dark brow arched over his left eye. 'No?'

'Of course not.' She pulled at her lip momentarily with her teeth. 'Don't get me wrong—I'm happy about your donation to the school, but I'm not in this for what I can get for myself. I'm not that sort of person.'

'Is your fiancé rich?'

Eliza felt the searing penetration of his cynical gaze. The insurance payout from the accident, along with the modest trust fund his late father had bequeathed Ewan had provided a reasonably secure income for the rest of his life. Without it, he and his mother, who was his chief carer, would have really struggled. 'He has enough to provide for his…I mean our future.'

'What does he do for a living?' Leo asked.

She looked at him numbly. What could she say? Should she tell him about Ewan's accident? Would it make a difference to how he thought of her? Explaining the accident would mean revealing her part in it. She could still see Ewan's face, the shock in his eyes and the pain of rejection in every plane and contour of his face. He had looked as if she had dealt him a physical blow. Even his colour had faded to a chalk-white pallor. For so long since she had wondered if she could have prepared him better for her decision to end things. It must have come as such a dreadful shock to him for her to announce it so seemingly out of the blue. She had been struggling with their relationship for months but hadn't said anything. But over that time she had found it harder and harder to envisage a future with him. Her love for him had been more like one would have for a friend rather than a life partner. Sex had become a bit of a chore for her. But she had felt so torn because he and his mother were the only family she had known after a lifetime of foster home placements.

And he had loved her.

That had always been the hardest thing to get her head around when it came to her final decision to end things. Ewan had loved her from the first moment he had helped her pick up the books she had dropped on her first day of term in sixth form after she had been placed with yet another foster family. She'd been the new kid in town and he had taken her under his wing and helped her to fit in. Being loved by someone had been a new experience for her. Up until that point she had always felt out of place, a burden that people put up with because it was the right thing to do for a kid in need. Being loved by Ewan had made her feel better about herself, more worthy, beautiful even.

But she hadn't loved him the same way he loved her.

'He has his own business,' she finally said, which was in a way not quite a lie. 'Investments, shares, that sort of thing.'

Marella came in just then, which shifted the conversation in another direction once they had taken their places at the table.

Eliza didn't feel much like eating. Her stomach was knotted and her temples were throbbing, signalling a tension headache was well on its way. She looked across at Leo and he didn't seem to be too hungry either. He had barely touched his entrée and took only a token couple of sips of the delicious wine he had poured for them both. His brow was furrowed and his posture tense. She sensed a brooding anger in him that he was trying to control for the sake of politeness or maybe because he was concerned Marella would come in on them with the rest of their meal.

'You blame me, don't you?' Eliza said into the cavernous silence.

His eyes were like diamonds, hard and impenetrable. 'What makes you say that?'

She drew in a sharp breath as she put her napkin aside. 'Look—I understand your frustration and despair over your daughter's condition but I hardly see that I'm in any way to blame.'

He pushed back from his chair so quickly the glasses on the table rattled. 'You lied to me,' he said through tight lips. 'You lied to me from the moment we met.'

Eliza rose to her feet rather than have him tower over her so menacingly. 'You lied to yourself, Leo. You wanted a wife and you chose the first woman to fit your checklist.'

'Why did you come on to me in that bar that night?

She found it hard to hold his burning gaze. 'I was at a loose end. I was jet-lagged and lonely. I have no other excuse. I would never do something like that normally. I can't really explain it even now.'

'Let me tell you why you did it.' His top lip curled in disdain. 'You were feeling horny. Your fiancé was thousands of miles away. You needed a stand-in stud to scratch your itch.'

'Stop it!' Eliza clamped her hands over her ears. 'Stop saying such horrible things.'

He pulled her hands down from her face, his fingers like handcuffs around her wrists. The blood sizzled in her veins at the contact. She felt every pore of her skin flare to take more of him in. Her inner core contracted as her body remembered how it had felt to have him thrusting inside her. His first possession four years ago had been rough, almost animalistic and yet she had relished every heart-stopping, pulse-racing second of it.

'You still want it, don't you?'

'No,' she said but her body was already betraying her. It moved towards him, searching for him, hungering for him, *aching* for him.

'Liar.' He brought her chin up, his eyes blazing with fiery intent.

'Don't do this,' she said but she wasn't sure if she was pleading with him or herself.

'You still want me. I saw it that first day when I came to your flat.'

'You're wrong.' She tried to deny it even as her pelvis brushed against his in feverish need.

He grasped her by the bottom and pushed her hard into his arousal. 'That's what you want, isn't it? You're desperate for it, just like you were four years ago.'

Eliza tried to push him away but it was like a stick insect trying to shift a skyscraper from its foundations. 'Stop it,' she begged. 'Please stop saying that.' A bubble of emotion rose in her throat. She tried to swallow it back down but it refused to go away. She didn't want to break down in front of him. She hated that weakness in her, the one where she became overwhelmed and crumbled emotionally. It was the abandoned little seven-year-old girl in her who did that.

She wasn't that little girl any more.

She was strong and independent.

She *had* to be strong.

She had to survive.

She had to withstand the temptation of losing herself in the sensual world of Leo Valente, the one man who could dismantle her carefully constructed emotional armour. Her armour had been just fine until he had come along. It had always stood her in good stead. But now it was peeling off her like a sloughed skin, leaving her exposed and raw and vulnerable.

'I'm sorry…' She squeezed her eyes tightly closed for a moment. 'I just need a little minute…'

He dropped his hold as if she had suddenly burned him. 'Save your tears.' He scraped a hand through his hair. 'It's not your pity I'm after.'

Eliza forced her eyes back to his hardened cynical gaze. 'Right now I'm having a little trouble figuring out what it is you actually want from me.'

'I told you. I want you to fill in for Kathleen. That's all I want.'

She watched as he strode to the other side of the room, his movements like his words: clipped and tense. Was it true? Was that *all* he wanted from her? What if he wanted more? Wasn't it too late? An unbridgeable chasm separated them. He'd had a child with another woman. She was still tied to another man. Even if they wanted to be together, how could she desert Ewan when it was her fault he was sitting drooling in that chair?

Maybe this *was* about revenge. It pained her to think Leo would stoop to that. Was he so bitter that he had to make her suffer? What good would it do to either of them to spend a month at war over what had happened four years ago? It wouldn't change anything. Their history would still be the same. Their future would still be hopelessly unattainable.

'You should go to bed.' Leo turned to look at her again. 'Alessandra is not an easy child to manage. You'll need all your reserves to handle her.'

'I'm used to dealing with difficult children,' Eliza said. 'I've made a career out of it.'

'Indeed you have.' He gave her a brief on-off movement of his lips that was a paltry imitation of a smile. 'Goodnight, Eliza.'

She felt as if she was being dismissed again. It didn't sit comfortably with her. She wanted to spend more time with him, getting to know the man he was now. Understanding the agony he was going through in handling a blind, motherless child. He seemed lonely and isolated. She could see it now that she knew what had put that guarded look in his eyes and that tension in the way he held his body. Who was helping him deal with his little girl's disability? Was anyone supporting him? She had met parents of special needs kids before. They carried a huge weight of responsibility on their shoulders. They had told her how shocking and devastating it had been to find they were now members of a club they had never intended to join: the autism club, the hearing impaired club, the learning disabled club—the not quite perfect club. And in most cases it wasn't a temporary membership.

It was for life.

'Leo…' She took a step towards him but then stopped when she saw the dark glitter of his gaze. 'I think it's important for Alessandra if she senses that we are friends rather than enemies.'

'How do you propose we do that?'

Eliza felt the mesmerising pull of his gaze. He was so close she could see the dark pepper of his stubble and her fingers twitched to reach up and feel its sexy rasp against her fingertips. She looked at his mouth, her stomach clenching as she remembered how passionately those lips could kiss and conquer hers. Her insides coiled as she thought of how he had explored every inch of her body with his lips and tongue. Was he remembering it too? Was he replaying every erotic scene in his head and feeling the reaction reverberate through his body? 'I…I think it's important we be civil to each other…'

'Civil?' Those fathomless dark eyes burned and seared as they held hers.

'Yes…civil…polite…that sort of thing.' She swallowed a tight little restriction in her throat. 'There's no need for us to be trading insults. We're both mature adults and I think it's best if we try and act as if we… um, like each other…a bit…at least while we're in the presence of Alessandra.'

'And what about when we are alone?' One of his brows lifted in a sardonic arc. 'Are we to continue to pretend to like each other—*a bit*?'

Something about his tone sent a shiver to the base of Eliza's spine. Being alone with him was something she was going to have to avoid as much as possible. The temptation of being in his arms had always been her downfall. Hadn't his rough embrace just proved it? He had only to touch her and her body burst into hungry flames of need. He said he didn't want her, but she saw the glitter of lust in his eyes. He could deny it all he liked but she could feel it like a third presence in the room. It hovered there between them, a silent but ever-present reminder of every erotic interlude they had shared.

His body *knew* hers intimately.

He knew how responsive she was to his touch. He knew how to make her flesh hum and sing. His touch on her body was like a delicate, priceless instrument being played by a maestro. No one could make her body respond the way he did. He was doing it now just by looking at her with that dark assessing gaze. It stroked her as it moved over her body. She felt the fizz and tingle of her lips as his gaze lingered there as if he was recalling how they had felt against his own. She felt a prickly stirring in her breasts when his gaze moved over them. Was he remembering how her tight nipples had felt against his teeth and tongue? Was he remembering how she had whimpered in pleasure as his teeth had sexily grazed her sensitive flesh? She felt the heat of arousal between her thighs even without him lowering his gaze that far. Was he remembering how it had felt to plunge his body into hers until they had both careened into mindless oblivion?

'I'm not here to spend time alone with you.' She gave him an arch look. 'I'm here to look after your daughter. That's what I'm being paid to do, isn't it?'

His gaze was inscrutable but she could see a tiny muscle clenching on and off in his jaw. 'Indeed it is.' He moved to the door. 'I'm going out for a short while. I don't know what time I'll be back.'

'Where are you going?' She mentally grimaced. She hadn't meant to sound like a waspish wife checking up on him.

He gave her a satirical look. 'Where do you think I might be going?'

Eliza felt her stomach plummet in despair. *He had a mistress.* No wonder he had pulled away from her. He already had someone else who saw to those needs. Who was she? Was it someone local? Had he set her up in a villa close by? Please don't let it be their villa—the villa where she had spent those blissful three weeks with him.

She set her mouth in a contemptuous line. 'Nice to

see you haven't let the minor inconvenience of widowhood and single parenthood get in the way of your sex life.'

His dark eyes glinted warningly. 'You are not being paid to comment on any aspect of my private life.'

'Did you get her to sign a confidentiality agreement too?' She threw him an icy glare. 'Did you pay her heaps and heaps of money to keep her mouth shut and her legs open?'

The silence was so tense it rang like the high-pitched whistle of a cheap kettle.

Eliza felt his anger. It was billowing in the air between them like invisible smoke. It sucked all the oxygen out of the room until she found it hard to breathe. She had overstepped the mark. She had let her emotions gallop out of control. She had revealed her vulnerability to him.

'Isn't jealousy a little inconsistent of you, given you're wearing another man's ring?' he asked in a deceptively calm tone.

She forced herself to hold his gaze. 'Relationships are not meant to be business contracts. You can't do that to people. It's not right.'

His lip curled mockingly. 'Let me get this straight—*you're* telling me what's right and wrong?'

She drew in a sharp breath to try to harness her spiralling emotions. 'I'm sorry. I shouldn't have said anything. It's none of my business who you see or what arrangements you make in order to see them.'

'You're damn right it's none of your business.'

Eliza bit down on her lip as he strode out of the room, flinching when he clipped the door shut behind him. The sound of his car roaring to life outside was like a glancing blow to her heart. She listened to him drive out of the villa grounds, her imagination already torturing her with where he was going and what he would be doing when he got there.

CHAPTER FIVE

LEO UNMOORED HIS motor launch and motored out to a favourite spot where he could look back at the twinkling lights fringing the Amalfi coast. He dropped anchor and sat on the deck, listening to the gentle slap of the water against the hull and the musical clanging of the rigging against the mast of a distant yacht as the onshore breeze passed through. A gibbous moon cast a silver glow across the crinkled surface of the ocean. It was the closest he got to peace these days, out here on the water.

It was laughably ironic that Eliza thought he was off bedding a mistress. He hadn't been with anyone since Giulia had died ten months ago. Not that his relationship with her had been fulfilling in that department. He had tried to make it work a couple of times in the early days, but he had always known she was lying there wishing he were someone else.

Hadn't he done the same?

He hadn't wanted to hurt her by treating her as a substitute, so in the end they had agreed on a sexless arrangement. He could have had affairs; Giulia had told him to do whatever he had to do and she would turn a blind eye, but he hadn't pursued it. He had the normal urges of any other man his age, but he had ignored them to focus on his responsibilities as a parent and his ever-demanding career.

But his physical reaction to Eliza was a pretty potent reminder that he couldn't go on ignoring the needs of his body. He had wanted her so badly it had taken every ounce of self-control not to back her up against the nearest wall and do what they both did so well together. His groin was still tingling with the sensation of her body jammed tightly against his. He had felt the soft press of her beautiful breasts against his chest. He had desperately wanted to cover her mouth with his, to rediscover those sensual contours, to taste the hot sweetness of her.

He had intended to keep his distance during her short stay. He had been so confident he would be able to keep things on a business level between them. But, reflecting on it now, he could see how that call from Kathleen when he was in London for his meeting had completely thrown him. He was used to having his life carefully controlled. His domestic arrangements ran like clockwork. He had come to rely heavily on his staff, almost forgetting they had lives and families and issues of their own. When Kathleen had begged him for some time off he'd had to think on his feet and the first person he had thought of was Eliza. He'd told himself it was because she was a talented teacher and used to handling difficult and needy children. But what if the subconscious part of him had made the decision for a completely different reason?

He still wanted her.

Who was he kidding? Of course he still wanted her. But would a month be enough to end this torment that plagued him? Those three weeks he'd had with her had never left his memory. He could recall almost every passionate moment they had spent together. The memory of her body lived in his flesh. When he looked at her he felt his blood stir. He felt his heart rate rise. He felt his skin tingle in anticipation of her silky touch. The need to possess her was a persistent ache. Seeing her again had brought it all back. The blistering passion she evoked in him. The heat and fire of her response that made him feel as if she was his perfect mate—that there was no one else out there who could make him feel the way she did. It was going to be impossible to ignore the desire he had for her when every time he came within touching distance of her his body reacted so powerfully.

But wouldn't an affair with her create more problems, which he could do without right now?

On the other hand, he was used to compartmentalising his life. He could file his relationship with her into the temporary basket. Wasn't that what she would want? It wasn't as if she was going to end her engagement for him. She'd had four years to do so and yet she hadn't.

He didn't understand how she could sell herself so short. What was she getting out of her relationship with her fiancé that she couldn't get with *him*? He had offered her riches beyond measure, a lifetime of love and commitment, and yet she had thrown it back in his face. Why? What tied her to a man who *still* hadn't married her? He didn't even *live* with her. What hold did he have over her? Or was Eliza keeping a 'fiancé' up her sleeve so she could flit in and out of any shallow little hook-up that took her fancy? The ring she wore didn't look like a modern design. What if she just wore it for show? What if it was her get-out prop? '*Sorry, but I'm already taken*' was a very good way of getting out of a relationship that had run its course. She might have picked the ring up at a pawn shop for all he knew. If there was an actual fiancé Leo was almost certain she wasn't in love with him. How could she be when she looked at him with such raw longing? He was sure he wasn't imagining it. From the first moment he had laid eyes on her he had felt an electric connection that was beyond anything he had felt before or since.

But this time he wouldn't be offering her anything but an affair. He gave a twisted smile. A shallow hook-up was what he would offer. He would set the rules. He would set the boundaries and he would enforce them if he had to. He would not think about the morality of it. If she was willing to betray her fiancé—if there was one—then it was nothing to do with him.

She could always say no.

By two a.m. Eliza had given up on the notion of sleeping. It wasn't the jetlag or the strange bed. It was the restlessness of her body that was keeping her from slumber. A milky drink usually did the trick but could she risk running into Leo by going downstairs to get one? She hadn't heard him return, but then, why would he need to? He had plenty of staff to keep his household running while he indulged in an off-site affair with his latest mistress.

Eliza slipped on a wrap and went downstairs. There was enough moonlight coming in through the windows to light her way. Just as she was taking the last step down, the front door opened. She gave a little startled gasp and put her hand up to the throat where her heart seemed to have jumped. 'Leo?'

He gave her a wry look. 'Who else were you expecting?'

Eliza pursed her lips. 'I wasn't expecting anyone. And I wasn't waiting up for you, either.'

A mocking glint shone in his dark eyes. 'Of course not.'

She jutted her chin at him. 'I was on my way to the kitchen to get a hot drink.'

'Don't let me stop you.'

Eliza looked at his tousled hair. *Bed hair. Just had wild sex hair.* It maddened her to think he could just waltz in and parade his sexual conquests like a badge of honour. 'How was your evening? Did it live up to your expectations?'

Even in the muted light she could see the way his mouth was slanted with a cat-that-got-the-canary smile. 'It was very pleasurable.'

Jealousy was like an arrow to her belly. How could he stand there and be so…so *blatant* about it?

'I just bet it was.'

'You would know.'

Her brows shot together. 'What's that supposed to mean?'

His smile had tilted even further to give him a devilish look. 'You've had first-hand experience at spending many a pleasurable evening with me, have you not?'

Eliza tightened her mouth. She didn't want to be reminded of the nights she had spent rolling and screaming with pleasure in his bed. She had spent the last four years *trying* to forget. She threw him a dismissive look. 'Sorry to burst the bubble on your ego, but you haven't left that much of an impression on me. I can barely recall anything about our affair other than I was relieved when it was over.'

'You're lying.'

Eliza gave him a flinty glare. 'That's what really irks you, isn't it, Leo? It still rankles even after all this time. I was the first woman to ever say no to you. You could have anyone you wanted but you couldn't have me.'

'I could have you.' His eyes burned with primal intent. 'I could have you right now and we both know it.'

She gave a scornful laugh that belied the shockingly shaky ground she was desperately trying to stand on. 'I'd like to see you try.'

His eyes scorched hers as he closed the distance between them in a lazy stroll that sent an anticipatory shiver dancing down the length of her spine. She knew *that* look. It made her blood race through the circuitry of her veins like high-octane fuel. It made her heart thud with excitement and her legs tremble like a tripod on an uneven floor. It made her core clench with an ache that had no cure other than the driving force of his body.

He took her by the upper arms, his fingers digging into her flesh with almost brutal strength. 'You should know me well enough by now to know how foolish it is to throw a gauntlet down like that before me.'

Eliza suppressed another little shiver as she flashed him a defiant look. 'I'm not scared of you.'

His fingers tightened even further as he jerked her hard against him. 'Then perhaps you should be.' And then his mouth swooped down and slammed against hers.

It was a bruising kiss but Eliza was beyond caring. The crush of his mouth on hers brought all of her suppressed longings to the surface of her body like lava out of a volcano. She felt the raw need on her lips where his were pressed so forcefully. She felt it in her breasts as they were pushed up against his chest. She felt it unfurling deep in her core, that twisting, twirling, torturous ache that was moving throughout her body at breakneck speed.

How had she gone for so long without feeling this feverish rush of passion? It was like waking up after a decade of sleep. Every pore of her skin was alive and sensitised. Every muscle and sinew was crying out for the stroke and glide of his touch.

His tongue stroked hers until she was whimpering at the back of her throat. His hands were still hard on her upper arms, his fingertips gripping her with bruising force, but she relished in the feel of his commanding hold. His proudly aroused body was pressed intimately against her. She felt the hard ridge of him against the femininity of her body. The barrier of their clothes was torture. She wanted him naked and inside her, filling her, stretching her—making her feel alive in a way no one else could. She moved against him, speaking in a silent and primal feminine language that was universal.

But, instead of answering the call to mate, he dropped his hold and pulled back from her. He wiped the back of his hand across his mouth as if to remove the taste of her. It was a deliberately insulting gesture and she wanted to slap him for it. But she would rather die than show him how much he had hurt her.

'You've certainly got the Neanderthal routine down pat,' she said, pushing back her hair with a flick of her hand. 'I'm surprised you didn't haul me upstairs by the hair to your lair.'

His dark eyes mocked her. 'Surprised or disappointed?'

She held his look with a sassy one of her own. 'I wouldn't have done it, you know. I wouldn't have slept with you.'

The corner of his mouth kicked up cynically. 'No?'

'I was playing with you.' She straightened her wrap over her shoulders with fastidious attention to detail. 'Seeing how far you'd go.'

When she finally brought her gaze back to his another involuntary shiver trickled down her spine at the sexy, *knowing* glint shining there.

'You know where to find me if you feel like playing some more. My room is three doors down from yours. You don't have to knock. Just come right in. I'll be waiting for you.'

Eliza gave him a crushing look. 'Your confidence is seriously misplaced.'

His mouth tilted sardonically as he turned to make his way up the stairs. 'So is yours.'

Eliza was up early the following morning. Not that she had slept much during the night. The needs Leo had awakened made her feel restless and twitchy. All night long her mind had raced with a flood of memories of their past affair—racy little scenes where she had pleasured him or he had pleasured her. Erotic little flashbacks of her lying pinned beneath his rocking body, or her riding him on top until she gasped out loud. They all came back to haunt her—to torture her with the gnawing ache of want that refused to be suppressed. Was that why he had stepped back when he did? He wanted to make her *own* her need of him. He was playing with her like a cat did with a hapless mouse.

She wasn't going to let him break her. She knew he wanted her pride as a trophy. He wanted to have all the power, to be able to control what happened between them this time around. She understood his motivations. She had hurt him. She *regretted* that.

But on the battleground between them was a small defenceless child.

It wasn't fair to let Alessandra get hurt by the crossfire. Any arguments they had would have to be conducted in private. Any resentment would have to be shelved until they were alone.

As she was dressing after her shower Eliza noticed her upper arms bore the faint but unmistakable imprint of his fingers where he had gripped her the night before. It made her belly quiver to think he had branded her with his touch. She slipped on a three quarter length cardigan to cover the marks. She didn't want to have to explain to Marella or to Laura, the agency girl, how they had got there.

Laura was all packed up ready to leave when Eliza went to the nursery suite. 'Alessandra's still asleep,' she said, nodding towards the little girl's room. 'That's the best she's slept since I've been here. She's been a little terror the whole time. I don't think she's slept two hours straight before. You must have a magic touch.'

'I don't know about that,' Eliza said with a self-deprecating smile.

Laura lugged her backpack over one shoulder. 'I'd better get going. I have a ride waiting for me downstairs.' She offered her hand. 'Good luck with it all. I don't envy you having to answer to Leo Valente. He's quite intimidating, isn't he?'

'He's just being a protective father.'

Laura grunted. 'Yeah, well, I wouldn't want to get on the wrong side of him. Did you know him before or something? I don't mean to pry, it's just that last night I kind of got the impression you two knew each other.'

'I met him briefly a few years ago.' Eliza knew she had to be careful what she said. The confidentiality agreement Leo had made her sign made her think twice before she revealed anything about her previous connection with him. She couldn't risk being quoted out of context. She had no reason to believe he wouldn't be true to his word over the consequences of speaking out of turn. There was a streak of ruthlessness in him now that hadn't been there before. Didn't last night prove it?

'You dated him?' Laura probed.

'Not for long. It wasn't serious.'

Laura gave her a streetwise smile. 'Maybe you could have another crack at it. He's got loads and loads of money. He'd be quite a catch if you could put up with the foul temper.'

'I'm already engaged.'

Laura glanced at her left hand. 'Oh, I didn't realise. Sorry. When's the big day?'

'Yes, when is the big day?' Leo's deep voice spoke from behind them.

Eliza felt her face flood with colour as his gaze hit hers. She wondered how long he had been there. Long enough if that brooding look was anything to go by. 'Laura is just leaving, aren't you, Laura?'

'Yes,' Laura said and made a move for the door. 'I'll see myself out. Bye.'

A prickly silence filled the room once the young woman had left.

'I'd prefer you to refrain from gossiping with the hired help,' Leo said in a clipped tone. 'It's in your contract.'

'I wasn't gossiping. I was simply answering her questions. It would've been rude not to.'

'You're not here to answer questions. You're here to look after my daughter.'

Eliza returned his hardened glare. 'Is that *really* why I'm here? Or it is because you have an axe to grind? Revenge is a dirty word, Leo. It's a dirty deed that could turn out hurting you much more than it hurts me.'

His cleanly shaven jaw locked with tension. 'I'd have

to care about you for you to be able to hurt me. I care nothing for you. I only want your body and you want mine. Last night proved it.'

Anger pulsed in her veins at his arrogant dismissal of her as a person. 'Do you really think I would allow myself to be used like that? To be pawed over like some cheap two-bit hooker you hired off a dark alley?'

There was a condescending glitter in his eyes as they warred with hers. 'I'd hardly call a million pounds cheap. But you can forget about bargaining for more. I'm not paying it. You're not worth it.'

'Oh, I'm worth it, all right.' She put on her best sultry come-to-bed-with-me look. 'I'm worth every penny and more.'

He grasped her so suddenly the breath was knocked right out of her lungs. She felt the imprint of his fingers on the bruises he had left the day before but her pride would not allow her to wince or flinch. 'You want me just as much as I want you. I know the game you're playing. You want to drive up the price. I've sorted out your school, but it's *your* bank account you want sorted out now, isn't it?'

Eliza couldn't stop herself from looking at his mouth. It was flat-lined and bitter now, but she remembered all too well how soft and sensual it could be when it came into contact with hers. Desire flooded her being. She felt the on-off contraction of it deep in her core. He was the only man who could reduce her to this—to this primal need that would settle for nothing less than the explosive possession of his body. Could she withstand this temptation? Could she work for him without giving in to this desperate longing?

'I don't need your money.'

He gave one of his harsh laughs. 'But you'd like it all the same. You're starting to realise what you've thrown away, aren't you?'

'I always knew what I was throwing away.'

His top lip curled. 'Are you saying you have regrets?'

She arched her brow pointedly. 'Don't we all?'

He held her gaze in a stare-down that made the base of her spine fizz like sherbet. 'My only regret is I didn't see you for what you were at the outset. You're a classic chameleon. You can change in the blink of an eye. I had you pegged as an old-fashioned girl who wanted the same things I wanted. But you were not that girl, were you? You were never that girl. You were a harlot on the hunt for sensory adventure and you didn't care where you got it.'

'Why is it such a crime for a woman to want sensory satisfaction?' Eliza asked. 'Why does that make *me* a harlot? What does that make *you?* Why are there no equally derogatory names for men who want to be satisfied physically? Why do women have to feel so bad about their own perfectly natural needs that you men seem to take for granted?'

'What's wrong with your fiancé that he can't give you the satisfaction you want or need?'

The question was like a punch to her chest. 'I'm not prepared to answer that.'

'Does he even exist?'

Eliza looked at him numbly. '*What?*'

'Is he a real person or just someone you made up to use as a get-out-of-jail-free card?' His eyes were hard as they drilled into hers. 'It's a handy device to have a fiancé in the background when you want to get out of an affair that's not going according to plan.'

She swallowed against the lump in her throat. Ewan did exist, but not as he used to be. And it was *her* fault. His life was as good as over. He would never feel the things he used to feel. He could never say the words he used to say. He couldn't even think the thoughts he used to think. He existed…but he didn't. He was caught between the conscious world and the unconscious.

'You're so fiercely loyal to him. But is he as loyal to you?'

Eliza lowered her gaze as she fought her emotions back down. 'He's very loyal. He's a good person. He's always been a good person.'

'You love him.'

She didn't need more than a second to think about it. 'Yes…'

The silence hummed with his bitterness.

How was she going to survive a month of this? What good was going to come out of his attempt to right the wrongs of the past? Nothing could be gained from this encounter. He was intent on revenge but they would both end up even more damaged than they already were. She couldn't fix Ewan and she couldn't fix Leo. She had ruined two lives, three if she counted Samantha.

And what about *her* life—the plans she had made were nothing but pipe dreams now. She wouldn't be able to have the family she wanted. She wouldn't be able to have the love she craved.

She was trapped, just like Ewan was trapped.

Eliza turned to the nursery, desperate to get away from the hatred she could feel pouring out of Leo towards her. 'I'm going to check on Alessandra. She should be awake by now.'

'My daughter's orientation and mobility teacher will

be here at ten,' he said. 'Tatiana works with her until lunchtime twice a week. You can either have that time to yourself or observe some of the things she is helping Alessandra with. I don't expect you to be on duty twenty-four hours a day.'

Eliza looked at him again. 'Aren't you worried that she's going to be upset by my being here for such a short time? It sounds like a lot of people are coming and going in her life. It's no wonder she gets upset and agitated. She doesn't know who is going to walk in the door next.'

'My daughter is used to being managed by carers,' he said. 'It's a fact of life that she will always need to have support around her.'

She held his gaze for a beat that drummed with tension. 'I meant what I said last night. I think you should get Kathleen to call her each day. It will give her something to look forward to and it might make the time go a little quicker for her.'

His jaw seemed to lock for a moment but then he released a harsh-sounding breath. 'I'm not sure if Kathleen will be back. I got an email from her this morning. Her family want her to move back to Ireland. She's still thinking about it. She's going to tell me what she's decided in a couple of weeks' time.'

Eliza swallowed. 'Does that mean you'll want me to stay longer?'

His gaze became steely as it nailed hers. 'Your contract is for one month and one month only. It's not up for negotiation.'

'But what if your daughter wants me to stay?'

'One month.' The words came out clipped through lips pulled tight with tension, those bitter eyes hardening even further. 'That's all I'm prepared to give you.'

'Would you really put your plans for revenge before the interests of your daughter?'

'This is not about revenge.'

She made a sceptical sound in her throat. 'Then what *is* it about?'

His eyes roved her body in a searing sweep that made her skin prickle with heat and longing. The memory of his bruising kiss was still beating beneath the surface of her lips. The need he had awakened was secretly pulsing in the depths of her body—an intense ache that refused to go away. She felt it travel from her core to her breasts as his gaze travelled the length and breadth of her body. 'I think you know what this is about.'

Lust.

It wasn't a word Eliza particularly liked, but how else could she describe how he made her feel? From the very first moment she had met him he had triggered this earthy response in her. She knew he was experienced—*very* experienced. She had come to the relationship with much less experience, but what she had lacked in that department she had more than made up for in passion. Her response to him had shocked her then and it still shocked her now. Didn't that kiss last night prove how dangerous it was to get too close to him? He would dismantle her emotional armour within a heartbeat. Making love with him would unpick every stitch of her carefully constructed resolve. She could not afford to let that happen. Going back to her bleak and lonely life in England would be so much harder to bear if she experienced the mind-blowing pleasure Leo offered. How would she settle for the bitter plate of what fate had dished up to her if she got a taste of such sweet paradise again?

Eliza threw him a contemptuous look born out of the fear that he would somehow see how terrifyingly vulnerable she was to him. 'And just because you want something, you just go out and get it, do you? Well, I've got news for you. I'm not on the market.'

He came up close with that slow, leisurely stroll he had perfected. She refused to back away but instead gave him the full wattage of her heated glare as she steeled herself for the firm grasp of his hands on her arms.

But he didn't.

Instead he gently brushed the back of his bent knuckles down the curve of her cheek in a barely touching caress that totally ambushed her defences. She felt her composure crack as her throat closed over. Tears formed and stung at the back of her eyes. Her chest felt like an oversized balloon was inflating inside it, taking up all the space so her lungs could no longer expand enough to breathe.

'Why are you doing this?' Her voice was not much more than a thread of sound. 'Why now? Why couldn't you have let things be?'

His expression had lost its steely edge and was now almost wistful. 'I wanted to make sure.'

'Sure of…of what?'

'That I didn't make the worst mistake of my life the night you told me you were engaged.'

Eliza swallowed a walnut-sized knot of emotion. 'You…you had a right to be upset…' She couldn't look at him. She lowered her gaze again and stared at her engagement ring instead.

There was the sound of Alessandra waking in the nursery—the rustle of bedclothes and a plaintive wail.

'I'll go to her.' Leo moved past and Eliza listened as he greeted his little daughter. He spoke in Italian but she could hear the love in his voice that was as clear as any translation. '*Buongiorno, tesorina, come ti senti*?'

Was it wrong to wish he could look upon *her* as his treasure too?

CHAPTER SIX

WHEN ELIZA CAME into the nursery Leo had Alessandra in his arms. 'I'll carry her downstairs for you but I won't be able to join you for breakfast,' he said. 'I have an online meeting in a few minutes.'

'Good morning, Alessandra,' Eliza said, reaching out to touch the child's hand that was gripping her father's shirt. 'It looks like we've got a date for breakfast.'

The little girl huddled closer to her father's chest. 'I want to have breakfast with *Papà*.'

Eliza exchanged a brief glance with Leo before addressing the child again. 'I'm afraid that's not possible today. But I'm sure *Papà* will make a special effort to have breakfast with you when he can.'

Alessandra's thin shoulders slumped as she let out a sigh. 'All wight.'

Once Leo had placed his daughter in her high chair in the breakfast room he kissed her on the top of the head and, with a brief unreadable glance at Eliza, he left.

Marella, the housekeeper, came bustling in, cooing to the child in Italian. '*Buongiorno, angioletta mia, tutto bene?*' She turned to Eliza. 'You have to feed her.' She nodded at the food in front of the child. 'She can't do it herself.'

'But surely she's old enough to do some of it on her own?'

'You'll have to discuss that with Signor Valente,' Marella said. 'Kathleen always feeds her. Tatiana, the O and M teacher, is trying to get Alessandra to do more for herself but it's a slow process.'

Eliza settled for a compromise by guiding Alessandra's hands to reach for things on her plate such as pieces of fruit or toast. The little girl was reluctant to drink from anything but her sippy cup so Eliza decided to leave that battle for another day. She knew how important it was to encourage Alessandra to live as normal a life as possible, but pushing her too fast, too soon could be detrimental to her confidence.

Tatiana, the orientation and mobility teacher arrived just as Marella was clearing away the breakfast things. After introducing herself, Tatiana filled Eliza in on the sorts of things she was doing with Alessandra while Marella momentarily distracted Alessandra.

'We're working on her coordination and spatial awareness. A sighted child learns by watching others and trying things for themselves, but a vision-impaired or blind child has no reference point. We have to help them explore the world around them in other ways, by touching and feeling, and by listening and using their sense of smell. We also have to teach what is appropriate behaviour in public, as they don't have the concept of being seen by others.'

'It all sounds rather painstaking,' Eliza said.

'It is,' Tatiana said. 'Alessandra is a bright child but don't let that strong will fool you. When it comes to her exercises she's not well motivated. That is rather typical of a vision-impaired child. They can become rather passive. Our job is to increase her independence little by little.'

'She seems small for her age.'

'Yes, she's on the lower percentile in terms of height and weight, but with more structured exercise she should catch up.'

'Is there anything I can do to help while I have her on my own?'

'Yes, of course,' Tatiana said. 'I'll write out a list of games and activities. You might even think of some of your own. Signor Valente told me you are a teacher, yes?'

'Yes. I teach a primary school class in a community school in London.'

'Then you're perfect for the job,' Tatiana said. 'What a shame you can't be here permanently. Kathleen is a sweetheart but she gives in to Alessandra too easily.'

'The post is only for a month,' Eliza said, automatically fingering the diamond on her left hand. 'I have to get back, in any case.'

'Don't get me wrong,' Tatiana said. 'Leo Valente is a loving father, but like a lot of parents of children with special needs, he is very protective—almost too protective at times. I guess it's hard for him, being a single parent.'

'Did you meet Alessandra's mother before she died?' Eliza asked.

Tatiana's expression said far more than her words. 'Yes and I still can't work out how those two ended up married to each other. I got the impression from Giulia it was a rebound relationship on his part.' She blew out a breath as her gaze went to where Alessandra was sitting in her high chair. 'I bet that's a one-night stand he's regretted ever since.'

Eliza could feel a wave of heat move through her cheeks. *I'm sure it's not the only one,* she thought with a searing pain near her heart. 'Leo loves his daughter. There can be no doubt of that.'

'Yes, of course he does,' Tatiana said. 'But it's probably not the life he envisaged for himself, is it? But then, lots of parents feel the same when they have a child with a disability. It's hard to get specialised nannies. Children with special needs can be very demanding. But to see them reach their potential is very rewarding.'

'Yes, I can imagine it is.'

'At least Signor Valente has the money to get the best help available,' Tatiana said. 'But it's true what people say, isn't it? You can't buy happiness.'

Eliza thought of Leo's brooding personality and the flashes of pain she had glimpsed in his eyes. 'No…you certainly can't…'

The morning passed swiftly as Tatiana worked with Alessandra in structured play with Eliza as active observer. There were shape puzzles for Alessandra to do as well as walking exercises to strengthen her muscles and improve her coordination. The little toddler wasn't good at walking on her own, even while holding someone's hand. Her coordination and muscle strength was significantly poorer compared to children her age. And, of course, what was difficult to the little tot was then wilfully avoided.

Eliza could see how a tired and overburdened parent would give in and do things for their child that they should really be encouraging them to do for themselves. It was draining and exhausting just watching the little girl work through her exercises and, even though Tatiana tried to make the session as playful as possible, Alessandra became very tired towards the end. There was barely time for a few mouthfuls of lunch before she was ready for her nap.

Eliza sat in the anteroom and read a book she had brought with her, keeping an ear out for any sign of the little girl becoming restless. An hour passed and then half of another but the child slept on. She could feel her own eyelids drooping when Marella came to the door with a steaming cup of tea and a freshly baked cup cake on a pretty flowered plate.

'You don't have to stay here like a prison guard.' Marella placed the tea and cake on the little table by Eliza's chair. 'There's a portable monitor. Its range is wide enough to reach the gardens and the pool. Didn't Signor Valente show you?'

'No…I expect he had too many other things on his mind.'

Marella shook her head sadly. 'Poor man. He has too much work to do and too little time to do it. He is always torn. He wants to be a good father but he has a big company to run. He'll drive himself to an early grave just like his father did if he's not careful.'

Eliza lowered her gaze to the cup of tea she was cradling in her hands. She thought of Leo getting through each day, feeling overly burdened and guilty about the competing demands of his life. Who did he turn to when things got a little overwhelming? One of his mistresses? How could someone he was just having sex with help him deal with his responsibilities? *Did* he turn to anyone or did he shoulder it all alone? No wonder he seemed angry and bitter a lot of the time. Maybe it wasn't just *her* that brought out that in him. Maybe he was just trying to cope with what life had thrown at him—just like she was trying to do, with limited success.

'I can imagine it must be very difficult for him, juggling it all.'

'After you've had your tea, why don't you take a

stroll out in the garden?' Marella said. 'I'll listen out for the little one. I'll take the monitor with me. I'll be on this floor in any case. I have to remake the bed the agency girl was using.'

Eliza could think of nothing better than a bit of sunshine. It seemed a long time since she had been in the fresh air. The villa was becoming oppressive, with its forbiddingly long corridors and large gloomy rooms. She put her cup down on the table. 'Are you sure?'

'But of course.' Marella shooed her away. 'It will do you good.'

The sun was deliciously warm as Eliza strolled about the gardens, the scent of roses thick and heady in the air. Was it her knowledge of Alessandra's blindness that made the colours of the roses seem so spectacular all of a sudden? Deep blood reds, soft and bright pinks and crimson, variegated ones, yellow and orange and the snowy perfection of white ones. Even the numerous shades of green in the foliage of the other plants and shrubs stood out to her as she wandered past. She went past the fountain and down a crushed limestone pathway to a grotto that was protected by the shade of a weeping birch. It was a magical sort of setting, secluded and private—the perfect place for quiet reflection. She slipped off her cardigan and sat on the wrought iron bench, wondering how many couples through the centuries had conducted their trysts under the umbrella-like shade of the lush and pendulous branches.

The sound of a footfall on the stones of the pathway made Eliza's heart give a little kick behind her ribcage. She stood up from the seat just as Leo came into view. He looked just as surprised to see her. She saw the camera-shutter flinch of his features in that nanosecond before he got control and assumed one of his inscrutable expressions.

'Eliza.'

'Marella told me to take a break. She's listening out for Alessandra. She's got the monitor. I didn't know you had one; otherwise—' she knew she was babbling but couldn't seem to stop '—she told me it would be all right and—'

'You're not under lock and key.'

Eliza tried to read his expression but it was like trying to read one of the marble statues she had walked past earlier in the long wide gallery in the villa. She wondered if he had come down here to be alone. Perhaps it was his private place for handling the difficulties of his life. No wonder he resented her presence. She was intruding on his only chance at solitude.

'I'd better head back.' She turned to pick up her cardigan that she'd left on the seat.

'What have you done to your arms?'

'Um—nothing.' She bunched the cardigan against her chest. It was too late to put it back on.

His frown brought his brows to a deep V above his eyes. 'Did I…?' He seemed momentarily lost for words. 'Did I do that to you?'

'It's nothing…really.' She began to turn away but he anchored her with a gentle band of his broad fingers around her wrist.

His touch was like a circle of flame. She felt the shockwave of it right to the secret heart of her. Her skin danced with jittery sensations. Her heart fluttered like a hummingbird and her breath halted in her throat like a horse refusing a jump.

'I'm sorry.' His voice was a deep bass—deeper than organ pipes. It made her spine loosen and quiver. It spoke to the primal woman in her, especially when he ever so gently ran one of his fingers over the marks he had made on her flesh. 'Do they hurt?'

'No, of course not.' She was struggling to deal with her spiralling emotions. Why did he have to stand so close to her? How could she resist him when he was close enough for her to sense his arrantly male reaction to her? If she moved so much as an inch she would feel him.

Oh, how she wanted to feel him!

Could he see how much she ached for him? How desperate she was to have it taken out of her control, to be swept away to a world where nothing mattered but the senses he awakened and satisfied.

'I'd forgotten how very sensitive your skin is.' His fingers danced over her left forearm, leaving every pore screaming for more of his tantalising touch.

Eliza swallowed convulsively. This was going to get out of hand rather rapidly if he kept on with this softly-softly assault on her senses. She could fend him off when he was angry and bitter. She could withstand him—only just—when he was brooding and resentful.

But in this mood he was far more dangerous.

Her need of him was dangerous.

She pulled back from his loose hold but it tightened a mere fraction, keeping her tethered to him—to temptation. 'I...I have to go...' Her words sounded desperate, her breathing even more so. She fought to control herself. She didn't want him to see how close to being undone she was. 'Please...let me go...'

'That was my mistake four years ago.' He brought her even closer, his hands going to the small of her back, pressing her to his need. 'I should never have let you go.'

'It wasn't a mistake.' She tried to push against his chest but he wouldn't budge. 'I had to go. I didn't belong with you. I *don't* belong with you.'

His hands gripped her wrists, gently but firmly. 'You keep fighting me but you want this as much as I do. I know you do. I *know* you want me. I feel it every time you look at me.'

'It's wrong.' Eliza was close to breaking. She couldn't allow herself to fold emotionally. She had to be strong. She had to think of poor Ewan. It was her fault he had been robbed of everything. He would never feel love again. He would never feel passion or desire.

Why should *she* feel it when he no longer could?

'Tell your fiancé you want a break.'

'I can't do that.'

'Why not?'

'He wouldn't understand.'

'Make him understand. Tell him you want a month to have a think about things. Is that so much to ask? For God's sake, you're giving him the rest of your life. What is one measly month in the scheme of things?'

Eliza tried to control her trembling bottom lip. 'Relationships can't be turned on and off like that. I've made a commitment. I can't opt out of it.'

His dark eyes glittered. 'Are saying you can't or you won't?'

She forced herself to hold his challenging look. 'I won't be used by you, Leo.'

One of his hands burned like a brand in the small of her back as he drew her closer. 'What's all this talk of me using you?' His voice was still low and deep, making her resolve fall over like a precariously assembled house of cards. 'You want the same thing I want. There doesn't have to be a winner or a loser in this. We can both have what we want.'

Eliza could feel the slow melt of her bones. She could feel that sharp dart of longing deep inside her body, the need that longed to be assuaged. Was it wrong to want to feel his passionate possession one more time? To explore the intense heat that continued to flare between them? But would one month be enough? How could it *ever* be enough? Experiencing that earth-shattering pleasure again would only leave her frustrated and miserable for the rest of her life. She would always be thinking of him, aching for him, *missing* him. It had been hard enough four years ago. He had lived in her body for all this time, making her even more restless and unhappy with her lot in life.

But it *was* her lot in life.

There was no escaping the fact that Ewan's life had been destroyed and that she had been the one to do it. How could she carry on with her life as if it didn't matter?

Of course it mattered.

It would always matter.

With a strength Eliza had no idea she possessed, she pushed back from him. 'I'm sorry…' She moved away from him until she was almost standing in the shrubbery. 'You're asking too much. It's all been too much. Finding out about your daughter's blindness… seeing how hard it is for her and for you. I can't think straight…I'm confused and upset…'

'You need more time.'

She squeezed her eyes closed for a moment as if that would make all of this go away. But when she opened them again he was still standing there, looking at her with his unwavering gaze.

'It's not about time…' She bit down on her lower lip. 'It's just not our time…' *It was never our time.*

He tucked a loose strand of her hair behind her ear. Her skin shivered at his tender touch, the nerves pirouetting beneath the surface until she was almost dizzy with longing. 'I've handled this appallingly, haven't I?' he asked, resting that same hand on the nape of her neck.

Eliza wasn't sure how to answer so remained silent. His hand was strong and yet gentle—protective. She longed to be held by him and never let go. But the past—their past—was a yawning canyon that was too wide and deep to cross.

He let out a rough-sounding sigh and, stepping away from her to look out over the rear garden, that same hand that had moments ago caressed her was now rubbing at the back of his neck as if trying to ease giant knots of tension buried there. 'I'm still not sure why I came to you that day in London. I needed a nanny in a hurry and for some reason the first person I thought of was you.' His hand dropped to his side as he turned and looked at her again. 'But maybe it was because I wanted you to see what my life had become.' His expression was tortured with anguish and frustration. 'I've got more money than I know what to do with and yet I can't fix my child. I can't *make* her see.'

Eliza felt his frustration. It was imbedded in every word he had spoken. It was in every nuance of his expression. He was in pain for his daughter—physical and emotional pain. 'You're a wonderful father, Leo. Your role is to love and provide for her. You're doing all that and more.'

'She needs more than I can give her.' He dragged a hand over his face. It pulled at his features, distorting them, making him seem older than his years. 'She needs her mother. But that's another thing I can't fix. I can't bring her mother back.'

'That's not your fault. You mustn't blame yourself.'

He gave her a weary look. 'Giulia was already broken when I met her. But I probably made it a thousand times worse.'

'How did you meet her?'

'In a bar.'

Eliza felt her face colour up. 'Not a great place to find lasting love…'

He gave her a look she couldn't quite decipher. 'No, but then people at a crossroads in their lives often hang out in bars. I was no different than Giulia. We'd both been disappointed in love. She'd been let down by a long-term lover. In hindsight, I would have been much better served—and her, for that matter—if I'd just listened to what had been going on in her life. She needed a friend, not a new lover to replace the one she'd lost.'

'What happened?'

His gaze dropped to the gravel at his feet as he kicked absently at a loose pebble. 'We had a one-night stand.' His eyes met hers again. 'I know you might find this hard to believe, but I don't make a habit of them. I regretted it as soon as it was over. We had no real chemistry. In some ways I think she only went through with it because she wanted to prove something to herself—that she could sleep with another man after being with her lover for so long.' He took a breath and slowly released it. 'She called me a month later and told me she was pregnant.'

'You must have been furious.'

He shrugged one shoulder. 'I wasn't feeling anything much at that stage. I guess that's why I offered to marry her. I truly didn't care either way. As far as I was concerned, the only woman I wanted wasn't available. What did it matter who I married?'

Eliza ignored the flash of pain his words evoked and frowned at him. 'Why was marriage so important to you? Most men your age are quite content with having affairs. They wouldn't dream of settling down with one person for the rest of their life, even when there is a child involved, especially one that wasn't planned.'

'My father loved my mother,' he said. 'It ended badly, but he always instilled in me that it was worth committing to one person. He didn't believe in half measures. His philosophy was you were either in or you were out. I admired that in him.

'I tried my best with Giulia. I gave her what I could but it wasn't enough. At the end of the day we didn't love each other. No amount of commitment on my part could compensate for her guilt over Alessandra's blindness. She just couldn't handle it. She rejected her right from the start. In her mind, it was as if someone had handed her the wrong baby in the hospital. She couldn't seem to accept that this was what life was going to be like from now on.'

'I'm sure there are a lot of parents who feel that way,' Eliza said.

He scored a pathway through his hair, as if even thinking about that time in his life made his head ache. 'The thing was, Giulia didn't want to have *my* baby. She wanted her ex's child.'

Eliza's frown showed her confusion as it pulled at

her forehead. 'But you said she deliberately set out to get pregnant, that she set you up.'

He gave her another weary look. 'It's true. But the thing is, I could have been anyone that night. She wanted to hit out at the man who'd let her down so badly. She wasn't thinking straight. On another night she might not have done it, but of course once it was done it was too late to undo it. She wasn't the type to have an abortion and, to be honest, I didn't want her to. We were both responsible for what happened. I could have walked away from her that night. But, in a way, I think I was trying to prove something too.'

Eliza sank her teeth into her lip, thinking about how devastating all this had been for him. His life had changed so swiftly and so permanently. And *she* had been part of that devastation when she had rejected his proposal. Was she always destined to ruin other people's lives? To make them desperately unhappy and destroy the life they had envisaged for themselves?

'I'm sorry…I can see now why you feel I'm partly to blame for how things have turned out. But who's to say we would've had a great relationship if I had been free to marry you?'

His dark eyes meshed with hers. 'Do you seriously doubt that we couldn't have had a satisfying relationship after what we shared during those three weeks?'

She turned away from his penetratingly hot gaze and folded her arms across her middle, cupping her elbows with her crossed over hands. 'There's much more to a relationship than sex. There's companionship and emotional honesty and closeness. The best sex in the world doesn't make up for those things.'

'Is that what you have with your fiancé? Emotional closeness?'

'I should get back…' Eliza glanced towards the villa. 'Alessandra will be well and truly awake by now. Marella will be wondering what's happened to me.'

She started back along the pathway but she didn't hear Leo following her. She glanced back when she got to the fountain but he had disappeared from sight. She gave an uneven sigh and, with a little slump of her shoulders, made her way inside the villa.

CHAPTER SEVEN

ALESSANDRA HAD ONLY just woken when Eliza came back to the nursery. 'I've got a special surprise in store,' she said as she lifted her out of the cot.

'What is it?' Alessandra asked, rubbing at one of her eyes.

Tatiana had explained to Eliza that eye-rubbing was something a lot of vision-impaired children did. But while it gave temporary comfort similar to sucking a thumb, as the child got older it was less socially acceptable. Tatiana had advised that distracting the child from the habit was the best way to manage it, so Eliza gently pulled her hand away and circled her tiny palm with the finger play, *Ring a Ring o' Roses.*

Alessandra giggled delightedly. 'Do it again.'

'Give me your other hand.'

The little girl held out her hand and Eliza repeated the rhyme, her heart squeezing as she saw the unadulterated joy on the toddler's face. 'Again! Again!'

'Maybe later,' Eliza said. 'I have other plans for you, young lady. We're going for a walk.'

'I don't want to walk. Carry me.'

'No carrying today, little Munchkin,' Eliza said. 'You've got two lovely little legs. You need to learn to use them a bit more.'

She took the little tot's hand and led her out to the landing and then down the stairs. She got Alessandra to feel the balustrade as she went down and to plant her feet carefully on each step before taking another. It was a slow process but well worth it as by the time they got down to the ground floor she could tell Alessandra was a little more confident.

'Now we're going to go outside to the garden,' Eliza said. 'Have you been out there much?'

'Kathleen used to take me sometimes but then she got stinged by a bee. I cried because I thought it was going to sting me too.'

'Don't worry; I won't let you get stung.' Eliza gave the little child's hand a gentle squeeze of reassurance. 'There's a lot of lovely things to smell and feel out there. Flowers are some of the most beautiful things in nature but the really cool thing is you don't have to see them to appreciate them. Lots of them have really lovely perfumes, particularly roses. I bet after a while you'll be able to tell them apart, just from smelling them.'

Once they were out in the garden, Eliza led Alessandra down to one of the rose gardens. She picked some blooms and held them to the child's little nose, smiling as Alessandra sniffed and smiled in turn. 'Beyootiful!' she said.

'That's a deep red one,' Eliza said. 'It's got a really rich scent. Here's a bright pink one. Its scent is a little less intense. What do you think?'

Alessandra pushed her nose against the velvet bloom. 'Nice.'

'Feel the petals,' Eliza said. 'There aren't any thorns on this one. I checked.'

The little girl fingered the soft petals, discovering each fold, her face full of concentration as if she was trying to picture what she was feeling. 'Can I smell some more?'

'Of course.' Eliza picked a yellow one this time. 'This one reminds me of the sunshine. It's bright and cheerful with a light, fresh fragrance.'

'Mmm.' Alessandra breathed in the fragrance. 'But I like the first one best.'

'That was the red one.' Eliza put them in a row on the ground and got Alessandra to sit on the grass beside her. 'Let's play a game. I'm going to hand you a rose and you have to tell me which colour it is by the smell. Do you think you can do that?'

'Will I know my colours after this?'

Eliza looked at the tiny tot's engaging little face and felt her heart contract. 'I think you're going to be an absolute star at this game. Now, here goes. Which one is this?'

Leo was coming back from speaking to one of the gardeners working on a retaining wall at the back of the garden when he saw Eliza and his little daughter sitting in a patch of sunshine on the lawn near the main rose garden. Eliza's attention was focused solely on Alessandra. She was smiling and tickling his daughter's nose with a rose. Alessandra was giggling in delight. The tinkling bell sound of his little girl's laughter sounded out across the garden. It was the most wonderful sound he had ever heard. It made something that had been stiff and locked inside his chest for years loosen.

He watched as Eliza rained a handful of rose petals from above Alessandra's head. Alessandra reached up and caught some of them, crushing them to her face and giggling anew.

He could have stood there and watched them for hours.

But then, as if Eliza had suddenly sensed his presence, she turned her head and the remaining petals in her hand dropped to the lawn like confetti.

He closed the distance in a few strides and his little daughter also turned her head in his direction as she heard him approach. '*Papà*?'

'You look like you are having a lot of fun, *mia piccola*.'

'I know my colours!' she said excitedly. 'Eliza's been teaching me.'

Leo quirked one of his brows at Eliza. 'You look like you're enjoying yourself too.'

'Alessandra is a very clever little girl,' she said. 'She's a joy to teach. Now, Alessandra, I'm going to pick some more roses. Let's show *Papà* how clever you are at distinguishing which one is which.'

Leo watched as she picked a handful of roses and came back to sit on the lawn next to his daughter. Alessandra's expression was a picture to behold. She held up her face for the brush of each velvet rose against her little nose. She breathed deeply and, after thinking about it for a moment, proudly announced, 'That's the pink one!'

'Very good,' Eliza said. 'Now, how about this one?'

'It's the red one!'

Leo looked on in amazement. How had she done it? It was like a miracle. His little daughter was able to tell each rose from the others on the basis of its smell but somehow Eliza had got her to associate the colour as well. Even though, strictly speaking, Alessandra hadn't learned her colours at all, it was a way to make her distinguish them by another route. It was nothing less than a stroke of genius. He felt incredibly touched that Eliza had taken the trouble to work her way through a task that had seemed insurmountable so that his little girl could feel more normal.

'OK, now, how about this one?' Eliza held up a white one and Alessandra sniffed and sniffed, her little face screwing up in confusion.

'It's not the yellow one, is it? It smells different.'

'You clever, clever girl!' Eliza said. 'It's a white one. I tried to trick you, but you're too clever by half. Well done.'

Alessandra was grinning from ear to ear. 'I like this game.'

Leo looked down at Eliza's warm smile. It made that stiff part of his chest loosen another notch. He imagined her with her own child—how natural she would be, how loving and nurturing. It wasn't just the trained teacher in her, either. He was starting to realise it was an essential part of her nature. She genuinely loved children and wanted to bring out the best in them. No wonder she had been recognised as a teacher of excellence. She cared about their learning and achievement. He could see the joy and satisfaction on her face as she worked with Alessandra. Sure, he was paying her big money to do it, but he suspected it wasn't the money that motivated her at all.

Why couldn't *she* have been Alessandra's mother?

'You're scarily good at this game,' Eliza said. 'I'll have to be on my toes to think of new ones to challenge you.' She got to her feet and took one of Alessandra's hands in hers. 'We'd better get you inside, out of this hot sun. I don't want you to get sunburnt.'

Leo moved forward to scoop his daughter up to carry her back to the villa but she seemed content to walk, albeit gingerly, by Eliza's side. He watched as she toddled alongside Eliza, her little hand entwined with hers, her footsteps awkward and cautious, but, with Eliza's gentle encouragement, she gradually gained a little more confidence.

'Four steps, Alessandra,' Eliza said as they got to the flagstone steps leading to the back entrance of the villa. 'Do you want to count them as we go?'

'One…two…three…four!'

Eliza ruffled her hair with an affectionate hand. 'What did I tell you? You're an absolute star. You'll soon be racing about the place without any help at all.'

Marella appeared from the kitchen as they came in. 'I've been baking your favourite cookies, Alessandra. Why don't we let Papà and Eliza have a moment while we have a snack?'

'*Grazie*, Marella,' Leo said. 'There are a few things I'd like to talk to Eliza about. Give us ten minutes.'

'*Sì, signor*.'

Leo met Eliza's gaze once the housekeeper had left with his daughter. 'It seems I was right in selecting you as a suitable stand-in for Kathleen. You've achieved much more in a day with Alessandra than she has in months.'

'I'm sure Kathleen is totally competent as a nanny.'

'That is true, but you seem to have a natural affinity with Alessandra.'

'She's a lovely child.'

'Most of the people who deal with her find her difficult.'

'She has a disability,' she said. 'It's easy to focus on what she can't do, but in my experience in teaching difficult children it is wiser to focus on what they *can* do. She can do a lot more than you probably realise.'

A frown pulled at his brow. 'Are you saying I'm holding her back in some way?'

'No, of course not,' she said. 'You're doing all the right things. It's just that it's sometimes hard to see what she needs from a parent's perspective. You want to protect her but in protecting her you may end up limiting her. She has to experience life. She has to experience the dangers and the disappointments; otherwise she will always live in a protective bubble that has no relation to the real world. She needs to live in the real world. She's blind but that doesn't mean she can't live a fulfilled and satisfying life.'

He moved to the other side of the room, his hand going to his neck, where a golf ball of tension was gnawing at him. 'What do you suggest I do that I'm not already doing?'

'You could spend more time with her, one on one. She needs quality time with you but also quantity time.'

Guilt prodded at him. He knew he wasn't as hands on as he could be. No one had played with him as a child. His mother had been too busy pursuing her own interests while his father had worked long hours to try and keep his company from going under. Leo wanted to be a better parent than his had been, but Alessandra's blindness made him feel so wretchedly inadequate. It had paralysed him as a parent. What if he did or said the wrong thing? What if he upset her or made her feel guilty for having special needs? Giulia, in her distress, had said unforgivable things in the hearing of Alessandra. He had tried to make up for it, but there were times when he wondered if it was already too late.

'I'll try to free up some time,' he said. 'It's hard when I'm trying to juggle a global business. I can't always be here. I have to rely on others to take care of her.'

'You could take her with you occasionally,' she said. 'It would be good for her.'

'What would be the point?' He threw her a frustrated glance. 'She can't *see* anything.'

'No, but she can feel, and she would be with you more than she is now. You are all she has now. The bond she has with you is what will build her confidence and sustain her through life. Stop feeling guilty. It's not your fault she's blind. It wasn't Giulia's fault. It's just what happened. Those were the cards you were dealt. You have to accept that.'

'You're not a parent. You know nothing of the guilt a parent feels.'

Her eyes flinched as if he had struck her. 'I know much more about guilt than you realise. I live with it every day. I *agonise* over it. But does it change anything? No. That's life. You have to find a way to deal with it.' Her gaze fell away from his as she pushed back a strand of her hair off her face.

Leo frowned as he narrowed his gaze to her left hand. 'Where's your ring?'

She glanced down at her hand and her face blanched. 'I don't know…' She looked up at him in panic, her eyes wide with alarm. 'It was there earlier. I have to find it. It's not mine.'

'What do you mean, it's not yours?'

She shifted her gaze again, her demeanour agitated. 'It's my fiancé's mother's. It's a family heirloom. I have to find it. It must have slipped off somewhere. It's a bit loose. I should've had it adjusted, but I—'

'It's probably in the garden where you were playing with Alessandra,' he said. 'I'll go and have a look.'

'I'll come with you,' she said, almost pushing him out of the way in her haste to get out of the door. 'I have to find it.'

'One of the gardeners will pick it up if it's out there,'

Leo said. 'Stop panicking. It didn't look all that valuable.'

She met his gaze with her distressed one. 'It's not about the monetary value. Why does everything have to be about money to you? It's got enormous sentimental value. I can't lose it. I just can't. I have to find it.'

'I trust my staff to hand it in if they find it. You don't have to worry. No one is going to rush it off to the nearest pawn shop.'

Her brow was a fine map of worried lines. 'You don't understand. I have to find it. I don't feel right without it on my finger.'

He grasped her flailing hand and held it firm. 'Why? Because you need it there as a reminder, don't you? Your fiancé is thousands of miles away but without that ring there to prod your conscience you could so easily forget all about him, couldn't you?'

She pulled out of his hold and dashed out of the room. Leo heard the slapping of her flat shoes along the marbled floor.

He followed at a much slower pace.

He would be perfectly happy if the blasted ring was *never* found.

Eliza looked everywhere but there was no sign of her ring. She went over every patch of the lawn. She went over the rose beds and the pathways but there was no trace of it anywhere. Her rising panic beat a sickening tattoo in her chest. How would she explain it to Samantha? It was so careless of her to have neglected to get it tightened. How would she ever make it up to her? It wasn't just any old ring. It was a symbol of Samantha's lifelong love for her husband Geoff and now *she* had lost it.

Leo had come out and spoken to the gardener before he joined her. 'Any sign?'

Eliza shook her head, her stomach still churning in anguish. 'Samantha will be devastated.'

'Samantha?'

'My fiancé's mother.' She wrung her hands, her eyes scanning the lawn in the vain hope that the sunlight would pick up the glitter of the ring. 'I don't know how I'll ever tell her. I have to find it. I *have* to.'

'The gardener will keep on looking. You should come indoors. You look like you're beginning to catch the sun.'

Eliza glanced at her bare arms. They were indeed a little pink in spite of the sunscreen she had put on earlier. She suddenly felt utterly exhausted. Losing the ring was the last straw on top of everything else. That telltale ache had started deep inside her chest. The tears were not far away. She could feel them burning like peroxide behind her eyes. She put her hand up and pinched the bridge of her nose to try and stop them from spilling.

'*Cara.*' Leo put a gentle hand on her shoulder. 'You're getting yourself in such a state. It's just a ring. It can be replaced.'

She shrugged off his hold and glared up at him with burning resentment. 'That's just *so* typical of you, isn't it? If you lose something you just walk out and get a new one. That's what you did when you lost me, wasn't it? You just went right on out and picked up someone else to replace me as soon as you could.'

The garden seemed to go into a stunned silence after her outburst. Even the light breeze that had been teasing the leaves on the trees had suddenly stilled, as if in shock at the bitterness of her words.

Eliza bit her lip as she lowered her gaze. 'I'm sorry…

That was wrong of me. You had a perfect right to move on with your life…'

There was another tense beat of silence.

'I hope you find your ring.' He gave her a curt nod and turned and strode across the lawn, back past the fountain until finally he disappeared out of sight.

CHAPTER EIGHT

WHEN ELIZA CAME downstairs after putting Alessandra to bed there was an envelope with her name on it propped up on the kitchen counter.

'That's your ring,' Marella said as she came out of the pantry. 'Signor Valente found it in the grotto. He was out there for ages looking for it.'

'That was…kind of him…' Eliza fingered the ring through the paper of the envelope. 'I think I'd better get it tightened before I wear it again.'

Marella cocked her head at her as she picked up a cleaning cloth. 'How long have you been engaged to this fiancé of yours?'

'Um…since I was nineteen…eight years.'

'It's a long time.'

She shifted her gaze from the penetrating black ink of the housekeeper's. 'Yes…yes, it is…'

'You're not in love with him, *sì*?'

'I *love* him.' Had she answered *too* quickly? Had she sounded *too* defensive? 'I've always loved him.'

'That's not the same thing as being in love,' Marella said. 'I see how you are with Signor Valente and him with you. He stirs something in you. Something you've tried for a long time to suppress, *sì*?'

Eliza felt a wave of colour wash over her cheeks. 'I'm just the replacement nanny. I'll be gone in four weeks.'

Marella gave the counter top a slow wipe as she mused, 'I wonder if he will let you go.'

'I'm absolutely certain Signor Valente will be enormously pleased to see the back of me,' Eliza said with feeling.

Marella stopped wiping and gave her a level look. 'I wasn't talking about Signor Valente.'

A telling silence slipped past.

'Excuse me…' Eliza forced a polite smile that felt more like a grimace. 'I have to check on Alessandra.'

When Eliza came downstairs an hour later Marella was just leaving to attend a family function.

'There is a meal all set up on gas flamed warmers in the dining room,' she said as she tied a nylon scarf around her neck. 'I think Signor Valente is in the study. Will you be all right to handle dishing up? Don't worry about clearing up afterwards. I can do that in the morning.'

'I wouldn't dream of leaving a mess for you to face in the morning,' Eliza said. 'I'm perfectly capable of dishing up and clearing away. Have a good evening.'

'*Grazie.*'

Eliza glanced towards the study once the housekeeper had left. Should she wait until Leo came out for dinner to thank him for finding her ring or should she seek him out now? She was still deciding when the door suddenly opened.

He saw her hovering there and arched a brow. 'Did you want me?'

I want you. I want you. I want you. It was like a chant inside her head but it was reverberating throughout her body as well. She could feel that on-off pulse deep in her core intensifying the longer his dark, mesmerising gaze held hers.

'Um…I wanted to thank you for finding my ring,' she said, knowing her cheeks were burning fiery red. 'It was very thoughtful of you to take the time to keep looking.'

'It was behind the seat in the grotto. You must've lost it when you picked up your cardigan.' His dark gaze glinted satirically. 'I'm surprised you didn't notice it missing earlier.'

Eliza set her mouth. 'Yes, well, I'm going to get it tightened so it doesn't happen again.'

He reached for her hand before she could step away. She sucked in a breath as those long, strong, tanned fingers imprisoned hers. Her heart started a madcap rhythm behind her breastbone and her skin tingled and tightened all over. 'W…what are you doing?' Was that her voice, that tiny mouse-like squeak of sound?

His gaze went to her mouth, lingering there. She felt her lips soften and part slightly, her response to him as automatic as breathing. His fingers were warm and dry around hers. She imagined them on other parts of her body, how it had felt to have them caress her intimately, her breasts, her inner thighs, the feminine heart of her that had swelled and flowered under his spine-tingling touch. Her insides clenched with longing as she thought of the stroke of his tongue against her—that most intimate of all kisses. How he had seemed to know from their first time together what she needed to reach fulfilment.

She could see the memory of it in his gaze as it came back to mesh with hers. It made her spine shiver to see that silent message pass between them…the universal language of making love.

Passionate, primal—primitive.

'*Ho voglia di te—ti voglio adesso.*' His words were like a verbal caress, all the more powerfully, intoxicatingly stimulating as they were delivered in his mother tongue.

Eliza swallowed as her heart raced with excitement. 'I don't understand what you just said…' *But I've got a pretty fair idea!*

Those dark eyes glittered with carnal intent as he grasped her by the hips and, with a little jerk forwards, he locked her against his erection. She felt it against her belly, the thunder of his blood mimicking the sensual cyclone that was happening within her own body. Her breasts ached for his touch. She could feel them swelling against the lace constraints of her bra. Her mouth tingled in anticipation of his covering it, plundering it. She sent the tip of her tongue out to moisten the surface of her lips. Her need of him was consuming her common sense like galloping, greedy flames did to a little pile of tinder-dry toothpicks.

'I want you—I want you now.' He said it this time in English and it had exactly the same devastatingly sensual impact.

'I want you too.' It was part confession, part plea.

He splayed a hand through her hair, gripping her almost roughly as his mouth came down on hers. It was a kiss that spoke of desperate longing, of needs that had for too long gone unmet, of a man wanting a woman so badly he could barely control his primitive response to her. It thrilled Eliza to feel that level of desire in him because it so completely and so utterly matched her own.

The stroke and glide of his tongue against hers set

her senses aflame. She undulated her hips against him, whimpering in delight as he in turn growled deep in his throat and responded by pressing even harder against her.

His hands moved over her body, skating over her breasts, leaving them tingling and twitching in their wake. She wanted more. When had she not wanted more from him? She wanted to feel his hands on her, flesh-to-flesh, to feel their skin in warm and sensual contact.

Her hands went to the front of his shirt, pulling at it as if it was nothing but a sheet of paper covering him. Buttons popped and a seam tore but she didn't hold back. Her mouth went to every bit of hard muscled flesh she uncovered. From the dish at the base of his neck just below his Adam's apple, down his sternum, taking a sideways detour to his flat dark male nipples, rolling the tip of her tongue over them in turn, before going lower in search of his belly button and beyond.

'Wait.' The one word command was rough and low. 'Ladies first.'

A shiver ran over her. She knew what he was going to do. The anticipation of it, the memory of it made her legs tremble like leaves in a wind tunnel.

He picked her up in his arms, carrying her effortlessly to the sofa inside his study. She felt the soft press of the cushions as he laid her down, those dark eyes holding hers with the unmistakable message of their sensual purpose, thrilling her from her tingling scalp to her curling toes.

He came back over her, but only to shove her dress above her hips. One of his hands peeled off her knickers, the slow but deliberate trail of lace as he pulled them down over her thigh to her ankles, another masterstroke of seduction in his considerable arsenal. She kicked off the lace along with her shoes, snatching in a quick breath as he bent his head to the swollen heart of her.

The intimacy of it should have appalled her given the current context of their relationship, but somehow it didn't. It felt completely natural for him to be touching her like this. To be touching and stroking her body as if it were the most fascinating and delicately fragrant flower he had ever seen.

'You are *so* beautiful.'

Oh, those words were like a symphony written only for her! She didn't feel beautiful with anyone else. No one else could make her body sing with such perfect harmony the way he did.

He took his time, ramping up her arousal to the point where she was sure she was going to scream if he didn't give her that final stroke that would send her careening into oblivion.

'Please…*oh, please…*' The words came out part groan, part gasp.

'Say you want me.'

'I want you. I want you.' She was panting as if she had just run up a steep incline. 'I want you.'

'Tell me you want me like no other man.'

She dug her fingers like claws into the cushioned sofa, her hips bucking as he continued his sensual torture. 'I want you more than anyone else… Oh, God. *Oh, God…*' Her orgasm splintered her senses into a starburst of feeling. It rattled and shook her body like a ragdoll in a madman's hands. It went on and on until she finally came out the other side, limbless and spent and breathless.

Leo moved up her body and set to work on removing her dress and bra. Eliza lifted her arms up like a child as he uncovered her flesh. She sighed with bone-deep pleasure as he took her breasts in his hands.

How had she gone so long without this exquisite worship of her body? Her flesh was alive with intense feeling. Shivers were still cascading down her spine like a waterfall of champagne bubbles. The very hairs on her head were still dancing on tiptoe. Her inner core was still pulsating with the aftershocks of the cataclysmic eruption of ecstasy that had rippled through it.

His hands gripped her hips once more as his body reared over hers. Somehow he'd had the foresight to apply a condom. She vaguely recalled him retrieving one from his wallet in his back pocket before he had shucked his trousers off.

He kissed her again, his mouth hard and yet soft in turn. It was a devastatingly seductive technique, yet another one he had mastered to perfection. She felt his erection poised for entry against her. She opened her legs for him, welcoming him with one of her hands pressed to the taut and carved curve of his buttocks, the other behind his head, pulling his mouth back down to hers as her ankles hooked around his legs.

He surged into her with a groan that came from deep at the back of his throat. It bordered on a rougher than normal entry but she welcomed it with a groan of pleasure. He seemed to check himself and then started to move a little more slowly, but she pushed him to increase his pace with little encouraging gasps and whimpers and further pressure from her hands pressing down on his buttocks.

She felt the rocking motion of his body within hers. She heard the intervals of his breathing gradually increase. She felt the tension in his muscles as they bunched up under the caress of her hands. The friction of his body within hers sent off her senses into another tailspin of anticipatory delight.

But still he wasn't intent on his own pleasure.

He was still focused on bringing about another delicious wave of hers and brought his fingers down to touch her. The way he seemed to know how much pressure and friction she needed to maximise her pleasure was the final undoing of her. The continued thrusting of his body and the delicate but magical ministration of his fingers were an earth-shattering combination. She was catapulted into another crazily spinning vortex of feeling that robbed her of all sense of time and place.

It was all feeling—feeling that was centred solely in her body.

But as she was coming down from the heights of human pleasure her mind resumed enough focus to register his powerful release. It sent another shockwave of pleasure through her body. She had felt every moment of that powerful pumping surge as he lost himself. There was something about that total loss of control that moved her deeply. It had always been this way between them. A mind-blowing combustion of lust and longing, and yet something else that was less easily definable…

As she moved her hands to the front of his body she noticed the pale circle on her bare left ring finger. It was a stark reminder of her commitment elsewhere.

Her stomach sank in despair.

She wasn't free.

She wasn't free.

She pushed against his chest without meeting his gaze. 'I want to get up.'

He held her down with a gentle but firm press of his hand on her left shoulder. 'Not so fast, *cara*. What's wrong?'

Eliza couldn't look at him. *Wouldn't* look at him. She stared at the peppery stubble on the bulge of his Adam's apple instead. 'This should never have happened.'

He took her chin between his finger and thumb and forced her to meet his gaze. 'Why is that?'

Her eyes smarted with the tears she resolved she *would not* shed in front of him. 'How can you *ask* that?'

His gaze quietly assessed hers. 'You still feel guilty about the natural impulses you have always felt around me?'

She lowered her lashes, chewing at her lip until she tasted the metallic sourness of blood. 'They might be natural but they're not appropriate.'

'Because you're still intent on tying yourself to a man who can't give you what you want or need?'

She continued to valiantly squeeze back the tears, still not looking at him. 'Please, let's not go over this again. I'm here with you now. I'm doing what you asked and paid me to do. Please don't ask me to do any more than that.'

He released a gusty sigh and got up, dressing again with an economy of movement Eliza privately envied. She felt exposed, not just physically—even though she had somehow managed to drag her discarded dress over her nakedness—but emotionally, and that was far more terrifying.

'Contrary to what you might think, I didn't pay you to sleep with me.' His voice was deep and rough, the words sounding as if they had been dragged along a gravel pathway. 'That is entirely separate from your position here as nanny to my daughter.'

She gave him a pointed look. 'Both are temporary appointments, are they not?'

His eyes were deep and dark and unfathomable. 'That depends.'

'Is Kathleen coming back?'

'She hasn't yet decided.'

'I thought you said my month-long contract was not up for negotiation,' Eliza said with a little frown. 'If she decides not to return, does that mean you'll offer me the post?'

'That also depends.'

She arched her brow. 'On what?'

'On whether you want to stay longer.'

Eliza chewed at her lip. If things had been different, of course she would stay. She would live with him as his lover, as his mistress, his daughter's nanny—whatever he wanted, she would do it because she wanted him so much.

But things *weren't* different.

They were exactly the same as they had been four years ago. It didn't matter what she wanted. It was the shackles of her guilt that would always make her forfeit what she wanted. How could she stay here with Leo and leave her other life behind? It was a fanciful dream she had to erase from her mind, just as she'd had to do in the past.

Eliza thought of little Alessandra, of how attached the child had become to her in such a short time. It wasn't just that the little girl was looking for a mother substitute. Eliza had latched onto her with equal measure. She looked forward to their time together. She felt excited about the ways in which Alessandra was growing and developing in confidence and independence. It wasn't just the teacher in her that was being validated, either. It was the deep-seated maternal instinct in her that longed to be expressed. Alessandra was responding to that strong instinct in her to love and protect and nurture.

If things were different, *she* would have been Alessandra's mother.

There was still a fiendish pain inside her chest at the thought of another woman sharing that deeply bonding experience with Leo. She so desperately wanted to be a mother. Each birthday that passed was a painful, gut-twisting reminder of her dream slipping even further out of her grasp.

Eliza brought her gaze back to his once she was sure she had her emotions hidden behind a mask of composure. 'Staying longer isn't an option…'

'Driving up the price, are we, Eliza?' A ripple of tension appeared along his jaw, his dark eyes flashing at her with disgust. 'That's what you're doing, isn't it? You want me to pay you a little extra to stay on as my mistress. How much do you want? Have you got a figure in mind?'

She took a steadying breath against the blast of his anger and turned away. 'There's no point talking to you in this mood.'

A hard hand came down on her forearm and turned her back to face him. His eyes blazed with heated purpose. She felt it ignite a fire in her blood where his fingers were wrapped around her wrist like a convict iron.

The tension in the air crackled like sheet lightning over a wide open plain.

'Don't turn away from me when I'm speaking to you,' he rasped.

Her chin went up and her eyes shot him their own fiery glare. 'Don't order me about like a child.'

His dark eyes glinted menacingly as they warred with hers. 'I'm paying you to obey my orders, damn it.'

Eliza felt a trail of molten heat roll down her spine but still her chin went even higher. 'You're not paying me enough to bow and scrape to you like a simpering servant.'

Those fingers burned her flesh like a brand. That hard-muscled body tempted her like an irresistible lure. Those dark eyes wrestled with hers until every nerve in her body was jangling and tingling with sensual hunger.

Heat exploded between her legs.

She could almost feel him there, that pounding surge of his body that triggered something raw and earthy and deeply primitive inside her.

'How much?' His eyes smouldered darkly. 'How much to have you in my bed for the rest of the month? How much to have you bowing and scraping and simpering to my every need?'

A reckless demon made her goad him. 'You can't afford me.'

'Try me. I have my limit. If you go over it I'll soon tell you.'

Eliza thought of the small house where Ewan and his mother lived in Suffolk. She thought of how much the bathroom needed renovating to make showering him easier for Samantha. She thought of the heating that needed improving because Ewan, as a quadriplegic, had no way of controlling his own body temperature. And then there were the lifting and toileting and feeding aids that always seemed to need an upgrade.

It all cost an astonishing amount of money.

Money Leo Valente was willing to pay her to be his mistress for the rest of the month.

Her heart tapped out an erratic tattoo. Maybe if she took the money it would make her feel less guilty about sleeping with him while she was engaged to Ewan. It would make it impossible to treat their relationship as anything but a business deal.

Well, perhaps not impossible…but unlikely.

He would have her body but she wouldn't sell him her heart.

Eliza met his hardened gaze with her outwardly composed one even as her stomach nosedived at the extraordinary step she was taking. 'I want two hundred and fifty thousand pounds.'

His brows lifted a fraction but, apart from that, his expression gave nothing away. 'I'll see that you get it within the next hour or two.'

'So—' she hastily disguised a tight little swallow '—it's not…too much?'

He brought her up against the trajectory of his arousal, the shock of the contact sending a wave of heat like a furnace blast right through her body. 'I'll let you know,' he said and sealed her mouth with the blistering heat of his.

CHAPTER NINE

WHEN ELIZA WOKE the following morning her body tingled from head to foot. She turned her head but the only sign of Leo having shared the bed with her was the indentation on his pillow beside her.

And his smell…

She breathed in the musk and citrusy scent of him that clung to the sheets as well as her skin. His love-making last night had been as spine-tingling as ever, maybe even more so. For some reason the fact that he was paying her to sleep with him had made her stretch her boundaries with him. It had been heart-stopping and exciting, edgy and wonderfully, mind-blowingly satisfying.

The door of the bedroom opened and he came in carrying a cup of tea and toast on a tray. He was naked except for a pair of track pants that were slung low on his lean hips. 'I've already checked on Alessandra. Marella's giving her breakfast downstairs.'

'I'm sorry…' Eliza frowned as she pulled the sheet up to cover her naked breasts. 'I overslept…I didn't hear her on the monitor.'

'It didn't go off.' He put the tray down on her side of the bed. 'I took it with me. She woke up while I was down making the tea.'

She pushed a matted tangle of hair off her face with a sweep of her hand. This cosy little domestic scene was not what she was expecting from him. It caught her off guard. It made her feel as if she was acting in a play but she had been given the wrong script. She didn't know what was expected of her. 'You seem to be having some problems with your human resources department,' she commented dryly.

His dark glinting eyes met hers as he sat on the edge of the bed beside her. 'How so?'

She gave him an ironic look. 'Your housekeeper is acting as the nanny and your nanny is acting like the lady of the manor—or should I say lady of the villa?'

He trailed the tip of his index finger down the length of her bare arm in a lazy, barely touching stroke that set off a shower of sparks beneath her skin. 'Marella enjoys helping with Alessandra. And I quite enjoy having you playing lady of the villa.'

Eliza shivered as that bottomless dark gaze smouldered as it held hers. 'Wouldn't lady of the night be more appropriate?' she asked with a pert hitch of her chin.

A line of steel travelled from his mouth and lodged itself in his eyes. 'What do you want the money for?'

She gave a careless shrug and shifted her gaze to the left of his. 'The usual things—clothes, jewellery, shoes, salon treatments, a holiday or two.'

He captured her chin and made her look at him. 'You do realise I would have paid you much more?'

Her stomach quivered as his thumb grazed the fullness of her bottom lip. 'Yes…I know.'

He measured her gaze with his for endless, heart-chugging seconds. 'But you didn't ask for it.'

'No.'

'Why not?'

She gave another careless little shrug. 'Maybe I don't think I'm worth it.'

His thumb caressed her cheek as he cupped her face in his hand, his gaze still rock-steady on hers. 'Why would you think that?'

Eliza felt the danger of getting too close to him, of allowing him to see behind the paper-thin armour she had pinned around herself. She had to stay streetwise and smart-mouthed. She couldn't allow him to see any other version of herself.

The real version.

'You get what you pay for in life, wouldn't you agree?' She didn't pause for him to answer. 'Say my price was a million pounds. I figure this way you only got a quarter of me.'

His gaze continued to hold hers unwaveringly. 'What if I wanted all of you?'

Eliza felt a momentary flare of alarm in her chest. She had experienced his ruthless intent before. It was dangerous to be inciting it into action again. What he wanted he got. He wouldn't let anything or anyone stand in his way. Hadn't he already achieved what he'd set out to achieve? She was back in his bed, wasn't she? And it didn't look as if he was going to let her out of it any time soon. She held his look with a steady determination she wasn't even close to feeling. 'The rest of me is not for sale.'

His thumb moved back and forth over her cheek, slowly, mesmerizingly, that all-seeing, all-knowing gaze stripping away the layers of her defences like pages being torn from a cheap notepad. 'So which part have I bought?' he asked.

'The part you wanted.'

'How do you know which part I wanted?'

'It's obvious, isn't it?' She brazenly stroked a hand down his naked chest to the elastic waistband of his track pants, giving him her best sultry look. 'It's the same part I want of you.'

She heard him suck in a breath as her hand dipped below the fabric. She felt his abdomen tense. She felt the satin of his skin, the hot, hard heat of him scorching her fingers as they wrapped around him. Her body primed itself for his possession and she didn't care how sweet or savage it was going to be.

She yanked his track pants down further and bent her head to him, teasing him mercilessly with her tongue. He groaned and dug his fingers into her scalp but he didn't pull away, or, at least, not at first. She drew on him, tasting the essence of him, swirling her tongue over and around him, making little flicking movements and little cat-like licks until finally he could stand no more.

'Wait,' he gasped, trying to pull back. 'I'm going to—' He let out a short, sharp expletive as she went for broke. She had him by the hips and dug her fingers in hard. Her mouth sucked harder and harder, wanting his final capitulation the same way he went for hers—ruthlessly.

He came explosively but she didn't shy away from receiving him. He shuddered and quaked, finally sagging over her like a puppet whose strings had been suddenly severed.

Eliza caressed her hands over his back and shoulders, a slow exploratory massage of each of his carved and toned muscles. He had loved her massaging him in the past. And she had loved doing it. He had carried a lot of tension in his body even back then. There was something almost worshipful about touching him this way, with long and smooth strokes of her palms and fingers, rediscovering him like a precious memory she thought she had lost for ever. 'You've got knots in your shoulders. You need to relax more.'

'Can't get more relaxed than this right now.'

'I'm just saying…'

He lifted himself up on his elbows and locked gazes with her. 'We're doing this the wrong way around. It's not the way I usually do things.'

She tiptoed her fingers over his pectoral muscles. 'You're paying me to pleasure you. That changes the dynamic, surely?'

He pulled her hand away from his chest and sat upright, his expression contorted with a brooding frown, his gaze dark and disapproving. 'I know what you're doing.'

'What am I doing?'

'You're playing the hooker card.'

She gave a little up and down movement of one shoulder. 'If the shoe fits I usually wear it. I find it's more comfortable that way.'

'Is that really how you want to play things?'

Her brow arched haughtily. 'Do I have a choice?'

He held her gaze for a long pause before he let out a breath and got to his feet. He scraped a hand through his hair before he dropped it back down by his side. 'The money is in your account. I deposited it an hour ago.'

'Thank you.' She gave him a look. 'Sir.'

There was another tight pause before he spoke. 'I have to go to Paris on business. Marella has agreed to be here to help you with Alessandra. I don't expect you to be on duty twenty-four hours a day.'

'How long will you be away?'

'A day or two.'

'Why don't you take us with you?' she asked. 'It's a shortish trip. It shouldn't be too hard to organise. It would be a little adventure for Alessandra. It will build her confidence to travel and mix with other people other than just you and Marella and me.'

His jaw tightened like a clamp. 'Maybe some other time.'

Eliza suspected his 'maybe some other time' meant *no* other time. What did he think was going to happen to Alessandra if she stepped outside the villa for once? How was his little girl supposed to live a normal life if he kept her away from everything that was normal? 'You can't keep her hidden away for ever, you know.'

'Is that what you think I'm doing?'

'No one even knows you have a child, much less that she's blind.'

'I don't want my daughter to be ridiculed or pitied in the press.' His gaze nailed hers. 'Can you imagine how terrifying it would be for her to be hounded by paparazzi? She's too young to cope with all of that. I won't allow her to be treated like a freak show every time she goes out in public.'

'I understand how you feel, but she needs to—'

He stabbed a finger in the air towards her, his eyes blazing with vitriolic anger. 'You do *not* understand. You don't have any idea of what it's like to have a child with a disability. She can't *see*. Do you hear me? She can't see and there's not a damn thing I can do about it.'

Eliza swallowed unevenly, her heart contracting at the raw emotion he was displaying. He was angry and bitter but beneath all that was a loving father who was truly heartbroken that he could do nothing to help his little daughter. Tears burned in the back of her throat for what he was going through. No wonder he was always so tense and on edge. 'I'm sorry…'

He drew in a tight breath and released it in a slow, uneven stream. 'I'm sorry for shouting at you.'

'You don't have to apologise…'

He came back to where she was still sitting amongst the pillows, a rueful look on his face as he brushed a flyaway strand of her hair off her face. 'I know you're only trying to help but this is a lot for me to handle right now.'

She lowered her gaze again and bit at her lip. 'I shouldn't have said anything…'

He stroked the pad of his thumb over her savaged lip. 'Of course you should. You're an expert on handling children. I appreciate your opinion although I might not always agree with it.'

'I just thought it would be good for Alessandra to stretch her wings a bit.' She met his gaze again. 'But the press thing is difficult. I can see why you want to protect her from all of that. But sooner or later she'll have to deal with it. She can't stay here at the villa for the rest of her life. She needs to mix with other children, to make friends and do normal kid stuff like go to birthday parties and on picnics and play dates.'

He studied her features for a measured pause. 'I might have to go back to London some time next week. If you think Alessandra would cope with it then maybe we could make a little holiday out of it. Maybe take her to Kew Gardens or something. Smell a few roses. That sort of thing.'

Eliza gave him a soft smile and touched his hand where it was resting on the bed beside her. 'She's a very lucky little girl to have such a wonderful father like you. There are a lot of little girls out there who would give anything to be loved by their fathers the way you love her.'

His fingers ensnared hers, holding them in the warmth of his hand. 'You've never told me anything about your father. I remember you told me when we first met that your mother died when you were young. Is he still alive?'

She shifted her gaze to their joined hands. 'Yes, but I've only met him the once.'

'You don't get on?'

'We haven't got anything in common.' She traced a fingertip over the backs of his knuckles rather than meet his gaze. 'We live in different worlds, so to speak.'

He brought her hand up to his mouth and kissed her bent fingers, his eyes holding hers in a sensual tether that sent a wave of longing through her body. 'Your tea and toast are cold. Do you want me to get you some more?'

'You don't have to. I'm not used to being served breakfast in bed.'

He took her currently bare ring finger between his thumb and index finger, his eyes still meshed with hers. 'Doesn't your fiancé treat you like a princess?'

Eliza couldn't hold his gaze. 'Not any more.'

A silence dragged on for several moments.

'Why do you stay with him?'

'I'd rather not talk about it.'

He pushed up her chin to lock her gaze with his. 'Has he got some sort of hold over you? Are you frightened of him?'

'No, I'm not frightened of him. He's not that sort of person.'

'What sort of person is he?'

She flashed him an irritated look. 'Can we just drop

this conversation? I'm not comfortable about talking about him while I'm being paid to be in your bed.'

'Then maybe I should make sure I get my money's worth while you're here, *sì*?' He pinned her wrists either side of her head, his eyes hot and smouldering as his hard aroused body pressed her down on the mattress.

Even if her hands were free, Eliza knew she wouldn't have had the strength of will to push him away. Her lower body was on fire, aching with the need to feel him inside her. He released one of her hands so he could rip away the sheet that was covering her, his hungry gaze moving over her like a burning flame.

His mouth swooped down and covered hers in a searing kiss, his tongue driving through to meet hers in a crazy, lustful, frenzied dance. Her breasts swelled beneath the solid press of his chest, her nipples going to hard little peaks as they rubbed against him.

He reached across her to find a condom in the bedside cabinet drawer but he didn't take his mouth off hers to do it. He kissed her relentlessly, passionately, drawing from her the sort of shamelessly wanton response she'd only ever experienced with him. She used her teeth like a female tiger in heat, biting and nipping and tugging at his lower lip, teasing him with little flicks of her tongue against his, shivering in delight when he did the same back to her.

Once the condom was on he entered her with a thick, surging thrust that made her gasp out loud. There was nothing slow and languid about his lovemaking. It was a breathtakingly fast and furious ride to the summit of pleasure. She felt the pressure building so quickly it was like a pressure cooker about to explode. Her body needed only the slightest bit of extra encouragement from his fingers to send her over the edge into a tumultuous release that made her head spin along with her senses.

But he wasn't stopping things there.

Before she had even caught her breath he flipped her over on her stomach, straddling her from behind, those strong hands of his on her hips as he thrust deep and hard, again and again until she was shivering with pleasure both inside and out.

There was something so wickedly primal and earthy about this dominant position. She felt as if he was taming her, subduing her even as he pleasured her. She heard his breathing rate increase as he fought for control, the grip on her hips almost painful as he thrust above her.

She raised her bottom just a fraction and the change of friction set off an explosion of feeling that shuddered through her like an earthquake: tremor after tremor, aftershock after aftershock, until finally she came out the other side, totally spent and limbless.

His hands tightened on her hips to hold her steady as he came. She felt every spasm of his body. She heard those harsh, utterly male groans of ecstasy that delighted her so much.

Did he experience the same rush of pleasure with the other women he slept with? Was it foolish of her to think she was somehow special? That what he experienced with her was completely different than with anyone else? That the sensational heat of their physical connection was the real reason he had brought her back into his life, not just as a fill-in nanny for his daughter?

Leo turned her back over and looked at her for a long moment. It wasn't easy to read his expression. Was he, like her, trying to disguise how deeply affected he was by what they had both shared? 'I want you to promise me something.'

Eliza moistened her kiss-swollen lips. 'What?'

'If we go to London next week, there is to be no physical contact with your fiancé.'

His sudden change in mood was jarring to say the least. But then, what had she been expecting him to say?

'What are you going to do?' she asked. 'Keep me under lock and key?'

A flinty element entered his gaze as it held hers. 'I am not having you go from my bed to his and back again. Do I make myself clear?'

She resented him thinking she would do such a thing, even though she knew it was perverse of her to blame him given she hadn't told him the truth about her situation. She wondered if she should just tell him. Maybe he would understand her painful dilemma much more than she gave him credit for. Sure, she'd left it a bit late, but she might be able to make him understand how terribly conflicted she felt.

'Leo…there's something you need to know about Ewan—'

'I don't even want you to speak his name in my presence,' he said. 'I will not share you with him or anyone. I've paid for your time and I will not be short-changed or cuckolded.' He got off the bed and picked up his track pants and roughly pulled them back up over his hips.

Her pride finally came to her rescue. She swung her legs off the bed and, with scant regard for her nakedness, stalked over to where he was standing and poked her index finger into the middle of his chest like a probe. 'How dare you tell me who I can and can't speak about in your presence?' she said. 'I don't care how much money you pay me. I will *not* be ordered about by you.'

His eyes glittered as he stared her down. 'You will do as I say or suffer the consequences.'

She curled her lip at him. 'Is that supposed to scare me? Because, if so, it doesn't.' *It did, but she wasn't going to admit that.*

His mouth was a thin line of ruthless determination. 'You want a job to go back to at the end of the summer break? Then think very carefully about your behaviour. One word from me and your career as a teacher will be well and truly over.'

Outrage made her splutter. 'You can't do that!'

His hardened look said he could and he would. 'I'll see you when I get back.'

CHAPTER TEN

IT WAS ALMOST a week before Eliza saw Leo again. Apparently the project he had in Paris had developed some issues and he needed to be on site to handle the difficulties. She had no doubt his work was demanding and time consuming, but in this instance she wondered if he had deliberately taken himself out of the picture to regroup. He didn't speak to her for long each time he called—just long enough for her to give him updates on what Alessandra was doing. The conversations were stiff and formal, just like a powerful employer to a very low-ranked employee. It riled her deeply, but she was nearly always with Alessandra when he called so she had no recourse. She had considered calling him when Alessandra was in bed asleep but had always talked herself out of it out of stubborn and wilful pride.

Alessandra clearly missed her father being around, but she seemed to accept he had to go away to work from time to time. Eliza enjoyed being with the little girl, even though at times it was challenging to think of ways to help her become more independent. Some days Alessandra was more motivated than others. But it was lovely to have the one on one time with her after coming from a busy classroom where she had to juggle so many children's educational and social needs.

Tatiana, the orientation and mobility teacher, came for another session and was thrilled to see how Alessandra had improved over the week. To Eliza it had seemed such painfully slow progress, but Tatiana reassured her that Alessandra was doing far better than other vision-impaired children her age.

The one challenge that Eliza was particularly keen to attempt was taking Alessandra for a walk outside the villa or even down to one of the cafés in Positano. She had spoken to Marella about it in passing, but while the housekeeper thought it was a great idea, she had reservations over what Leo would say.

'Why don't you ask him about it when he next calls?' Marella said.

Eliza knew what he would say. *No.* She wanted to present it as a fait accompli to show him how well his little girl was coping with new experiences. She took comfort in the fact that no one would know who she was so there would be no threat of press attention.

Their first walk outside the villa grounds was slow, but Eliza took comfort in the fact that Alessandra seemed to enjoy the different smells and sounds the further they went. She couldn't help feeling incredibly sad as she looked down at the exquisite beauty of the scenery below. The bluey-green water of the ocean sparkled in the sunshine, boats, frightfully expensive-looking yachts and other pleasure craft dotted the surface, but Alessandra could see none of it. It seemed so cruel to be robbed of such pleasure in looking at the glorious array of nature. But then, if Alessandra had never seen it, would she miss it the way a sighted person would if their vision was suddenly taken away?

Their second outing was a little more adventurous. Eliza got Giuseppe to drive them down to Spiaggia

Fornillo, the less crowded of the two main beaches in Positano. It had been quite an achievement getting the little girl to walk on the pebbly shore with bare feet but she seemed to enjoy the experience.

'Have you ever been swimming?' Eliza asked Alessandra as they made their way back to the villa in the car.

'Kathleen took me once but I didn't like it.'

'I didn't like swimming at first either,' Eliza said, giving the little girl's hand a gentle squeeze. 'But after you get over the fear part and learn to float it's one of the nicest things to do, especially on a hot day.'

That very afternoon Eliza took Alessandra down to the pool in the garden for a swimming lesson. With plenty of sunscreen to protect the little girl's pale skin, she gently introduced her to the feel of the water by getting her to kick her legs while she held her, gradually working up to getting used to having water trickle over her face. Alessandra was frightened at first, but gradually became confident enough to float on her back with Eliza keeping her supported by a gentle hand beneath her shoulder blades and in the dish of her little back.

'Am I swimming yet?' Alessandra asked, almost swallowing a mouthful of water in her excitement.

'Almost, sweetie.' Eliza gave a little laugh. 'You're getting better all the time. Now let's try floating on your tummy. You'll have to hold your breath for this. Remember how I got you to blow bubbles into the water before?'

'Uh huh.' Alessandra turned on her stomach with Eliza's guiding hands and gingerly put her face in the water. She blew some bubbles but soon had to lift her head to snatch in a breath. She gave a few little splutters but didn't seem too fazed by the experience.

'Well done,' Eliza said. 'You're a right little water baby, aren't you?'

Alessandra grinned as she clung to Eliza like a little frog on a tree. 'I like swimming now. And I like you. I wish you could stay with me for ever.'

Eliza's heart contracted sharply at the unexpected love she felt for this little child. 'I like you too, darling.' *And I wish I could stay for ever too.*

A tall shadow suddenly blocked the angle of the sun and she turned and saw Leo standing there with an unreadable expression on his face. 'Oh…I didn't realise you were back…Alessandra, your father is home.'

'*Papà*, I can swim!'

'I saw you, *mia piccola*,' Leo said, leaning down to kiss her on both cheeks. 'I'm very impressed. Is there room in there for me?'

'Yes!'

Eliza didn't say a word. She wasn't sure it was wise to share the pool—even as big as it was—with that tall, intensely male, leanly muscled body. Wearing a bikini when accompanied by a blind toddler was quite different from wearing it when there was a fully sighted, full-blooded man around, especially one who had seen her in much less. She felt the scorch of his gaze as it went to the curve of her breasts, which were showing just above the line of the water she was standing in. She felt her insides clench and release with that intimate tug of need she only felt when he was around.

A silent message passed between their locked gazes.

Eliza gulped as he stood back up and tugged at his tie, pulling it through the collar of his shirt to toss it to one of the sun loungers on the sandstone terrace beside the pool.

His shirt was next, followed by his shoes and socks.

The sun caught the angles and planes of his taut chest and abdomen, making him look like a statue carved by a master of the art.

Marella came out on to the terrace at that point with a tray of iced drinks. 'I think it might be time for Alessandra to get out of the heat, *sì*?' she said with a twinkling and rather knowing smile.

Eliza felt a blush rush over her face and travel to the very roots of her hair. 'It's my job to see to her—'

'*Grazie,* Marella,' Leo said smoothly. 'I think Eliza could do with some time to relax.' He bent and scooped Alessandra out of her arms. 'I will be up later to tuck you into bed, *tesorina*. Be good for Marella.'

Once Marella and the child had gone Eliza was left feeling alarmingly defenceless. She covered her chest with her arms, shivering even though the sun was still deliciously warm on her neck and shoulders. 'What are you doing?' she asked.

His hands were pulling his belt through the lugs of his trousers. 'I'm joining you in the pool.'

'But you're not wearing bathers…are you?'

A dark brow lifted in an arc. 'I seem to remember a time when you didn't think they were necessary.'

'That was before. It was different then. This place is like Piccadilly Circus. There are staff about everywhere.'

He unzipped his trousers and she watched with bated breath as he stood there in nothing but his black underwear. He already had the beginnings of an erection, which was no surprise given how her own body was reacting. 'Have you missed me, *cara*?'

She gave her head a haughty little toss. 'No.'

He laughed and slipped into the water beside her, cupping the back of her head with one of his hands as he pressed a hot kiss to her tight mouth. It didn't stay tight for long, however. All it took was one erotic sweep of his tongue for her to open to him with a sigh of bliss. He tasted salty and male with a hint of mint. It was ambrosia to her. She responded greedily, giving back as good as he gave, her tongue tangling, duelling and seducing just as his was doing to hers. Her breasts were jammed up against his chest, the water-soaked fabric abrading her already erect nipples.

His other hand ruthlessly undid the strings of her bikini top and it floated away from her body like a four-legged octopus. He cupped her free breasts with his hands, caressing her, teasing her with his warm, wet touch. He took his mouth off hers to feast on each breast in turn. Eliza arched back in pleasure as his teeth and his tongue grazed and salved in turn. Her nerves went into a sensual riot beneath her skin. They jumped and danced and flickered with longing. That deepest, most feminine ache of all pulsed relentlessly between her legs. She could feel his hard erection pressing against the softness of her belly. It awoke everything that was female in her. She rubbed against him to get more of that wonderful friction.

He made a guttural sound in his throat as he undid the strings of her bikini bottoms at her hips. The scanty fabric fell away and his fingers went to her, delving deep.

It wasn't enough. She wanted more. She wanted *all* of him.

She pulled at his underwear to free him to her touch. She wrapped her hand around him, rubbing him, teasing him, and pleasuring him as his mouth came back to hers in a passionately hot kiss that had undercurrents of desperation.

He suddenly pulled back from her, breathing hard, his eyes glazed with desire. 'I haven't got a condom.'

'Oh…' Disappointment was like an enervating drug that made her sag as if all of her muscles were weighted by anvils.

His eyes gleamed at her as he backed her against the side of the pool. 'Why the long face, *tesoro mio*? We can be creative, *sì*?'

Her body tingled at the thought of just how creative his lovemaking could be. But then, she too could be innovative when it came to giving him pleasure. She slithered against him, from chest to thigh, ramping up his need for her with the same merciless intent he had been using on her.

He took her by the waist and lifted her up to a sitting position on the edge of the pool. It was shamelessly wanton to open her legs in full view of the villa but she was beyond caring.

The first stroke of his masterful tongue made her shudder, the second made her gasp, and the third made her cry out loud as the ripples started to roll through her. 'Don't stop, don't stop, *don't stop…*' She clung to his hair for purchase as her body shattered around her.

He gave her a sexy smile as she came back to her senses. 'Good?'

She gave a little shrug that belied everything she had just felt. 'OK, I guess.'

'Minx.' He pulled her back into the water to hold her against him. 'I should punish you for lying. What do you think would be a suitable penance?'

Send me back to my old life. Eliza gave herself a mental shake and forced a smile to her lips. 'I don't know…I'm sure you'll think of something.'

His brows moved together. 'What's wrong?'

'Nothing.'

He cupped her cheek, holding her gaze with his. 'Are you still angry with me?'

Eliza was starting to wonder where her anger had gone. As soon as he had appeared on the pool deck she had forgotten all about their tense little battle of wills the day he had left to go to Paris. Her feelings about him now were much more confusing…terrifying, actually. She couldn't afford to examine them too closely.

'Does it matter to you what I feel?' she asked. 'I'm just an employee. I'm not supposed to feel anything but gratitude for having a job.'

His expression became brooding as his hand dropped away from her face. 'So we're back to that, are we?'

'You're the one who engineered this,' she said, struggling to keep her emotions in check. 'You come marching back in my life and issue orders and stipulations and conditions. I don't know what you want from me. You keep changing the goalposts. I just don't know who I'm supposed to be when I'm with you.'

He looked at her for a lengthy moment. 'Why not just be yourself?'

She gave a little cough of despair. 'I don't even know who that is any more.'

His hands came down on the tops of her shoulders, a gentle but firm hold. His eyes were very dark as they meshed with hers, but not with anger this time. 'Who was that girl in the bar four years ago?'

Eliza twisted her lips in a rueful manner. 'I'm not sure. I hadn't met her before that night. She came as a bit of a surprise to me, to be perfectly honest.'

He started massaging his thumbs over the front of her shoulders, slowly and soothingly. 'She came as a bit of a surprise to me, too. A delightful one, however.'

She felt a wave of sadness wash over her. How very different things would have been if she had been free to commit to the relationship he had wanted. 'Did you really fall in love with me back then?' She was shocked she had asked it but it was too late to take the words back. They hung in the silence for a beat or two.

'I think you were right when you said I was looking for stability after my father died. Losing him so suddenly threw me. I think it's hard for an only child—no matter how young or old—to deal with the loss of a parent. There's no one to share the grief with. I panicked at the thought of ending up like him, all alone and desperately lonely.'

'I'm sorry.'

He gave her shoulders a little squeeze before he dropped his hands. 'You'd better get some clothes on. You're starting to get goose bumps.'

Eliza watched as he effortlessly hauled himself out of the pool. He was completely unselfconscious about being naked. He stepped into his trousers and zipped them up without even bothering to dry himself. He bent to pick up his shoes and, flinging his shirt and tie over one shoulder, walked into the villa without a backward glance.

When Eliza came down to the *salone* later that evening Leo was standing with his back to the room with a drink in his hand. There was something about his posture that suggested he was no longer in that mellow mood he'd been in down by the pool. He turned as she came in and gave her a brittle glare. 'Alessandra informed me you'd taken her outside the villa grounds on not one, but two occasions.'

She straightened her shoulders. 'We didn't go very far. She'd never been to the beach before.'

'That's completely beside the point.' His eyes blazed with anger. 'Do you have any idea of the risk you were taking?'

'What risk is there in allowing her to walk down the street or put her feet in the ocean, for God's sake? I was with her the whole time.'

'You went expressly against my instructions.'

Eliza frowned at him. 'But you said we'd go to London next week. I thought it would be good preparation for that.'

'I said I'd *think* about it.'

'That's not the way I heard it. You said if I thought Alessandra would cope with it then we'd make a little holiday out of it. I was preparing her to cope with it and she did very well, all things considered.'

Anger pulsed at the side of his mouth. 'Did anyone see you? Were there paparazzi about?'

'No, why should there be?' she asked. 'No one knows who I am.'

'That could change as soon as we are seen in public together.' His eyes pinned hers. 'Have you thought of how you're going to explain *that* to your fiancé?'

Eliza raised her chin defiantly. 'Yes, I have thought about it. I'll tell him the truth.'

His brow furrowed. 'That I'm paying you to sleep with me?'

She gave him an arch look. 'It's the truth, isn't it?'

He shifted his gaze and let out a gust of a breath. 'It wasn't why I asked you to come here.'

'So you keep saying, but it's pretty obvious this is what you wanted right from the start.'

He took a large swallow of his drink and put it down,

his muscles bunched and tight beneath the fine cotton of his shirt. 'You haven't forgotten you're forbidden to speak to the press, have you?'

'No.'

He faced her with a steely look. 'You're not very good at obeying rules, are you, Eliza?'

'You're very good at making them up as you go along, aren't you?' she tossed back.

His mouth started to twitch at the corners. 'I wondered when she would be back.'

She frowned again. 'What...*who* do you mean?'

'The girl in the bar—that spirited, feisty, edgy little temptress.' His eyes glinted darkly. 'I like her. She turns me on.'

She made a huffy movement with one of her shoulders, trying to ignore the wave of heat that was coursing through her at that smouldering look in his gaze. 'Yes, well, I liked the guy by the pool this afternoon much more than the one facing me now.'

'What did you like about him?'

'He was nice.'

'Nice?' He gave a laugh. 'That's not a word I would ever use to describe myself.'

'You were nice four years ago. I thought you were one of the nicest men I'd ever met.'

His dark eyes gleamed some more. 'Even though I practically ripped the clothes from your body and had wild, rough sex with you the first night we met?'

'Did I complain?'

'No.' His frown came back and the ghost of a smile that had been playing about his mouth disappeared. 'Why did you come up to my room with me that night?'

'I told you—I was tipsy and jet-lagged and feeling reckless.'

'You were taking a hell of a risk. I could have been anyone. I could have hurt you—seriously hurt you.'

'I trusted you.'

'Foolish, foolish girl.'

Eliza felt a shiver run up along her arms. She could see the desire he had for her. She could feel it pulsing like a current in the air between them. 'The way I see it, you were taking a similar risk.'

The ghost of a smile was back, wry this time as it tilted up one corner of his mouth. 'I find it hard to see what you could have possibly done to hurt me. I'm almost twice your weight.'

But I did hurt you, she thought. *Isn't that why I'm here now?*

'Are you going to pour me a drink or do I have to jump through hoops first?' she asked.

'No hoops.' He came to stand right in front of her. 'Just one kiss.'

She tilted her head back and held his dark brown gaze pertly as the blood all but sizzled in her veins. 'Is that an order?'

He tugged her against his rock-hard body, his eyes scorching hers. 'You bet it is.'

CHAPTER ELEVEN

WHEN ELIZA BROUGHT Alessandra downstairs for breakfast the next morning Leo intercepted them at the door. He reached for his daughter and held her close against his broad chest. Seeing such an intensely masculine man hold a tiny child so protectively made Eliza's heart instantly melt.

Was it her imagination that he seemed a little more relaxed this morning? It wasn't as if he was particularly rested, but then, neither was she. Their lovemaking last night had been particularly passionate and edgy. She could still feel the little pull of tender muscles where he had thrust so deep and so hard inside her. It was such a heady reminder of the breathtaking mastery he had over her body. But as much as she loved the heart-stopping raciness of his lovemaking, there was a tiny part of her that secretly longed for something a little more emotional. Maybe he didn't have the capacity to feel emotion during sex. It was just a physical release for him, like any other bodily need being attended to, like hunger and thirst. But it wasn't like that for her… or at least not now…

'I thought we could have breakfast out on the water this morning,' Leo said. 'Would you like that, *mia piccola*?'

'In the pool?' Alessandra asked.

'No, on my boat.'

'You have a boat?' Eliza asked.

'It's moored down at the marina. I thought Alessandra might enjoy being out on the water. I've never taken her on it before. Marella's packing us up a picnic to take with us.'

Eliza could see he was making an effort to spend more time with his daughter. He was relaxing his tight control over where she could go. She could also see what a big step it was for him to take. A trip out on a boat might be a relatively simple and rather enjoyable adventure for a sighted child, but in Alessandra's case there were many considerations to take into account. Her experience of the outing would be different but hopefully no less enjoyable. Besides, she would be with her father and that was clearly something that made her feel loved and special.

'Breakfast on the water sounds lovely, doesn't it, sweetie?' she addressed the little girl.

Alessandra hugged her arms tightly around her father's neck and smiled. 'Can I take Rosie with me?'

'Who's Rosie?' Leo asked.

'Rosie is the toy puppy Eliza made for me,' Alessandra said. 'She has long floppy ears and a tail just like a real puppy.'

Leo met Eliza's gaze over the top of his daughter's little head. 'Eliza is a very clever young lady. She is talented at many things.'

'I want her to stay with me for ever,' Alessandra said. 'Can you make her stay with us, *Papà*? I want her to be my *mamma* now. She tucks me in and reads me stories and she cuddles me lots and lots.'

Eliza felt emotion block her throat like a scrubbing brush stuck halfway down. She blinked a couple of times and shifted her gaze from Leo's. Alessandra needed someone there *all* of the time, someone she could rely on—someone to love her unconditionally.

Hadn't *she* felt the same desperate ache for stability and love as a child? Throughout her lonely childhood she had clutched on to various caregivers in an attempt to feel loved and cherished. Whenever she had been sent to yet another foster placement, she had blamed herself for not being pretty enough, cute enough or lovable enough. The constant pressure of wondering whether she was doing the right thing to make people love her had worn her down. She had eventually stopped trying and at times had deliberately sabotaged the relationships that could have most helped her.

But Alessandra wasn't a difficult child to love. Eliza loved all children—even the most trying ones—but something about Leo's little girl had planted a tiny fishhook in her heart. She felt it tugging on her whenever she thought of the day when her time with her would come to an end. Leaving Leo would break her heart, leaving his daughter would rip it from her chest.

'I'm afraid that's not possible,' Leo said in a matter-of-fact tone. 'Now, let's go and get that picnic, shall we?'

Leo's motor launch was moored amongst similar luxury boats down at the marina. It was a beautiful vessel, sleek and powerful as it carved through the water. The sun was bright and made thousands of diamonds sparkle across the surface of the sea. It was a poignant reminder that little Alessandra couldn't see the beauty that surrounded them. But she was clearly enjoying being in the fresh air with the briny scent of the sea in the air. She lifted her face to the breeze as the boat moved across the water and giggled in delight when a spray of moisture hit her face. 'It's wetting me!'

'The ocean is blowing you kisses,' Eliza said and dropped a kiss on the top of the little girl's wind-tousled hair. She looked up and caught Leo's gaze on her. 'It's a gorgeous boat, Leo. Have you had it long?'

'I bought it just before Alessandra was born.' He brushed back his hair off his face with one of his hands, and although he was wearing reflective sunglasses she could see the crease of a frown between his brows. 'I thought it'd be a great thing to do as a family. Get out on the water, sail into the sunset, get away from the madding crowd, so to speak.' His mouth twisted ruefully. 'I only ever take it out on my own, mostly late at night when Alessandra's fast asleep in bed when Kathleen or Marella are on duty. I suppose I should think about selling it.'

Eliza looked at his wind-tousled hair and her heart gave a little leap of hope. 'Is that where you went the other night? Out here on the boat…alone?'

His expression was self-deprecating. 'Not quite what you were expecting from a worldly playboy, is it?'

Eliza was conscious of Alessandra sitting on her knee but she hoped the unfamiliar English words would not compromise her innocence. 'When was the last time you were…um…a playboy?'

'I took my marriage vows seriously, even though nothing was happening in that department, more or less since that first night. We agreed to leave things on a platonic basis. In the time since she…left us ten months ago…' he glanced at his daughter for a moment before returning his gaze to hers '…I've had other more important priorities.'

Eliza stared at him in shock. For the last four years

he had not been out with a variety of mistresses. He hadn't been with *anyone.* Like her, he had been concentrating on his responsibilities, trying to do the best he could under difficult and heart-wrenching circumstances. The night she had thought he had been having bed-wrecking sex with some casual hook-up, he had actually been out on his boat—*alone*. Probably spending the time like she did back in her life in England, tortured with guilt and desperation at how life had thrown such a devastating curve ball.

Alessandra shifted on Eliza's lap. 'I'm hungry.'

Eliza ruffled the little tot's raven-black hair. 'Then let's have breakfast.'

Leo met her gaze and gave her a smile. 'How about you set up the picnic in the dining area while I teach this young lady how to steer a motor launch?'

'Can I steer it? Can I really?' Alessandra asked with excitement. 'What if I run into something?'

He scooped her up in his arms and carried her towards the bow. 'You'll have me by your side to direct you, *mia piccola*. We'll be a team. A team works together so no one gets into trouble. We look out for each other.'

'Can Eliza be part of our team?' Alessandra asked. 'For always and always?'

Eliza blinked back a rush of tears and looked out at the ocean so Leo couldn't see how much his little girl's request had pained her. Why was life always so full of such difficult choices? If she chose to stay she would be abandoning Samantha and Ewan. If she chose to leave she would be breaking not only her own heart, but also dear little Alessandra's.

As for Leo's heart…did he still have one after what happened between them four years ago? She had a feeling he had closed off his heart since then. Yes, he loved his daughter, but he would allow no one else to get close to him.

'She's a part of our team for now,' he said in a deep and gravelly tone. 'Now, let's get your hands on the wheel. Yes, just like that. Now, here we go—full steam ahead.'

On the way back to the marina after breakfast, Leo glanced at Eliza, who was sitting with his daughter on her lap, holding one of her little hands in hers with an indulgent smile on her face. To anyone looking from the outside, she would easily pass for Alessandra's biological mother with her glossy mahogany hair and creamy toned skin.

Although he had paid an enormous sum of money to engage her services as a nanny, he suspected she would have been just as dedicated if he had paid her nothing. She seemed to genuinely care for his daughter. He had seen her numerous times when she hadn't known he was watching. Those spontaneous hugs and kisses she gave Alessandra could not be anything but genuine.

Even his housekeeper, Marella, had commented on how much happier Alessandra seemed now that Eliza was there. Truth be told, he had found it a little unnerving to see Eliza's relationship grow and blossom with his daughter. He hadn't planned on Alessandra getting so attached to her so quickly. He had felt confident Alessandra's relationship with Kathleen would override any new feelings she developed for Eliza.

And, as much as he hated to admit it, the villa did seem more of a home with the sound of laughter and footsteps going up and down the corridors. Eliza had enhanced his daughter's life in such a short time. Her swimming lessons and her trips to the beach had built his daughter's awareness of the world around her. Eliza's competence and confidence in exposing Alessandra to new things had helped give him the confidence to take this outing today. She had shown him that he could afford to be more adventurous in taking Alessandra out and about more. His little girl might not be able to see the things he so desperately wanted her to see, but she had clearly enjoyed the sunshine and the fresh air and the sound of the water and the sea birds. How much more could he help her experience?

But how could he do it without Eliza?

When they returned from the trip to London there would be less than ten days left before Kathleen returned. She had emailed him and told him she wasn't going to stay in Ireland with her family after all. A couple of weeks ago he would have been thrilled by that announcement.

But now…he wasn't sure he wanted to think about how he felt.

Eliza hadn't been wearing her engagement ring but he had noticed it swinging on a chain around her neck a couple of times. She took care never to wear it when they were in bed together but it irked him that she still clung to it. He knew she wasn't in love with the guy and yet he didn't like to fool himself that she was in love with him instead.

Their arrangement was purely a sexual one, not an emotional one. He was happy with that. Perhaps happy was not the best choice of word—content, satisfied…

OK, frustrated was probably a little closer to how he was feeling. He always felt as if she gave everything of herself physically when they were together but there was a part of her that was still off-limits.

What perverse facet of his personality craved that one elusive part of her that she refused to offer him? It wasn't as if he loved her. He had sworn he would never allow himself to be that vulnerable again. Hadn't he learnt that lesson the hard way in childhood? He had loved his mother and look how she had walked out as if he had meant nothing to her.

He flatly *refused* to let anyone do that to him again.

He had been caught off guard with Eliza four years ago. The sudden death of his father had left him reeling. He had seen something in Eliza that had spoken directly to his damaged soul. He had felt as if they were kindred spirits. He knew that it sounded like some sort of crystal ball claptrap, but it had stayed with him all the same—the sense that they had both experienced bitter disappointment in life and were searching for some way of soothing that deep ache in their psyche. Their physical connection had transcended anything he had experienced before. Even now his body was humming with the aftershocks of their lovemaking last night. No one pleasured him the way she did. He suspected no one pleasured her the way he did, either.

But she wasn't going to stay with him for ever. He wasn't going to ask her to. He would have to let her go when the time was up. He would have no need of her as a nanny now that Kathleen was coming back.

And those other needs?

Well, there were other women, weren't there? Women who wanted what he wanted: a temporary, mutually satisfying arrangement with no feelings, no attachment and no regrets once it was over.

He had lived the life of a playboy before. He could do it again.

* * *

Eliza was sitting on deck with Alessandra fast asleep against her shoulder as Leo docked the vessel when she caught sight of a photographer aiming a powerful-looking lens their way. 'Um…Leo?'

He glanced across at her. 'What's wrong?'

She jerked her head in the direction of the cameraman. 'It might be just a tourist…'

'Take Alessandra below deck,' he commanded curtly.

'I don't think—'

'Do as I say,' he clipped out.

Eliza rose stiffly to her feet and, putting a protective hand to the back of the little child's head, went back down below deck. She tucked Alessandra into one of the beds in one of the luxury sleeping suites and gently closed the door. She sat in the lounge and fumed about Leo's curt manner. She understood he wanted to protect his little daughter but the bigger the issue he made out of it the more anxious Alessandra might become. She felt it would be better to explain to Alessandra that there were journalists out and about who were interested in her Papà's life and that it was part and parcel of being a successful public figure.

And how dare he speak to *her* as if she was just a servant? They were lovers for God's sake! It might be a temporary arrangement and all that, but she refused to be spoken to as if she had no standing with him at all.

Leo came down to the lounge after a few minutes, his expression black with anger. 'When I ask you to do something I expect you to do it, not stand there arguing about it.'

Eliza got abruptly to her feet and shot him a glare. 'You didn't ask me. You *ordered* me.'

His mouth tightened until his lips all but disappeared. 'You will do as I ask or order, do you hear me?'

She glowered at him. 'I will not be spoken to like that. And what if Alessandra had been awake? What's she going to think if she hears you barking out orders as if I'm nothing to you but yet another obsequious servant you've surrounded yourself with to make your life run like stupid clockwork?'

His dark gaze took on a probing glint. 'Are you saying you want to be more to me than an employee?'

Eliza rued her reckless tongue. 'No…no, I'm not saying that.'

'Then what are you saying?'

She blew out a tense little breath. What *was* she saying? She wanted to be more to him than a temporary fling but he was never going to ask her and she wasn't free to accept if by some miracle he did. 'I'm saying you have no right to order me about like a drill sergeant. There will always be journalists lurking about. You have to prepare Alessandra for it. She's old enough to understand that people are interested in your life.'

He scraped a hand through his hair, making it even more tousled than the wind had done. 'I'm sorry. I was wrong to snap at you. It just caught me off guard seeing that guy with that camera up there.'

'Was it a journalist?'

'Probably. I'm not sure what paper or agency he works for. It doesn't seem to matter. The photos go viral within minutes.' His expression tightened. 'I can't stand the thought of my daughter being the target of intrusive paparazzi. I'm not ready to expose her to that.'

'I know this is really hard for you,' Eliza said. 'But Alessandra will feel your tension if you don't relax a bit. Other high profile parents have to deal with this stuff all the time. The more you try and resist these people, the more attractive you become as a target.'

'You're probably right…' He gave her a worn down look. 'I always swore I would never let her go through a childhood like mine. I want to protect her as much as I can. I want her to feel safe and loved.'

'What was it like during your childhood?'

He sucked in another breath and released it in a whoosh. 'It certainly wasn't all tartan picnic blankets and soft cuddly puppies. I think my mother needed to justify her decision to leave by publicly documenting a whole list of infringements my father and I had supposedly done. I was just a little kid. What had I done other than be a kid? My father…well, all he had done was love her. The press made the most of it, of course. The scandal of my mother's affair was splashed over every paper in the country but she didn't seem to care. It was as if she was proud to have got away from the shackles of domesticity. It destroyed my father. He just crumpled emotionally to think he wasn't enough for her—that she had sold out to someone who had more money than him.'

Eliza could understand now why he had such a fierce desire to keep Alessandra out of the probing eyes of the media. He had been caught in the crossfire as a child. How distressing it must have been to have all those private issues made public. She put a hand on his arm. 'You weren't to blame for your parents' problems.'

He looked down at her for a long moment, his gaze deep and dark. 'How did your mother die?'

She dropped her hand from his arm and turned away, folding her arms across her body. 'What has that got to do with anything?'

'You've never told me. I want to know. What happened to her?'

Eliza blew out a breath and faced him again. What was the point of hiding it? She was the product of despair and degradation. It couldn't be changed. She couldn't miraculously whitewash her background any more than he could his. 'Drugs and drink robbed her of her life. They robbed me of both my parents when it comes down to it. I suspect my father was the one who introduced her to drugs. He's serving time in prison for drug-related offences. The one and only time I visited him he asked me to drug run for him. It might seem strange, given that familial blood is supposed to be thicker than water, but I declined. I guess it had something to do with the fact that I was farmed out to distant relatives who weren't all that enamoured with the prospect of raising a young, bewildered and overly sensitive child. The only true family I've known is my fiancé's. So, as to tartan picnic blankets and puppies… well, I have no experience of that, either.'

He put a gentle hand on her shoulder. 'I'm sorry.'

Eliza gave him the vestige of a smile. 'Why are you apologising? It's not your fault. I was already royally screwed up when I met you.'

His eyes roved her face, lingering over her gaze as if searching for the real person hiding behind the shadows. 'Maybe, but I probably made it a whole lot worse.'

'You didn't.' She put her hand on his chest, feeling his heart beating slow and steadily underneath her palm. 'I was happy for those three weeks. It was like stepping into someone else's life. For that period of time I didn't have a care in the world. It was like a dream, a fantasy. I didn't want it to end.'

'Then why did you end it?'

Her hand slid off his chest to push through the curtain of her windswept hair. 'All good things have to come to an end, don't they? It was time to move on. Soon it will be time to move on again.'

'What about Alessandra? You've been very good for her—even Tatiana says so. And it's easy to see how attached she's become to you.'

Eliza felt that painful little fishhook tug on her heart again. 'She'll cope. She'll have Kathleen and Marella and, most importantly, she'll have you.'

'Will you miss her?'

'I'll miss her terribly. She's such a little sweetheart.' *I wish she were mine.*

'And what about me?' His eyes were suddenly unreadable. 'Will you miss me too?'

Eliza's heart gave another painful contraction at the thought of leaving him. Would their paths ever cross again? Would the only contact be seeing him from time to time in a gossip magazine with some other woman on his arm? How would she bear it? What if he *did* decide to marry again? He might go on to have another child, or even more than one. He would have the family she had longed for while she would be stuck in her bleak, lonely life back at home, trapped in an engagement with a man who could not free her from it even if he wanted to.

She forced a worldly smile to her lips. 'I'll certainly miss picnics on luxury launches and swanning about in a villa that's as big as an apartment block.'

'That wasn't what I was asking.'

'Just what exactly *are* you asking?' She gave him a pointed look. 'It's not like you want me to stay with you permanently—Kathleen is coming back. You won't need me any more.'

'We'd better get going.' His expression was a mask of stone. 'I have some work to see to before we leave for London tomorrow.'

'We're leaving *tomorrow*?'

'The bursar of your school wants to meet with me. He spoke of a project you had proposed to the board for young single mothers on parenting practices and counselling, especially for those with children with special needs. I'd like to look at it a little more closely. It sounds like a good idea.'

Eliza had trouble containing her surprise. 'I don't know what to say…'

His eyes were hard as they held hers. 'Don't go attaching anything sentimental to my interest. I have a lot of money and, like a lot of wealthy people, I want to make a difference where it counts. There are other schools and charities that are in just as much, if not more, need of funds. I have to choose the ones I think are most productive in the long run.'

'This means so much to me,' she said. 'It's been a dream of mine for so long to do something like this. I don't know how to thank you.'

'I don't want or need your thanks.' He moved to the suite where Alessandra was sleeping. 'Meet me at the car. The paparazzi guy should have left by now.'

CHAPTER TWELVE

ELIZA DIDN'T SEE Leo until the following morning, just as they were about to leave for London. She had waited for him last night but he hadn't come to her.

She was still so deeply touched that he was considering doing more for her school. She wasn't sure what was behind his motivation, she was just grateful that he was contemplating supporting the project that was so very dear to her heart.

Had he softened in his attitude towards her? Dare she hope that he would no longer hate her for how she had rejected him all those years ago? Was this the time to tell him about Ewan? He had expressly forbidden her to speak of her fiancé, but maybe during this trip to London she could find a quiet moment to explain to him her circumstances. He came across as such a hard-nosed businessman, but she knew he had a heart. She had seen it time and time again when he was with his tiny daughter. She caught faint glimpses of it when she found his gaze on her, as if he was studying her, trying to put things together in his head. She desperately wanted him to understand her situation. As each day passed she felt more and more that he had a right to know. She could not leave him without telling him why she had made the choice she had.

'Signor Valente wants a quick word with you in the study,' Marella said as she bundled Alessandra into her arms. 'I'll get Alessandra settled in the car. Giuseppe will take the bags.'

Eliza went through to the study, where she found Leo standing behind his desk looking out at the garden. He turned as he heard her footfall and picked up a newspaper off his desk and handed it to her with an unreadable expression. 'The press have identified you as my new mistress.'

She took the paper and looked at the photo of her, standing on the deck of his boat with Alessandra asleep against her shoulder. The caption read: *New stepmother for tragic toddler heiress Alessandra Valente? London primary schoolteacher Eliza Lincoln has been identified as the mystery woman in Leo Valente's life.*

Eliza swallowed thickly. What if Samantha saw this? Would it hit the press back in Britain? What would Samantha think of her? She had told her a version of the truth rather than tell her an outright lie. She'd said she was visiting an old friend in Italy to fill in for the regular nanny who was taking a little break. She hadn't said the old friend was actually the man she had met and fallen in love with four years ago. Now it would be splashed over every newspaper in the country that she had gone off and had a clandestine affair. Samantha would be so dreadfully hurt. She would feel *so* betrayed.

'You might want to warn your fiancé in case this gets picked up by the British tabloids,' Leo said as if he had read her thoughts.

She chewed at her lower lip. 'Yes…'

'I suspect there will be quite a lot of press attention when we arrive in London,' he said. 'It will blow over after a day or two. Remember you are forbidden to comment on anything to do with your time with us here.'

Eliza straightened her shoulders as she handed him back the paper. 'I haven't forgotten.'

The flight to London went without a hitch but, as Leo had predicted, there was a cluster of photographers waiting outside for a glimpse of the young Englishwoman who had been spotted on his boat with his little girl the day before. The click, click, click of camera shutters going off sounded like a heavy round of bullets being discharged.

'Miss Lincoln, what does your fiancé Ewan Brockman think of you spending the last couple of weeks with billionaire Leo Valente in his luxury villa on the Amalfi coast in Italy?'

Eliza totally froze. How on earth did these people find out this stuff? What else did they know? For all these years Samantha had been adamant Ewan's condition should be kept out of the press. She had done everything she could to keep Ewan's dignity intact and Eliza had loved and respected her for it. Who had released his name? Someone at school? Only Georgie knew of the extent of Ewan's condition. Had a journalist pressed her for details? That was another phone call Eliza should have made. She should have warned Georgie to keep quiet if anyone approached her to comment on her private life.

'Miss Lincoln is my daughter's fill-in nanny,' Leo said before Eliza could get her mouth to work. 'She will be returning to her fiancé in a matter of days. Please give us room. My daughter is becoming upset.'

It was true—Alessandra was starting to whimper in distress, but Eliza had a feeling it had more to do with Leo's statement that she was leaving them to go back to her old life rather than the surge of the press. She cuddled the little girl close to her chest and, keeping her head down against the flashing cameras, she walked into the hotel with Leo until they were finally safe in their suite.

It didn't take long to settle Alessandra, who was tired after the journey. Marella, who had travelled with them, offered to babysit while Leo and Eliza went out for a meal.

'Are you sure this is wise?' Eliza asked as Leo closed his phone after booking a table at a restaurant.

'We need to eat, don't we?'

'Yes, but surely a meal in our suite would be perfectly fine?' She fiddled with the chain around her neck with agitated fingers. 'What's the point in deliberately entering the fray? They'll just hound us all over again.'

He gave her an ironic lift of his brow. 'You were the one who said I shouldn't hide Alessandra away.'

'We're not talking about Alessandra,' she said stiffly. 'We're talking about me, about *my* reputation. People are going to get hurt by all that stuff they're saying about me.'

'I take it you mean your fiancé?' His eyes were hard as stone as they held hers.

Eliza still hadn't had either the time or the privacy to call Samantha. Any moment now she expected her phone to ring, with Samantha asking her what the hell was going on. It was making her nervy and jumpy. A headache was pounding at her temples and a pit of nausea was corroding the lining of her stomach like flesh-eating acid. 'I don't like being called your mistress.'

'It's the truth, isn't it?'

'Not for much longer.' She scooped up her bag and

slung it over her shoulder. ‘Let’s get this over with. I want to get back as quickly as possible and go to bed.’

He gave her a smouldering look as he held the door open for her. ‘I couldn’t have put it better myself.’

They were halfway through dinner at an exclusive restaurant in Mayfair when Eliza’s phone audibly vibrated from inside her bag. She had set it to silent but hadn’t thought to turn off the vibration and illumination component. She tried to ignore it, hoping that Leo hadn’t heard, but the glow every time it vibrated was visible through the top of her bag.

‘Aren’t you going to answer it?’ he asked.

‘Um…it can wait.’ She picked up her glass of wine and took a little sip to settle her nerves.

The phone vibrated again.

‘Sounds like someone really wants to talk to you,’ he said.

Eliza knew it was pathetic of her to keep putting off the inevitable. It was a lifetime habit of hers to procrastinate, hoping that things would go away or be resolved on their own, but it was only prolonging the agony. Wasn’t that why she was in this mess? She should have been honest right from the word go with Ewan. She shouldn’t have waited for months and months without saying anything, letting him believe everything was fine when it wasn’t. Hadn’t she learned her lesson by now? She had to face things, not hide from them. ‘Um…will you excuse me?’ She rose to her feet. ‘I won’t be long.’

There was no one in the lipstick lounge adjacent to the restroom, so Eliza sat on a chintz-covered chair and pressed Samantha’s number. ‘Hi, it’s me.’

‘Oh, darling,’ Samantha said with an audible sigh

of relief. 'I'm so glad you called back so quickly. I'm bringing Ewan up to London to see the specialist tomorrow. You know how we've been on that waiting list for months and months? Well, there's been a sudden cancellation. I know you're probably tied up with your little nanny job, but I was hoping since you're back in London for a couple of days that you could come with me. Do you think you could get an hour or two off? You know how hard I find managing him all by myself. I called the agency and asked for a respite carer to come with me but there's no one available at such short notice. I was just hoping you could come with us. I know it's a lot to ask.'

Eliza felt her insides twist into cripplingly tight knots of guilt. How could she say no? She knew it wasn't the physical support with Ewan that Samantha was after. She knew how much hope Samantha had invested in seeing this particular specialist. She also knew Samantha was going to be completely shattered when the specialist gave her the same prognosis every other specialist she had taken Ewan to had done.

How could she let her face that all by herself?

Leo would be tied up with his work most of the day as well as his meeting with the bursar so it shouldn't cause too much of a problem. Marella probably wouldn't mind giving her a couple of hours. She needn't even ask Leo's permission. He would probably say no in any case. He would probably assume she was going against his orders and sneaking in a passionate session with her fiancé.

If only he knew…

'Of course I'll come with you,' she said. 'Text me the address and the time and I'll be there.'

'You're an angel,' Samantha said. 'I honestly don't know what I'd do without you.'

Eliza took an uneven breath and slowly released it. 'I thought you were calling about the stuff in the press… I guess you've seen it by now, otherwise you wouldn't have known I was here. I should have called you first to warn you. I'm sorry. It all sounds so horribly sordid.'

'Oh, sweetie, don't worry about that,' Samantha said. 'I know what the press are like. They make up stuff all the time. You can't believe a word you read these days. It's just pure sensationalism. I know you would never leave Ewan.'

Eliza felt guilt come down on her like a tower of bricks. *But I had left him!* The words were jammed in her throat, stuck behind a wall of strangling emotion.

'See you tomorrow, darling,' Samantha said. 'Love you.'

'Love you, too.' Eliza gave a long, heavy sigh as she switched the phone off. And, taking a deep breath, she got to her feet and walked back to where Leo was waiting for her.

He stood up when she came back to the table. 'Is everything all right?'

Eliza gave him a brief forced smile as she sat down. 'Of course.' She picked up her wine glass and cradled it in both hands to keep them occupied.

'Who was it?'

'Just a friend.'

'Eliza.'

She brought up her gaze and her chin. 'Yes?'

'I don't need to remind you of the rules, do I?'

'Would you like to screen all my calls while you're at it?' She put her glass down with a little clunk. 'Or how about you scroll through my emails and texts?'

He frowned and reached for his own wine glass. 'I'm sorry. I don't want to spoil our truce.'

'Truce? Is that what you call this?' She waved a hand to encompass the romantic setting.

'Look, I don't want to spend the only time we have alone together arguing. That wasn't the point of going out to dinner this evening.'

'What *is* the point?' Was it to make her fall in love with him again and then drop her cold? Was it to make her feel even more wretched about her other life once this was over?

He took one of her tightly clenched hands and began to massage her stiff fingers until they softened and relaxed. 'The point is to get to know one another better,' he said. 'I've noticed we either have mad, passionate sex or argue like fiends when we are alone. I want to try doing something different for a change.'

Eliza looked at her hand in his, the way his olive skin was so much of a contrast to her creamy one. She felt the stirring of her body the longer he held her. Those fingers had touched every part of her body. They could make her sizzle with excitement just by looking at them. It was becoming harder and harder to keep her emotions hidden away. She wasn't supposed to be falling in love with him again. She wasn't supposed to be dreaming of a life with him.

That was not an option for her.

She raised her gaze back to meet his. 'What did you have in mind?'

He smiled a slow smile that made his eyes become soft and warm, and another lock on her heart loosened. 'Why don't you wait and see?'

An hour later they were on a dance floor, not in an exclusive nightclub or a hotel ballroom, but on the balcony of their hotel suite. Champagne was in an ice bucket, romantic music was playing from the sound system and the vista of the city of London was spread out below them in a glittering array of twinkling lights and famous landmarks.

Eliza was in Leo's arms, dancing like Cinderella at the ball. The clock had moved way past midnight but this was one night she didn't want to end. She had never considered herself a particularly good dancer but somehow in Leo's arms she felt as if she was floating across the balcony, their bodies at one and their footwork perfectly in tune, apart from a couple of early missteps on her part.

She leaned her head against his chest and breathed in the warm citrus and clean male scent of him. 'This is nice…'

His hand pressed against the small of her back to bring her closer. 'Where did you learn to dance?' he asked.

She looked up at him with a rueful smile. 'I know, I'm rubbish at it, aren't I? I've probably mashed your toes to a pulp.'

He gave a deep chuckle and kissed her forehead. 'Don't worry. I can still walk.'

Eliza laid her head back down against his chest as she thought of Ewan sitting in that chair, his legs and arms useless, his once brilliant brain now in scattered fragments that could no longer connect.

The line of that old nursery rhyme played inside her head, as it had done so many times over the last five and a half years: *All the King's horses and all the King's men couldn't put Humpty Dumpty together again...*

CHAPTER THIRTEEN

THE NEXT DAY, Leo got back earlier than he'd expected from his meetings. He had particularly enjoyed the one with the community school bursar. He had made a commitment to the school and he couldn't wait to tell Eliza about it. The project she had set her heart on would go ahead, no matter how things turned out when her time with him was up.

Last night he had sensed a shift in their relationship. In the past they had had sex, last night they had made love. He had felt the difference in her kisses and caresses. He wondered if she had sensed the difference in his.

Did it mean she might reconsider her engagement? He had done a quick Internet search on her fiancé but he hadn't uncovered much at all. It surprised him for in this day and age just about everyone had a social media page or blog or website. Was the man some sort of recluse? It had niggled at him all day. After what had come out in the papers yesterday, why hadn't the guy stormed into the hotel and punched Leo's lights out? It didn't make sense. If Ewan Brockman loved Eliza, then surely he would have come forward and demanded an explanation.

It was time to have a no holds barred conversation

with her. Something wasn't quite adding up and he wasn't going to stop digging until he found out what it was—and there was no time like the present.

Leo came into the suite to find Marella sitting on the sofa with a book while Alessandra was having a nap in the next room.

'Where's Eliza?' he asked as he put his briefcase down.

'She went to do a bit of shopping,' Marella said, closing the book and putting it to one side. 'She's only been gone a couple of hours. I told her to take all the time she wanted. She should be back soon. Why don't you call her and meet her for a drink? I'll give Alessandra her bath and supper.'

'Good idea.' He gave her an appreciative smile and reached for his phone. He frowned as the call went through to message bank. He sent her a text but there was no response.

'She's probably turned her phone off,' Marella said.

'Did she say where she was intending to shop?'

Marella pursed her lips for a moment. 'I think she said something about going to Queen Square.'

He frowned as he put his phone back in his pocket. Queen Square was where the world-renowned UCL Institute of Neurology was situated. He'd driven past it a couple of times on previous trips to London. Great Ormond Street Hospital was close by. Why was Eliza going there? Sure, there were plenty of shops in the Bloomsbury district, but why had she told Marella she was going to Queen Square of all places?

Leo saw her from half a block away. She was standing talking with an older woman in her fifties outside the UCL Institute of Neurology. The older woman looked very distressed. She kept mopping at her eyes with a scrunched up tissue. Eliza was holding the hand of a gaunt young man in his late twenties who was strapped in a wheelchair, complete with breathing apparatus and a urinary catheter that was just visible under the tartan blanket that covered his thin, muscle-wasted legs.

Leo felt as if someone had thrown a ninety-pound dumb-bell straight at his chest.

Her fiancé.

He swallowed against a monkey wrench of guilt that was stuck sideways in his throat. Her fiancé was a quadriplegic. The poor man was totally and utterly incapacitated. He didn't even seem to be aware of where he was or whom he was with; he was staring vacantly into space. Leo watched as Eliza gently wiped some drool from the side of the young man's mouth with a tissue.

Oh, dear God, what had he done?

Why hadn't she told him?

Why the hell hadn't she told him?

He didn't know whether to be furious at her or to feel sorry for her. Why let him think the very worst of her for all this time? It all made horrible sense now that he had seen her fiancé with his very own eyes. It wasn't a normal relationship. How could it be, with that poor young man sitting drooling and slumped in his chair like that? Was that why she had taken the money he had offered her? She had done it for her fiancé.

His gut churned and roiled with remorse.

He had exploited her in the worst way imaginable.

Leo turned back the way he had come. He needed time to think about this—to get his head around it all. He didn't want to have it out with her on the street with her fiancé and his mother—he assumed it was his mother—watching on. He took a couple of deep calming breaths but they caught on the claws of his guilt that were still tearing at his throat.

Eliza had turned down his marriage proposal because she had honoured her commitment to her fiancé. It took the promise of *in sickness and in health* to a whole new level. She hadn't done it because she hadn't loved *him*. His instincts back then had been right after all. He had felt sure she had fallen in love with him. He had felt sure of it last night when she had danced in his arms on the balcony and made love with him with such exquisite tenderness.

He had felt his own feelings for her stirring beneath the concrete slab of his denial where he had buried them four years ago.

He thought back to all the little clues she had dropped about her fiancé. If only he had pushed a little harder he might have got her to trust him enough to tell him before things had gone this far. Was it too late to undo the damage? Would she forgive him?

His heart felt as if someone had slammed it with a sledgehammer.

What did it matter if she did or not? She was still tied to her fiancé. She still wore his ring, if not on her finger then around her neck.

Close to her heart...

Eliza got back to the hotel a little flustered at being later than she'd planned. Samantha had taken the news hard, as she had expected. There was no magical cure for Ewan. No special treatment or miraculous therapy that would make his body and mind function again. It was heartbreaking to think of Samantha's hopes being dashed all over again. What mother didn't want the best for her child? Wasn't Leo the same with Alessandra?

He would move heaven and earth to give his little girl a cure for her blindness, but it wasn't to be.

Samantha had been so upset Eliza had found herself promising to spend the rest of the summer break with her and Ewan once she got back from Italy. Even as the words had come out of her mouth she had wished she could pull them back. She felt as if she was being torn in two. Leaving Leo for the second time would be hard enough, but this time she would be leaving Alessandra as well.

Could life get any more viciously cruel?

Eliza opened the door of the suite and Leo turned to face her from where he was standing at the window overlooking the view. Her heart gave a little jolt in her chest. She had hoped to get back before he did. 'I'm sorry I'm late…' She put her handbag down and put a hand to her hair to smooth it back from where the breeze had teased it loose. 'The shops were crazily busy.'

His eyes went to her empty hands. 'Not a very successful trip, I take it?'

Her heart gave another lurch. 'No…no, it wasn't…' She tried to smile but somehow her mouth wouldn't cooperate. 'Where's Alessandra?'

'With Marella in the suite next door.'

'I hope you didn't mind me having a bit of time to myself.' She couldn't quite hold his gaze.

'I seem to remember telling you before that you are not under lock and key.' He wandered over to the bar area of the suite. 'Would you like a drink?'

'Um…yes, thank you.'

He handed her a glass of chilled white wine. 'Shopping is such thirsty work, *sì*?'

Eliza still couldn't read his inscrutable expression.

'Yes…' She took a sip of her drink. 'How did your meeting with the bursar go?'

'I've decided to bankroll your project.'

She blinked at him. 'You…you have?'

'I read your proposal in detail.' His expression remained masklike. 'There are a few loose ends that need tying up, but I think it won't take too much time to sort them out.'

Eliza forced her tense shoulders to relax. Was there some sort of subtext to this conversation or was she just imagining it? It was hard to gauge his mood. He seemed as if he was waiting for her to say something, or was she imagining that too? 'I can't thank you enough for what you're doing. I'm not sure why you're doing it.'

'You can't guess?'

She flicked over her dry lips with her tongue. 'I'm not foolish enough to think it's because you care something for me. You've made it pretty clear from the outset that you don't.' *Apart from last night, when it had seemed as if he was making love with her for the very first time.*

There was a silence that seemed to have a disturbing undercurrent to it. It stretched and stretched like a too thin wire being pulled by industrial strength strainers.

'Why didn't you tell me?' Leo asked.

'Tell you what?'

He let out a stiff curse that made her flinch. 'Let's stop playing games. I saw you today.'

Her stomach clenched. 'Saw me where?'

'With your fiancé. I assume that's who the young man in the wheelchair is?'

'Yes…'

His frown was so deep it joined his eyebrows like a bridge over his eyes. 'Is that all you can say?'

Eliza put her glass down before she dropped it. 'I was going to tell you.' She hugged her arms across her body. 'I would've told you days ago but you forbade me to even speak his name out loud.'

'That is not a good enough excuse and you know it.' He glared at her, but whether it was with anger or frustration she couldn't quite tell. 'You could've insisted I listen. You could've told me the first day I came to see you. For God's sake, you could've told me the first night we met. And you damn well *should've* told me the night I proposed to you.'

'Why?' She tossed him a glare right on back. 'What difference would it have made?'

'How can you *ask* that?' His tone was incredulous. 'I wanted to marry you. I still want to marry you.'

Eliza noticed he hadn't said he loved her. He just wanted a wife and a stepmother for his daughter. Wasn't that what the press had said? 'I'm not free to marry you.'

He came over and put his hands on her shoulders. 'Listen to me, Eliza. We can sort this out. Your fiancé will understand. You just have to tell him you want to be with someone else.'

She pulled out of his hold and put some distance between them, her arms going across her middle again. 'It's not that simple…' She took a breath that tore at her throat like talons. 'It's my fault he's in that chair.'

'What do you mean?'

She looked at him again. 'I ended our relationship. He left my flat upset—devastated, actually. He was in no fit state to drive. I should never have let him go. It was my fault. If I hadn't broken our engagement that night he would still be a healthy, active, intelligent, fully functioning man.' She choked back a sob. 'I can't even tell him I'm sorry. He doesn't have any understanding of language any more. He's little more than a body in a chair. He can't even breathe on his own. How can I tell his mother I want to be with someone else after what I've done to her son?'

'You didn't tell her you'd broken off the engagement?' Leo asked with a puzzled frown.

Eliza shook her head. 'When I got the call, she was already at the hospital. She was shattered by what the doctors had told her about his condition. He wasn't expected to make it through the night. How could I tell her then?'

'What about later?'

'I couldn't…' She took another shaky breath. 'How could I? She would think—like everyone else would—that I was trying to weasel my way out of a life of looking after him. It would be such a cruel and selfish and heartless thing to do.'

'Aren't you being a little hard on yourself? Would you have expected him to give up his life if you had been the one injured?'

Eliza had thought about it but had always come up with the same answer. 'No, because he would never have broken up with me without warning. He would have prepared me for it, like I should've done for him. We'd been together since I was sixteen. It was wrong of me to dump it on him like that. He loved me so much. And look at what that love has cost him. It's only fair that I give up my future for him. I owe him that.'

'You don't owe him your future,' Leo said. 'Come on, Eliza, you're not thinking rationally. His mother wouldn't want you to give up your life like this. Surely she's told you to move on with your life?'

Eliza gave him a despairing look. 'I'm all she has left. She lost his father when Ewan was a little boy. Now she's as good as lost him, too. How can I walk away from her now? I'm like a daughter to her and she's been like a mother to me. I can't do it. I just can't.'

'What if I talk to her? I'll make her understand how it's unfair of her to expect so much of you.'

Eliza shook her head sadly. 'You're so used to getting whatever you want, but sometimes there are things you just can't have, no matter how hard and desperately you wish for them.'

'Do you think I don't know that?' he asked. 'I have a child I would do anything on this earth to help.'

'I know you would and that's exactly what Samantha is like. She's a wonderful mother and a wonderful person. It would devastate her if I was to go away and live with you in Italy.'

'What if we moved to London? I could work from here. It would be a big adjustment but I could do it. There are good schools for the blind here. Alessandra will soon adjust.'

Eliza pulled her emotions back into line like a ball of loose yarn being wound up rapidly and tightly. 'I can't marry you, Leo. You have to accept that. Once the month is up I have to come back to my life here. I've already promised Samantha to spend the last couple of weeks of the holidays with her and Ewan.'

'You *do* have a choice. Damn it, Eliza, can't you see that? You're locking yourself away out of guilt. It's not going to help anyone, least of all your fiancé.' He sent his hand through his hair again. 'I suppose that's why you took the money. It was for him, wasn't it?'

'Yes…'

'Why didn't you ask for more?'

'I was uncomfortable enough as it was, without exploiting your offer.'

He gave an embittered laugh. 'Let's say it how it was. It wasn't an offer. I blackmailed you. I can never forgive myself for that.' He moved to the other side of the room as if he needed the distance from her to think.

'I'm sorry...' Eliza broke the silence. 'I've handled this so badly. I've made it so much worse.' She took a deep shuddering breath as she finally came to a decision. 'I'm not going to go back with you to Italy tomorrow. It wouldn't be fair to Alessandra. It will make it so much harder when the month is up.'

He swung around to glare at her. 'What...you're just going to walk away? What about the contract you signed? Are you forgetting the terms and conditions?'

'If you decide to act on them, then I'll have to face that if and when it happens.'

'I'll withdraw my offer for your project. I'll tell the bursar I've changed my mind.' His jaw was clenched tight, his eyes flashing at her furiously.

Eliza knew it was risky calling his bluff but she hoped he would come to understand this was the best way to handle things—the cleanest way. 'Will you say goodbye to Alessandra for me? I don't want to wake her now. It will only upset her more.'

His look was scathing. 'I never took you for a coward.'

'It has to be this way.'

'Why does it?' His eyes flashed at her again. 'Are you really going to stand there and deny that you love me?'

Eliza steeled herself as she held his gaze. 'I have never said I loved you.'

A muscle flicked in his cheek and his eyes hardened. 'So it was always just about the money.'

'Yes.'

His lip curled mockingly. 'And the sex.'

She gave him her best worldly look. 'That too.'

He sucked in a breath and moved to the window overlooking the leafy street below. 'I'll have Marella send your things to you when we get back.'

'Thank you.' Eliza moved past to collect her things from the suite.

'I won't say goodbye,' he said. 'I think we've both said all that needs to be said.'

Except I love you, Eliza thought sadly as she softly closed the door as she left.

CHAPTER FOURTEEN

ELIZA SPENT THE first week with Samantha and Ewan in Suffolk in a state of emotional distress so acute it made her feel physically ill. She couldn't sleep and she could barely get a morsel of food past her lips. Every time she thought of Leo or Alessandra her chest would ache as if a stack of heavy books was balanced on it. But she had no choice but to keep what she was feeling to herself as Samantha was still dealing with her heartbreak over the hopelessness of Ewan's situation.

But towards the middle of the second week Samantha seemed to pick herself up. She had even been out a couple of times in the evening while Eliza sat with Ewan. She hadn't said where she was going or whom she was going with and Eliza hadn't asked. But each time Samantha returned she looked a little less strained and unhappy.

'Darling, you don't seem yourself since you came back from the nanny job,' Samantha said as she watched Eliza push the food around her plate during dinner. 'Is everything all right? Are you missing the little girl? She's rather a cute little button, isn't she?'

'Yes, she is. And yes, I do miss her.'

'What a pity she's blind.' Samantha picked up her

glass of lemonade. 'But that's not the worst thing that can happen to a person, is it?'

'No…it isn't.'

'I would've loved a daughter,' Samantha said. 'Don't get me wrong—I loved having a son. No mother could have asked for a better one than Ewan. And I've been so fortunate in having you as a surrogate daughter. I can't thank you enough for always being there for me and for Ewan.'

Eliza put her cutlery down and gripped her hands together on her lap underneath the table. It had been brewing inside her for days, this pressing need to put things straight at last. She could no longer live with this terrible guilt. She wanted to move on with her life. She could no longer deny her love for Leo. Even if he didn't love her, surely she owed him the truth of her feelings. 'Samantha…there's something you need to know about that night…I know it will be hard for you to hear and I don't blame you for thinking I'm just making it up to get out of this situation, but it's my fault Ewan had the accident that night.'

The silence was long and painful.

'I broke off our engagement,' Eliza continued. 'Ewan left my place so upset he should never have got behind the wheel of that car. I should never have let him leave like that. I'd bottled up my feelings for so long and then that night I just couldn't hold it in any longer. I told him I didn't love him any more. He was devastated.' She choked back a sob. 'I know you can't possibly forgive me. I will never forgive myself. But I want to have a life now. I want to be with Leo and his little girl. I love him. I'm sorry if that upsets you or you think it's selfish but I can't live this lie any more. I feel so wicked to have accepted the love you've given so freely and so generously when all this time I've been lying to you.'

Samantha let out a deep uneven sigh. She suddenly looked much older than her years. She seemed to sag in the chair as if her bones had got tired of staying neatly aligned. 'I suppose it's only right that you lied to me.'

'What do you mean?'

Samantha gave her a pained look. 'I've been lying to you too for the last few years.'

'I don't understand…' Eliza frowned in puzzlement. 'What do you mean? How have *you* lied to me? I'm the one who covered up what happened that night. I should have told you at the hospital. I should have told you well before this.'

Samantha took a deep breath and released it in a jagged stream. 'He told me.'

Eliza was still frowning in confusion. 'Who told you what?'

'Ewan.' Samantha met her gaze levelly. 'He told me you'd broken up with him.'

Eliza felt her heart slam against her ribcage as if it had hit a brick wall at high speed. 'When did he tell you?'

Samantha's throat moved up and down like a mouse moving under a rug. 'I called him just a minute or two after he'd left your place.' Her face crumpled. 'I'm so sorry. I should've told you before now. I've been feeling so wretchedly guilty. It was my fault. I was on the phone to him just moments before he crashed into that tree.' She gave a ragged sob and dropped her head into her hands. 'He told me you'd ended your engagement. He was upset. I told him to pull himself together. I was furious with him for being so surprised by your ending things. I'd seen it coming for months. He was livid. I'd never heard him so angry. He hung up on me. It was my fault. I caused his accident.'

'No.' Eliza rushed over to wrap her arms around Samantha. 'No, please don't blame yourself.'

'I knew you were unhappy,' Samantha sobbed into her shoulder. 'I knew it but I didn't say anything to him or to you. I wanted it to all work out. I wanted you to be the daughter I'd always longed for. I wanted us to be a family. That's all I wanted.'

Eliza closed her eyes as she held Samantha tightly in her arms. 'You're not to blame. You're not in any way to blame. I'm still that daughter. I'll always be that daughter and part of your family.'

Samantha pulled back to look at her. 'There's something else I want to confess.'

'What is it?'

'I've met someone.' She blushed like a teenager confessing to her first crush. 'He's a doctor at the clinic I take Ewan to. He's been wonderfully supportive. We've been on a few dates. That's where I've been going the last couple of nights. It's happened very quickly but we have such a lot in common. He has a daughter with cerebral palsy. I think he's going to ask me to marry him. If he does, I've decided I'll say yes.'

Eliza smiled with genuine happiness. 'But that's wonderful! You deserve to be happy.'

Samantha gave her a tremulous smile. 'I've been so worried about telling you, but when I saw all that fuss in the press about you and Leo Valente, I started to wonder if it might finally be time for both of us to move on with our lives.'

Eliza blinked back tears. 'I'm not sure if I have a future with Leo, but I want to tell him I love him. I think I owe him that.'

Samantha grasped her hands in hers. 'You must tell him how you feel. You don't owe Ewan anything. He is happy, or at least as happy as he can ever be. He's not aware of anything other than his immediate physical comfort. Robert has explained all that to me. It's helped me come to terms with it all. Ewan is not the same person now. He can never be that person again. But he's happy. And you and I need to be happy for him. Will you promise me that?'

'I will be happy for you and for Ewan. I promise you.' Eliza took off the chain from around her neck and handed Samantha the engagement ring. 'I think you're going to need this.'

Samantha clutched it tightly in her hand and smiled. 'You know something? I think you might be right.'

Eliza arrived at Leo's villa at three in the afternoon. Marella answered the door and immediately swept her up in a bone-crushing hug. 'I knew you'd come back. I told Signor Valente and Alessandra you'd be back. They've been so miserable. Like a bad English summer, *sì*?'

Eliza smiled in spite of the turmoil of her emotions. 'Where is he? I should've phoned first to see if he was at home. I didn't think…I just wanted to get here and talk to him as soon as I could.'

'He's not here,' Marella said. 'But he's not far away. He's at the old villa.'

'The one he had four years ago?'

'Sì,' Marella nodded. 'He thinks it would be better for Alessandra. I agree with him. This place is too big for her.'

Eliza felt her heart lift. 'Is she here?'

'She is sleeping upstairs. Do you want to see her?'

'I'd love to see her, but I think I'd better talk to Leo first.'

Marella beamed. 'I think that is a very good idea.'

Eliza pushed open the squeaky old wrought iron gate of the villa that was tucked into one of the hillsides that overlooked the stunning views of the coast below. The garden was very neglected and the villa needed a coat of paint but it was like stepping back in time. The scent of lemon blossom was tangy in the air. The cobblestones underneath the thin soles of her ballet flats were warm from a full day of sun. The birds were twittering in the trees and shrubbery nearby, just as they had four years ago.

She walked up the path to the front door but before she could reach up to use the rusty old knocker the door opened. Leo looked as if he had just encountered a ghost. He stared down at her, his throat moving up and down as if he couldn't quite get his voice to work.

Eliza dropped her hand back down by her side. 'I came to offer my services as a nanny but it looks to me that what you really need is a gardener and a painter.'

'I already have a nanny.' His expression was difficult to read but she thought she saw a glint in those dark eyes.

'Do you have any other positions vacant?' Eliza asked.

'Which position did you have in mind?'

She gave a little shrug of her shoulder. 'Lover, confidante, stepmother, wife—that sort of thing. I'm pretty flexible.'

A tiny half smile tugged at the edges of his mouth. 'Do you want a temporary post or are you thinking about something a little more long-term?'

Eliza put her hands on his chest, splaying the fingers of her right hand so she could feel the steady beat of his heart. 'I'm thinking in terms of forever.'

'What makes you think I'd offer you forever?'

She searched his features for a moment. Had she got it wrong? Had she jumped to the wrong conclusion? 'You do love me, don't you? I know you haven't said it but nor have I. And I do. I love you so much. I've always loved you. From the moment I met you I felt you were the only person for me.'

He put his arms around her. 'Of course I love you. How can you doubt that?'

She tiptoed her other hand up to the stubbly growth on his jaw. 'I've put you through hell and yet you still love me.'

He cupped her face in his hands. 'Isn't that what true love is supposed to do? Conquer everything in its path and triumph over all in the end?'

'I didn't know it was possible to love someone so much.'

'A couple of weeks ago you walked out of my life and I didn't think you'd be back. It was like four years ago all over again. What's changed?'

'*I've* changed,' she said. 'I've finally realised that life dishes up what it dishes up and we all have to deal with it in our own way and in our own time. I will probably always feel sad and guilty about Ewan. I can't change that. It's just what is. But I'm not making his life any better or worse by denying myself a chance at happiness. He would want me to live his life for him. I'm going to do my very best to do that. And my new life starts now, here with you and Alessandra. You are my family, but I have to say I need to keep a special corner open for Samantha. She's the most amazing surrogate mother in the world and I don't want to lose her.'

Leo put his arms around her and hugged her tightly. 'Then you won't,' he said. 'I need a mother, too, and Alessandra desperately needs a hands-on grandmother. Do you think she would have enough love to stretch to us as well?'

Eliza smiled as she hugged him tight. 'I'm absolutely sure of it.'

* * * * *

THE RINGS THAT BIND

BY
MICHELLE SMART

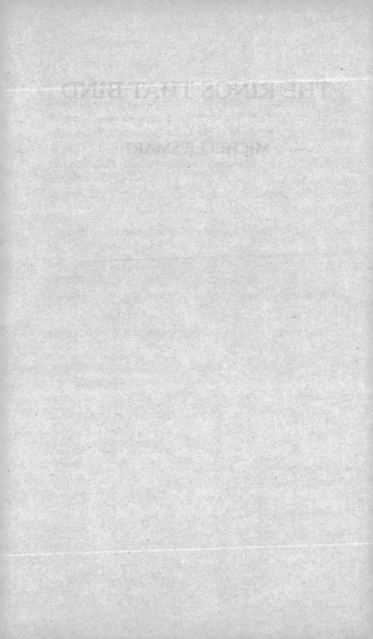

Michelle Smart's love affair with books began as a baby, when she would cuddle them in her cot. This love for all things wordy has never left her. A voracious reader of all genres, her love of romance was cemented at the age of twelve when she came across her first Mills & Boon book. That book sparked a seed and, although she didn't have the words to explain it then, she discovered something special— that a book had the capacity to make her heart beat as if she were falling in love.

When not reading, or pretending to do the housework, Michelle loves nothing more than creating worlds of her own featuring handsome brooding heroes and the sparkly, feisty women who can melt their frozen hearts. She hopes her books can make her readers' hearts beat a little faster too.

Michelle Smart lives in Northamptonshire with her own hero and their two young sons.

To Gilly

CHAPTER ONE

ROSA BARANSKI SAT on the kitchen worktop, ostensibly waiting for the coffee percolator to finish, and gazed down at the slate tiles. She hated the flooring. Even with the benefit of under-floor heating it always felt so cold.

It was incredible to think she had once lived in a house of the same proportions as the place she currently called home. In that, her first children's home, she had shared the house with forty other children and an ever-rotating shift of adults. The home had been a hub of noise and chaos, something she had hated until she had discovered how terrifying silence could be and how loneliness could destroy your soul.

Back then, her bedroom had been around the same size as the one she had now. Then, she had shared it with four other girls.

In those dark days and nights she had dreamed of escape.

Around two decades on, and for entirely different reasons, she had come to the painful conclusion that she needed to escape again. At least now she had the power simply to leave.

But she could not do anything until she had spoken to Nico. However much her stomach churned at the thought, she could not leave without an explanation. It wouldn't be fair.

For what seemed the hundredth time she read the text message on her phone, her stomach twisting at the bland, almost curt words that leapt off the screen. It was from her brother.

She'd received it a week ago and could not stop reading it. She should delete it but she couldn't. It was her only tangible link to him.

Shifting her position in order to peer out of the window, she felt her belly do a funny skipping thing as she spotted the sleek black Maserati crunch slowly over the long gravel driveway before disappearing from view.

Nicolai was home.

The dread coursing through her bloodstream was reminiscent of the first time she had met him. She had attended an interview for the role of his temporary PA, providing maternity cover for his regular PA, who had gone into early labour.

She had sat in a large waiting room with five other potential candidates. She hadn't been able to help but notice that the secretary who had been placed in charge of them visibly braced herself every time she knocked on his office door. The other candidates must have noticed it too. All of them had sat in hushed, almost reverential silence.

If Nico Baranski's reputation had not already preceded him, the sight of the candidates' faces after they had been interviewed would have been enough to terrify them. One by one they left his office ashen-faced. One woman had been blinking back tears.

Rosa had been the last to go in.

By that point her nerves had been shredded.

She had entered the plush, masculine office and been confronted with an immovable body behind a huge oak desk and a hard, unwavering stare.

She had breathed a visible sigh of relief.

Far from the living embodiment of an ogre her febrile mind had conjured during the long wait for her turn, Nicolai Baranski was but a mere mortal. An enormously well-built, gorgeous mortal, but a mortal all the same.

Her relief had been so great her nerves had disappeared.

When he had finally spoken, inviting her to sit in rapid Russian, she had responded in kind without missing a single beat.

Only by the flicker of an eyebrow had he shown any response to her fluency.

'It says on your résumé that you studied Russian at university and then spent a year working in St Petersburg for the Danask Group after your graduation, before transferring back to London,' he had said, flipping through a pile of paper in front of him.

'That is correct.'

He looked up, the brilliance of his light green eyes piercing her. 'Your references are excellent. You are clearly a valued member of the Danask Group. Why do you want to leave?'

'I have gone as far as I can and I am looking for a new challenge. I have already worked my notice with them,' she added, knowing this position needed to be filled quickly.

'How many other jobs have you applied for?'

'None. This is the only one I thought suitable.'

'You do realise the job involves a lot of travel?'

'That is one of the reasons I applied.' The idea of escaping London and her deteriorating home life sounded wonderful. Not that she would say such a thing to him. Rosa kept a strict demarcation between her business and her personal life.

'You will often be required to leave the UK at short notice.'

'I will carry a travel case at all times for such eventualities.'

'You should know I am not interested in hiring someone who clock-watches.'

'I am aware of your reputation, Gaspadin Baranski,' she replied, matching his coolness of tone. 'You pay an excellent salary for good reason.'

He studied her with narrowed eyes before pulling a document wallet out of his top drawer and handing it to her. 'Translate that for me.'

The document was in Russian. She scanned it for a moment before translating. When she was done, Nico leaned back on his chair, a thoughtful expression on his face. 'When can you start?'

And that was it. The job had been hers. She had started immediately.

Now, she inhaled deeply and slowly, pulling the ponytail at the back of her head as tight as she could.

If there was one thing she had learned it was that when there was a potentially unpleasant job to do it was better to face it head-on. Get it over with. Even if it meant telling her husband news for which she had no way of knowing how he would react.

It wasn't until she heard movement from the door connecting the house with the underground garage that she snapped out of her stupor and jumped down, wincing as her bare feet hit the cold floor.

Shoving the phone into her pocket, she used all her powers of concentration to keep her hands steady and pour coffee into the waiting mug without spilling it everywhere.

Would he even bother seeking her out? Or would he hide away in his study as he so often did nowadays?

She listened to the sound of the study door being opened, followed less than a minute later by the sound of the same door closing. Muted footsteps grew closer until he was there, leaning nonchalantly against the kitchen doorframe, filling the space, arms folded across his broad chest.

'Hello, Rosa.'

'Hello, Nico.' She threw him a brief smile, praying he couldn't see the way her knees knocked together. Even though it was Sunday, and he had spent a good portion of the day travelling, he was impeccably dressed in a crisp white shirt, an incredibly snazzy silver-and-pink tie, and tailored dark grey trousers. It made her pale blue jogging bottoms and white T-shirt look positively grungy by comparison. 'Good trip?'

He considered, folding his arms across his chest. 'It could have been worse. I'm not yet convinced they are the kind of people I wish to do business with.'

Which undoubtedly meant he would *not* be investing in the mineral extraction facility he had spent the best part of a week scrutinising.

'Coffee?'

He nodded. 'Where's Gloria?' he asked, referring to their housekeeper.

She opened a cupboard and pulled a mug out. 'Her grandson has a bad dose of chicken-pox and she wants to give her daughter a break, so I've given her the weekend off.'

A furrow appeared on his brow. 'Why would you do that?'

Rosa rolled her eyes and poured coffee into the mug before adding a splash of milk. A few drops spilled onto the granite worktop. She wiped it absently with her wrist. 'I did it because she was worried about her daughter.'

'Her daughter is a fully grown woman.'

'That doesn't mean Gloria has abdicated her maternal feelings.' Not that Rosa knew anything about being the recipient of maternal feelings. Not since the age of five, when her mother had abandoned her. She held the mug out to him. 'Besides, it worked in my favour. I need to talk to you.' And she would prefer not to talk in front of an audience.

'That can wait for a minute. I have something for you.' Unfolding his arms, Nico produced a small gift-wrapped package and handed it to her, taking his mug in exchange. 'Happy birthday.'

Stunned at the gift—two days too late—she stared up at him. 'Thank you.'

His light green eyes sparkled. 'You're welcome. I'm sorry I didn't make it back in time to take you out.'

'Don't worry about it. Business comes first.' She tried to speak without rancour. Business always came first. In effect, their whole marriage was nothing more than a business transaction.

When she had agreed to what could only be described as a marriage of convenience, she could not have known there would come a point when something she accepted as part of the pact they had made would start to eat at her. She could not have known that something inside her would shift.

The idea of marriage—indeed, the deed itself—had come about in California. They had spent over a week there, working on the purchase of a mining facility. Once the final contract had been signed Nico had insisted on treating the whole team to a meal to celebrate.

They had been the last two standing. After ten days of continuous slog, Rosa had been ready to let her hair down. To her surprise, Nico had been in the mood to cut loose too.

When he'd suggested a drink in the bar that jutted out over the calm ocean she had readily agreed.

It was the first time they had been alone together in what could have been described as a social setting.

They had settled in a corner, the lapping ocean surrounding them. On Nico's instructions the bartender had brought two shot glasses and a bottle of vodka to their table.

Nico had poured them both a hefty measure and raised his glass. 'To Rosa Carty,' he had said with an approving nod.

'To me?'

'The most efficient PA in the western hemisphere.'

She had been flummoxed at the unexpected compliment. 'I just do my job.'

'And you do it superbly. I am the envy of my compatriots.'

Before she could respond her phone buzzed for the ninth time that evening.

'Who keeps messaging you?' he asked with a definite hint of irritation.

'My ex,' she muttered, firing a text back.

'Your ex? If he is an ex, why is he contacting you?'

'It's personal.'

He leant forward. 'We are off the clock now, Rosa. We are socializing, not preparing a board meeting. Tell me.'

They might be 'off the clock', as he so eloquently put it, but there was no mistaking a direct order. 'I changed the locks of my flat before coming to California. He's not very happy about it but I'm fed up with him turning up and letting himself in whenever he feels like it.'

A shadow crossed Nico's eyes. 'Has he threatened you?'

'Not in a physical sense. He's convinced that if he keeps the pressure up I'll go back to him.' She straightened her spine. 'But I won't. Sooner or later he'll get the message.'

'When did you end it?'

'Two months ago.'

'You'd have thought he'd have got the message by now.'

As if proving his point, her phone buzzed again.

Before she could open the message he reached over and removed the mobile from her hand.

'If you keep answering you'll only encourage him,' he said in a no-nonsense manner.

'If I don't answer he sends twice as many.' As she spoke Nico's smartphone beeped in turn.

He looked at the screen, then back at Rosa. 'How long were you with him?'

'Three years.'

He held his smartphone up. 'I enjoyed the grand total of two dates with Sophie before she started hinting at making things *permanent*.' His lips tightened. 'I ended it but she will not accept it. It is always the same. Women always want to make things permanent.'

'That's because you're such a catch,' she said, snatching her phone back. 'How old are you? Thirty-five?'

'Thirty-six,' he corrected.

She looked back down at her phone and read the latest pleading message. 'Well, then—they all think you're ready to settle down.'

'Not with one of them.' He downed his shot of vodka and then tapped the side of Rosa's full glass. 'Your turn. And if you don't turn your phone off I will throw it in the ocean.'

'Try it,' she said absently, her attention focused on the screen in front of her. She had tried everything to make Stephen get the message. Being nice. Being cruel. None of it was getting through to him.

Before her finger could even touch the keypad to form a response Nico took the phone out of her hand and threw it over the railing and into the ocean. It made a lovely splashing sound before disappearing into the dark water.

The anger that surged through her blood at this high-handed, outrageous act was as unexpected as the deed itself.

She stared at him in disbelief.

There was no contrition. He simply sat there with one brow raised, his features arranged into a perfect display of nonchalance.

She could never have known then that less than twelve hours later she would marry him.

But she *had* married him. And now she had to deal with the consequences.

Walking over to the long breakfast bar, grabbing her mug of coffee on the way, she hooked a stool out with her foot and took a seat. Her stomach was doing funny flipping motions and she could not take her eyes off the beautiful gift-wrapping. It must have taken him ages to get it so perfect.

It was not until she turned the gift upside down to unwrap it that she saw the sticker holding the ribbon to the box. She recognised the insignia on it and knew in an instant that it had been professionally gift-wrapped. She tried not to let dejection set in. So what if he hadn't wrapped it himself? He had thought of her.

Tearing it open, she found a bottle of expensive perfume.

Nico took the stool opposite and gazed at her expectantly. Black stubble had broken out on his chiselled jawline which, combined with his neatly trimmed goatee, gave him a slightly sinister yet wholly masculine air. His usually tousled black hair was even messier than usual. Rosa found herself fighting her own hands to stop herself from smoothing it down—an urge that had been increasing over recent months, and an urge that only served to prove that the course of action she was about to take was for the best.

She looked back at the gift. 'It's lovely. Thank you.' Then she made the mistake of turning it over in her hand and catching sight of the duty-free label on the bottom.

It brought to mind the old T-shirt she recalled one of her foster sisters continuously wearing: 'My dad went to Blackpool and all he brought me was this lousy T-shirt'. Most likely it was the only gift the child's father *had* brought her.

In Nico's case he had been to Morocco. And all he had brought her was some duty-free perfume. As a birthday present.

If she hadn't known how offended he would be she would have laughed. Although generous to a fault, Nico was simply not wired to lavish gifts on people. He hadn't even bought her a Christmas card—had been astonished to receive the gift of a silk tie and cufflinks from her.

She would bet none of his lovers had ever been kissed off with an expensive piece of jewellery. His brain did not work that way. The very fact that he had bought something for her touched her deeply, lodging a crumb of doubt into her certainty.

'So, what did you do for your birthday?' he asked as if he *hadn't* stood her up at the very last minute, as if she *hadn't* been all dressed up and waiting for him.

Since she had stopped working for him he had stood her up at the last minute a couple of times. She tried very hard to be philosophical about it—with his line of work, and the different time-zones he travelled between, it couldn't always be helped.

When she had worked for him they had spent around half their time abroad. Since she had left Baranski Mining three months ago they had shared a roof twenty-nine times. She had counted.

She had never been able to shake the feeling she was being punished for having the temerity to refuse his offer of a permanent role.

His failure to return home for her birthday had felt like having a twisting knife plunged into her heart.

'Stephen took me to La Torina.'

'Stephen?'

For the ghost of a second she could have sworn his sensuous lips tightened, that the pupils of his eyes pulsed. She blinked, certain she was imagining it, and found his features arranged in their usual indifference.

She nodded, challenging him, *willing* him to make something of it.

'Do I take it Stephen is the sender of the flowers on the reception table?'

'Yes. Aren't they beautiful?' She took a sip of her coffee and waited for some form of reaction from him.

'They certainly brighten the room up.' His tone was casual. They could be discussing a dull day at the office. 'Did you sleep with him?'

She didn't flinch or hesitate, simply held her chin aloft in silent defiance. 'Yes.'

Her stomach clenched as she gazed into the piercing green eyes of the man she had married. She searched intently, looking for a sign of *something*—some form of emotion, something to show he cared. But there was nothing to be found. There never had been. It shouldn't matter. After all, emotions had never been part of the deal between them.

Their marriage hadn't been all bad. For the most part it had been good—at least until she had left Baranski Mining. They had worked fantastically well together, both professionally and socially.

She remembered one evening when they had attended a charity auction and the auctioneer had had a large dollop of cream stuck to his ear. She and Nico had sat there like robots, not daring to look at each other, the corners of their mouths twitching with mirth. It hadn't meant anything, but it had been one of those rare moments when she had felt perfect alignment with him.

It was a moment of togetherness, and they had become few and far between.

And it *did* matter.

His indifference hurt more every time she looked at it.

'I would say good for you,' he said, studying her closely. 'It is time you took a lover. But there is something ironic about you falling into bed with the man you married me to escape from.'

The irony had not been lost on her either.

If Stephen had called ten minutes earlier the outcome would have been very different.

She had just come off the phone to Nico, and he had given her a brusque explanation of why he wouldn't make it back in time to take her out for her birthday.

She'd been all dressed up with nowhere to go.

And she'd made the mistake of reading her brother's text message for possibly the hundredth time.

It had been one of the lowest points of her life.

Then Stephen had called to wish her a happy birthday. If she hadn't felt so heartsick she would have hung the receiver up. Instead she had found herself agreeing to a meal.

Company. That was what she'd craved. Freddy Krueger could have offered her a date and she would have accepted.

'Nico, I—'

'Let us pause this conversation for a minute,' he interrupted, getting to his feet. 'It has been a long day. I could use a proper drink and something comfortable to sit on.'

A drink sounded good to her. Lord knew she needed something to numb the curdling of her belly. Because, for all the seeming indifference of his words, Nico's powerful body was taut with tension, like a coil waiting to spring free.

She followed him through to the spacious living room and curled up on the sofa while he poured them both a hefty measure of vodka.

It was certainly a day for irony. Vodka had played its part in the start of their marriage and now it would play its part in its demise. She took a long sip, welcoming the numbing burn of the clear liquid, before placing it on the coffee table.

She waited until he had settled in the sofa opposite before speaking. Her words came out in a rush. 'Nico, this isn't working.'

'What isn't working?'

'This.' She threw her arms in the air and gave a rueful shrug. 'Us. Our marriage. I want out.'

CHAPTER TWO

ROSA WAS UNNERVED by Nico's stillness. He leant forward, his muscular forearms resting on his thighs, his glass cradled between his large hands. 'Are you getting back together with Stephen?'

'No...'

His eyes did not leave her face. 'You left him because he suffocated you.'

'I'm not getting back with Stephen.'

'He wouldn't take no for an answer,' he continued. 'You were on the verge of getting a restraining order against him when you married me.'

'I know.' She expelled stale air through her teeth and closed her eyes. She had no wish to explain the utter desperation she had felt on her birthday, the horrendous feeling that there was not a soul in the world who cared if she lived or died. 'Sleeping with him was a mistake that will not be repeated.' A huge mistake. A massive mistake of epic proportions. But it did have one advantage—it had allowed her to see the enormous error she had made marrying Nico.

'Is there someone else?'

'No. There is no one else.' How could there be?

'Then why do you want to leave?'

She wished he wouldn't look at her with such menacing stillness. Nico always kept his cards close to his chest, but she couldn't help feeling as if he were trying to penetrate through to her brain and dissect the contents. If only she had the slightest clue as to what he was thinking.

'Because it isn't working for me any more.' She reached for a squishy cushion and cuddled it to her belly, hoping the comfort would quell the butterflies raging inside. 'We agreed from the start that if either of us wanted to leave we could, without any fuss. Nico, I want a fresh start. I want a divorce.'

Nico remained still as he stared hard at the woman he had married, his eyes flickering down to the gold band she wore on her finger. A ring *he* had put there.

'I am well aware of what we agreed, Rosa. However, it is unreasonable for you to suddenly state you want a divorce and not give me a valid reason.'

'There is no single valid reason.' She tugged a stray lock of her ebony hair behind her ear. 'When we agreed to marry it seemed the perfect solution for both of us—a nice, convenient open marriage. No emotional ties or anything messy…' Her husky voice trailed off. 'I don't know exactly what I want from a marriage—I don't know if I even want a marriage—but, Nicolai, I do know I want something more than this.'

It was the use of his full first name that convinced him she was serious. She had addressed him by his shortened name since they'd exchanged their wedding vows. That, and the fact they were speaking in English.

Rosa adored the Russian tongue. They rarely spoke her native language when together.

His hands tightened around his glass and he took a long sip of the clear, fiery liquid. Rosa was a lot like vodka. Clear and pure-looking, but with a definite bite. In her own understated way she did not take crap from anyone.

He pursed his lips as he contemplated her, sitting there,

studying him with an openness he had always admired. He had admired her from the start.

After his PA had gone into early labour he'd had no choice but to approach an employment agency to fill the role. There had been no one in his employ suitable for it.

The agency had duly sent six candidates—all of whom, they'd assured him, were fluent in Russian. By the time he had interviewed the first five he'd been ready to sue the agency. The candidates had been useless. Never mind that their Russian had been far from fluent, he doubted they could have organised a children's party.

And then in had walked Rosa Carty, the model of calm efficiency.

Her Russian was flawless. Perfect. He would trust her to organise a state funeral.

He had offered her the position immediately and she had started on the hoof, with no training or guidance. She had stepped into the breach as if she had always been there.

She had never flirted with him, had never dressed as anything but the professional she was, had never brought her private life to the office. She had been perfect.

Marriage had always been an institution he admired but one he had long accepted would not be for him.

Five months on and he had been in his office with Serge, his finance director and an old friend from his university days. They had been going over the figures for his buyout of a Californian mine when there had been a sharp rap at the door and Rosa had walked in.

He had known immediately something was wrong. She would never have dreamt of interrupting a meeting unless it was important.

'We have a slight problem,' she had said in her usual understated fashion. 'There is a discrepancy with the output figures.'

She had lain the offending document before him and pointed to a tiny section highlighted in pink. The figure in question had been out by less than an eighth of one per cent, but in financial terms equated to over a million pounds.

At least ten pairs of eyes, including his own, had gone through the document. Rosa was the only person to have picked up on the error.

After agreeing on an action plan, she had set off to implement it. He'd had no doubt the whole thing would be rectified by the end of the day.

'Your PA is really something,' Serge had said with a shake of his head when she'd left the office. 'When Madeline comes back from maternity leave can I have Rosa in my department?'

Nico had shrugged noncommittally. Even at that stage he had known he wanted to keep Rosa as his PA—had been busy strategising ways to keep her working directly for him without landing himself with a lawsuit from a disgruntled Madeline.

'Is she married?' Serge had asked with a sudden knowing look in his eyes. 'She is exactly the kind of woman a man like you should marry.'

If Serge hadn't been one of his oldest friends Nico would have fired him on the spot for insubordination.

'There is nothing worse than a newly married man,' he said drily.

'Marriage has been the making of me,' Serge countered amiably. 'Seriously, my friend, Rosa would be perfect for you. She's got the same coolness as you. You have mentioned breaking into the Middle East. Socialising is a big part of their business culture and marriage is very much respected. Rosa would be an asset to you. Besides,' he continued with a flash of his teeth, 'a man can't stay happy all his life!'

Days later he had travelled to California with Rosa and

an army of workers. As the days passed, Serge's words had kept repeating in his head.

By their last day he had almost convinced himself that his friend could be on to something.

He had engineered things so that he and Rosa were alone after the celebratory meal, sitting in the balmy night air, drinking vodka. Usually his employees' private lives and private time were strictly off-limits, but that night he had wanted to test if their compatibility in the office could be matched in a social setting.

The constant buzz of her phone had driven him to distraction. Well, it had been more the fact that she'd kept ignoring him to answer those annoying messages that had irritated him. And the fact that he'd disliked her responding to someone who was so clearly deranged. So he'd thrown her phone into the ocean.

She had simply glared at him, a small tick playing under her left eye. 'That was unnecessary.'

'Every time you respond you give him false hope,' he pointed out. 'The only way to be rid of him is to cut all communication. I will replace your phone. Now, drink your shot.'

For the breadth of a moment he thought she would throw the glass at him.

Instead she lifted the shot and downed it. In one. Done, she slammed the glass back on the table and eyeballed him with caramel eyes that swirled with amusement. 'There. Happy now?'

A bubble of laughter climbed his throat. He had never imagined his starchy, temporary PA possessed a personality.

'So you never contemplated marrying…?'

'Stephen,' she supplied with a hiccup. She put her hand to her mouth and threw him a wry smile. 'No. Never in a million years would I have married him. Although I'd love to marry *someone*, right now, just to get him off my back.' She shook her head. 'I do like the idea of marriage, but I'd be a rubbish wife. I'm married to my work and I much prefer my own company.'

Nico nodded, understanding. 'I like the idea of a wife who can accompany me to functions and hold an intelligent conversation.' He chose his words carefully. 'But the thought of all that *emoting* couples are supposed to do leaves me cold.'

'Tell me about it,' she agreed with pursed lips.

He looked, at her—*really* looked at her. Serge's assessment had been right. Rosa would be an asset to any businessman. And *he* would be that businessman.

She could be a female version of him! Both were perfectionists. Both were dedicated to their work. Nico had long wanted marriage for the respectability it afforded, but after Galina—his one heavy entanglement and the only failure in his life—he had known he was not cut out for relationships. He was not made that way.

'We could marry,' he said idly, watching closely for her reaction.

The vodka Rosa had just poured into her mouth was spat out.

'Think about it,' he said, warming to his theme. 'We would be perfect together.'

'Yes,' she said, pulling a face once she had finished choking. 'And all those socialites would have to stop harassing you for marriage.'

'More importantly, from your perspective, Stephen would get the picture that you are never coming back. But that's neither here nor there. You are a woman of great intellect. We work well together. There is no reason we could not have a successful marriage.'

'This all sounds fabulous,' she said, with a roll of her eyes. 'But there are a couple of slight problems.'

'Which are?'

'One: we don't fancy each other.'

Even Nico was vain enough to bristle slightly at that remark. 'That means there is no chance of us falling into bed and messing things up by letting emotions get in the way.' Although, looking at her, he had to admit there was something appealing about her in a fresh-faced, pretty kind of way. Not that he would ever be tempted to do anything about it. No. Rosa was not his type at all.

'Two.' She ticked the number off on her fingers. 'I don't believe in mixing business with pleasure.'

'Neither do I. But as this is a business proposal that would not be a problem.'

Her eyes suddenly widened. 'My God, are you serious?'

'Absolutely. Think about it, Rosa. We would be perfect together. We both want marriage…'

'Just not to anyone who would expect us to compromise our lives for it,' she finished with an unexpected sparkle.

'This calls for a drink.' He poured them both another hefty measure of vodka and chinked his glass to hers. On the count of three they downed them.

Done, Nico reached for his smartphone and started a search.

'We can marry here, tonight, in California,' he said, reading quickly. 'As long as we've got our passports, we're good to go.'

'Excellent.' She pulled her briefcase onto her lap and rummaged through it.

'What are you doing?'

'Looking for a pen and some paper.'

'What for?'

She had looked at him, amusement written all over her face. 'If we're going to get married it's only right we make a contract for it. Shall I write it in English or Russian?'

And that had been it. They had married, still slightly tipsy, the next morning.

Not once had he been given cause to regret their impulsive decision—the only impulsive decision he had made in his thirty-six years.

And now she had the nerve to sit there, eleven months on, and tell him she had *changed her mind.*

Not only that, but she had slept with her ex.

A wave of nausea rolled through his stomach—so violent he almost retched.

He was in no position to complain. He should be able to accept that. They had made an agreement that theirs would be an open marriage. As long as they exercised discretion they could sleep with whomever they chose.

Was he not a modern, twenty-first-century man? He had no right to feel possessive about a woman who was his wife in name only.

Intellectually, he knew all the right things to think.

Under the surface of his skin, though, his latent Neanderthal had reared up and punched him hard, right in the solar plexus.

She had slept with someone else. That little gem had lodged in his chest and was piercing into him with regular stabbing motions.

She had slept with someone else and had the nerve to think that *she* could call the shots.

He had bought her a birthday present. The first personal gift he had ever bought a woman. *And she had slept with someone else.*

Had she slept with her ex as punishment for him not returning in time for her birthday? With any other woman the answer would be a resounding yes. But Rosa was not made in the same mould as other women. Or so he had thought.

'You should have told me you were unhappy.' As he spoke,

something rancid nibbled away at his gut—which he tried to quash with another sip of his vodka.

She threw him a wan smile. 'I'm not unhappy—more lonely, I guess.'

'That would not have been a problem if you had taken the job permanently when I offered it to you.'

It was an issue that still rankled. A week before Madeline, his original PA, had been due to return from maternity leave, she had dropped the bombshell that she would not be coming back. He'd hidden his delight, wished her well, and promptly offered the job to his wife.

She had refused to take it. She'd turned his generous offer down, just as she'd refused all subsequent offers of employment within the Baranski Mining empire.

Ever since he had accrued enough money to purchase Reuben Mining and turn it into Baranski Mining no one had ever refused him anything.

'Nico, I was lonely when I worked for you.'

How was that even possible? They had spent nearly every waking hour together.

He took another long sip of his vodka. 'I do hope this decision will not affect our trip to Butterfly Island,' he said, struggling to keep an even tone. He must be more exhausted than he had appreciated, because his mood was darkening as rapidly as his musings. And the rolls of nausea were increasing.

She sighed and pulled out the band holding her ponytail, before immediately gathering all the stray locks and tying it up again, stretching her creamy skin taut.

He preferred it when she wore her silky black tresses loose, as she did on the occasions when they accompanied each other to social functions. With her hair loose, her angular features softened, her caramel eyes, under which purple smudges currently resided, became rounder.

'We are due to fly there in a fortnight,' he reminded her tightly. 'We had an agreement and I expect you to honour it.'

The new PA he had appointed three months ago, when Rosa had refused the job, had proved herself to be spectacularly useless. And the one he had hired after sacking that one. And the next. As he had found since Rosa had moved on, when compared with his wife's calm, dedicated efficiency, they were all useless.

Rosa's eyes widened a fraction. 'You *expect*?' she questioned in that husky voice he usually found so soothing.

'Yes. A commitment is a commitment. Like our marriage.'

Dimly he recalled a conversation one evening about how his plans for mineral mining in the Indian Ocean were firming up. He was readying for the contractual stage now, which meant he would need a Russian-speaking assistant to accompany him to Butterfly Island for the contract completion. He remembered complaining of the impossibility of finding someone and training them up in time, which was when Rosa had offered to accompany him instead. Just as he had hoped she would. She had landed a job working as a translator for another London-based Russian firm, but was willing to use her holiday entitlement to assist him.

'I know.' Her nose wrinkled. She gave a little shiver and rubbed her arms, pushing her full breasts together; unaware that the late-afternoon sunlight filtering in through the big bay window illuminated her white T-shirt, making it virtually transparent.

He averted his eyes and willed away the tingles of awareness spreading through him.

What the hell was the matter with him? His wife had told him she'd slept with her ex and wanted a divorce, and his body was *still* capable of reacting to her?

Although she was not his type, intellectually he was aware

that Rosa was an attractive woman. That awareness had been growing in recent months. There had even been times when…

No. He had never allowed the idea of anything physical between them to take root. If it had been anyone but Rosa he would not have thought twice about acting on it, but he had never been able to shake the feeling that sleeping with her would be akin to opening a can of worms.

Maybe he should have done.

'I would be grateful if you could take someone else in my place.'

Her words cut through his inappropriate meanderings.

'Impossible. It is far too short notice.'

She arched an eyebrow. 'Rubbish. You employ plenty of linguists of both nationalities.'

He fought to keep his tone even. 'But none as good as you—as you well know. And even if I could find and train someone at such short notice, it is *you* I want.'

'Really?'

The inflection in her tone made him pause. Somehow he didn't think she was referring to work.

'I'm sorry, Nico, but it's out of the question. I know it is an inconvenience, but two weeks is by no means too short notice.'

Two weeks to find another Rosa was impossible.

'I've been looking on the internet and we can sort the divorce out ourselves.'

'What are you talking about?'

'Our divorce,' she said evenly. 'There's no point in us appointing lawyers. I don't want anything from you, and unless you want something from me—'

'I don't recall agreeing to any divorce,' he cut in, the grip on his glass tightening.

She had it all figured out. She seriously thought she could

tell him she wanted a divorce and then waltz off into the moonlight.

The nausea rolled up into his throat and lodged there, burning his vocal cords.

She seriously thought he would let her go.

Her warm eyes chilled and narrowed. 'Actually, you did. When we married. Remember?'

He forced his throat to work. 'That was eleven months ago. My feelings on the matter have changed.' Hell could freeze over before he let her leave.

'Well, mine haven't. As far as I'm concerned, my feelings on divorce are the same as they were then.' She got to her feet and stood as tall as her short, curvy frame would allow. 'I'm sorry if my decision somehow inconveniences you—I had assumed you wouldn't be bothered—and I'm sorry if somehow I have disappointed you, but, Nicolai, I can't stay in this sham of a marriage for a second longer.'

Sadness rang in her eyes before she turned and headed for the door.

'Where do you think you're going?'

Her spine became rigid. 'To collect my belongings. I packed earlier.'

'And where do you intend to go? To *Stephen*?'

As he spoke her lover's name the glass in his hand shattered.

CHAPTER THREE

ROSA VACUUMED THE last tiny shard of glass from the thick carpet.

Her hands had finally stopped shaking, but her heart still thundered painfully against her ribs.

Nico's face…

When that glass had shattered there had been a moment when she had thought his face would crack too.

Other than the usual business talk, it seemed he had barely noticed her existence in months. He might not have cared that she had slept with someone else, but she had been a fool to hope he would give her a divorce without putting up a fight.

She should have known better. If there was one thing she knew about her husband it was that he did not like to lose. At anything.

She had known Butterfly Island would be a problem—after all, he seemed to spend the majority of their limited time together bitching about the latest unfortunate to be appointed the role of his PA—but she had put that down to his being miffed that she had refused the job. Her husband's success and power had put him in the unfortunate position of seldom being denied anything he wanted. He had not taken her refusal to continue working for him well—had taken it as a personal slight. Which, of course, it had been—but not in the way he assumed.

By the time her contract with Baranski Mining had expired Rosa's feelings towards him had become far too complicated for her even to consider staying on. She had fervently hoped some distance from him would settle the weird hormones unleashed by their working so closely together. It hadn't worked. She had been left rattling round their huge home alone while he travelled the globe, rarely spending more than a couple of nights in London at any one time.

She had missed him. God help her, she had missed him.

She was wedging the vacuum back in the cupboard when Nico came out of the downstairs bathroom, where he had been washing shards of glass off his hand. Somehow the shattered glass hadn't even nicked him. The man must be made of Teflon.

She had no idea what he had done to his hair, but even taking into account its usual messiness it was sticking up as if he'd rubbed a balloon on it.

For some reason this tugged at her.

The cool façade had definitely cracked.

His features were arranged in their usual indifference, but the pulse in his jaw was working double-time. This was the closest to angry she had ever seen him.

Closing the cupboard, she took a deep breath. 'In answer to your question, I'm going to stay at a hotel until the lease on my flat expires.' Thank God she'd had the foresight to grant her tenants only a short-term lease. She missed her cosy flat dreadfully. But at least in a hotel she wouldn't be alone, and in the meantime she could start hunting for a new flatmate to share with.

If there was one thing she hated it was living alone. Marrying Nico had, at the time, been a godsend. With Stephen gone, she had been trying to find a flatmate—someone who was happy to share a home with her without wanting to spend every evening drinking wine and having girly chats.

Nico's mad idea had been the answer to every prayer she'd had. He wouldn't expect anything from her other than intellectual stimulation. In return she would have his name and a ring on her finger. Symbols that she belonged to someone. And he wore *her* ring. A metaphorical symbol that he belonged to her too.

'I think not.' His green eyes had darkened into an almost sinister gleam. 'You see, Rosa, under no circumstances will I allow you to leave. I do not want a divorce. Go up to your room and unpack—you're not going anywhere.'

Rosa reared back and stared at him. Surely he hadn't just said what she thought he had? 'You won't *allow* me to leave?'

His mouth formed a thin, grim line. 'You are my wife.'

'Exactly. I am your wife—not your possession.'

'In certain cultures that is one and the same thing.'

'Well, luckily for me we're in the UK, and not some backwards country where women have no voice.'

'I will never agree to a divorce.'

She studied him carefully, half expecting him to crack a smile and say he was joking. Surely he could not be serious? However, she did have one more ace up her sleeve—no one could ever accuse her of being anything but thorough. 'If you won't agree to a divorce I will apply for an annulment. This marriage was never consummated. Therefore it is void.'

Not bothering to wait for a response, Rosa walked away. Determined to keep a cool head, she walked steadily up the stairs to her suite, placing a hand to her chest in a futile attempt to temper her thundering heart.

Thankfully she'd had the foresight to pack earlier—a job that had taken less than an hour.

Heavy footsteps neared her and mentally she braced herself.

Nico crossed the threshold into her bedroom, his features so taut he might have been carved from ice. His eyes, though… His eyes shimmered with fury.

'You do realise you can't stop me?' she said coldly.

He folded his arms across his chest, accentuating the breadth of his physique. Nico really was a mountain of a man, filling the space around him, dwarfing everything in the vicinity. 'I think you'll find I can.'

'By using force?' She didn't believe he would do that. Not for a second. He might be over a foot taller than her, and packed full of solid muscle, but she knew perfectly well he would never use that to his advantage.

His lips curved into a cold smile. 'I don't need to use physical force, Rosa. I have other advantages to stop you leaving.'

'Why are you being like this?' She forced her voice to remain calm. 'Why can't you just accept I want out?'

'I'll tell you why,' he said, stalking towards her, his eyes glittering. 'You see, *daragaya*, I have just learned that not only have I been cuckolded but, to add insult to injury, you want to humiliate me too.'

It was the casual, almost sneering way he called her *his darling wife* that did it. Something inside of her snapped. Gazing up at him, mere feet away, close enough for her to feel the heat emanating from his powerful body, she said, 'Cuckolded? Humiliated? What planet are you on? How many women have you slept with since we married?'

Oh, he had been discreet. She would give him that. But there was no way a man as overtly masculine as Nico would go eleven months without sex.

'Do not try to twist the subject. We are not talking about me. We are talking about you and the fact you want to advertise to the world that we never have consummated our marriage.'

'You know damn well I won't be doing anything of the sort.'

'You think the press won't leap on a nugget like that? You think I want to be the butt of everyone's gossip? To know friends and business acquaintances will speculate over the reasons you and I never had sex?'

Rosa turned her face away, a slow burn crawling up her neck.

Lord, she did not want to *think* of them having sex. It was bad enough dreaming about his hard, naked body taking her passionately and then waking up in the morning with a burning need deep inside her, knowing there was nothing she could do about it other than take as cold a shower as she could bear and push it from her mind. At least she could control her conscious thoughts.

She took a step away from him—away from that citrusy, masculine scent that was starting to swirl around her senses. 'I don't relish that scenario any more than you, but if you refuse a divorce you will leave me no other option than to go down the annulment road.'

'I will deny it,' he said, staring at her unsmilingly. 'I will tell the courts that you are a fantasist.'

'You would lie under oath?'

The ring of shock in Rosa's eyes was all too apparent.

In truth, Nico had shocked himself.

Would he really go that far? Under ordinary circumstances the answer would be a resounding no. But these were far from ordinary circumstances.

Her suitcases sat neatly by her bedroom door. A sign of her intent.

Of her defiance.

Without any pause for thought, he reached for the nearest, flicked the clips to spring it open and tipped the contents into a heap on the floor.

'I will do whatever is necessary to uphold my reputation,'

he said, staring intently into her startled eyes. He clenched his hands into fists and held them tightly by his sides to prevent them doing the same to the other suitcase. He had made his point. 'You are a Baranski and will remain a Baranski for as long as I deem necessary.'

Rosa backed away from him like a wary cat, tugging at her ponytail, loathing written all over her pretty face. 'I'll be a Carty again before you can blink,' she said, her chest rising up and down with rapid motion. 'I'll change my name back by deed poll if necessary. And if you think upending my possessions is going to make me stay, then you are delusional.'

He would never have guessed his starchy wife was capable of anger. Irritation, yes. Mild annoyance on a bad day, maybe. But full-blown anger? No.

She had not even raised her voice but he could feel it—those tiny ripples of fury kept under the tightest of reins.

What would it be like to unleash that passion? A passion he had blithely ignored over the eleven months of their marriage, not even aware of its existence.

It had been there all along. And another man had been the recipient of it.

The knowledge lingered in his senses like a pungent smell.

And it made him react in ways he had never believed himself capable of.

'I have a proposition for you,' he said, breaking the taut silence.

Her eyes narrowed in suspicion.

'I do not want a divorce or an annulment. I like our marriage—it suits me very well.' And he was damned if he was going to let it end on her terms. If they were going to divorce it would be on *his* terms and his terms only.

'It doesn't suit *me*.'

Clamping down on the fresh flash of rage that followed this little declaration, he forced his voice to remain calm. 'I realise that. However, as you have done so much research you must be aware that we cannot divorce until we have been married for a year—which in our case is a whole month away.'

'That doesn't mean we can't start the ball rolling,' she said, displaying the stubbornness he had always admired in her when she had worked for him, working regular twelve hour days in an effort to ensure everything was in perfect order.

It was the same stubbornness she had displayed when she'd refused his every overture to work with him permanently.

With a flash of insight he realised the more he tried to force her to comply the more she would dig her heels in. Her obstinancy was liable to take the form of an immovable object.

Why had he never noticed how sexy such stubbornness could be?

He squashed the thought away.

'Give me a month—until the date of our first anniversary—to change your mind,' he said, in the most reasonable voice he could muster. 'Come to Butterfly Island with me as planned—you're a first-class PA and linguist, and there is no one capable of doing the job as well as you. Do that and I will grant you a divorce. Refuse, and I will fight you every inch of the way.'

'I won't change my mind.'

'That remains to be seen. But unless you give me the next month to try you will find yourself with one almighty fight on your hands.' Deliberately he stepped towards her, over the puddle of clothes, encroaching on her personal space—a move he had never made in all the time he had known her. 'I will contest it every step of the way. If I wanted, I could play dirty and drag it on for years. And guess what? I never lose.'

A small tick pounded under her left eye, so tiny it was barely perceptible. He had only seen that particular affliction once before. Smelling victory, he pressed on a little further, leaning close enough to smell her clean, feminine scent. He swallowed the moisture that formed in his mouth.

'One month, Rosa. I don't think that's a very long time to wait for a lifetime of freedom.'

She gazed back at him, the tiny tick still pounding, before she visibly hardened. 'I want it in writing.'

'I beg your pardon?' His lips curled. He had never been so insulted. 'I am giving you my word.'

'You gave me your word eleven months ago.'

'And you gave me yours. I am not the one planning to break my vows.'

For an age they simply stared at each other, neither bending. The tension between them had become so thick a steak knife would have had trouble cutting through it. Yet through the seeping tension he could not help but admire her. There were not many people brave enough to face him off.

Rosa caved in first. Extending her hand, she said, 'We will shake on it. One month, Nicolai. And if at the end you refuse to give me my divorce then I will show you just how dirty *I* can play.'

Her fiery declaration sent a frisson of excitement racing through his veins. As he reached for her hand he realised it was the first time their flesh had touched since they had exchanged their rings.

And as he walked back down the stairs, victory still ringing within him, Nico realised it had also been the first time he had set foot in her suite since she had moved in.

A black Jeep awaited them at the landing strip that constituted Butterfly Island's airport.

It was roasting hot, the heat shimmering like waves off the ground. Even though Rosa had had the foresight to change into a light, cotton summer dress, her skin was dampening by the second.

It had been eighteen hours since they'd left London and she was shattered. The thirteen hour flight on Nico's plush private jet hadn't been too bad, but she had been far too wired to sleep. Unlike Nico, who had the amazing knack of being able to sleep on command.

Fortunately she'd had a pile of documents to read through to keep her occupied. She'd devoted all her spare time over the past fortnight in getting up to speed on the contracts. There had been little else for her to do. Nico had been as elusive over the past two weeks as an escaped hamster.

The one-hour connecting flight to Butterfly Island on a four-seat Cessna had been a more cramped affair. Nico had sat in front of her. They had been close enough to touch—close enough for her to smell him.

She had spent the flight breathing through her mouth.

A squat, elderly gentleman who looked dressed for a safari, in a cream pocketed shirt, cream shorts, a panama hat and long white socks, got out of the Jeep and strode over to them. For his part, Nico had relaxed his strict business attire by removing his jacket and tie and rolling up his sleeves.

'Nicolai—as always, it's a pleasure to have your company.'

'Likewise.' Nico shook the offered hand vigorously. 'Allow me to introduce you to my wife, Rosa. Rosa, this is Robert King—owner of Butterfly Island and King Island.'

His wife? Nico had introduced her as his *wife*? In the eight months she had continued working for him after their quickie wedding he had never introduced her as anything other than his assistant. They had agreed that when it came to business it was best to keep things on a professional footing.

Before she could think about this in any depth she was pulled into the American's arms. 'Wonderful to meet you, Rosa. Your husband has told me all about you.' He released her, but kept hold of her forearms so he could look at her. 'Nicolai, you never told me what a beauty she was.'

Nico placed an arm around her waist in what could only be described as a possessive manner, forcing a reluctant Robert to release her. Rosa, already reeling at being called a *beauty*, was so shocked at this unexpected and blatant show of possessiveness that she froze.

'Rosa's beauty speaks for itself,' said Nico in his gravelly tones. 'Now, have all the arrangements been made?'

She was not sure if she'd imagined it, but she could have sworn Robert dropped him a quick wink. 'Everything's in hand.'

The minor stupor caused by Nico's introduction and his unprecedented hold on her receded, and she extracted herself from his arm. 'It's wonderful to meet you too, Mr King, but—as I'm sure *my husband* has already informed you—I have accompanied him as his assistant and not his wife.'

'His assistant, eh?' Robert's wink was a lot more obvious this time. 'I get you, I get you. Say no more. Now, you folks must be exhausted after all that travelling. Let's get you to your accommodation so you can freshen up. Oh—and, Rosa? It's Robert.'

The air-conditioning in the Jeep had been turned to full blast. Rosa welcomed the freshness after the stifling heat of the airstrip. It was the only thing she did welcome as the men started to talk business. Robert didn't exactly freeze her out of the conversation but all his attention was focused on Nico. She had a feeling if she offered an opinion he would ruffle her hair and tell her not to worry her pretty head about it. It was infuriating, but not half as infuriating as Nico's obliviousness to it.

She comforted herself with the knowledge that once Robert had seen her work he would see for himself that she was there *not* out of the virtue of being Nico's wife but out of the virtue of being good at her job.

Still, it made for an uncomfortable journey—at least for her.

Butterfly Island was small by anyone's standards. According to her research, its circumference was only a touch over nine miles. They reached the complex where they were to stay for the next fortnight in less than ten minutes.

To Rosa's eyes it certainly lived up to its high-class honeymoon resort billing. When over the past fortnight she'd allowed herself to think of being in a lovers' paradise with the man who was her husband but not her lover, she had consoled herself that she would be too busy working to have time to witness any open signs of affection displayed by the other guests.

The driver pulled up outside a large, one-storey Tuscan-style villa.

'I'll leave you two to settle in.' Robert grinned, throwing her a wink. 'Get a good night's sleep and I'll get a golf-buggy to collect you after breakfast and bring you to the hotel. The conference room's all ready to go. And, Rosa—' he winked at her again '—the spa here has been named one of the best in the world. My staff have all been instructed to give you preferential treatment on anything you desire.'

'That is very kind. I'll be sure to remember that.' She smiled. The shimmering heat of the day and the ambient atmosphere of the island had already started working its magic on her. What was the point in getting antsy? He was an old man. She would change his mind soon enough. 'See you in the morning.'

Entering the villa, she tightened her ponytail and sighed with pleasure.

'Shall I take your luggage to your bedroom?' the driver asked, depositing their cases on the terracotta floor.

'I shall deal with it,' Nico said, slipping him some local currency.

Once they were alone, he turned to Rosa. 'I need to check in with the Moscow office, so take a look around.'

Leaving him to it, she headed off into the open-plan living quarters, which were as airy and sophisticated as one would expect for a villa of this calibre. On the gleaming dining table stood a bucket of champagne on ice, a large bowl of fresh fruit and a vase of the prettiest, most delicious-smelling flowers she had ever seen or sniffed. Tucked away discreetly in a corner to the rear was a large, fully equipped office, which she gave a cursory once-over before heading to the patio doors. Inspecting the office could wait. She would spend the next fortnight virtually chained to the desk.

She stepped out onto the decking. A sprawling lawn ran down to a sandy-white beach.

Bubbles of excitement started thrumming through her veins. Dozens of co-mingling scents converged under her nose, from fragrant flowers and freshly cut grass to the salty scent of the sea.

Rosa closed her eyes. She had travelled to many countries with Nico during her time as his PA. Relaxation had never been on the agenda. This trip would be no different. She was here to work.

All the same…

They'd always stayed in luxurious accommodation, but it had always been functional rather than beautiful.

Butterfly Island was stunning. This villa was stunning.

Wistfulness clutched at her belly. What would it be like if she were here with a lover? Someone she trusted enough to place her heart in his hands, who would not squeeze all the life out of it?

She scrubbed the image away—especially the image of Nico that kept trying to intrude. Finding another lover was the last thing on her mind. Sleeping with Stephen had been an act of folly—an act of desperation to purge the hurt that had almost consumed her whole.

CHAPTER FOUR

AFTER ONE LAST longing gaze at the beach, Rosa went back inside to search for the bedrooms. The first was easy to find, and immediately she chose it for herself. The bedroom, large and opulent, would be any honeymooner's dream. Its raised emperor four-poster bed even had the clichéd rose petals scattered all over the silk sheets. The *en suite* bathroom was *amazing*. The bath! She had never seen anything like it: sunken, with gold taps around the edges, it was large enough to swim in.

To stake her claim, she chucked her handbag on the bed and then left it to find Nico's bedroom.

A few minutes later, her brief good mood having plummeted, she found Nico in the partitioned office, his laptop open, still talking on his smartphone.

He took one look at her face and disconnected the call.

'What is wrong?' he asked. 'You look as if someone has stolen your luggage.'

She stood before him. 'There's only one bedroom.'

She waited for his disapproval.

He leaned back in the Captain's chair and stretched out his long legs. 'Naturally there is only one room.'

'What do you mean, "naturally"? I was assured by Camilla, or Emily, or whoever it is that currently runs your

London office, that a two-bedroomed villa had been reserved for us.'

'I changed it.'

Her chin nearly hit the floor. 'Why did you do that?'

'Because we are married, and married couples rarely sleep in separate beds. Unless, of course, they are not sharing conjugal relations.'

She shook her head slowly, wishing she could slap the smug arrogance off his face. 'You clever bastard.'

'I shall take that as a compliment.'

'It wasn't meant to be.' She knew exactly what he was playing at. 'I'm not sharing a bed with you. I assume it is enough that people *think* we are sleeping together?'

He shrugged nonchalantly. 'I do not control how other people think.'

'You'll have to sleep on the sofa.'

'I think not. I will be sleeping on that big, comfortable bed. If you wish to join me…?' He raised an eyebrow in invitation.

She blinked in shock.

Had that really been a suggestive tone in his voice? Surely not…

Unnerved, she took a step back.

Nico sat up and rested his forearms on his thighs, openly studying her. 'Does the thought of sharing a bed with me scare you?'

'Of course not,' she lied, inching back a little further—as far as the edge of the desk. He was still too close, but there was no way she was going to scurry off like a frightened rabbit just because he was close enough for her to smell his fruity scent.

They had worked side-by-side for the best part of a year and his scent had hardly ever been a problem for her—at least not until the last few months of her tenure. That had been one of the reasons she had turned down his offer of a permanent position. Nico smelled far too good for her sensibility.

'Then what is your problem?' His eyes gave a sudden gleam. 'Worried I won't be able to keep my hands off you?'

'Don't be ridiculous.' As if Nico had *ever* looked at her with anything other than platonic eyes.

'Why would you think that ridiculous? You're an attractive woman—sharing a bed with you would be a temptation for any man.'

To her horror, she felt her neck burn. She turned her head, unable to look at him, suddenly scared of what he would see. 'Now you *are* being ridiculous.'

His voice dropped to a murmur. 'I've thought about you a lot these past few weeks.'

She fixed her gaze on a pretty landscape painting on the wall. 'Sure you have.'

He had the audacity to laugh, with a low, gravelly timbre that sent tiny tingles dancing on her skin.

'You are angry with me for not spending any time with you. That would have been easily rectified if you were still working for me. You would have travelled with me.'

'Your ego astounds me.' She paused to swallow a lump that had formed in her throat. 'However, if your idea of getting me to change my mind about our marriage was to leave me alone for a fortnight, it was one heck of a rubbish plan.'

'I had matters to arrange and business to tie up before this trip.' He leaned closer and cupped the curve of her neck. 'Did you miss me?'

His unexpected action caught her off-guard. She would not have been more surprised if he had told her he was gay. She could understand the arm around her waist when they had been with Robert—Nico was doing all in his power to set her up to look a liar and a fool if she went down the annulment route—but *this*?

She had to fight with everything she had not to respond to the feel of his warm palm against her sensitised skin. She would *not* fall into his blatant trap.

'No.' She pulled away from his clasp—his second touch in less than an hour. 'I didn't miss you. Now, will you stop playing games? It's making me uncomfortable.'

His lips curved slightly. 'I am not playing games.'

'That's what it feels like.'

'You agreed to give me the chance to prove our marriage deserves another shot.'

'So far you have failed spectacularly. And pretending you find me attractive is not the way to go about it either.' Not after eleven months of complete uninterest.

'Have you considered that maybe I am not acting?'

The breath caught in her throat. If she hadn't already known how indifferent he was to her physically, she might almost have believed him.

She dragged air into her lungs and took a step to the side. 'Actually, no. I don't believe that for a second. You don't find me attractive. You're just using your masculinity to try and drive me into some kind of feminine stupor. You think I will fall for your charms and thus save you the unpleasantness of a public divorce—and save you from the hundreds of women who will come beating on your door, begging to be the new Mrs Baranski.'

He stilled, his eyes narrowing. 'You have me all figured out.'

'You're an easy read.'

What else could it be? Their marriage hadn't just been platonic, it had been positively frigid. Intellectually, they got along beautifully. They could talk business until the sun came up. But there had been no physical contact of any kind, not even when they had drunk more vodka together than was good for them. They would attend functions where couples were together in every sense of the word—holding hands, sneaking kisses. For all their cordiality, she and Nico wouldn't even wipe a fragment of lint from each other's clothing.

It was what she had signed up to. But she'd had no idea when she drew up that stupid contract that it would come to hurt so much and gnaw at her insides.

'If I were to tell you I find you incredibly sexy, would you think I was lying?'

'We both know I am not your type.' Even when passing her a mug of coffee he made a concerted effort not to touch her.

'Maybe my tastes are becoming more discerning.'

'Unluckily for you, *my* tastes aren't. If you think I want to share a bed with a man who has a deli counter of blondes queuing for a space in his bed, you have another think coming. Believe me, that was a strong positive for me when we made our no-sex pact.'

Nico studied her, his brow furrowed. 'Yet you were willing to share a bed with the ex-boyfriend you married me to escape?'

'There were numerous reasons I married you. Escaping Stephen was only one of them. Not having sex with you was another.'

He rose to his feet and flashed a smile. A dangerous smile. A predatory smile. 'Maybe if we had made sex part of our deal you would not be wanting to leave me. You certainly would not have needed to seek physical attention or *flowers* from your ex.'

Her incredulity at his arrogance was matched only by the heavy swirl of heat settling in her core.

Fighting it, she straightened to her full five foot three inches and speared him with a quelling look. 'Don't even go there. Don't even think about it. It's not going to happen. Not now. Not ever.'

'Ah, *daragaya*, but things have changed. You agreed to

give me a month to change your mind. And as we have never had sex before…' His words trailed off as he leaned over, and then he whispered into her ear. 'I guarantee one night with me and you will find your ex wanting. You will certainly never want to leave.'

It was the warmth of his breath in her ear, skewering her senses, that prevented her from slapping him. Tingles bounced on every millimetre of skin, her core thickening and nestling in the apex of her thighs, burning her.

'You're sick,' she dragged from her arid throat. 'You're like a child with an unwanted toy. You don't want to play with it, but the second another child picks it up you decide you want it after all. Well, I am not a toy. And I will not be treated as one.'

Nico had to admire her poise. Rosa walked away with her back straight and her hips gently swaying. She had not once raised her voice.

Yet that same fury she had displayed when she had told him of her wish to divorce was there, bubbling under the surface.

That passion, ripe for unleashing—how clearly he could see it now.

The logical part of his brain kept telling him to let her go, to give her the divorce she so obviously wanted and get on with his life.

He happened to believe that this time the logical part of his brain was wrong.

Maybe she was right in her 'child with a toy' analogy.

Her declaration a fortnight ago had released something within him—a fighting spirit more ruthless than in any business dealing he had ever conducted.

Nico hated to lose. He had spent the past fortnight ensuring he would win.

He and Rosa were bound by a piece of paper and two bands of gold. Nothing more. He had failed to appreciate that she was not an automaton. She was a sexual being, with needs and desires like everyone else. It was only natural she would seek gratification. On reflection, the only thing that should surprise him was how long it had taken her.

What he had *not* expected was the ugly, putrid feeling residing deep in his guts at the knowledge of what she had done.

He could not stop thinking about it.

She had gained satisfaction with another.

The thought of another man pawing *his wife* made his skin crawl.

The thought of his wife pawing another man made him want to punch a wall.

And now all bets were off.

Rosa's desire for a divorce meant whatever agreement they had made was null and void.

Soon she would share that delectable body with *him*. Her husband.

He hadn't intended to come on to her so soon, but the little stunt he had just pulled had proved one thing: he recognised the signs of feminine desire and in his strait-laced wife he had seen them. She wanted him. He would use that latent desire and play with her until she was begging for *his* possession, whimpering with the pleasure only *he* could give her, until all thoughts of another were eradicated from her mind.

He would make things so good she would never want to leave.

Rosa was buried nose-deep in paperwork when she heard the front door of the villa open. Every limb and digit froze.

She was determined every document would be faultless. There was nothing worse than thinking you had it word-perfect only for Nico to read through the documents and find a misspelled Russian word or an incorrect tense. Admittedly that had only happened twice, but that had been enough for her to determine it would not happen on this, their last trip together.

Not that she *should* be busting a gut for the man. Throughout their marriage he had treated her with nothing but professional courtesy. All right, maybe that was exaggerating things a little—whenever she had accompanied him to functions they had always had fun together, but it had been strictly platonic fun. Now it was all long, lingering glances and murmured comments that could be twisted into something intimate if she so chose.

She did not choose.

It would be obvious to a blind man what Nico was up to.

Soon he would make his move. And she would be ready for it.

A waft of citrusy musk wafted under her nose and she reached for her cup of cold coffee, washing away the saliva that had formed, Pavlov's Dog–style, in her mouth.

'How are you getting on?' To her intense irritation he placed one hand on her desk, the other on the back of her chair, and peered over her shoulder to see what she was working on.

'Fine, thank you.' She didn't dare move. He was so close his breath was tickling her hair, making her aware of the heat emanating from his powerful body. She could feel it now, that heat, and her whole body was alive and tingling at his proximity.

'Good. It is time to stop. We're going out for dinner.'

'Go without me. I've far too much work to do.' Actually, she didn't. She had been pleasantly surprised to find there was only a fraction of the expected workload, the reduction assisted by the half-dozen translators Nico had flown over to help her. At the rate she was ploughing through it she could be back in London within a week.

'Impossible. We are dining with Robert and his wife.'

'In that case I *definitely* have far too much work to do. And can you please move back and stop invading my personal space?'

His response to her request was to lean over her shoulder and flip the lid of her laptop shut.

Rosa's spine stiffened, then froze. She stared at the now closed laptop with widening eyes, her hands curling into fists as fury simmered through her veins. 'I've just spent three hours working on that document,' she said through gritted teeth.

'And now you have finished. Your working day is over.'

'I hadn't saved it.'

'Your laptop is configured to auto-save every five minutes. Any loss will be minimal.'

How *dared* he sound so reasonable? How dared he? '*I* decide when my working day is over. Not you.'

'Rosa, I do not recall giving you a choice in the matter. You are calling it a day and that is that. Now, go and get ready for dinner.'

Her frustrations spilling over, she deliberately shoved her chair back and 'accidentally' rammed it into Nico's legs. He jumped back.

'Sorry,' she lied, hastily getting to her feet.

He did not look in the least perturbed, simply threw her a lazy, knowing smile which she longed to slap off his face.

Keeping a good distance between them, she folded her arms across her chest and glared at him. 'You *do* realise Robert King thinks I'm here on a free jaunt? He probably thinks you've appointed me as your PA as some kind of tax dodge.'

She had absented herself from the meeting between Nico and Robert that morning in the hotel conference room with the excuse that she needed to ensure all the other translators had settled in. In reality she had left the conference room because if she had stayed another minute she would have been liable to throw her laptop at Robert King. It would not have been half as bad if Nico had not allowed Robert's misconceptions to continue.

'Why do you care what he thinks?' he asked. 'You're excellent at your job and he will realise it soon enough.'

'I don't like people making assumptions about me.'

Nico stored this little nugget of information away. It was extremely rare for Rosa to let slip anything personal about herself, however innocuous. He knew she was devoted to her job, knew her favourite food, knew she loved all things Russian, knew she could not sleep when travelling, knew she disliked raised voices and knew she was an orphan. Until now, that had been it.

Now he could add a dislike of people judging her to the list. Briefly he wondered where this dislike had come from, but pushed the thought away. It shouldn't—didn't—matter to him. It was the information itself he required.

Know your enemies. Know their weaknesses. The who, what, where, when and why were superfluous.

However, she did have a valid point about Robert's attitude towards her. Rosa was damn good at her job, and as smart as a whip, which was the main reason their marriage had been such a success—at least from his perspective. She was a good sounding board and able to see the bigger picture with the barest of facts. He had become accustomed to confiding in her about business, had almost come to rely on it.

His mouth filled with a bitter taste as he was reminded that, unless he changed her mind, one day some other man was going to get the benefit of that excellent brain.

He had done nothing to prevent Robert forming the wrong

opinion of her but he should feel no guilt. All was fair in love and war, and this was definitely war. He had taken a perverse pleasure in seeing her reduced to the status of wife and pretty trinket hanging on his arm.

His independent wife clung to her professional status like a second skin. She clung to her professional status around *him* like a second skin. She never let her guard down for a single second. Not even when she confessed infidelity. Always that wall was between them. He had facilitated its construction with her.

Well, he was going to tear it down—every last brick. By hook or by crook he would bring out that hidden womanly side, a side she had been happy to share with someone else.

Now he had got over his shock about her wanting to leave him he was able to think rationally. He could not in all conscience force her to stay if she was determined to go. It would be intolerable for them both. But neither was he prepared to let her go without sampling that fabulous body for himself and making her see how good things could be between them. Goddammit, she was his *wife*.

One thing he had learned about women was that one night in his bed was enough for them to start talking about *feelings*. Had he not married Rosa because she was nothing like those women?

Rosa was emotionally closed off. It was preposterous to imagine she would lie in bed and discuss *feelings,* or that she would expect him to share his.

His solution was perfect. The more he thought about it, the more it made sense. They would continue with their perfect marriage and in the evenings he would share her bed and her delectable body. That would stave off her loneliness and put paid to her ridiculous idea of divorce.

He smothered a sudden burst of mirth at the recognition

that at least he wouldn't have to worry about her hearing wedding bells.

'Rosa, I will make it clear to Robert tonight that you are more than just my wife, that you are an excellent translator and PA.'

'You most certainly will not,' she said, in what sounded uncannily like exasperation. 'That would be even worse.' She adopted a childish voice. *'Oh, Mr King, have I told you how well my little wife sings? She's so good she could be on a talent show.'*

Despite himself, Nico laughed. 'I get your point. I will try for subtlety. How does that sound?'

She narrowed her eyes. 'Better. Obviously it would have been better not to get us into this position in the first place. If you had just introduced me as your PA, like you always used to do, we would not have this problem.'

'I don't have any problem with it—I'm proud to call you my wife.'

Satisfaction drove through him as he witnessed the colour spread up her neck. He was only speaking the truth.

'But naturally I do understand why the situation would irk you.'

'Irk?' The caramel in her eyes darkened. 'Yes, I would say the situation *irks* me. I've worked too hard for my professionalism to be reduced to nothing but a bit part in your life.'

He could understand that too. And the guilt that had been hanging around him like a bad smell reeked a little bit stronger. Nico understood hard work. How else did a boy from a backward Siberian mining town break free and conquer the world?

'Is there something wrong with your neck?' he enquired.

'Sorry?'

'You keep kneading it. You were doing it this morning.'

'Oh.' For a moment she looked a little stunned. 'I cricked it last night.'

'Cricked?'

'I strained it. I woke up with it. I'll take some ibuprofen for it soon.'

'Is it from sleeping on the sofa?'

The look she gave him could only be described as a *'well, duh'* look.

He smiled. 'That is what happens when you allow pride to dictate your actions. There was a perfectly good bed for you to sleep in—there still is.'

'Or you could do the gentlemanly thing and offer to sleep on the sofa tonight.'

'I could,' he agreed. 'But I won't. The bed is plenty big enough for both of us. I promise I will not try anything with you.' He paused deliberately before continuing, 'That is not to say *you* cannot try anything with me.'

That delicious colour flared across her face and neck again. 'There you go again, making innuendoes and flirting with me.'

'That was not innuendo. It was fact. I would be delighted if you were to seduce me.'

Rosa looked as if she were about to bolt, so Nico raised his hands in a sign of peace. 'Robert and Laura are expecting to dine with us and it would be wholly embarrassing if I were to arrive solo.'

Deliberately he played to her sense of fairness—another trait he had forgotten to tuck away in his mental box of her characteristics.

From the pursing of her lips he could tell she was thinking about it. He pressed a little harder. 'All you have done since we left London is work. You need to take a break.'

'All right,' she relented grudgingly. 'I'll come with you. But I don't want a late night.'

'Not a problem. We have a busy day tomorrow, so an early night will do us both good.' Not that he would confide what type of busy day they would be sharing. If he were to tell her he was certain she would hijack a yacht and sail all the way to the mainland to catch a flight home.

'I'll go and get ready.' She slid past him and grabbed her handbag from the desk.

A tiny brown mole on the nape of her neck caught his attention. He had never noticed it before. Did she have others…?

A weird compulsion to press a kiss to it and taste that creamy skin crept through him. Before he could act on it she'd walked off, leaving him to blow out tiny puffs of air, struggling to control the ache spreading through his loins.

His physical reaction to a tiny mole perplexed him.

His growing physical reaction to *her* perplexed him.

All this flirting was becoming a major turn-on—which was strange in itself as he was not a man given to flirting. But Rosa's reaction to it was such an unexpected delighted that the more he did it, the more he wanted to do it.

Maybe he had been telling the truth when he'd said his tastes were becoming more discerning?

Women had always been an exotic mystery to him. He enjoyed sex, but he found intimacy on any other level repellent. He had certainly never before become fixated on a *mole*.

He was sure some psychoanalyst would put his repulsion down to being brought up solely by an undemonstrative father. Since leaving the Siberian mining town where he'd grown up, Nico had learned that some men displayed physical affection towards their children. Not his father. Mikhail Baranski was a real man's man: hard-drinking and hard-working. He had provided for Nico, but expected his son to take care of himself. All Nico's knowledge about physical affection and intimacy came from books. When he'd left home and moved to

Moscow he had assumed relationships would be as easy to conduct as they were in the books. But they weren't.

It had taken his relationship with Galina for him to realise he simply wasn't wired for it. Emotions and affection were for other people. Not for him. He had sampled failure once and had no intention of tasting it again.

His marriage to Rosa had been the perfect solution to this inbred aversion to intimacy. He had a discreet woman of intelligence to share his life, without any of the mumbo-jumbo sex seemed to provoke in the female of the species—the mumbo-jumbo that was totally alien to him.

CHAPTER FIVE

'WILL I DO?'

Nico looked up from his laptop and appraised his wife, who had just made an appearance from the bedroom.

She posed before him, hands on hips, chin cocked upwards. 'I assume the dress code is casual?'

She had finally released her ebony hair from the confines of that dreadful ponytail she favoured. She'd had it cut since the last time he had seen her wear it loose. Her silky locks still fell in waves down her back, but the front had been feathered, softening her angular features. Tonight she had opted for simplicity, wearing a demure dusky-pink dress that flared slightly to her knees and matching it with silver sandals with heels that added a good four inches to her short, curvy frame. Her concession to make-up was a touch of mascara and some pale pink lipstick. She looked wickedly pretty, but beneath the truculent expression he detected a hint of apprehension in her eyes.

He searched for the right words to tell her how beautiful she looked.

'You look fine,' he said. 'I'd better get ready. I've opened a bottle of white—it's in the fridge.'

He showered quickly and methodically, trying to banish the glimmer of hurt his off-hand compliment had briefly evoked in Rosa's eyes.

At first glance she was just a reasonably attractive woman. It wasn't until you studied her face and became trapped in the depth of those striking caramel eyes that you became aware of her radiant yet understated beauty. Unlike most other women, whose beauty faded after a couple of dates, becoming—dared he say it?—a touch boring, Rosa's beauty increased with each subsequent look. There was always something new to see: a new profile of her snub nose if looked at from a new angle, lines that appeared depending on whether she was smiling or frowning, lips that changed colour depending on her tiredness and mood.

By the time he had dressed, donning a short-sleeved navy linen shirt and charcoal chinos, and left the bedroom, Rosa was back at her desk. It didn't surprise him.

'What are you doing?'

She jumped and slammed down the lid of her laptop. 'Nothing.'

'Nothing? Really? Then why have your cheeks gone red?'

'It's personal.'

'Did you remember to save it before you closed the lid?' he asked pointedly.

Rosa's cheeks coloured even brighter. Her face tight, her lips clenched into a thin line, she got up from her chair and stalked past him, grabbing a small clutch bag off the table. 'Are we going?'

Nico briefly debated opening her laptop and doing a thorough investigation into what she had been up to.

'If we don't leave now we'll be late,' she reminded him. 'And we wouldn't want to be late for Robert and Laura, would we?'

What would his demanding answers achieve? He knew who she had been in touch with. If she hadn't been corresponding with Stephen why else would she be so evasive?

Swallowing the bile that had risen in his throat, and making a mental note to check out her laptop after she had fallen asleep, Nico locked the front door behind them and they set off.

'Why have you removed your shoes?' he asked, after glancing at her and realising she had shrunk. The top of her head was once again barely level with his armpit.

'Believe me, these shoes are not made for walking.'

'So why wear them?'

'I'm not. I'm carrying them.'

'Your feet will get cut.'

'This pathway's so smooth I bet Robert's had the sweepers out.'

There was not a lot he could say to that type of logic—especially when his mind was still consumed with rabid, ugly thoughts.

He had to know.

'Have you heard from him?'

'Who?'

'Stephen.'

Her answer came succinctly. 'No.'

'Do you think you will hear from him again?'

A mirthless sound that might have been some form of laugh escaped from her throat. 'Nico, it was a disaster. I should never have gone out with him…' Her voice trailed off before she added quietly, 'I doubt Stephen will ever want to see me again.'

But did she want to see *him* again? For some reason the question stuck in his throat.

And if she hadn't been corresponding with Stephen then what *had* she been up to on the laptop?

'How did you meet up with him again?' he asked, keeping his voice on a nice, even keel. 'I thought you had cut him out of your life?'

'I had.'

Deliberately he let the silence envelop them.

'I bumped into him a couple of months ago at the dealership when I went to buy my new car.'

'You have a new car?'

'Yes.'

'What did you get?'

'A Fiat 500.'

'Ah, yes. I recall seeing it in the garage. I assumed it was Gloria's. Why didn't you go for something more selective?'

'By "selective" I assume you mean more expensive?'

'*Da.* If it was a matter of cost, I would have been happy to pay for it.'

'That's very generous, Nico, but I've made it perfectly clear I don't want your money.'

'You are my wife, Rosa. I appreciate ours is not a conventional marriage but it still means something. If you need anything you only have to ask.' In eleven months of marriage she hadn't asked for anything from him. She really was—had been—the perfect wife.

They arrived at the hotel, pausing for a moment so Rosa could put her shoes back on before walking into the lobby. He felt her stiffen beside him and knew without asking that she had seen Laura King, who was propped against the bar, towering over her diminutive husband.

At the functions they'd attended as a married couple he had noticed the way Rosa's generous smile would not quite meet her eyes when she was introduced to the starlets and models that littered the social scene. Often he had wondered if she disapproved of them—an irrelevant question he had never before felt compelled to ask.

She'd displayed the same stiffness then as she was displaying now, with Laura looming towards her.

It suddenly dawned on him that it was not disapproval she felt. He didn't know what it could be—and neither should he care—but in that brief moment of understanding a strange compulsion swept through him, an impulse to wrap his arm around her and offer reassurances that everything would be fine.

Internally he recoiled. The idea of offering comfort, or reassurance, or *anything* of a physical nature beyond sex, was anathema to him. He didn't have a clue what the requirements of such an act were, and nor would he know the right words to say.

His rare bout of indecision was steamrollered over by Robert swooping on Rosa and pulling her into an exuberant embrace.

'You look beautiful, Mrs Baranski.' He beamed, letting her go but taking her hand and planting a kiss on it.

Robert King was easily in his seventies, and Butterfly Island was but a small part of his empire. King Island, an uninhabited island he also owned, was to be used as a base for Nico's miners. If the contracts were not signed Nico could forget about mining offshore.

At that precise moment, though, Nico wanted nothing more than to pull the old man away from his wife and tell him to keep his liver-spotted hands to himself.

But of course he did nothing of the sort, and nor did he understand where this primitive, possessive urge had come from. He could only assume the heat of the day had somehow got to him.

Robert made the introductions and then led them through to the restaurant, which was as lush and opulent as the rest of the resort.

Rosa could not help but wish they were dining outside, in one of the beachside restaurants, where the soft breeze would cool them naturally, rather than inside with the air-conditioning turned on full-blast. She shivered and rubbed her arms, wishing she could move a little closer to Nico and take advantage of his body heat.

Robert looked at Nico. 'Red or white?'

'Do you have Pouilly-Fumé on your wine list?' Nico asked

'We certainly do.' Robert clicked his fingers and a waiter, who had been hovering on the sidelines, practically flew over.

'Do you want white too, Rosa?' Nico asked pointedly.

Rosa suppressed a smile.

Now that she was seated, and had got over her shock at seeing Robert's wife, she had started to relax a little.

Somewhere in her imaginings she had conjured up an image of an elderly, yet perfectly coiffured and immaculately dressed lady—a kind of glamorous gran. The reality was markedly different. Laura King, who wasted no time in bragging that she had once worked as a model, was a good forty years her husband's junior, and stood a good foot taller than him too. She was stunning: ultra-tanned and toned, with long sun-bleached blonde hair that fell in a sheet to a pert derrière enhanced by a tiny gold dress.

In short, she was everything Rosa wasn't.

From feeling happy with the outfit she had selected, Rosa now felt utterly flat. She could not help but imagine Nico comparing the two women—his rather plain wife seated next to him opposed to the glittery beauty opposite.

Nico wouldn't have to pretend with Laura. He would want to make love to her for herself, and not out of ferocious pride. The same pride that would not allow anyone to know he had shared a roof with a woman for almost a year without once becoming intimate with her.

He would never have stood *Laura* up on her birthday.

It made her belly curdle and her blood simmer to know he only thought of her, Rosa, as an asset in his successful life. He wanted to keep this asset, neatly ticked off in the box marked 'wife', not because he didn't want to lose *her,* per se, but because he didn't want to lose. Full stop.

He would never want her for herself.

Whatever she wore, however much money she spent, Rosa would never be anything but a distant star compared with Laura's dazzling sun. Judging from the less than subtle glances being thrown her way, she had a feeling the Amazonian agreed.

'How long have you two been married?' Laura asked in a syrupy voice.

'Eleven months.'

'Eleven and a half months,' Nico corrected.

'Oh, so you're still newlyweds! And what are you planning for your first anniversary? Something special?'

'Oh, yes,' Rosa agreed sweetly. No way would she allow her feelings of intimidation to show. 'I'm planning to divorce him.' She cast a quick glance at Nico, to see how he had taken her off-the-cuff quip. His face was set in its usual impassive mask.

Laura squealed with laughter. 'That is so *funny*.'

'Isn't it? How long have you two been married?'

Laura fluttered her extended lashes at her husband. 'Three years. It feels like for ever—doesn't it, darling?'

The conversation went rapidly downhill. Laura completely dominated it, mostly throwing sugar-laced barbs at her husband and casting lingering eyes at Nico when she thought no one was looking. For his part, Robert seemed oblivious to his wife's behaviour, beaming throughout.

After the main course Laura excused herself to 'powder her nose', while Robert insisted there were new guests he needed to welcome.

'Are you all right?' Nico asked quietly once they were alone.

'Me? I'm fine.'

'She is a little…full-on.'

'Who? Laura? I can't say I noticed,' she lied, compressing her lips together.

'She is certainly a handful.'

Rosa fixed a thin smile to her face. It was the most she could manage.

'It seems to me Robert has his work cut out keeping her in line.'

'I doubt anyone could keep *her* in line,' she retorted tartly. Did Nico *have* to talk about that woman? 'Besides, they're made for each other.'

Nico raised a brow.

'He gets a beautiful young bimbo on his arm; she gets to inherit billions when he dies.'

'I've never known you to be such a cynic,' he mused.

She took a long sip of wine and then quickly put the glass back down. Her tongue was starting to loosen—a sure sign it was time to switch to water.

There was something else eating away at her too: a low, queasy ache that clutched at her chest and swirled in her belly, making her want to pounce on the Amazonian and tell her to keep her manicured mitts off her husband.

But Nico was not going to be her husband for much longer. In any event, she had no proprietorial rights to him. Theirs was an open marriage. There were no propriety rights. Even if he was trying to establish some for his own ends.

'So you think she is beautiful?' Nico asked, his voice mild, uninterested.

'Of course. Don't you?' She almost laughed. As if Nico would think Laura anything *but* a beautiful sun. Physically, she was exactly his type. No wonder he couldn't stop talking about her—and this from a man who never talked anything but business.

After a pause, Nico said, 'Anyone who spends that amount

of time, money and effort on herself could not look anything but beautiful.'

Flattened, Rosa nearly reached for her wine again, but then she froze, suddenly aware of Nico leaning over into her personal space. He put his mouth to her ear, close enough for her to feel the warmth of his breath.

All at once her heart-rate tripled.

Tingles of awareness spread throughout her skin, like hot treacle swimming under the surface, throbbing down low, deep in her core.

Her mouth ran dry as this one intimate moment consumed her entire being.

Whatever Nico had planned to whisper was cut off as Robert came back to the table, breaking the spell with an almost tangible snap.

'Excuse me, lovebirds,' he said, winking at them as he took his seat. 'Sorry to interrupt.'

'You are not interrupting anything,' Nico said with his usual calmness, draping a casual arm across Rosa's back.

Laura chose that moment to make a reappearance too. From the manic way she was speaking, and the amount of sniffing she was now doing, Rosa suspected she had taken the term 'powder her nose' literally.

There were not many people she disliked, but Laura King was fast becoming one of them. Generally she tried not to judge a book by its cover—even beautiful, leggy women—but if that woman fluttered her eyelashes at Nico one more time she swore she would stick a fork in her leg.

As consolation, she reminded herself that they only had around a week left on this island, and then she would never have to see Laura again.

She wouldn't have to see Nico again either.

She took her glass and finished the wine in one swallow.

'Is something the matter?' Nico asked.

She shivered. 'Someone walked over my grave.'

It was almost the truth. For that brief moment the thought of leaving him had felt like a bereavement.

She had to remind herself she was doing the right thing.

Marrying Nico had triggered something inside her. At first it had been so subtle she hadn't noticed it, but as time had gone on it had crept under her skin and into her psyche. No matter how hard she'd tried to keep her distance, no matter how hard she'd tried to keep their relationship professional and companionable, that something had fought to be heard.

She had run from it. She had refused to work permanently for him because of it, blithely covering her ears in a futile attempt to drown out the noise and pretend it didn't exist.

Well, she heard it loud and clear now.

Desire. Lust. Need. Whatever name you gave it, it amounted to the same thing.

She didn't want to need anyone—least of all Nico.

The sooner they completed this project the better.

Leaving Nico had never felt so imperative.

'You're looking peaky, lady.' Robert's booming voice broke through her red-coloured thoughts.

Nico's turned his head, his sharp eyes narrowing as he studied her. 'Another ghost?' he asked ironically.

'I think now would be a good time to let her in on the surprise you have arranged,' Robert said.

A sudden sense of dread washed over her. Whatever Nico had been plotting, it could not be good news.

His arrogant grin confirmed this opinion before he even opened his mouth. 'Robert has kindly agreed to let us take a little trip on one of his yachts. Just the two of us. It's my anniversary present for you.'

Rosa was glad Nico had declined Robert's offer of a golf-buggy to drive them back to their villa. She needed fresh air to think, and this clear, warm night with a delicious breeze from the ocean was the perfect setting to do just that. Well, it would be if she was alone, not walking by the side of the man who had put her in such a pickle.

'Are you not going to remove your shoes?'

'Sorry?'

'Your crippling shoes.' Nico stopped and nodded at her feet.

'Right. Yes. You're right.' Her head was full of so much confusion she had completely forgotten her feet were killing her. Of course now he had mentioned it she felt the full force of her shoes' constriction and quickly took them off. But not before debating stamping on his foot first.

Why did he have to display proper concern at the moment when she wanted nothing more than to bodily harm him?

'When are you going to start scolding me?' he asked, with a definite hint of anticipation.

'What's the point?' She shrugged tightly. 'You're clearly one step ahead of me.'

When Nico had made his announcement he had placed his hand on her thigh and squeezed it gently. To the casual observer it would have been a sign of affection. To Rosa it had been a warning.

He had been counting on her not making a scene and, goddamn him, he had counted correctly.

She would sooner cut her thumbs off than have a scene in public—or a scene anywhere, for that matter.

And so she had smiled sweetly and thanked Nico and Robert for the lovely, thoughtful gesture. At the same time she had placed her own hand on Nico's thigh. She had tried hard not to notice the muscular strength as she dug her nails in as hard as she could and said, 'You conniving bastard,' in Russian.

He had translated this to the rapt Kings as, 'You are a wonderful husband.' At least Robert had looked rapt. Rosa's one small consolation was that Laura's immovable face had looked positively sulky.

How she had longed to lash out at him properly—still longed to. How dared he manipulate her in such a fashion?

The fury racing through her was only matched by the tendrils of excitement unfurling in her stomach—tendrils she wanted to find scissors for and snip dead.

All these emotions were terrifying. The only way she could cope was to suck it up and ride it out. In no way, shape or form would she allow Nico to glean how deeply he'd affected her.

Was this how hormonal teenagers felt? Rosa had never been a proper hormonal teenager. Not for her the lashing out or falling off the rails that befell so many other adolescents. Who had there been for her to lash out at? The one person she had really wanted to kick out at, namely her mother, hadn't been there. Her mother had gone. No forwarding address. No Rosa.

Now the additional translators made sense. Nico could whisk her off for the day without affecting the contract schedule and everyone would think how romantic he was.

This one gesture more than any other killed the annulment idea stone-dead.

She would suck it up. It was only for one day. She could cope with Nico for one day.

'Did you bring a bikini?'

'No.' And if she had she wouldn't wear it in front of him.

'Why not?'

'We are supposed to be here to work, not go day-tripping on a yacht.'

'We are in one of the most beautiful locations in the world. Surely you brought some clothes to relax in?'

With the exception of a couple of dresses, the clothes she had brought were decidedly practical. She mentally ran through her wardrobe, trying to think of something suitable she could wear for a day's cruising.

'Never mind,' he said, interrupting her private musings. 'I'll arrange for a member of staff to bring a bikini for you from the resort boutique.'

'Can you make sure it's a *burkhini*?' she could not resist saying. She would bet Nico had never seen cellulite. At least not in the flesh.

'What is that?'

'Never mind.' She sighed. 'Go ahead. Do what you like. You generally do.'

'You're learning.'

They had arrived back at the villa. Nico dug his hand into his pocket for the key.

'Is your neck still hurting?' he asked as he unlocked the door, holding it open for her.

'Yes. And, no, I don't want a massage, thank you.' Her throat caught and she turned her face away. It shouldn't have surprised her that he had noticed something wrong with her neck—Nico noticed *everything*. Yet it had. His simple concern had touched her in a way she could hardly bear to think about.

'I do not recall offering one,' he said smoothly. 'However, I *am* prepared to do the gentlemanly thing and let you have the bed tonight.'

'Where will you sleep?'

'I will take the sofa.'

She stared at him, wondering what was going on in that conniving mind. He looked back at her with an openness she found suspicious, certain it was not simple concern dictating his offer.

'Why would you do that?'

He reached out and stroked a finger under one of her eyes. 'Believe it or not, *daragaya*, I am not a complete bastard. You have been working hard and need to rest.'

* * *

Nico felt her quiver, then stiffen beneath his touch, and experienced a frisson of satisfaction.

How easy it would be to kiss those plump, delectable lips. Rosa would certainly explode—although whether it would be an explosion of lust or an explosion of all the unleashed anger she was trying so hard to contain he could not say.

There would be plenty of time on the yacht for seduction. When it happened, he wanted her to be fully committed to it. He wanted Rosa begging for him.

He did not want her looking at him with eyes bruised from lack of sleep…eyes that no longer looked at him with total trust. Whenever she looked at him now it was with suspicion.

When she had looked at her ex, what had been ringing out of those caramel eyes? Had it been adoration?

She'd said sleeping with Stephen had been a disaster. The thought brought him no comfort. She had allowed another man to make love to her. He could not rid himself of the nasty taste that left in his mouth.

As cruel as he knew it was to think such thoughts, he hoped Stephen was an impotent flop.

When he, Nico, made love to Rosa, it would be the most satisfying, fulfilling event of her life.

But now was not the time to make his move. Rosa no longer trusted him. She was right not to. He needed to regain that trust.

But first he needed to check her laptop, and the easiest way to do that would be by letting her sleep in the bedroom with the door closed.

He dropped his hand and ran it through his hair. 'Go to bed, Rosa,' he said, 'Before I change my mind and join you.'

His lips twitched as she pointed her nose in the air and walked off, swinging her sandals.

An hour later, he threw the sheet back and swung his legs

off the sofa. Silently he padded to the office of the villa, pausing as he passed the bedroom. A dim glow seeped under the closed door. Rosa was still awake.

He filled his lungs with oxygen, debating whether to climb back into his makeshift bed and get some sleep.

Impossible. Until he knew what she had been doing his brain would not switch off. She had been up to something. That was a given. She had reacted like a startled rabbit and he wanted to know why. He *needed* to know why.

His antennae were on high alert. If he were a dog he would have an ear cocked. He flipped the lid of her laptop and turned it on. He flinched as the brief start-up tune rang out.

Keeping still, hardly daring to breathe, he waited for movement from the bedroom. Nothing.

The laptop finished loading. Adrenaline firing through his veins, his heart pounding, he clicked the mouse.

It was password-protected.

He muttered an oath under his breath and racked his brains, trying to think of what she would use. As much as it sickened him even to key in the letters, the first word he tried was *Stephen*. Invalid. A warning came up that he had two further attempts before the laptop shut itself down. At that moment he heard the distant sound of the toilet in the *en suite* bathroom flushing.

A cold sweat enveloped him.

What the *hell* was he playing at?

He was trying to hack into his own wife's laptop. What kind of sick puppy was he?

Clicking on the 'shutdown' icon, he closed the lid and moved stealthily back to the sofa.

All was quiet in the villa. All except the thunder that was his heart.

CHAPTER SIX

AFTER A LIGHT breakfast they made their way via golf-buggy to the harbour. Awaiting them, gleaming brightly in the calm ocean, stood the *Butterfly King*, a majestic yacht eighty feet long and three decks high.

'Is it to your liking?' Nico asked, unable to gauge Rosa's reaction to it because her lips had formed such a tight white line.

'It is nice and big—so, yes, I would say it is perfect.'

'Well, that's good to know,' he murmured, 'that you find big things perfect.' He laughed softly at the filthy look she threw at him. 'Shall we board?'

He really was going to have to put a stop to all these innuendoes, he thought ruefully a few minutes, later when the ache in his loins still refused to abate.

If he'd known how much fun it would be to flirt with his strait-laced wife he would have tried it months ago. She coloured so beautifully.

But then, their marriage had never been about flirting. Their marriage had been strictly business.

Now their marriage was open season—nothing was off-limits.

The Captain led them through to a plush saloon, where he introduced them to the four other crew members. 'I'll leave Jim here to show you around,' he said. 'It's time to set sail.'

'Can I order you any refreshments before I give you the grand tour?' Jim asked.

'I think we could both do with a coffee,' Nico said quickly. He wanted to make sure they were far from shore before he sprang his next surprise.

'I'd love a cappuccino, thank you,' said Rosa. She walked over to the wide window and gazed out, giving him an excellent view of her rear.

His wife had proper womanly curves. The cream linen trousers she wore accentuated the shape of her rounded bottom, and the pale pink blouse displayed her tiny waist. Not for the first time he marvelled that he had been so blind to it.

After they had finished their coffee, and he judged they had sailed far enough that she would not attempt to swim back to shore, he announced it was time for the tour.

'I thought Jim was going to do it,' she said.

'There is no need to disturb him. I am well acquainted with the yacht's interior.' He threw out his arms expansively. 'As you can see, this is the saloon. Through that door is the dining room, which leads on to the gym. The lower deck is of no relevance to us, but the upper deck…' He smiled.

Rosa did not trust that smile. And nor did she trust the gleam in his eyes. 'The upper deck, what?'

'Come. I will show you.'

As soon as they set foot inside the door at the top of the stairs she knew she had been right to be suspicious.

'Is this some kind of joke?'

The entire top deck was a suite. Not just any suite, either. This was a suite designed for lovers.

The bed, all scarlet silk sheets and soft, plump pillows, easily took up a third of the space. It did not so much dominate. The bed *was* the space. A whole cabal of honeymooners could sleep on it. Everything was designed around it.

Bed! Sex!

She might as well scream the words out because this suite was designed with nothing but sex in mind. Even the swimming pool—yes it had a heart-shaped swimming pool at one end through some patio doors—was an extension of the romantic and yet somehow erotic theme. Whoever had designed this suite should either be commended for an award or shot.

'Nice try,' she said, backing away. '*You* can spend the day in this boudoir. Me? I'm going to sit in the saloon and drink lots of vodka.'

'Look in the dressing room,' he instructed, pointing at a door.

She'd bet he'd had a minuscule bikini put there for her.

She was right. What she had not anticipated was the amount of other clothing neatly hung in there too.

Spinning round to face him, she put her hands on her hips. 'How long are we staying here?'

'A week.'

There was no other word for it. 'Bastard.'

When she would have walked out, there and then, he grabbed her wrist and pulled her to him. 'Come outside with me for a minute.'

'No. I'm going to see the Captain and demand he return us to shore.' She tried to shake him off but his grip was too strong.

'It will not make any difference.'

'Why? Have you paid him off?'

He didn't even have the decency to look shamefaced.

'You bloody well have, haven't you?'

Nico released his grip and tugged at her hand. He led her outside, past the swimming pool to the front of the yacht. She was so steaming mad she let him.

'Look at this scenery,' he said once they were standing side-by-side, holding on to the railings. 'Look at the calm of the ocean. You need a holiday. I need a holiday. Neither of us has taken any time off for over a year.'

She had to admit there was something rather soothing about the glistening ocean. 'Yes, I need a holiday. One far, far away from *you*. I can't believe you would do something so…so…' She scrambled around in her fried brain for the correct word. 'So sneaky.'

'I had to be sneaky because I knew you wouldn't agree to it otherwise.'

'Too right I wouldn't have.'

'Forgive me for being underhand. I am trying to save our marriage. Desperate times call for desperate deeds.' He gave her a crooked smile and lightly covered her hand with his. His wedding ring glistened under the beaming sun. 'You said you would give me a month, but it seems to me you have already made up your mind that our marriage is over.'

'Other than flirting with me, you haven't done anything to convince me otherwise.'

'I appreciate I was busy for the first two weeks, but a lot of that time was spent organising this.'

'Really?' She experienced a flicker of uncertainty.

'Really. I needed to ensure a good team of staff were left at the resort so you and I could take this week off and get to know each other properly.' Nico's features had a seriousness to them that had been missing in recent days. 'It seems to me that you are being unfair.'

'How have you worked that out?'

'You came to Butterfly Island with your mind made up. You promised to give me—us—another chance, but you didn't mean it, did you?'

'What's the point?' she said with a shrug, turning her focus back onto the open water. 'You only want our marriage to continue for your own convenience and ego.'

'My point exactly. You came here with preconceived ideas

about what I want and what my motives are and have not given two thoughts to the fact I genuinely want our marriage to work. For both of us.'

His low yet gentle tones made her squirm inside, like a naughty schoolgirl caught stuffing crayons in her pockets.

'How do you imagine that makes me feel?' he continued. 'Knowing you are only pretending? That in reality you are counting the days until you can be rid of me?'

This time she squirmed visibly. When he put it like that it did seem rather cold. She hadn't meant it to be. It was self-preservation. Nothing else.

'Give me this week, Rosa. Let us get to know each other properly—the way we should have done from the start.'

She wanted to. She didn't know where it came from, but she felt her chest expand, as if it were full of fluttering butterflies trying desperately to break free.

She had got by perfectly well on her own. In all the years she had been with Stephen she had always felt detached from him and that was the way she liked it. With Nico she could feel her detachment slipping. And it terrified her.

'But all this,' she said, turning around and waving an arm towards the suite. 'This doesn't feel like the action of a man trying to get to know me better. This feels like the action of a man trying to get into my knickers.'

How could she trust that he wanted *her* knickers off? *Her. Rosa.* Not his *wife*. Not his *asset*. Her. A woman he desired.

'Can it not be both?' His green eyes held hers, burning her with their intensity. 'I am not going to deny that I desire you. But I am prepared to wait until you are ready. You know you can trust me.'

'We always said no sex,' she said.

Cornered did not begin to describe how hemmed in she felt at that moment. She had trusted Nico enough to marry him, but that had not required any intimacy—nothing physical or emotional. Their marriage had given her the things she truly craved—stability and a feeling of belonging, of being a unit. Just sharing the same surname had been enough. At least it had been. For the first few months.

How could she trust that he wouldn't reject her like everyone else she had loved in her life? She couldn't. She didn't know how.

'That rule did neither of us any good, did it? The loneliness of an empty bed drove you into the arms of your ex. If our marriage is to continue, there is no doubt in my mind that sex needs to be a part of it. We need to have a proper marriage.'

Nico could see Rosa fighting a war with herself. Victory was within his grasp. He could smell it. He should have played to her sense of fairness from the start. After all, it was the thing he admired about her for above everything else.

That night in California, when the mad idea to marry had overtaken them and she had produced that piece of paper for them to write their contract, she could have made any number of demands on his fortune. But that was not Rosa's style. The first thing she had written was that neither would have a claim on the other's wealth. When he had queried this she had given that husky laugh and said, 'I don't want you thinking you can have a share of my flat. I earned it. You can keep all your billions. You earned them. I just want to keep my flat.'

She had been serious. For all the vodka they had consumed, he had known she was serious. Call him a fool—his lawyer, when they'd returned to England with the marriage certificate, certainly had—but he had trusted her.

Goddammit it, he had *trusted* her. Nico, the man who did not trust anyone, had trusted his wife. And she had slept with her ex.

The second point on the list had been no sex between them.

The third point had been to allow either of them to take

lovers so long as they exercised discretion. He had never dreamed Rosa would be the one to take advantage of that point.

Had she laughed with Stephen? Had he been the recipient of that throaty huskiness?

When had he, Nico, last heard that laugh?

He forced his mind back to the subject at hand. He had no intention of Rosa ever discovering how his veins burned with fury whenever he thought of them together.

'Give me this week. If at the end of it you still want to leave then I will not try to stop you. All I ask is that you keep an open mind. We can be good together. All you need to do is give us a chance to find out how good.'

He didn't realise he was holding his breath until, after long, interminable seconds, she finally inclined her head.

'It's obvious I'm stuck here, whether I like it or not. I'm not going to lie and pretend I'm thrilled at the way you have manipulated me. But I do get where you're coming from.' She turned her head and fixed her beautiful yet still wary eyes on him. 'I'm not going to make any promises other than I will *try* to keep an open mind about us.'

'I can't ask for any more than that.' He raised a hand and trailed the back of a finger down her cheek. She really had the most marvellous skin. 'Why don't you get changed into something with more of a holiday feel and I'll get us some drinks? We can sit out here, laze by the pool…the choice is yours.'

Her brow furrowed. 'The choice of what?'

'The choice to do what people on holiday do.'

'But I've never been on holiday before.'

'Seriously?'

A part of him thought she must be joking, while another part pointed out that neither of them had taken a break in the fifteen months they had known each other. They hadn't even bothered pretending to take a honeymoon. She had taken her holiday entitlement from her new job to accompany him as his assistant now, not expecting to be given the opportunity to let her hair down.

When, he wondered, did his wife ever let her hair down?

Had she let her hair down with Stephen?

'You can hardly talk,' she pointed out. 'When did *you* last take a holiday?'

That made him think. 'It must have been around eighteen months ago.' Before Rosa had come to work for him. 'But as a rule I like to take a week off every six months to recharge my batteries. In future it's something we can do together.'

Nico never holidayed with women. His relationships, if they could be called that, never lasted long enough. Once, he and Galina had discussed travelling together, or rather Galina had angled for it…

He swallowed and scratched the thought away. Travelling with Galina would have been a nightmare. She would have suffocated him.

He preferred going away with Serge and the rest of his old buddies from university, whether it was mountain climbing or trekking through the Amazon. Rosa was the only woman he would ever consider holidaying with. He doubted she could ever irritate him. She would certainly never try to suffocate him.

She gave a non-committal shrug. 'We'll see. I don't think I'm a holiday-type person.'

'What does that mean?'

'Holidays are things other people have. Not people like me.'

There was something in her voice, an almost confused ring, that pulled at him. It occurred to him that apart from reading the occasional book or watching the occasional film she rarely relaxed in the traditional sense.

Why had he never noticed that before?

'Everyone deserves a holiday,' he told her. 'Now, go and get changed and I'll meet you back out here shortly.'

Who had Nico shared his last holiday with? Rosa wondered, stepping into the dressing room and rifling through the items in there, all of which were marked with the name of a boutique from the King resort. She marvelled that they were the correct size, until she considered that *someone*—namely Nico—must have gone through her wardrobe. When had he done that? Back in London? At the villa? He had gone to huge trouble to make this happen, especially as the contract negotiations with Robert King were at such a delicate point.

She could not shake the feeling that she was being manipulated. Scratch that. *Of course* she was being manipulated—and blatantly so. He was not trying to hide it or make any excuses for it. Nico wanted their marriage to continue and was using all the means at his disposal to make it happen.

Was it possible his motives were sincere?

Was it truly possible he liked her enough as a person and desired her enough as a woman to fight to keep her in his life?

She could not wrap her head around it. Other than Stephen, people had generally fought to keep her *out* of their lives, not in it.

Deep in her belly was the sense that something was amiss. Try as she might to think of what it might be, she could not.

Maybe it would be best if she stopped thinking so much.

Settling on a black bikini, which she covered with a pair of denim shorts and a dusky-pink T-shirt, she smothered her exposed flesh with sunscreen and headed to the sundeck, studiously avoiding looking at the bed.

She had a whole day of Nico's sole company to get through before she could even contemplate sharing a bed with him—not just tonight but every night for the rest of the week. For once there would be nothing to distract her. No work. Nothing to keep her mind occupied from him.

He filled her mind too much as it was.

Rosa took a seat at an the outdoor table where a stack of boxes had been placed. Already bored with her own company, she took a look at them.

A moment later she almost choked when Nico strode up the stairs from the second deck to join her, carrying a couple of tall glasses. Not only had he removed his ever-present suit, but he had changed into a pair of knee-length canvas shorts. And nothing else. Nothing but hot, rippling muscle.

All of a sudden the heat of the day sank into her pores, making her feel clammy and bothered.

'You look hot,' he observed, taking a seat and pushing a glass towards her. 'This will cool you down.'

'What is it?'

'A cocktail.'

She sniffed the green concoction suspiciously. It smelled fresh and delicious. Taking a sip, she felt her eyes nearly pop out of her head. 'Blimey—this is strong. What's in it?'

He bestowed upon her an enigmatic smile. 'Enjoy it and leave the ingredients to me.'

'I never had you pegged as a cocktail fan.'

'When I was at university my dorm-mate threw a cocktail party. His cocktails were so disgusting I took over the bar.'

'I think you're yummy.'

She winced at the unintentional *faux pas*. But, seriously, how was she supposed to think straight with Nico's golden torso right in her line of vision? On the occasions when she had seen him in shorts and T-shirt for his daily jog she had been able to tune his incredible body out. That ability had now deserted her. But then, she had never seen him topless before—had never seen for herself the breadth of his shoulders or the dusting of silky black hair covering his muscular chest that continued down to the low-slung shorts resting on his hips.

'Sorry, I think *this*—the cocktail—is yummy.'

'Rosa, relax.' Nico's hand hovered in the air and for one breathless moment she thought he was going to touch her.

Relax? *Relax?* How could she relax when just being near him put her on hyper-alert?

'I'm not going to jump on you,' he murmured with a lazy curve of his lips. 'Not until you ask me to or, even better, jump on me.'

'You'll have a long wait,' she said. Even to her own ears her voice sounded feeble. If only he would cover his chest she would be able to think clearly.

His eyes darkened and gleamed. 'You will find I have incredible patience when it comes to something I really want.'

Rosa grabbed her cocktail and took a long sip, welcoming the cold liquid's cooling effect on her flushing cheeks. 'Pack it in, Nico. I've already told you I'm not making any promises.'

'I was merely making an observation,' he said smoothly, placing a hand on the boxes. 'What would you like to play? We have chess, Scrabble and backgammon. Or…' he wiggled an eyebrow '…we could play something else entirely.'

Despite herself she snickered. She had to admit there was something compelling about this irreverent, flirty Nico. She wondered if this was how he treated his lovers and immediately scratched the thought away.

'I'll play you at a board game but you'll have to choose which. I've never played any of them.'

He gave her the same look he'd given her when she told him she'd never had a holiday.

'That's no problem. I'll go back to the saloon and select some different games.'

'Don't worry about it,' she said. 'I doubt I'll know those

either. Why don't you teach me Scrabble? I've always wanted to learn that.'

It didn't take long for him to set the board up and go through the rules with her.

'Are you sure you've never played before?' he asked half an hour later. He had beaten her only by the skin of his teeth.

'Never,' she confirmed.

'Hmm.' He fixed disbelieving eyes on her. 'I think I'm in the hands of a Scrabble shark.'

Food was brought up for their lunch—a platter of refreshing fruits and cheeses. After they had demolished the lot Nico, unwilling to relinquish his bartending duties to anyone, made a pitcher of what he called 'a vodka cocktail', which had striped red and orange colours running through it.

Rosa won the second game. Fortified by more colourful cocktails than was good for her, she could not stop laughing about it—especially when Nico pretended to sulk.

'Ha!' she snorted. 'Beaten by a girl.'

'That's a very sexist remark, young lady,' he said, adopting a mock-grave voice.

She swept the tiles into the small green sack and flashed him a saccharine smile. 'That's because you're a very sexist man.'

His brows shot up. 'In what possible way am I sexist? I employ hundreds of women, many of them at senior or director level. I would employ more if the mining industry was not so male-dominated. We don't get enough women applying for positions.'

'That would be a valid point, but I don't think you see the women you employ as female.'

'You are confusing me.'

'It seems to me that if a woman isn't a tall, blonde stick-insect with silicone boobs you don't recognise her as a woman. She's just another drone in your employ.'

'If I were to flirt with any woman in my employ I would be asking for trouble. It's a sexual harassment lawsuit waiting to happen.'

'Possibly,' she conceded. 'Or it could just be that you don't fancy a woman who has to use her brains to earn a living rather than her body.'

'Ouch.' He winced. 'How does that theory explain why I fancy you?'

'It doesn't—but that's because you *don't* fancy me. Not really. You just don't like losing, and for me to leave our marriage means you'll have lost.'

CHAPTER SEVEN

FOR A MOMENT it felt as if Rosa had looked inside his head and scoffed at what she found.

'Which brings me to the second point of my argument,' she continued, her husky voice full of amusement. 'You married a drone instead of a stick-insect because you assumed marrying a high-maintenance supermodel would be hell on earth. Did you ever seriously consider marrying any of your lovers?'

Fascinated, Nico shook his head.

Rosa was pretty much bang on the money.

Growing up, he had had minimal contact with the opposite sex. For twenty-one years women had been a remote, alien species.

And then he had met Galina, the first woman to prove to him that females were not a mysterious sub-gender.

Beautiful, intelligent, emotionally needy Galina…

Whenever he thought about her he could still taste failure on his tongue. Thinking about her always served as a reminder of why it was for the best for him to divide the women in his life into two camps.

In the first camp were his lovers—beautiful socialites who looked good on his arm. He was not so immodest as not to know he was fortunate in his looks and physique, but when it came to socialites those particular attributes came a low second to the size of his wallet. He was certain he could look like the Hunchback of Notre Dame and they would still want him. The thought of marrying any of them filled him with horror. As sexy and as beautiful as they were, the thought of waking up to one of them, sharing a roof, the demands they would place on him, were all things he found intolerable.

In the second camp were the women who worked for him, women employed for their brains and not their looks. As he had found with Galina, intelligent women tended to be more emotionally literate too. A rigidly enforced dress code ensured none of them came to work dressed as if for a nightclub. This kept things on a professional basis for everyone.

Although he had always desired marriage for the respectability and stability it afforded, he had never expected to meet someone to whom he could make that commitment. He had never imagined meeting a woman who could straddle both camps.

That night in California when he had got to know the real Rosa, the woman under the starchy surface, he had been delighted to discover someone with an easy wit to match her quick brain. Her understated attractiveness had blossomed. She would, he had realised, make boring corporate functions tolerable without clinging like a limpet to his arm.

Best of all, she was vehemently against emotional entanglements. He had come to suspect that in Rosa, as in himself, that particular gene had been switched off.

But even emotionally illiterate people had physical needs. Rosa was no exception.

And neither was he.

The blossoming he had first spotted in California had now flowered into a sexy radiance of creamy skin hidden by far too much material. Soon, he vowed, Rosa would unpeel the clothing covering her delectable body and reveal herself to his willing, devouring eyes. And then he would devour her.

'There are a couple of things I want to correct you on,' he

said, his voice throaty. 'I do *not* regard my female employees as "drones". They are simply my employees, and they are afforded the respect they deserve for the quality of their work and not their gender.'

'Good comeback.' She nodded approvingly and raised her glass, taking another long drink through her straw.

'One other correction in your assessment.' He leaned across the table and dropped his voice, forcing her to lean closer so she could hear him. 'I *do* desire you, Mrs Baranski. And I would love nothing more than the opportunity to prove it.'

Rosa scowled and leaned back, folding her arms across her chest. 'Why do you have to spoil it? We were having a lovely conversation…'

'Discussing my faults?' he interjected.

'Absolutely.' She nodded. 'As I said, we were having a lovely conversation and you had to reduce it to a basic level.'

'Your cheeks are burning.'

'Thanks for pointing that out.'

'Do I make you hot?'

'Shut up.'

'You make *me* hot.'

'The only thing hot about you is the air that comes out of your mouth.'

'So harsh.' He sighed. 'And such a lie too.' Before she could splutter with outrage, he grinned. 'Shall we make it the best of three games?'

'Only if you promise to stop talking about sex.'

Once they had taken seven tiles each, he could not resist pressing her a little further. 'What do you think about making this game more interesting?'

'How?'

'If either of us gets a triple letter word the other has to remove an item of clothing.'

'You'd be naked in two goes.'

'One.'

'Oh…'

'Feeling hot again?' he purred, noting the colour of her neck.

'If you make one more lewd remark I'm abandoning the game.'

'Then I will win by default.'

Her pursed lips loosened, a smile beginning to crack out of all that sternness. 'You always have to get the last word in.'

He grinned again. As much as she tried to deny it, Rosa's immunity to him was weakening by the minute. He was scratching under the surface of her skin and piercing into the delicious flesh. Soon she would be his for the taking.

Her eyes narrowed, a shrewdness flickering in them. 'I'll make a deal with you. If I win this game you are not to talk about sex for the rest of the holiday.'

'And if *I* win?'

'If you win I'll get some earplugs.'

'I'll agree to one night—if you win I promise I will not talk about sex again until tomorrow morning.'

'That includes innuendo.'

'You have a deal.'

This would be an easy win. Rosa had played two games of Scrabble. She had picked it up quickly, but he had gone easy on her on the basis it was unfair to humiliate a novice. Not this time.

'When I win I can talk about sex all night if I so wish. I can tell you exactly what I would like to do with your ravishing body, how I spend inordinate amounts of time wondering what colour your nipples are and what they taste like…'

'Stop it.' Rosa's protest came out as a moan. The second he had mentioned her nipples she had become wholly conscious of how sensitised they had become—as her whole being had become. Her skin was almost dancing with awareness.

Listening to his gravelly voice purring the words in Russian, she had felt the blood in her system heating to unbearable levels.

She crossed her legs, as if the act could smother the pulsations between her thighs, and forced her voice to sound at least reasonably normal. 'You play dirty.'

His green eyes glittered. 'I like dirty. I especially like playing dirty with husky-voiced bombshells.'

He was impossible to talk to!

Growling under her breath, Rosa pulled a letter out from the green sack. 'Typical.' She had pulled out the letter X.

Naturally Nico pulled out a B. He didn't even try to hide his smirk. 'I shall start, then.'

It became immediately apparent that he was set on winning. All dirty talk stopped, and his focus was solely on the letters lined up in front of him.

Of course as soon as it was her turn the innuendoes started again.

'Stop trying to put me off,' she complained after her third move. He was already forty points ahead. 'That's bad sportsmanship.'

He smirked, although his eyes were creased in concentration. 'If you can't take the heat...'

'I should jump into the pool.'

'Sorry?'

'If I can't take the heat I should jump into the swimming pool.' She smiled in what she hoped was a seductive manner, suddenly compelled to give him a taste of his own medicine. She was making it too easy for him. Why should she be the only one to suffer? 'Maybe I should jump into the pool naked?'

Not taking her eyes off him, she slowly closed her lips around her straw and sucked.

'You are playing with fire,' he warned, grabbing the wrist holding the straw.

'Really?' She adopted a surprised look. 'We're only talking. If you would prefer I stop talking you only have to say. And then shut up too.'

He shook his head with incredulity before grazing a kiss across her knuckles. 'Game on.'

She blinked at the unexpected intimacy, but forced her mind to concentrate.

His next move took him eighty-three points clear.

Rosa had no intention of going down without a fight, but it was a lot harder than it should have been. Nico had dropped the verbal flirtation, but whenever it was her turn he would fix those green eyes on her and seduce her with them—at least until the sun got into them and he started squinting.

'That'll teach you,' she sniggered, placing three tiles on the board and clawing back thirty much needed points.

The game progressed slowly. As hard as she tried, she couldn't quite catch him, only able to shave off a few points here and there. She was twenty-six points behind when she removed the final tiles from the bag.

For an age Nico's face was scrunched in concentration. He took a sip of his cocktail, his eyes meeting hers with a look that could only be described as triumphant. Slowly, deliberately, he placed six of his tiles on the board.

'I think you'll find that comes to sixty-two points which puts me eighty-eight points ahead with only one tile left.'

Ouch!

'Do you want to admit defeat?'

'No chance.' She frowned and stared at her letters, waiting for them to magically form a super-duper…

Ha!

How she kept her face poker straight she would never know, but, after positioning her S at the bottom of Nico's last-laid word, she placed all her tiles on the board. 'I think you'll find that comes to thirty-six points, plus a bonus fifty points for using all my letters.'

The smirk playing on his lips vanished. Quickly he made his own calculations.

'So it's down to your last tile,' she observed. 'Let's have a look.'

With obvious reluctance he picked it up and held his palm open. It was a C, worth three points which would be deducted from his total and added to hers.

'Would it be in really bad taste for me to jump up and down and squeal like a banshee?' she asked.

'Yes.'

'Thought so.' She got to her feet. 'I can be gracious in victory. Seeing as you lost, you can pack the board away. I'm going for a shower—all this heat is getting to me. See you later, loser.'

Still sniggering, she went straight to the *en suite* bathroom and locked the door behind her.

Rosa had to give Nico credit—he'd stopped sulking by the time their evening meal was served. At least she assumed he had been sulking, seeing as he had whiled away the last hours of the afternoon in the saloon.

As the heat of the day had barely been dented, they decided to eat on the sundeck, consuming a bottle of chilled white wine with their meal.

'Is this what people do on holiday?' she asked, once she had cleared her coconut mousse with a contented sigh. 'Laze about doing not very much and consuming lots of alcohol? And not to forget beating their spouse at Scrabble?'

His lips quirked. 'Tomorrow I will teach you to play chess.'

'Sounds exciting.'

'You will need all your concentration.'

'I'm sure I'll cope.'

'Same rules as today?'

She pondered. 'Best of three—but no flirting or innuendo *at all* during play. Deal?'

He extended a hand. 'If we are going to make a deal we must seal it with a handshake.'

I'd much rather seal it with a kiss, she thought, before checking herself. Time to cut back on the alcohol. Her thoughts were becoming extremely wayward, running further away with every look at him. And, really, Nico *did* look stunningly handsome under the moonlight. More so than normal, which she had not thought possible. Somehow he made a pair of knee-length shorts and a green polo-shirt look sexy.

Surreptitiously wiping her palm on her skirt first, she took his hand, expecting a quick shake and then release.

Nico clasped his fingers over hers, pulling her hand close so he could examine it. 'Your hands are tiny,' he said, holding his hand to hers.

'I am half your size,' she commented, with a nonchalance that belied the swirls of heat pervading through her. To cover her nervous excitement she downed the rest of her wine.

'Tell me why you have never taken a holiday before,' he said, still gazing at her hand.

'There's nothing to tell. The opportunity was never there.' Why had she not snatched her hand away? And why had her heartbeat trebled, with pulses of excitement hopping across her skin?

'But you earn good money. It's not as if you can't afford it.'

'I've always had better things to spend my money on.'

'Such as?'

'Education. Rent and then mortgage. Food, fancy shoes and handbags. You know—the usual.'

'I know it well.'

He raised his eyes to meet hers. The intensity whirling in them had an effect that was almost hypnotic.

'Did your father ever take you on holiday—it *was* just you and your father, wasn't it?'

'Yes, it was just me and my father. And, no, we never went on holiday.' Nico released her hand and finished his wine. 'Coffee?'

'Please.'

The hand he'd released tingled so much she rammed it between her thighs, glad the moonlight prevented him from seeing the colour blazing across her neck and face.

He pressed the intercom and spoke quietly into it, all the while keeping his eyes fixed on her.

Past history was not something they had discussed. When they had decided to marry right there and then in California, she had asked if his parents would be disappointed not to attend. He had shaken his head.

'My mother died when I was a toddler,' he had said, as collected as always. 'And my father isn't a man for ceremony.'

It had not been mentioned or alluded to since by either of them.

Why was that?

How could you spend eleven months living with someone and know next to nothing about them other than how they took their coffee?

She had been too scared to ask. Not scared of Nico's reaction to any probing questions, but scared of *her* reaction. Sharing histories had felt an intimacy too far—way beyond the remit of their marriage pact.

But now, with the moonlight beaming above and a slight breeze tempering the warm glow from all the wine she'd consumed, it all seemed so irrelevant. She enjoyed Nico's company, she found him incredibly sexy—why not take the opportunity to get to know him better while she still had the chance? What did she have to lose?

Once their plates had been cleared and the coffee delivered, Rosa placed her elbows on the table and rested her chin on her hands, admiring the graceful way he poured the dark brown liquid. For such a large man there was an elegance about his movements she found more and more captivating.

'What was it like, growing up in Siberia?'

'Cold.'

'Hilarious. I'm curious, though—what *was* it like? Whenever I think of Siberia all I can think of is *Dr Zhivago*.'

'*Dr Zhivago* was written seventy years ago.'

'Exactly. Incidentally, it is my favourite book. But I am curious to know what it's really like.'

Nico poured a splash of milk into his cup. 'Why do you want to know?'

'Sheer curiosity. You're the one who said we should use this time to get to know each other better,' she reminded him pointedly. 'Unless you were only saying that in the hope I would drop my knickers?'

He looked up at her, his lips twitching, his eyes gleaming. He took a sip of the hot liquid. 'I lived in a small mining town. I cannot talk for the rest of Siberia because I never visited it.'

'What was your town like?'

'Small and boring. I learned to make my own amusements.'

'Did your father ever remarry?'

'No.'

'Did he ever come close?'

'No.'

'Why not?'

'I have no idea. I would imagine the dearth of women had something to do with it.'

'Why was there a dearth of women?'

'The town is in one of Siberia's remotest regions. The summers aren't too bad but the winters are cruel and long. There are very few families and most of them move on when their children reach school age.'

'Were there any children your age?'

'There were a couple of older boys I was educated with.'

'What about girls?'

'Girls?'

'You know—the humans with the x and y chromosomes.'

'It was the families with girls who got out the quickest. It was a man's town.'

'That must have been hard for you,' she observed, feeling a pang for the child Nico had been, cut off from the rest of civilisation with only a couple of friends and no female figure in his life.

He shrugged. 'It was my life. I knew no different.'

'But something must have made you want to leave it.'

'Books. My father is a voracious reader. He encouraged me to read so I would learn that our town was only a tiny atom in the world. He was determined his life would not be my life.'

Rosa's throat closed.

So they did have something in common other than a tendency towards workaholicism. Books. The need for escape. The knowledge that the hands they had been dealt did not have to define them for all eternity.

'Why did he not leave when you were a child, like the other families?'

'My father is a functioning alcoholic,' he stated flatly. 'He's the only drunk I've ever met who drinks his way through a bar with a book in his hand. Any hopes or ambitions were subverted by the bottom of a bottle.'

'Not all of them,' she countered, her heart in her throat. Nico had been raised by an alcoholic? Oh, the poor, poor child. 'He had hopes and ambitions for *you*.'

His eyes still held hers, but the light contained in them had been snuffed out. 'Those ambitions were not of the present. He would come home drunk in the middle of the night—I would be awake, waiting to make sure he had walked back safely—and tell me that he wanted a different life for me. He would say that if I worked hard and studied hard I would be able to leave the town and do anything I wanted.'

'He was right.'

'Yes, he was right,' he conceded. 'And it would sound idyllic—except he would be delivering these drunken lectures after I had spent the day taking myself to school and back, washing, cleaning and feeding myself because there was no thought in his head of doing those things for me.'

Rosa's eyes widened. 'You had to fend for yourself?'

'Always. I do not remember it ever being different.' He laughed mirthlessly. 'I could build a fire at five and was given housekeeping money when I was seven.'

Witnessing the horror in Rosa's eyes, Nico wished he could take back his words. He didn't even know why he was revealing so much. It was those damn unwavering eyes of hers. They contained far too much warmth. A man could throw himself into that swirling caramel if he wasn't careful.

'It wasn't as bad as I am making it sound,' he retracted, feeling an inordinate amount of guilt at his disloyalty. His father was not a bad man—something he had recognised even as a small child. 'There was an elderly woman who lived quite close by. I think she felt sorry for me. Sometimes she would bring a pot of stew to our house. She would never come in. Just leave it on the doorstep.'

Even now, decades on, he could still taste that stew. Even now, decades on, having dined in the world's finest restaurants and been catered for by the world's finest chefs, he had never tasted anything as good.

'My father took care of me as best he could,' he explained

quietly, not sure why he felt the need to make her understand, only knowing he did not want Rosa to think badly of the man who had raised him. 'I know that by today's standards he neglected me, but I never felt it. I am certain if I had not been around he would have drunk himself into an early grave.'

Rosa's hand covered his—just a light pressure, but enough to sear his skin.

'You do not need to explain your father to me, Nico,' she said, staring at him with eyes that contained a mixture of pity and…was that *envy*? Surely not? 'It took guts for him to keep you. He must love you very much.'

He wanted to move his hand, snatch it away, but the warmth transmuted from her skin acted like glue, binding them together.

Nico did not want her sympathy, or empathy, or whatever it was seeping from her. All he wanted was to hear her throaty laugh and watch those caramel eyes darken into chocolate as he took possession of her.

He could not remove his hand.

The easy, yet sexually charged atmosphere that had been swirling between them for days had tightened. The air was so thick it almost resembled a misty fog.

But this was so much more than mere sexual tension.

What the hell was he doing? He was supposed to be laying the path to seduction, not unbuttoning about things that rarely passed from his lips.

Slowly, he pulled his hand away. He wanted her hands to rest on him in passion, not sympathy.

'After my mother died of pneumonia my father had a duty to raise me.'

'But he could have absolved himself from that responsibility,' she contradicted with a flick of her ponytail.

'My father, for all his faults, would never have absolved himself from his responsibilities.'

'Then he is a better man than a lot of parents.'

It was on the tip of his tongue to ask what her comment meant, to probe the reason for the clouding of those eyes. But he did not want to hear it. Getting to know each other better did not mean learning each other's intimate secrets. The only intimacy he wanted from Rosa was in the bedroom.

He flashed a grin. 'It's getting late. Fancy a game of Scrabble before bed?'

Rosa did not trust Nico's grin. It was too…*fake*—as if he were a marionette having its strings pulled.

She could understand that. While he had defended his father, and in her mind it was evident his father had loved him, there was no escaping the fact that Nico's childhood had been harsh. Sometimes the past was too painful to talk about.

Some confidences were a confidence too far.

'If it's all the same to you, I think I'll go to bed.' She got to her feet and flashed a grin she knew looked every bit as fake as his. 'I'm all Scrabbled out.'

Nico's answering smile relieved some of the oppressive tension that had enveloped them, allowing her to breathe a little easier. 'Is this the part where you get some barbed wire and roll it down the centre of the bed?'

'Gosh, not only are you supremely intelligent and a whizz at making money, but you can read minds. Are there no limits to your talents?'

'None that I have discovered.'

'And so incredibly modest. Goodnight.'

'I'll be joining you soon.'

'Don't rush on my account. Go and find the crew. Watch the sun come up with them.'

His low chuckles followed her all the way into the suite.

CHAPTER EIGHT

IN THE *EN SUITE* bathroom, Rosa stripped down to her knickers, splashed water onto her face and cleaned her teeth. The skin that had been exposed to the sun had pinkened, and she wrinkled her slightly burned nose. Why couldn't her skin turn a lovely golden hue?

Nico had beautiful golden skin.

She blew out a puff of air. She really did not want to be reminded of his fantastic physique—not when she would shortly be sharing a bed with him. It had been bad enough spending the day with his gorgeous chest parked in her eye-line. There had been more than one occasion when she had wanted to yell at him to put a T-shirt on. But she had known perfectly well how he would react to that and had wisely kept her mouth shut.

A shiver ran through her. Would he keep to his side of their earlier wager?

Nico was a man of his word, she reminded herself. The chances of him reneging on it and starting a whole load of sex talk as she fell into slumber were extremely remote.

The thought made her feel surprisingly flat. Could that really be disappointment?

Lord knew how she would react if he *did* renege. Hopefully she would have the presence of mind to put a sock in his mouth. If her reaction from earlier was any indication, though, she would be a puddling wreck within seconds.

It was too unfair. Why did he have to possess a voice that was more molten than lava? Why could he not have some dreadful nasally whine, whereby dirty talk sounded ridiculous?

But then, Nico didn't even have to speak. Just thinking about him was becoming enough to turn her into a puddling wreck.

She felt as if she had learned more about him in a day than she had in the whole time she had worked for him and been married to him. His refusal to blame his father for such a harsh childhood, his attempts to mitigate it, humanised him, stripped back the layers to reveal the man beneath the towering powerhouse shell.

She forced herself to look at her reflection. Was she really so different from his usual lovers?

The answer was a resounding *yes*. Unless she was strapped to a stretching machine for a year and had a bucket of bleach tipped over her head she could never look like those lithe beauties. She'd probably need a nose-job too.

How could she trust that he really did want her for herself and not out of revenge? If he had an inkling of why she had slept with Stephen…

And how could she trust her own feelings around him? He had confided a part of his past to her and it had felt as if a stack of knives were ripping into her heart.

She had wanted to climb onto his lap and wrap her arms around him.

In all the years she had been with Stephen she had never felt that urge towards him—not even when his grandmother had died. She had hated herself for her coldness but she had not been able to cross that breach.

The last time she recalled giving physical comfort, she had

been in her early teens. A young girl, newly orphaned, had been brought into the care home whilst foster care was arranged for her. She had been placed in Rosa's dormitory for the night. Rosa had heard the devastated child whimpering in her sleep and had crawled into her bed. She had held the child in her arms, stroked her hair and soothed her until she had finally fallen asleep, clinging onto Rosa like a limpet.

The next morning the girl had left. Rosa had never seen her again. Over the years she had often thought of her, had often prayed the child had found a new family who loved and cherished her.

Hearing the patio doors to the decking area close, she blinked the past away and hurriedly donned the only suitable clothing she had found that could be used as nightwear.

She breezed past Nico and turned over the sheets on the bed. 'Is there a preference for which side you like to sleep?' she asked politely.

'Your side,' he said, his lips twitching.

'Not going to happen.'

'Can't blame a man for trying. By the way, what are you *wearing*?'

'This old thing?' She looked down at the cotton shirt that reached below her knees. 'Just something I found in your dressing room.'

'You've been going through my clothes?'

'I would apologise—but a), you went through my clothing at some point to get my dress size, and b), you didn't bother to arrange a decent set of pyjamas for me. There's no way on earth I'm going to wear those scraps of lace I assume are supposed to be nightwear.'

And no way was she going to admit that she had gazed at them for an inordinate amount of time, wondering what it would be like to wear such sexy, exotic apparel.

'So you thought you would help yourself to one of my shirts?'

'Got a problem with that?' she asked, raising a brow in challenge.

His eyes sparkled. 'I happen to think you look incredibly sexy in my shirt.

'Oh, go away.'

Chuckling, he disappeared into the *en suite.*

Rosa flopped onto her back and gazed up at the ceiling. When she had pilfered his shirt she had felt a sense of vindication at getting herself out of a pickle. Now the heat cresting through her made her wonder if she should have stuck to a pair of knickers and a T-shirt. Except the T-shirts in the dressing room were all tiny designer numbers that would cover her shoulders but not much else.

She had thought half a bottle of wine would send her into an immediate slumber, and silently cursed herself for having coffee.

Much as she tried to keep her mind occupied, away from any errant thoughts about what Nico might be doing in the bathroom and what state of undress he might be in, she was all too aware of the shower running.

She forced her mind to concentrate on anything but Nico, determined not to think of him naked, lathering under the steaming water. Anything would do. The economy. The pink designer shoes she had spotted on Bond Street.

She might as well tell herself not to think about purple elephants.

Grimacing, she forced herself to take deep breaths before jumping off the bed and helping herself to a bottle of water from the discreetly placed fridge.

She was getting back into bed when the bathroom door opened and Nico appeared, wearing nothing but a tiny towel across his snake hips. A waft of warm, citrusy steam followed in his wake and she sucked in a breath, moisture filling her mouth.

His black hair was damp, his golden skin a deeper bronze after a day of glorious sunshine. Seriously, had there *ever* been a finer specimen of the male form? He was truly magnificent—a Roman statue brought to life.

And, no matter how dispassionately she tried to see him, her body seemed to go into some form of meltdown. Could he not just *put some bloody clothes on*?

He looked at her and raised a brow.

'Please don't tell me I said that aloud?' she begged.

'Do you have a problem with my body?' he asked, with the arrogant look of one who knew his form was damn near perfect.

'Only when you're not wearing clothes.' That was a lie. She had a problem with him clothed too. But near-as-dammit naked…?

'Why? What is wrong with me?'

'Nothing.' And that was the precise problem.

Rosa had never considered herself a shallow person, but right then she wished he had a massive paunch and a hairy back. Anything had to be better than the reality, which was that she wanted nothing more than to run her fingers through the black silken hair covering his broad, muscular chest and taste his smooth skin.

Just like that, her belly flipped, and heat went rampaging through her blood. For a moment she stood paralysed, treacle-thick desire rooting her to the floor.

The beautiful golden chest in front of her eyes rose sharply. As if drawn by a magnet, she looked up, Meeting his gaze, she sucked in a breath.

The intensity in those green eyes…

Dear God, if she had wanted proof he really did desire her for herself, and not out of some stupid game or pride, it was there, resonating out of him—as pure and tangible a desire as she had ever seen.

The very air around them thickened. Heat was licking her bones, flowing low, deep into her pelvis, forming a physical ache in her core.

Every inch of her felt alive, as if she could feel the charge of every electron ever created on her skin. And her breasts…

Not since they had first started to develop had she been so aware of them. Without looking down she knew the nipples had puckered, were straining against the fabric of his shirt.

'Do you have a problem with me sleeping naked next to you?'

A problem? Yes, she would say she had a problem with that—the problem being her own desire to strip his shirt off and get naked with him.

'I think it would be gentlemanly for you to wear a pair of shorts,' she said, the words coming from a throat that felt ragged.

'Your wish is my command.' Turning his back to her, thus giving her an excellent view of his lean torso from behind and endless muscular legs, he stepped briefly into the dressing room, returning with a pair of black undershorts in his hand. 'Will these suffice?'

She swallowed. 'They'll do.'

Rosa realised she had been gawping at him like a hormone-filled teenager and hurriedly climbed back under the silk bedsheets, nestling into them like a cocoon, pretending not to be aware of Nico dropping his towel and stepping into the undershorts. She would not peek. No way. She would keep her eyes tightly closed.

The bed dipped.

She squeezed her eyes even tighter. Blocking her senses made a whole heap of sense.

The bed was huge, but she could still feel the heat from his body permeating through the sheets. It dipped again as Nico reached for the row of switches on the wall behind them and turned the lights off.

Rosa shivered as they were plunged into darkness. 'Could you keep the bathroom light on, please?'

After he'd fiddled with the switches, the suite was filled with a muted glow from the *en suite* bathroom.

'Thank you.'

'I didn't know you were afraid of the dark.' Nico said.

'I'm not,' she lied, keeping her back firmly to him, 'I just prefer to sleep with a light on. Goodnight.'

'Don't I get a goodnight kiss?'

'No. Go to sleep.'

Nico listened to Rosa's breathing—a deep, rhythmic sound that was strangely comforting. Such a different sound from the noisy snore that would reverberate throughout the small wooden house he had shared with his father. At times Nico had been quite certain the house would collapse from the drunken sound. Despite the noise being reminiscent of a pneumatic drill, he had taken comfort from it. It had meant his father was alive.

Self-sufficiency was not something he had been born with. It was a trait he had learned through necessity. Until he had left home for university in Moscow it had been just him and his father. In his dreams he still felt the terror he had known as a small child, when he would lie in bed night after night, praying to whoever was looking out for his father that he'd be brought home safely. And he did come home. Every night. No matter how deep his stupor, his father had never forgotten he had a son at home, waiting for him. Waiting for him with the light on.

Why did Rosa need a light on?

He rubbed his fingers into his temples, trying to eradicate

the question, the answer to which he had no business knowing. The only intimacy he wanted from Rosa was physical. Nothing more. The fact he had already revealed a little of himself earlier was cause for alarm. He could have answered her questions without going into detail. Which begged the question: why hadn't he?

The past was aptly named. Learn from history and move on, taking those lessons into the future but not dwelling on them.

Nico had learned that lesson well.

Naturally he had tried every trick in the book to get his father to straighten out, even going as far as to book him into an alcohol treatment facility in America that was reputed to be one of the toughest in the world. That was the day his father had taken him to one side.

'Nicolai, I cannot allow you to spend any more money on me. These people will not cure me.'

'How do you know that?' he had demanded. 'These people are the best at dealing with chronic alcoholics.'

'But, Nicolai, I do not want to be cured.' He had fixed remarkably clear, sober eyes onto him. 'If it were not for you I would have died a long time ago. Please, my son, stop trying. I do not want to meet reality.'

That was when he had realised it was pointless trying to save a man who did not want to be saved. All he could do was try and provide as safe an environment as possible for his father to pickle himself in.

Now Nico had the peace of mind knowing his father was in a warm home, with assistance at the press of a button. No more staggering over a mile every night in knee-deep snow and blizzards; his father lived in a ground floor apartment in Moscow, with a choice of bars within a short walk and a small army of unobtrusive carers ready to scoop him up if he should fall. He also had the comfort of knowing his father was a sociable drunk. He might not want to talk to anyone, but at least he preferred to drink with other humans around him.

His mind drifted to the picture of his mother he kept in his wallet. One of only a handful of pictures of Katerina Baranski left, it resided in the back of his wallet, rarely looked at, rarely thought about. But it was always there, always with him. How different would his life have been if she had lived beyond his second birthday?

Rosa sighed in her sleep, the muted sound a welcome distraction. Ruminating on the past was pointless. He turned his face to stare at her back, as stiff as a rod even in slumber. Only the top of her ebony hair was poking out beneath the cocoon of blankets she had made for herself.

Did Rosa have a picture of her parents in her wallet?

He felt a sharp pang in his chest. At least his father was still alive. Rosa had no one.

Rubbing his hand down his face, he closed his eyes.

He needed to get some sleep. His mind was all over the place, heading into dangerous territory.

The sooner the sun came up the better. Then he could advance his seduction of her and find some peace in knowing his marriage was intact.

The bed dipped.

Rosa's eyes snapped open.

Sitting at the foot of the bed, tray in hand, was Nico.

'I bring you breakfast,' he said, flashing his white teeth at her.

'What time is it?' she asked, placing a hand over her mouth to smother a yawn.

'Nine o'clock.'

She groaned and squeezed her eyes shut. It still felt like the middle of the night.

As ridiculous as she knew it to be, she had spent the night

rooted to the spot, not quite at the edge of the bed, too scared to move. Her limbs ached from being forced to remain in the same position for hours on end.

No matter how hard she'd tried, she had been unable to relax. She had been far too aware of the warm body lying mere feet away from her. Every time she had dozed off Nico's scent had wafted under her nose, yanking her right back into consciousness.

'Come on, lazy bones, sit up. Your breakfast is getting cold.'

It took a few moments, but somehow she managed to disentangle herself from the sheets that had smothered her all night and hoik herself upright. Now she was moving blood moved freely back to her limbs, which were all screaming obscenities at her.

'Have you been working out?' she asked, noting the sheen of perspiration soaking through his white T-shirt. He used their home gym regularly, but jogging was his preferred form of exercise. She guessed being stuck in the middle of the ocean limited his options for a good run.

'I have,' he said, placing the tray on her lap and removing the silver lid from the plate to reveal poached eggs on toast. A bowl of fruit and a glass of orange juice were placed next to it. He got to his feet. 'Coffee?'

'Yes, please.' She rubbed at her neck before taking a drink of the orange juice, which went some way to soothing her arid throat.

'Is your neck hurting again?'

She pulled a face.

'Would you like me to rub it better for you?'

'Would you like me to stab you with my fork?' Not taking her eyes off him, she stabbed it into an egg.

Amusement played on his lips. 'I have a weapon I can assault you with if you are so inclined.'

'Don't start,' she said, shaking her head. 'It's too early for innuendoes.'

'Our deal only lasted for a night,' he reminded her with a lopsided grin. 'You're now officially fair game.'

'Not until we've done three rounds of chess.' She winced as she felt another sharp twinge in her neck.

'It's hardly surprising you're having neck problems with the way you sleep,' Nico said, resting his arms back and openly studying her with his gorgeous green eyes. 'It was like sleeping next to a mannequin. Tell me—do all women sleep as if they are encased in concrete?'

'You should know—you've slept with enough of us.' She popped some egg and toast into her mouth.

'I have never slept with a woman in my life.'

Rosa stopped chewing and eyed him with suspicion. Swallowing the food, she almost choked. 'Nico, you have slept with *loads* of women.'

'That is inaccurate. I have never actually slept with a woman before.'

'Rubbish. You've slept with more women then I have digits and limbs. And eyes. And—'

'No.' He cut her off with an amused frown. 'I have had sex with a number of women, but I have never slept with any of them.'

She could not hide her incredulity. 'Seriously? You've never fallen asleep with a woman before?'

'I find women like cuddles after sex.' He spoke as if *cuddles* were a dirty word. 'But that is not for me.'

'What do you do, then?' she asked, horrified and fascinated all at once. 'Kick them out of bed the second you've come? Or do you come and run?' She laughed at her own joke, anything to hide the sickening churn of her stomach.

'It's not quite as sordid as you're trying to make out. I have never invited a woman into my bed, so that situation has never arisen. I simply thank them for a great evening and leave.'

'Ooh, what a gentleman you are. You really know how to make a woman feel special.'

'Is it not better than leading them on?'

The amusement in his eyes had dimmed a little, the intensity increasing. She had the strangest feeling he was trying to convey a message to her.

'I make it clear from the outset that I am not offering any sort of permanency. If I were to stick around afterwards and whisper endearments I would be lying and offering a false promise. I do not make false promises, Rosa, but neither do I set out to humiliate them. They know the score from the beginning. It's just sex. Nothing more, nothing less.'

She continued to meet his stare whilst chewing another forkful of egg, struggling to work out what he was trying to tell her.

Before she could ask he raised an arm and sniffed. 'I'd better have a shower before I start to smell.' He rose to his feet with his usual languid grace. 'Finish your breakfast. When you're dressed and ready, I'll give you a good thrashing at chess. Before I forget, you might want to put on a higher factor sun cream today—the Captain tells me it is going to be a scorcher.'

Thoroughly confused, she watched him retreat into the *en suite* bathroom.

The more she recalled his words, the more her brain became befuddled. Was it a warning or an explanation? Was he telling her that, even though he wanted to sleep with her, she was not to expect anything more? Or was he trying to tell her what his attitude *had* been?

She took a sip of her coffee and forced herself to think coherently.

Nico wanted their marriage to continue. He had spelt that

out more than once. He wanted their marriage to be a proper one. With sex.

Could she really do it? Could she really give herself to him? Because one thing was clear—if she were to give her husband her body, there was every danger she would give so much more with it.

CHAPTER NINE

'WHY DON'T YOU leave your hair loose?' Nico asked when Rosa joined him on the sundeck. As usual she had scraped it back into a tight ponytail.

'Because it's a pain in the bum and keeps getting in my eyes.' She took the seat opposite him and frowned down at the carved figures laid out in their respective starting positions.

'You have such beautiful hair. It's a shame you don't let it free.'

The simple sincerity in his voice reached inside her and knocked off a fragment of the wall surrounding her heart. She almost heard it smash. Her hands shaking, she tightened her hair further.

He smiled ruefully, pushing a piece of paper to her. 'I've written out what all the pieces are and the moves they can make. Have a read of it while I make us some cocktails.'

'Already?' She blinked and looked at her watch. 'It's not even eleven o'clock yet.'

'We're on holiday,' he said, as if that explained everything.

'And this is what people do on holiday?'

'Rosa, a holiday is a time to relax—and let your hair down,' he added with a smirk. 'Soon you will get into the swing of it.'

She gazed around at the gleaming ocean and the cobalt blue of the sky and sighed with pleasure. 'I never realised how wonderful it was to do nothing.'

'It is strange, yes?'

Although his eyes were covered with sunglasses, she could feel his gaze resting upon her.

'Yes,' she agreed, knowing exactly what he meant. 'It is a little strange.'

'You will get used to it. And when you do, you will realise regular breaks are essential to keep your brain firing on all cylinders.' He paused, a sensuous look flittering over his face. 'Do you know what would make you relax even more?'

Inexplicably, her mouth went dry. She shook her head.

'A massage. I think we should change the terms of our deal. I don't mean to sound superior, but there is little chance of you beating me at chess. If I win three games in row, I get to give you a full-body massage.'

'And that is supposed to be my forfeit?' Was that dry croak really her voice?

He removed his glasses, hitting her with the full power of his magnetic stare. 'No *daragaya*, that is to be my prize.'

After a beat, he rose.

'You can give me your answer when I return. I suggest you read through the moves while I am gone.'

Rosa watched him stroll away, her heart pounding erratically against her ribs. Idly she fingered the piece of paper and, despite the churning that was threatening to consume her whole, found her attention caught by the intricate sketches Nico had drawn to represent each piece. She had often noticed the strength of his hands and the dexterity of his long, capable fingers…

A thrill ran up her spine as she considered what it would be like to have those proficient fingers kneading her flesh, touching her…

Dear God, she should be dismissing his suggestion out of hand, but…

It felt as she had spent eleven months climbing in a very

slow, very steep rollercoaster, her anticipation and fear increasing the higher the carriage climbed. Now she had reached the top and could see the fall coming, but was helpless to get off—helpless to find the reverse button that would take her back to safety. There was nothing to stop gravity taking its course and plunging her over the top.

Think of the exhilaration of the ride.

But think of the consequences should the carriage come off the track.

Absently she kneaded the back of her aching neck.

'Thinking about what it would feel like to have me massage all that tension out of your system?'

Nico's voice broke her out of her tortured reverie. Her eyes flew to him. He was carrying a pitcher of light green liquid and two glasses, evoking an enormous sense of *déjà vu.* Which was not surprising, seeing as he had performed the same action only twenty-four hours before.

Yet twenty-four hours ago she had hardly dared allow herself to think about sleeping with him, too fearful of the powerful feelings such a thought provoked. Now…? Now the burn inside her, the ache… Now she didn't know if she even *wanted* to control it any more.

Nico was trying to create a proper marriage for them and she was letting fear block it. Surely it was time to step out of the shackles of the past and place her faith in a man she was already halfway to falling in love with?

Love?

She didn't even know what it was. Not really.

Love was a word bandied about too much.

Her mother had professed to love her. And then she had abandoned her.

She had taken her foster mother into her heart only to be rejected.

Stephen had professed to love her, but he wouldn't even let

her *breathe*. With Stephen she had always kept the essence of herself hidden, rigidly maintaining her barriers. He'd never even come close to breaking through.

With Nico those same barriers were crumbling. The foundations were shaking. Everything was conspiring to pull the last of her fortress down—the sun, the setting and most especially Nico. Everything about him awoke senses she hadn't been aware existed. He made her *feel*.

She straightened her spine and looked him square in the eyes. 'Yes. I have been thinking about that.'

He merely raised an eyebrow. 'And?'

Sometimes he was just too cool for school.

She picked up her glass and took a sip, then used her middle finger to slowly wipe the residue away from her mouth. 'And the answer is yes.'

His eyes gleamed with a vibrancy that made the breath catch in her throat. He held his glass aloft. 'To us.'

She chinked her glass to his. 'To us,' she echoed, striving vainly to match his collectedness.

A long, charged pause settled between them before he said, 'To make it more of a competition, I will remove three of my pawns for each of the games.'

'You're not worried I might pick it up as well as I picked up Scrabble?' she could not resist asking, her voice huskier than usual.

He shook his head. 'Chess is a game of strategy. It takes years of practice to become proficient at it. My father taught me to play when I was a young boy so I have decades on you.'

'How young?'

'Five.

'Crikey. That *is* young.' Automatically her thoughts flew to her own childhood, to being five years old. That was *the* most vivid age in her early memories. How could it not be?

It was the age she been ripped away from everything and everyone she loved.

She pushed the maudlin thoughts away. She was twenty-seven years old and had spent her entire life trying to be a good girl, trying to do the right thing. She had convinced herself that if she behaved one day her mother would come back and get her.

Her mother had never come back. She hadn't wanted her. And when, at the age of eight, she had finally been approved as a candidate for adoption: no one else had wanted her either.

She had spent the rest of her life pushing everyone away because of it.

She wanted Nico with a desperate, hungry craving she could no longer control. And he wanted her too.

He was right. They could be good together. But they would never know unless she took a chance.

Was she really prepared to risk what could be a happy future for them because of fear?

No. Not any more.

Today would be the next turning point in her life.

Today the barriers would come down.

She was in charge of her own destiny. That destiny was with Nico. She just had to trust…

Filling her lungs to stave off the nervous butterflies playing inside her chest, she placed her fingers at the hem of her T-shirt and slowly pulled it up, past her belly, past her bikini-covered breasts, and over her head.

Done, she locked eyes with him and felt an enormous thrill of power and excitement surge through her.

Nico took a long gulp of his cocktail.

'It's very hot,' she commented, in the most matter-of-fact voice she could muster.

'Da.'

If his eyes were any wider she figured they might just pop out of his head.

'I think I will take my shorts off too.'

Keeping her eyes fixed firmly on his stunned face, she stood up. She undid the button, then teased the zip loose and wriggled the shorts down her hips and thighs before letting them fall in a puddle at her ankles. Casually she stepped out of them and bent over to pick them up from the floor.

'You will burn,' he said hoarsely, his eyes hooded.

Rosa reached a hand behind her head and pulled her hair-band free, shaking her head to enable her hair to tumble over her shoulders. 'In that case I suggest we go inside. I forfeit the game.'

Nico did not think he had ever been so aroused—not even when he had first seen a picture of a naked woman at the grand old age of nineteen.

This…

How could he ever have thought she was merely pretty? She was beautiful. And how could he ever have thought implanted breasts on 'stick-insects'—as Rosa so eloquently referred to his previous lovers—were attractive? Compared to the creamy, inviting wonder of Rosa's voluptuous figure… there *was* no comparison.

Slowly, he extended a hand. 'If you are forfeiting then I win by default. It is time for me to claim my prize.'

Rosa's chest rose and fell, and the beautiful caramel swirls of her eyes pulled him to her. With only the slightest hint of hesitation she threaded her fingers through his, allowing him to steer her, keeping their fingers laced together.

Nico locked the patio doors behind them before turning to face her.

She stood at the foot of the bed, watching him. It was as if a hook caught in his chest when he caught a glimmer of apprehension in her eyes, confirming his suspicions that she was not quite as blasé as she was trying to portray.

Ridiculously, this touched him.

His usual sleek lovers oozed sexual confidence, knew they looked fantastic clothed or undressed.

Not one of them could hold a torch to Rosa.

A bottle of massage oil had been left on the dressing table, as he had instructed.

'You were confident,' she observed, uttering her first words since she had forfeited.

'I always play to win.'

He stepped over until he stood before her. Unable to resist, he snaked a hand around her neck and gathered that thick mass of hair, inhaling the sweet fragrance. He felt her tremble, heard her breath quicken.

Heat licked through him, as deep a burn as he could stand. He released his hold on her and took a step back, unable to tear his eyes away. 'It is traditional for a massage to be given naked.'

The caramel darkened to chocolate. Keeping her eyes fixed on his, she moved her hands behind her back and unhooked the top of her bikini, then slid the straps down past her shoulders and let it drop to the floor.

For an age all he could do was gaze at her, completely transfixed. Those magnificent breasts he had been dreaming about were more perfect than in his deepest imaginings.

Rosa was all woman—a glorious, hourglass gift from the heavens.

He sensed her arousal. He could see it in the puckering of the perfect pale rose nipples, hear it in the shallowness of her breath, feel it in the heat emanating from her curvy form.

Her fingers tugged at the bikini bottoms.

'No,' he said hoarsely. 'Keep those on.' He did not think he could trust himself if she were to reveal the core of her womanhood to him. Not yet. Not until he had regained some control.

Closing his eyes, he took deep breaths. 'I need you to lie on your stomach.'

When she was lying flat on her belly, her head resting on a pillow, he removed a condom from his wallet and threw it onto the bed before divesting himself of the restrictive shorts. Shamelessly naked, he climbed onto the bed and knelt beside her.

Her ebony hair was spread around her shoulders. With tender care, he gathered it together and swept it down the side of her neck, tucking it under her chin. Her eyes were closed.

She jolted when the first drops of oil hit her back but made no sound.

At first he worked on her neck and the top of her shoulders, determined to release the tension that had been dogging her since their arrival on Butterfly Island, slowly working his way downwards across the sweep of her back. He could not help but marvel at the dewy softness of her skin, his fingers kneading into buttery flesh so reminiscent of a Botticelli painting.

How could he ever have thought lean stick-insects were desirable?

Gradually he reached the top of her rounded buttocks.

So far she had made not the slightest sound. Nothing. Surely she could not have fallen asleep?

That question was answered a moment later when he tugged down on her bikini bottoms and she raised her bottom in the air to assist him.

Nico had to stop what he was doing and check himself. The ache in his loins was no mere pain. It was torture. Pure torture.

Only when he was certain he had control did he slide the bikini bottoms down her smooth, shapely legs and throw them onto the floor. He pressed a kiss to the small of her back and had to check himself again when a tiny whimper escaped from her throat.

Spreading her legs, he knelt between them and rained kisses all over her back, simultaneously massaging her buttocks, her thighs, her waist, touching every part of her, then returning to knead that glorious bottom.

When his lips reached the base of her neck he traced a finger down the cleft between her buttocks, gratified beyond measure when she raised them again for him. Gently he inserted a finger into her velvet warmth and groaned aloud as he was welcomed into her hot moistness.

Another whimper escaped from her throat.

He clamped a hand on her shoulder and finally turned her over.

The sight that greeted him would be forever etched into his memories.

Rosa's cheeks were flushed, her eyes dilated. Her plump lips were a screaming invitation to be kissed…

Nico did not need a second invitation.

Stroking the stray strands of hair off her face, he took possession of the soft plumpness.

The first press of his lips to hers scorched him. If it were possible to combust with a kiss, this was the closest any human had come. The fire that burned through him was almost too much to bear, and when he snaked his tongue into the sweetness of her parted lips he almost pulled away, the intensity too much for any mere mortal to handle…

But then one of Rosa's arms wound around his neck.

Her hand palmed the base of his skull, her fingers scraping through the bristles of his hair, forcing him closer, deepening the kiss, driving away all errant thoughts. He was helpless to do anything but succumb.

He kissed her like a drowning man reaching air, and she responded with the same greedy, furious need, their tongues clashing in a rhythmic duel in which they would both be winners.

Kissing had always been a sop. He had never seen the need for it other than as a means to a greater end.

But he could kiss Rosa for ever—could plunder her mouth with his tongue and lips for eternity. She tasted like nectar.

Her response blew his mind. Her kisses, her touch, all turning the raging burn in his veins into thick lava. She shifted and writhed beneath him, parting her legs, hooking an ankle around his thigh in wordless invitation.

'Not yet,' he murmured into her mouth, before breaking away and trailing kisses down the delicate arch of her neck, further down, until he caught a pink puckered nipple in his mouth.

Her helpless moan fired his fervour. Her small hands cradled his scalp, her back arching in response.

Rosa's breasts were perfection in themselves. Soft and plump and gloriously ripe. He kissed and caressed and sucked and moulded, his free hand trailing down to the mound between her legs, splaying his fingers through damp, downy hair.

He had never been so turned on in his life.

Why, he wondered dimly as he smothered the other glorious nipple with his mouth, did so many women feel the need to display the core of their femininity and turn it into an exhibition? Not Rosa. All of Rosa's secrets were hidden, waiting to be discovered.

'Nico, please—I need you inside me.'

Her husky voice was little more than a whimper. And he needed to be inside her too. Forget the long, languorous bout of lovemaking he had envisaged for them. This was too much. He needed her now.

'Condom.' That was the only word he could manage. A

raging fire was consuming every part of him. He stretched out an arm and snatched the foil wrapper.

Unwilling to break physical contact, still resting between her thighs, he shifted onto his hip. While he ripped the foil with his teeth and unrolled the condom onto an erection that had ever ached more, Rosa wound her arms around his neck and rained kisses down his throat and across his collarbone, her soft lips burning his skin, her teeth nipping at his flesh.

Much more of this and he really would combust.

The condom securely on, Nico wrapped his arms around her tiny waist and pushed her back onto the pillow, possessing her mouth as he positioned himself above the welcoming folds between her legs.

She raised her hips and in one fluid movement he plunged deep into her tight warmth.

Dear sweet heaven…

His eyes flew open to find Rosa's fixed on him, on her face an expression of heavenly wonder.

He wanted to savour it, to relish the sheer, unadulterated pleasure of the moment. But he could not. He kissed her—a brutal clash of lips and teeth and tongue—and began to move, thrusting as deep inside her as he could go.

She moaned deeply, her fingers clasping his buttocks, driving him deeper and deeper, forcing the pace, demanding more, taking every inch of him until he feared he could hold on no further.

Her breaths were becoming shallow, her soft moans becoming longer.

Pulsations were starting to build inside him.

He screwed his eyes shut, fighting with all his might to hold on. This was too soon. Far too soon. He didn't want it to end. He wanted to drive into her tight warmth for ever.

And then her back arched, her muscles spasmed around him and he could hold on no more. With one last bucking thrust he let go and allowed the pulsations to rip through him in a burst of unprecedented exquisite pleasure.

Rosa could not help the laugh that escaped from her throat.

Nico lifted his face from its burial in her shoulder and gazed at her.

'Amazing…' She sighed. Stars were still blinding the back of her retinas. 'Bloody amazing.'

He kissed her—a full-bodied, sensual kiss that contained so much—before breaking away from her.

'I need to get rid of the condom,' he said regretfully, his voice hoarse.

'One more kiss,' she beseeched, yanking his head back down so they could exchange a kiss that was filled more with laughter than passion.

He pressed his lips to the tip of her nose. 'I'll be back in less than a minute.'

'I'll be counting.'

Stretching luxuriantly, she watched him pad over to the *en suite* bathroom.

It was cold without his warmth, so she nestled under the sheets to wait for his return.

She felt ridiculously like giggling.

So *that* was what an orgasm felt like.

This time she did giggle, smothering the schoolgirl sound with a pillow.

Who would have known? How could she ever have known making love to her husband would be so wonderful?

'What's so funny?' Nico came back into the room, stalking towards her, his brow raised and a quirk playing on his lips.

She shook her head. 'Nothing. I was just thinking.'

He got under the covers next to her. 'Thinking about what?'

'Thinking I can't believe we shared a roof for eleven

months and had no idea how incredible things could be between us.'

A pang of anxiety suddenly bloomed through her.

'It wasn't just me, was it?' she begged, turning onto her side to face him and sliding her hand around his waist. 'Tell me it was as good for you.'

He pulled her close so she was flush against him and breathed into her hair. 'How can you even question it?'

Her mind at ease, she buried her face into his chest, inhaling the citrusy scent that now contained a hint of musk.

Had she ever felt so…replete? Content? Whatever the word, all she knew was right at that moment it would take a crowbar to prise her away from him.

Nico had taken her to the stars and she never wanted to come back to earth.

CHAPTER TEN

'WAKE UP, SLEEPY HEAD.'

Nico's gravelly voice broke through Rosa's slumber. Instantly her brain switched to wakefulness.

As with the day before, he had brought her breakfast in bed.

Stretching, she covered a yawn and sat up.

What a difference a day made.

Twenty-four hours ago she had woken stiff and shattered. Today she felt as if she had slept for England. Not that she'd had that much sleep, considering they had still been making love when the sun began its ascent.

'What game are you planning to teach me today?' she asked, picking up the glass of orange juice.

A wicked gleam came into Nico's eyes. 'Today, *daragaya*, you and I are going on a trip.'

'Where to? The gym?' She guffawed at her own joke. Unbelievably, she was already wide awake, her entire being fizzing with delight, her heart so full she could believe it had been filled with a forest of rose petals.

He leaned down and grazed his teeth along the curve of her neck. 'Eat your breakfast and then change into one of those tiny bikinis that show off your beautiful body.'

'You want me to change?' she said, turning the sides of

her mouth down and fluttering her eyelashes at him. 'That's a shame. I was hoping we could spend the rest of the day in bed.'

Capturing her mouth in a kiss, he nipped her bottom lip gently. 'Nothing would please me more than to spend the rest of the week in bed with you, but as this is your first holiday I want you to remember it for more than fantastic sex.'

With hungry eyes she watched him retreat into the *en suite* bathroom and released a sigh of contentment.

Impulsively she pinched her forearm.

It hurt.

She threw herself back and gazed at the ceiling, a smile glued to her face.

This really was real.

For the first time since she was eight years old she wanted to hug herself with happiness.

An hour later they stood with the Captain on the main deck. The back of the yacht had been rolled open. Ahead of them, rising from the ocean like the kind of deserted island found in all good films, sat uninhabited King Island.

'You expect me to get on that?' she asked, pointing at the jet ski that had been brought out. The Captain had assured them that snorkelling gear and a picnic had been placed in its inbuilt storage box.

'That's how we're getting to the island,' Nico said, throwing her a life jacket. 'Now, put that on.'

She looked at the fluorescent material with doubt and not a little fear. 'Won't the orange clash with my sunburn?'

He simply stared at her, arms folded, brows raised.

'I don't see why we can't sail to the island like normal people,' she grumbled.

'Where would the fun be in that?' A gorgeous smile broke out on his poker-straight face. 'We're on holiday. Let's make the most of it.'

She stared uncertainly at the jet ski. To her eyes it was a huge, fat, two-seater motorbike with the wheels missing.

'I'll be driving it,' he said, clearly reading her mind. 'You will be perfectly safe. You just have to hold on tight to me.'

Despite herself, those now familiar bubbles of excitement started causing a riot in her belly. In her heart she knew Nico would never do anything that would put her in harm's reach. When she had given herself to him she had given more than just her body and her heart. She had given him her trust.

Before she could act, Nico closed the gap between them, pulled the life jacket from her hands and manhandled her arms into it. 'That's better,' he said, a smirk playing on his lips as he zipped it up securely.

She glared at him. 'I am perfectly capable of putting a life jacket on myself, thank you.'

'If you'd dithered any longer the sun would have been setting.'

Despite herself, she laughed, shaking her head at his high-handed arrogance—an arrogance tempered by the amusement in his eyes.

Naturally he eschewed her demands that he too wear a life jacket, jumping onto the machine dressed only in a pair of long navy swimming shorts.

Holding on to the handlebars, he flashed his white teeth. 'Well? Are you getting on? Or do you want me to carry you on?'

'You wouldn't dare,' she said, knowing perfectly well that he would dare. He wouldn't think twice about it.

Not giving him the chance, she climbed on behind him, wrapped her arms around his waist and they were off.

Her head pressed into his back, she clung to him. Over the ocean they flew, cutting through bobbing waves, the speed making her hair splay in all directions, the spray of salt water tempering the blazing heat of the sun on her semi-naked form.

All too soon they came to a stop on a smooth white beach.

'That was fantastic!' she exclaimed with a beam of delight.

Nico grinned and took her hand to steady her wobbly legs as she climbed off. 'Exhilarating, isn't it?'

'Can we do it again for longer?'

He mock-bowed. 'Your wish is my command. But let us explore the island and eat first.'

King Island was much smaller than Butterfly Island, and much less verdant, but it contained the same tropical feel. If a castaway should appear with a parrot on his shoulder she wouldn't bat an eyelash. As far as Rosa was concerned, it was perfect.

Hands clasped together, they traversed the beach, paddling through the shallow water before finding a small cove that was perfect for their picnic, away from any prying eyes on the yacht.

Nico unpacked their feast of goodies. For a while they ate in companionable silence. The sun beamed down, and the fresh scent of shrubbery and exotic flowers filled Rosa's senses with such warmth and contentment she feared she could explode from the joy of it all.

Was this how normal people felt? What normal people experienced? The heady rush of falling in love, of embracing the pleasures life had to offer instead of hiding away in a self-built fortress?

'How long after the contracts are signed will you start building here?' she asked, referring to the accommodation and facilities that were to be built there for the offshore workers.

'Within weeks.'

She sighed sadly.

'What's the matter?'

'It seems a shame to spoil all this beauty.'

He reached out a hand and tilted her chin. 'You have seen

the plans. Robert and I agreed the only development done here would be sympathetic to the landscape. I promise you I will keep to my word.'

'I know.' She smiled. Impulsively, she darted up and pressed a kiss to his lips. 'You're a good man, Nicolai Baranski.'

For a moment darkness clouded his eyes, before he blinked it away and flashed a mocking grin. 'Don't tell anyone else that.'

She looked at him carefully, looking for a clue as to what could have caused that brief cloud. Apart from a gleam in his eye there was nothing to be found.

She shoved the image away to be pondered another time. Right then everything was perfect, and she didn't want anything to intrude and mar it.

She wrapped her arms around his neck. 'I wouldn't dream of telling anyone. After all, we have your reputation to protect.'

Hooking an arm around her waist, he lowered her onto her back and nuzzled her neck. 'Speaking of protecting reputations, you *do* realise it has been a whole four hours since this bad Russian playboy has made love to his beautiful English wife?'

'Then I suggest we do something about it,' she said, her words coming out in tiny gasps as she felt his erection press against her thigh.

Her gasps soon turned into soft mews when Nico divested her of her bikini and got down to some serious reputation-salvaging…

After a day spent exploring King Island and each other, and a mammoth, exhilarating ride on the jet ski, they'd returned to the yacht for dinner, which they'd eaten on the sundeck.

Now they were both sprawled on the bed, as naked as the

day they had been born, watching *Dr Zhivago* on a cinema screen which was connected to the internet.

'How many times have you watched this?' Nico asked, carefully placing a trail of cherries along her spine.

She shrugged and pressed a foot against his leg. 'No idea.'

He tapped her bottom. 'Don't move.'

She cocked her head back and speared him with a look. 'You're distracting me.'

'That was my intention.'

Her eyes gleamed. 'Carry on.'

Carry on? He could make love to her all night.

Luckily they still had another four days together. That would be plenty of time to get this mass of unprecedented desire out of his system. Life could then return to normal, with the added bonus of sharing his beautiful wife's body every night when he was in the UK. Unless, of course, he could convince her to take a permanent role as his PA.

One by one he ate the cherries off her back, then got down to some proper distraction business.

Even the moon had disappeared by the time they were finally spent and he turned the light off.

Sleepily, she prodded him with her foot. 'Keep it on.'

'Right. Sorry.' He fiddled with the switches until he found the bathroom light and turned it on, filling the cabin with a dim, warm glow. Curiosity finally got the better of him. 'If you're not afraid of the dark, why do you like to have the light on?'

'I can see if anyone sneaks into the room.'

Thinking she had made a joke, Nico started to laugh, but then he remembered all the times he had passed her room at night and seen a dim glow seeping from under her doorframe. He had always assumed she was reading or watching television. How many times had he fought his yen to open the door…?

He blinked the thought away.

'Do I take it someone once came into your room in the dark and scared you?'

She yawned and snuggled into him. 'Nico, it's late and I'm shattered. Can we have this conversation in the morning?'

'No.' He should be shattered too. Physically, he was. But his brain was still fully wired. 'You always shy away from discussing your past or anything personal.' So did he. Normally. But right then he did not feel normal. Not by a long chalk.

'That's the way we always liked it.'

'If someone has hurt or scared you it is my business to know.' And when he learned *who* had hurt and scared Rosa he would track that person down and give them the fright of their life. No one hurt his wife. *No one.*

'It was a long time ago. All children are hurt and scared at some point.'

He forced his voice to stay even, trying to control the wild flurry of his thoughts. 'What happened?'

'Nothing *happened*,' she said quietly. 'There were a couple of bullies in one of the children's homes I lived in for a while. They thought it was funny to sneak into the younger kids' rooms and scare us.' She raised her head and rested her chin on his chest. 'One particularly well-executed torment was to hide under our beds and then, after the lights had been turned out, to grab our legs. In my case, the monster under the bed was two fourteen-year-old girls.'

The hairs on his arms rose. Everything she had said made his skin crawl, but out of everything one pertinent fact leapt out at him. 'You lived in a children's home?'

'Yes.'

His voice became hoarse. 'When? Why?'

She was silent for a few moments, as if weighing up

whether or not to confide in him. 'My mother abandoned me to Social Services when I was five.'

Blood rushed to his brain, the pressure inside his head pounding with the weight of a dozen hammers. 'Your mother *abandoned* you?'

It took guts for him to keep you. He must love you very much. Her words echoed around his head. Why hadn't he paid attention to the wistful tone in which those words had been delivered?

'I thought you were an orphan.' He raked a hand through his hair as he distinctly recalled her stating when they'd married that her parents were both dead. He had never questioned her on this—had assumed she had been an adult when they'd died.

'My dad died when I was a baby,' she said, and the light in her voice that had been so prevalent throughout the day had diminished into a dispassionate tone he recognised but could not place. 'My mum died a couple of years ago.'

'Did you go back to live with her?' he asked hopefully. The thought of Rosa living in the care system tore at something inside of him.

'No. She never came back for me.'

Silence rent the cabin, the proportions of which seemed to have shrunk into a tiny bubble. The only movement was his fingers, running through her hair like a comb.

He knew he should leave it there. They had made love. That did not mean he had to know her innermost secrets. He did not know what had compelled him to question her in the first place.

'Tell me,' he commanded in a voice that was not quite steady.

Her chest lifted as she expelled a long sigh. 'There isn't much to tell. My parents were really young when they had me—only sixteen. Dad was a bit of a hothead, by all accounts, and died in a motorbike accident. Then her own mother died and my mum couldn't cope raising me on her own.'

He swallowed. 'They told you this?'

Her head moved, her thick hair tickling his chin. 'I was allowed to see my file when I turned eighteen.' A touch of sadness crept into her voice. 'I always thought—hoped—I was dumped because she couldn't afford to keep me. I thought the social worker was protecting me from something terrible, like drug abuse or…or something. But money and drugs didn't have anything to do with it. She just didn't want me back. Social Services held out for three years in the hope she would take me back before approving me as a candidate for adoption.'

Nico swore under his breath.

'Unfortunately eight-year-olds aren't at the top of any potential adopters' wish-lists.'

He closed his eyes at the matter-of-fact, fatalistic tone to her voice and wrapped his arms around her, as if the very act could protect her and keep her safe. How could anyone treat a child in such a manner?

And what kind of a monster was he, to live with someone, to forge a life with them—yes, an unconventional life, but a life all the same—and not know something so fundamental about her?

'Could your mother have been suffering from depression?' he suggested, his brain scrambling to think of something that would explain such heartless behaviour. 'She had lost your father and her own mother in a short space of time.'

'I tracked her down five years ago.'

There was that catch in her throat again—a catch that leapt out and jumped right into his heart.

'She was embarrassed to see me. I think it shamed her, having me on her doorstep, reminding her of a life she had tried to forget. She'd remarried and had another child. A boy.

A brother I never knew existed. She was polite, but…' Her voice was fading, becoming little more than a whisper. 'She didn't want me there. It was obvious. I gave her my details but I never heard from her again.'

'I'm sorry.' His words sounded ridiculous to his own ears. How could a mere *sorry* compensate for a lifetime of abandonment?

'What for?' Surprise laced her husky voice.

'I never knew.'

'It's not something I shout about.' She disentangled herself from his tight hold and rolled onto her back. He could see her profile, her snub nose pointing upwards as she gazed at the ceiling. 'Us care-home kids have a bad rep. Most people think kids in care are drug-addicted no-hopers. We're expected to fail. And for the most part we do.'

'*You* didn't fail,' he said, outraged on her behalf.

'I was lucky. I had a social worker who believed in me, and at one point I was placed with a foster family who were fanatical about the need for a good education. It was through them that I learned I had a good brain and a talent for languages—Dacha, the foster mum, was Russian.'

'Did she teach you the language?'

'Only a few words and phrases—I only stayed with them for a year—but I learned to love the sound of it. Russian is a beautiful language.'

'Why did you only stay with them for a year?'

'They had a baby of their own so I had to move out.'

'What? Because they had a baby?'

'The baby needed a nursery. I had the only spare room.'

There was that dispassionate tone again—the tone that sliced through his skin and into his core. 'Stupid me thought they were going to adopt me.' She sighed deeply, then rolled onto her side again and snuggled back into him. 'Can we stop talking about this now? I'm tired and I need to get some sleep.'

Nico knew he should heed her request and drop the subject. Rosa's past was none of his business. He had got what he wanted. He had proved they were compatible in bed—hell, *compatible* was an understatement. Together they were spectacular.

Now she belonged to him and no one else. He could share her brain, her wit and her body. Everything else was superfluous.

And yet…

'What about your brother?' he asked. He couldn't let the matter drop. The need to find some light for her was becoming of the utmost importance. *Please*, let there be some light. 'Have you met him? How old is he?'

'He's twenty.' Quickly Nico did the maths. Rosa's brother had been born just two years after she had been abandoned. 'He called to let me know our mother had died—he'd found the letter I gave her with my contact details on it.'

'That was good of him.'

'He called *after* the funeral. Out of courtesy. I've only had contact with him once since. Now, can I please go to sleep?'

Nico's hands balled into fists even as he kissed the top of her head and wished her a reluctant goodnight.

There was still so much he wanted to know.

How did a child go through what she had been through and grow up to be such a *good* person? There was nothing in Rosa's personality to hint at her traumatic childhood and adolescence.

Or was there?

Maybe the clues were there if you searched hard enough.

She was personable. Everyone liked her. But could anyone say they *knew* her? Really knew her? He suspected the answer to that was no. Rosa did not have a single close friend.

No wonder she had jumped at the idea of marrying him. She had been effectively alone since early childhood—and what was it she had said to him when they were scribbling their marriage contract? *'This will suit me perfectly. I've always liked the idea of being part of a couple—well, being part of a unit—but...'* There she had shrugged, her nose wrinkling. *'The rest of it...no, thank you. My head is private.'*

Nico had thought he understood what she could not articulate. They were two of a kind. Emotional intimacy repulsed them both.

Now he wondered if it really did repulse her, or if it were just a barrier she had erected to protect herself.

What had changed? Why did she want to leave a marriage that gave her everything she needed without having to put up with the nonsense she didn't want?

The answer became obvious.

Rosa wanted more. She had said so herself the day she'd asked for a divorce. He had simply misinterpreted it.

He had spent two days and nights making love to her, blithely unaware of the emotional damage she had sustained.

His stupid pride had been so injured when she'd had the temerity to sleep with another man, that not once had he properly considered *why* she had ricocheted back into her ex-boyfriend's arms. He had assumed her loneliness was of a sexual kind.

A roll of nausea swelled in his stomach, beads of perspiration breaking out on his forehead.

He pulled her closer. She felt so good in his arms. Better than he could ever have imagined.

But Rosa needed something he could never give her. She needed someone to love her.

If they'd had this conversation before—even two days ago—he would never have made love to her.

He had married her believing she had the same emotional deficiency as himself.

He could not have got it more wrong if he had tried.

He expelled a shuddering breath.

'Are you okay?' she said into his chest, her voice thick with sleep.

'Everything is fine.' He traced his fingers lightly across her back. 'Get some sleep.'

That was the first lie he had ever told her. Everything was *not* fine.

Nico was incapable of returning love. He was incapable of reciprocating emotion. This deficiency on his part had already caused one woman real pain. He would not allow it to damage Rosa too. She deserved—hell, she *needed*—so much more than he could ever give.

What he needed was to end this. He needed to end this now. Before she gave her heart to him. Before he caused her any more damage.

CHAPTER ELEVEN

ROSA LAY LIKE a starfish in the swimming pool, letting the morning heat be absorbed into her skin. A smile played on her lips—the same smile she had woken with, even though she had been alone in the bed. Nico must have gone for his morning exercise, which had put paid to her idea of surprising him with breakfast in bed.

It would have been wonderful to do something nice for him. Whatever his motivations, there was no denying that he had gone out of his way to ensure that this, their first holiday together—and her first holiday ever—was as relaxing as it could possibly be. All she wanted was to make a gesture to show how much she appreciated everything he had done.

It was hard to credit that she had married him believing herself to be safe. Marrying a control freak like Nico—a man she had believed incapable of affection or empathy—had seemed ideal for what she had needed. Looking back, she was glad she hadn't known how her feelings towards him would change. If she'd had a crystal ball she never would have married him.

Thank God she didn't have a crystal ball.

Under that tough, controlling exterior lay a loyal and thoughtful man and a thrillingly tender lover. And he cared. He really cared.

She could no more have stopped herself from falling in

love with him than she could have stopped the blazing sun from rising.

When he had still not appeared after she had spent thirty minutes lazing in the pool, she ordered breakfast for herself. She was halfway through a bacon sandwich when he appeared from the stairs on the second deck, wearing only a pair of gym shorts with a towel slung round his neck.

'Morning.' She beamed, rising from her chair in anticipation of his kiss.

Nico nodded briefly and looked at his watch. 'Good morning. Did you sleep well?'

'Wonderfully, thank you. How did you sleep?'

'Fine.' He looked at his watch again.

'You snuck out of bed early. Was I snoring?'

Only the briefest glimmer of a smile curved his lips, but he still did not look at her. 'Not at all.'

She swallowed a throat that had suddenly and inexplicably gone dry. 'Have you eaten?'

'Yes. I need to shower. Finish your breakfast. I'll join you in a while.'

Her heart thundering painfully against her ribs, she watched him disappear into their suite.

He closed the patio door behind him.

Dimly aware she was still standing, she sat back down.

Nico had not looked her in the eyes once during that short exchange.

Her stomach rolled. She gazed at the bacon sandwich still in her hand and placed it back on the plate. Her appetite, which mere moments ago had been ravenous, had deserted her.

If she had not lived with Nico for nearly a year she would have shrugged off his strange mood, putting it down to him not being a morning person. Plenty of people weren't—herself included.

Nico was not one of them. Nico awoke early every morning, firing on all cylinders. Especially after his morning workout.

She didn't realise she had nibbled her little fingernail down too far until he returned a good half-hour later. By then her breakfast had been cleared away and a fresh pot of coffee brought to the sundeck.

'I did debate ordering us a cocktail each,' she said as he took the seat opposite. 'But I thought you would only complain it didn't match your standards.' Deliberately she kept her tone light, hoping the unease rippling through her was nothing but the workings of a paranoid mind. Her paranoia had been fed a little more by the polo shirt he wore, which covered his chest.

'Very wise.' The tiniest ghost of smile played on his lips. His eyes were unreadable.

'So, what do you fancy doing today?' she asked, chattering madly to fill the tense silence that had appeared between them. 'As we're in the middle of the open ocean I'm guessing another trip to a deserted island is out of the question. Are there many other board games you can teach me? I'd love to learn backgammon…'

'Rosa, we need to talk.'

Her mouth shut with a snap.

He poured them both a coffee and slid her cup to her. 'The divorce you want…I am in agreement.'

Her lips parted, forming a perfect O. But nothing came out. If she'd had sails he would have literally knocked the wind out of them.

Nico rested his elbows on the table and took a sip of his coffee. Finally he looked at her. 'I don't want you to get the wrong idea—the past couple of days have been great—but in hindsight I think our becoming lovers was a mistake.'

Frozen, she continued to gaze at him, unable to blink.

There was nothing to read on his face. It held the same dispassionate expression it had contained when she had told him she wanted a divorce.

'I misunderstood what you meant when you said you wanted more from a marriage,' he continued. 'I took it to mean you wanted sex to be a part of it. I did not realise you were looking for something deeper. If I had known of your history I would never have allowed us to sleep together.'

Deep inside her belly all the lovely, warm, mushy feelings that had been swirling there since they had first made love solidified into compacted ice. Her blood thickened into slush; her head was a pounding torment of hammers.

Forcing deep breaths into her lungs, she counted to ten before dredging up a smile. 'I really don't know where you got the idea I wanted something deeper, Nico,' she said. Thank God her vocal cords were working properly. 'I said I wanted something more than what we had. I never actually said *what* I wanted, or said I wanted it with *you*.' It gave her enormous, bitter satisfaction to witness disconcertion flittering across his features. 'But you are right in one respect—the last couple of days *have* been great. I really feel as if I've had a proper holiday, so thank you for that. I'll be sure to include regular breaks in my schedule. And you're excellent in bed. Congratulations.'

Nico blanched—whether at her saccharinely sweet delivered words or the *faux* sincere manner in which she was delivering them, she couldn't have cared less.

'And congratulations for managing the equivalent of three days with me,' she continued. 'Is that a record for you? But, *purlease*, it *was* only sex—and, as great as it was, I have no interest in pursuing a deeper relationship with a man who has the emotional maturity of a walnut.'

His eyes glittered, a deep crease furrowing in his brow. 'Rosa, I never—'

'A word of advice,' she interrupted, getting to her feet. 'When you're standing in a deep hole, stop digging.'

'Where are you going?' he asked as she walked off towards the cabin.

'To get some suncream,' she called back over her shoulder. 'It looks like today is going to be another scorcher and I don't fancy burning—I'd hate to clash with the life jacket should the yacht capsize.'

When she had disappeared from view Nico took a deep breath and closed his eyes.

That had been harder than he'd expected. Much harder. Through his extended workout he had been mulling over the best choice of words to use. He had known he could not put it off, but for once there had been inertia in his body's response. For once the thought of ending a relationship had caused his stomach to cramp.

He hadn't lied. They truly had been great together. The past three days had been the best of his life. If ever there was a woman he *could* love, Rosa would be the one.

But he did not know how to love. He did not know how to give a woman what she needed. And the last thing he wanted was to hurt the one woman in the world he liked and respected.

It had hurt his heart to look at her.

When he had said what needed to be said he had forced his eyes to stay locked on her, forced himself to witness the shock she had not been quick enough to hide.

Her shock had not lasted long. He should have known she would not react in the way he'd anticipated. Not for Rosa the tantrums and sulks he had become accustomed to. Apart from her initial shock, she couldn't have cared less.

Had he really read her so wrong?

Had her childhood hardened her so much that she was incapable of loving too?

The thought should dispel some of his nagging guilt. It did not.

Rosa's shock had been real. That tiny tic of hers, although barely perceptible, had been revealing.

It was not long before she came back out to the sundeck in a black bikini, white shorts and dark sunglasses. She marched over to him.

'Could you put some suncream on my back, please?' She thrust the bottle into the hand he automatically stretched out. Not waiting for an answer, she turned her back to him and lifted her ponytail.

He had no good reason to refuse.

'Are we going to return to Butterfly Island before schedule?' she asked whilst he poured the thick cream onto the palm of a hand.

'I will speak to the Captain shortly.' Using brisk motions he slathered the cream onto her back, wishing his fingers didn't delight in the buttery skin. He counted four moles and compressed his lips tightly together. His skin tingled. He was filled with the need to slip a hand round and cup one of those full…

'Good. It is pointless continuing with this cruise when there is work we can be getting on with. Are you done?'

He blinked and quickly moved his hands away. 'Yes.' He clenched them into fists lest he gave in to the urge to slap her perfectly rounded bottom.

'Thank you.' She flashed him a quick smile and padded over to the pool.

Nico supressed a groan as she casually stripped off the shorts and placed them neatly on a lounger. She then unfolded a towel, spread it out on the adjacent lounger, and settled down under the blazing sun.

He must be mad, he reflected, gritting his teeth at the ache rampaging through his loins. If he had kept his mouth shut for a couple more days he could be down there, lazing by the pool, with the most responsive, intuitive woman he had ever been blessed to make love with.

Until today he had never ended a relationship before it had run its course. Admittedly, it didn't take long for him to become bored with a lover, but Rosa was different. He had never had a lover like Rosa before.

He dragged his fingers through his hair and got to his feet. It was time to tell the Captain they needed to change course and return to Butterfly Island.

With a pang of dread he acknowledged they would have to spend at least one more night together.

Her eyes hidden behind the thick sunglasses, Rosa watched Nico leave the sundeck.

She wanted to throw up. If it were not for her pride she would be holed up in the bathroom at that very minute.

At least she had managed to salvage some dignity from the situation. But then, having spent her life coping with rejection, she had become an expert at handling it.

This time would be no different.

Nico spent the rest of the day with the crew. The Captain had agreed to increase the speed they were sailing at. With any luck they should return to shore tomorrow evening. The Captain had also agreed to show him how the yacht was run, and he had thoroughly enjoyed exploring the bowels of the ship and learning of the mechanics behind it.

The sun had long set and thick clouds were encroaching over the sky when his thoughts turned to Rosa. All day her image had flickered at the back of his retinas, but he had refused to allow her space in his head. Thinking of her made his chest tighten too strongly for comfort.

He hoped she had remembered to eat. She had a habit of skipping meals when she was bogged down with work.

Then he remembered she had nothing to distract her from eating.

He found her sitting cross-legged under the covers of the enormous bed, working on a laptop set upon her knees. No doubt she had taken sanctuary indoors because of the brewing storm.

She lifted her head briefly and nodded at him.

'You're wearing glasses,' he said, blinking with surprise at the pink-rimmed frames.

'Well spotted.' Her focus went back to whatever she was doing.

'I didn't know you wore glasses.' How was that even possible?

'I have continuous-wear contact lenses, but the ones I had with me were nearing the end of their shelf-life. If I had known I would be away for longer than a day I would have made sure I brought my supplies with me.' She threw him an accusatory glare. 'Luckily I keep a spare pair of glasses in my handbag.'

He surveyed her warily. Rosa's frame was taut, as if she were contracting all her muscles. 'They suit you.'

Her lips tightened into a white line and she tapped furiously at the keys in front of her. 'Whatever.'

He raised a brow at the inflection of her tone. 'They *do* suit you.'

'Nicolai, I am perfectly aware glasses make me look like a troll. Please don't try to be nice to me.'

'I'm not trying to be nice.' He ran a hand through his hair and shook his head. For someone who professed to be cool about the turn their relationship had taken, she was acting extremely strangely. 'I don't know where you got the idea you look like a troll…'

'From the mirror—all right?' she snapped, slamming the lid of the laptop down and staring at him with a look of untamed wildness behind the clear lenses. Her eyes were strangely magnified. 'Believe me, I am well aware of how I look—of the ugly, vertically challenged frump who's reflected back at me.'

'You are *not* ugly,' he snapped back, outraged she could even think such a thing.

'I'm hardly the kind of long-legged, blonde-haired beauty you usually cavort with.' She pushed the laptop off her lap and slithered out from under the covers.

Nico had no idea what he could say to that last remark without making matters worse. For all her tightly controlled exterior something was clearly eating at her, and for once he didn't have a clue how to approach her.

She jumped off the bed, her braless breasts bouncing softly under a thin white vest. The only other item of clothing she wore was a pair of skimpy lace knickers. Knickers *he* had instructed be included in her wardrobe when seduction had been at the forefront of his mind.

At this stage seduction should be the last thing on his mind, but watching her stride forcefully across the cabin floor, he felt that familiar ache well inside him. If he was being honest with himself the ache hadn't really left him, had been a constant reminder of how mind-blowing things had been between them.

'Where did you get the laptop from?' he asked, coughing to clear the lump that had formed in his throat. He needed to get away from personal territory. He had opened a big enough can of worms the day before, by pumping her for information that should have been left alone.

'Patrick lent it to me,' she said, referring to one of the

crew members. She stepped into her dressing room, leaving the door open. He watched as she rummaged through some drawers.

'What were you working on?'

'It's personal.' She bent over to step into the yellow skirt she had selected. Anyone else and he would suspect her of being deliberately provocative. Instead he could feel the taut anger reverberating through her, pulsing through the physical distance she had placed between them and hitting him with the force of a Taser.

He should let it go. Hadn't he learned by now that with Rosa he should leave well enough alone, if only for his own sanity?

His mind flickered back to their last night on Butterfly Island and her suspicious behaviour before they had gone to dinner. 'Is this what you were doing the other night, before we went to dinner with Robert and Laura?'

Why was he even pretending to care?

Deep inside Rosa's bones a fire raged—a fire she had spent the day obstinately refusing to admit even existed. For the first time since she had married Nico the fire had nothing to do with lust or desire. This was rage—a simmering inferno of anger. And now, with him conversing so casually, acting as if nothing had happened—as if he hadn't dumped her and then left her to her own lonely devices for the day—the inferno was approaching boiling point.

She would not allow it to spill over. Whatever happened, she would never let him know the utter devastation he had wrought.

She answered him only when she was certain her tongue could be kept under control. A stupid thing, to think a tongue could take a life of its own, when it was her brain and consciousness that controlled it, but over the past few days it felt as if all the control she had spent years cultivating and perfecting was being ground into dust.

'Yes,' she said, zipping the skirt and smoothing it down. 'It's what I was doing the other night.'

'And are you going to share what you have been doing with *me*?'

'If you must know, I've been trying to trace my father's family.'

He was silent before cautiously asking, 'Are you having any luck?'

'No.'

'What sites have you tried?'

She closed the dressing room door and told him briefly of the ancestry and genealogy sites she had signed up to.

'Have you searched on the social networking sites?'

She threw him a look of disdain and immediately wished she hadn't. Looking at him hurt. 'I've searched everywhere. I've got copies of his birth and death certificates, but the only thing I know for certain is he was an only child. His parents died young. His father was an only child too, but his mother had a sister who emigrated to Australia decades ago. In the year I've been searching she's the only possible surviving relative I've found. I have no idea where in Australia she is, or if she's married or…anything.'

'I know a good private investigator in Australia,' he said. 'If you give me your great-aunt's details I can get him to look into it.'

'No, thank you,' she said stiffly, forcing her legs to walk past him to the stupidly enormous bed. 'I'm happy to take my time. I have no intention of reaching out to her.'

Nico was the last person she wanted help from. All she wanted from him was his signature on the divorce papers.

How dared he lead her on? How dared he say he wanted a proper marriage when all he'd really wanted was to get into her knickers? She had trusted him, and all along he had been pretending, playing a role.

She could hear his brain ticking. She wouldn't put it past him to hire the investigator whether she agreed to it or not.

'What about your mother's family?' he asked quietly.

She carefully picked up the laptop. 'All dead. My mother was the only child of elderly parents—her mother was forty-four when she had her. In those days that really was old to be a mother.' Unwilling to continue the conversation a second longer, she tucked the laptop under her arm. 'I need to get this back to Patrick before he finishes for the evening.'

'I'll come with you,' Nico offered.

'I'm quite capable of walking down two flights of stairs on my own,' she said tersely. She didn't want to be anywhere near him.

In fact, she decided, as she passed through the saloon, she would spend the night in here. The leather sofas were comfortable and it would be easy enough to borrow a blanket. Anything had to be better than sharing a bed with a man for whom two nights with her had most definitely been enough.

CHAPTER TWELVE

NICO FOUND HIMSELF checking his watch for the umpteenth time. Rosa should have returned to their suite hours ago.

He would not check on her. Even he had been able to recognise the 'get lost' vibes she had been expelling. Although it went against the grain, he knew he needed to respect her need for space. If he had considered her needs in the first place he would never have got them into this mess.

Leaving her alone for the day had been a bad move on his part. Who could blame her for working all the hours humanly possible when such darkness resided in her head? And why the hell hadn't he left all talk of divorce until they were back on *terra firma*?

But how could he have lived with himself if he had continued to make love to her knowing she believed things between them were something they were not?

Nausea rolled in his stomach with the same motion as the rolling yacht. The incoming storm was proving strong enough to overpower the state-of-the-art stabilisers. He hoped Rosa wasn't outside in it.

Turning onto his side, he stared at her pillow before rolling back and staring at the ceiling. He took another look at his watch.

Screw it. He would never get any sleep until he knew she was all right.

He pulled on a pair of shorts before walking down the steps to the second deck. The saloon was empty. All the rooms on the deck were empty.

The thick storm clouds that had been brewing over them had burst; fat drops of rain were falling like a sheet, the noise almost deafening. His concern was on the verge of turning into something deeper when he spotted her outside. She was leaning on the railings, gazing out into the black nothingness, seemingly oblivious to the wind and rain lashing around her.

His fear should have been allayed by the sight of her. Instead his pulse surged. There was something about the way she stood and her dishevelled appearance that raised his antennae.

He opened the door and stepped out into the storm. 'What are you doing out here?' he asked, forced to raise his voice to be heard over the crashing waves.

She spun around to face him, clutching the tall glass of clear fluid in her hand. 'Nothing.'

'Nothing?' He searched her face, his heart plummeting at the desolation he found there. Deliberately he kept his voice even and non-threatening. 'Please, Rosa, come away from the railing.'

'I'm not in the mood for your company.'

'Have you been drinking?'

'What's it to you?' she said stiffly. 'Now, please leave me alone.'

'Vodka and low railings do not go together—especially in a storm.'

'Why? Are you worried I might fall overboard?' She shook her head and rolled her eyes. 'Please, Nico, don't act as if you care.'

He winced. 'Of course I care.'

Any desolation cleared, her face transforming into an animalistic snarl. The glass in her hand went sailing past him and shattered on the wooden deck. Before he could process what she had just done she roared at him. 'How *dare* you come out here pretending you give a damn about me?'

Stunned at her words and actions, he blinked in astonishment. Nico had barely heard Rosa raise her voice before.

'Well? Are you not going to answer me?' she shouted. 'Or are you too busy thinking of some more good excuses to justify dumping me?'

'I didn't dump you...'

'Don't you dare lie to me!' she screamed, pounding her fists against his chest. 'Don't you bloody dare! I should have known better than to trust you! You're just like everyone else!'

'Rosa, stop it!'

Somehow he managed to gather her wrists together and pull her under the overhang, away from the pouring rain. She struggled. When he refused to relinquish his hold she kicked him in the shins. It would have hurt, but her wet feet were bare.

'Rosa, stop,' he commanded.

Whether it was the authority in his tone or her complete inability to wriggle out of his hold, she stopped struggling and gazed at him. To his horror, her magnified eyes filled and her chin wobbled a fraction.

'Tell me what's wrong with me,' she said, her voice now little more than a whisper. 'Please—just tell me. What is so wrong that no one wants me?'

He shook his head and swore under his breath. 'Rosa, there is nothing wrong with you.'

For a moment she looked as unsure and vulnerable as a child. Relinquishing his hold on her wrists, he reached a hand to her shoulder, but she stiffened at his touch and shrank away, back into the deluge.

The driving rain saturated her, making her appear smaller and more vulnerable than anything he could have conjured in his darkest nightmares. She seemed oblivious to it. 'All I've ever wanted was to feel as if I belong somewhere. But there is nowhere for me. I tried with Stephen. I really, really tried. But it wasn't there. I wanted to love him but I couldn't, and I *hurt* him. I hurt him as badly as my mother hurt me.'

He opened his mouth but she shook her head, her voice now full of despair.

'Do you know why I got together with him? Call me shallow, but it was because he said I was pretty. No one had ever called me that before. All my life I've known there's something wrong with me, that I'm ugly…'

'You are not ugly!' Nico could not stomach another word. Stepping forward, he palmed her cheeks and forced her to look at him. 'You are *not* ugly. And nor are you pretty. Rosa, you're *beautiful*—inside and out.'

She swiped him away. 'Then why don't you want me any more? I've been thinking it over and over and I can't think of any other reason. I put my trust in you. You said you wanted a proper marriage and I believed you. You're not a liar, Nico, so you must have meant it. But the second you got me into bed and became intimate with me you no longer wanted me. So please, I beg you, tell me what is wrong with me?'

Nico dragged his hand down his face, breathing deeply to catch hold of himself.

The pain in her eyes was almost more than he could bear to witness. All his worst fears were crashing down on him and it was so much worse than he could have imagined. 'You are one of the best people I have ever known,' he said, trying to process his thoughts into some semblance of order. 'You deserve someone who will love and cherish you, and I wish to God that someone could be me.'

'But it can't be you, can it? Two nights was enough for you to realise there is something rotten about me…'

'No!' For the first time in his life he pulled a woman into

his arms for the sole purpose of providing comfort. Wrapping his arms tightly around her so she couldn't wriggle free, he buried his face in her soaking hair and breathed her in. He felt her glasses dislodged against his chest and something inside him cracked.

'Listen to me,' he said, speaking into her hair. 'I *did* want a proper marriage, but my definition of that was for us to continue exactly as we were with sex thrown into the mix. I thought that was what you wanted too. I didn't realise how badly you needed something more. I wish I could be the one to give it to you but I'm not made that way.'

She tried to twist out of his hold but he kept her pressed against him. He could feel the warmth of her breath against his chest and dug his fingers into her scalp.

'Please, Rosa, just listen. You know I am not one for opening up. This is hard for me.'

But he had to try. He could never live with himself if she were to continue believing there was something inherently wrong with her that drove people away.

Lord, what had he done?

His selfish pride and monstrous ego had set off a chain of events he could never have predicted even with the benefit of a crystal ball. Rosa was the last person in the world he would ever want to hurt.

Only when she stilled did Nico resume his thread, uncaring of the rain lashing down on them both. 'You know I grew up without there being any women in my life?'

She nodded jerkily, her hair tickling his face.

'I didn't have my first girlfriend until I was twenty-one. We were together for six months and it is the only proper relationship I have had.'

Somehow her stiff form became even more rigid.

'Galina was the first woman I slept with. Until that point everything I knew about women and relationships came from books. I wanted what the books promised, but I soon learned I am not cut out for relationships. I am incapable of giving a woman what she needs. Galina wanted so much from me and I could not give it to her. I couldn't even spend a night sharing the same bed with her. She was convinced she could change me—I *wanted* her to change me—but it was futile. The more she tried, the more I withdrew. Eventually she'd had enough and walked away, but not before telling me I had something missing.'

Rosa sucked in a breath.

'She was right,' he said. He closed his eyes and inhaled her scent, filling his lungs with her sweetness. 'Galina gave six months of her life to a man who could not reciprocate her love. I wanted to reciprocate but I had never been shown how—and it was too late for me to learn. Non-sexual intimacy leaves me cold. That's why I have always gone with high-maintenance women since. They're so wrapped up in themselves they have nothing to give to anyone else.'

When he'd finished talking he took a deep breath. It was the longest speech he had ever made.

'So why not marry one of them?' she asked.

Slowly she withdrew her arms from around his waist and looked up at him, her eyes scrutinising his face for answers.

'Because I had no wish to tie myself to a woman whose idea of conversation was discussing the latest innovation in self-tanning.' His lips curved a touch. 'I married *you* because you are clever and independent and because you are incredibly beautiful.' The slight smile dropped. 'I also married you because I assumed your aversion to emotional entanglements meant you were the same as me. But you are *not* the same as me. You need someone who can love you and reciprocate the enormous amount of love you have inside you. You need someone who can support you and be a shoulder to lean on.

I can't be that man—I'm not equipped for it. I am too selfish and controlling and you will be better off without me.'

Even with the rain dripping over her face he could see the tears that continued to fall down her cheeks.

'Come,' he said, hooking an arm around her shoulder. 'We should get inside before we both contract pneumonia.'

'I need to clean up the glass.'

'I'll get a member of the crew to do it.'

'It's no bother.'

'You don't even know where the dustpan is.'

Rosa had no answer to that that. While Nico pressed the buzzer to notify the crew of the shattered glass she slipped away, up the steps to the third deck and into their cabin.

The enormous bed seemed to wink at her.

She didn't even have the energy to flash it the bird. All she wanted was to crash out.

Locking the *en suite* bathroom door behind her, she stripped her sopping clothes off and stood under the shower.

She kept it together, methodically cleaning herself before stepping out and towelling dry. It was not until she stood before the sink to brush her teeth and caught sight of her blurred reflection that her knees gave way and she slumped onto the floor, covering her ears to drown out the screaming in her head.

From starting full of such hope and happiness, the day had ended in nothing but darkness.

In its own way, Nico's childhood had been as difficult as her own. Growing up without physical affection had affected him badly, and any chance of him cultivating the semblance of a normal relationship had been snuffed out with one moment of failure.

What kind of twisted world did she live in where she finally found someone she trusted enough to place her heart in his hands only to learn he was unable to care for it? Or was it that he was unwilling to try?

Nico had pulled himself up and created a multi-national empire from nothing but his own blood and sweat. More than anything that proved he had the drive and motivation to succeed when the prize was something he really wanted.

But if there was one thing she knew about her soon-to-be-ex-husband it was that failure would not be tolerated, and being dumped by his first—only—girlfriend would definitely have been classified as failure.

The bloody coward.

'I was getting worried about you,' Nico said when she finally left the bathroom. He was sitting on the edge of the bed, wearing clean, dry shorts. He'd draped a towel over the dressing table chair.

Rosa gazed at him coolly. 'You have nothing to worry about. I just needed some time alone to collect my thoughts.'

For a moment they stared at each other, until he got to his feet. 'You take the bed. I'm going to get some sleep in the saloon.'

It was eerie how similar their thought processes could be. How long had it been since she'd formed her own intention to sleep in the saloon?

Clenching her teeth together, she jerked a nod. 'Take one of the blankets off the bed.'

'No, you'll need it.'

'I'll double the other one up. Please—take it.' Could she *be* any more polite? It certainly beat scratching his eyes out, but it was not, she assumed, half as satisfying.

'If you're sure?'

'I'm sure.' To prove it, she helped him remove the top blanket and folded it together for him, then thrust it with more force than necessary into his arms.

Done, his arms piled with pillows and the blanket, Nico cast her one last look which she was not quick enough to escape from. 'Are you sure you'll be all right on your own?'

'Of course I will.' She forced a smile. 'Goodnight.'

'Goodnight, Rosa.'

Alone, she was all too aware of the ferocious storm raging against the yacht. Yet it was nothing compared to the agonies taking place within her.

Slumping on the bed, she wrapped the remaining blanket around herself, then raised her arm to switch the lights off. Seeing as she had the cabin to herself, she opted to keep the dimmers above the bed on, dulling them to a muted glow.

Without Nico there the mattress felt much too large, as if she could roll over and over and never reach the edge.

Even with all the pillows he had taken there were still half a dozen left for her. She sniffed them in turn. None of them held his scent. Which was a good thing. Why torment herself further? She was no masochist. She hugged one to her chest and tried not to think of how much more comforting it would be if it smelt like her husband.

After two hours spent trying to fall asleep, she was on the verge of screaming or crying. It took everything she had to stop herself doing either.

She had spent the vast majority of her life sleeping alone. She had slept through storms before. Plenty of them.

But no other storm had been so loud. Somehow it was worse being inside and on the top deck. There was hardly anything to muffle the deafening noise.

At least worrying about the storm prevented her from thinking too much about Nico. She really didn't want to think about him, or about the future she had only just accepted could be hers but had been snatched away before she'd had a smidgeon of time to enjoy it.

As the minutes slowly passed the anger that had first

seeded when she had hidden in the bathroom fertilised and began to grow.

Had any of it been real?

They were so good together. As a lover, Nico was incomparable. Or maybe it was her reaction to him that was incomparable?

It had certainly felt real. There had not been an iota of doubt in her mind that the hedonistic rush she had experienced in his arms had been reciprocated. Surely he had not faked his desire for her?

Her experiences with men were limited in the extreme. Stephen had been the first man to get anywhere with her, and it had taken him months of trying for her to agree to a date. After sleeping with him for the first time she had been completely underwhelmed but, having nothing to compare it with, had not been too bothered. She would have been perfectly happy never to see him again but he had been so keen it would have been cruel to end it. Or so she had thought. Maybe it would have been better to have ended it then, before he had time to become more infatuated with her.

She'd never had any illusions, though. Stephen's infatuation had stemmed from her distance. Always he'd tried to chip away at her barriers, but he hadn't been able to smash them down fast enough. Rosa was too accomplished at rebuilding them.

Those barriers had been for her own protection. Being rejected and turned away by her Russian foster mother, a woman she had come to trust and love, had been the last straw. She had sworn *never again*. It had not been conscious. It had been self-protection.

Hindsight was a wonderful thing. Only now could she see how badly she had treated Stephen. She had refused to let him in. And then, after it was all over, she had committed the cardinal sin and—

A bolt of lightning streaked past the yacht, illuminating the cabin in a brief prism of light.

Burying her head under a pillow, she tried to muffle out the storm and her tormented thoughts.

No, she thought. Whatever wrongs she had done to Stephen, surely she did not deserve this burning pain stabbing into her chest, or the nausea just a deep breath away from spilling out? She had never meant to hurt him—especially in the manner she had at their final parting. But she had been so low. So vulnerable. The man she had longed to share her birthday with—her husband—had been too busy to return home. And she had needed human company so badly. With Stephen it had never been real. Not for her.

What she and Nico had shared *had* been real. For two perfect days and nights it had been real. At least for her.

The cabin door opened and she threw the pillow off her head and snapped her head up.

Nico stood at the threshold and gazed at her, his hair sticking up all over the place.

Did he realise his shorts were undone, resting on his hipbones by the slimmest of margins?

For a moment she forgot to breathe.

'I just wanted to check you were okay,' he said, sounding uncomfortable.

'Me? I'm fine.' She didn't know whether she wanted to kiss his face off or throw something at him.

'Liar.' His grin was weak. 'I'll leave you to sleep. Goodnight.'

About to wish him a goodnight in turn, Rosa opened her mouth. 'Was any of it real?'

He cocked his head back. 'Sorry?'

'You and me? What we shared? When me made love? When we explored King Island together? When you treated me like a beautiful princess? Did you mean any of it?'

She watched his magnificent chest rise sharply before he nodded, his eyes a burning fire of intensity. 'It was the best time of my life.'

His chest rose again and he twisted round to leave.

'Don't go.'

'Sorry?'

'Stay with me. Just for tonight.'

Leaning against the doorframe in a pose she found achingly familiar, he lasered her with his eyes, his brow knotted in concentration. 'Do you know what you are asking?'

She nodded.

She knew exactly what she was asking. What they had shared had been the most incredible experience of her life. She had come alive in his arms and it had been glorious. But, more than simply wanting a repeat, she needed to reclaim something. Her pride. This time tomorrow they would be back on Butterfly Island and the forced intimacy between them would be gone. This would be her last chance to let things end on *her* terms. She would no longer allow Nico to dictate everything.

Whether he admitted it to himself or not, he had used her. It had not been intentional, that much she could appreciate, but it did not change the facts. *My definition of that was for us to continue exactly as we were with sex thrown into the mix.* Had he seriously thought she would want a relationship based solely on sex?

All that time and energy he had spent on seducing her she had blithely believed he was attempting to build something special between them.

All that time he had known he would never be able to love her. Not because he was incapable, as he so obviously believed, but because he was too much of a bloody coward even to try.

He had smashed through every one of her defences with

the subtlety of a battering ram but was too scared to put his own defences on the line.

And to her that was unforgiveable.

Well, now it was her turn to use him. But she would not lower herself to using subterfuge. When they went their separate ways she would leave with her head held high.

CHAPTER THIRTEEN

ROSA THREW OFF the sheet and swung her legs off the bed. 'One last time,' she said, padding towards him.

Nico continued to stare at her, immovable, his face unreadable. Except for his eyes. His eyes burned with swirling intensity.

When she reached him, she placed her hands palm-down on his chest, savouring the rapid thrum of his heartbeat.

His chest heaved. His Adam's apple moved as he swallowed.

Looking down, she could see the outline of an erection straining against his shorts. A wave of power rushed through her.

Nico's desire was for *her*.

She lightly traced his smooth skin, the tips of her fingers lacing through the silky black hair, moving on to make circular motions around the dusky nipples which were almost in line with her mouth. Without thinking, she pressed a kiss to one whilst gently pinching the other.

His breathing deepened but he remained still. As she tasted the saltiness of his skin the ache that had lain dormant all day, submerged under a tsunami of anger and grief, roared back to life.

Nico roared back to life too, capturing her cheeks in his

hands and tilting her face upwards. 'You are playing with fire,' he said, his voice a thick groan.

She stared into those magnetic green eyes, which even without the benefit of her glasses were so clearly striking, and slid her hands up and over his shoulders, hooking them around his neck. 'Maybe. But this time I have no intention of getting burned. Now, kiss me.'

Bringing her face close enough to catch the warmth of his breath, he crushed her lips in a kiss that demanded full possession. And full possession was what she gave in return. In the fraction of a second their tongues were duelling, her body flattened against his.

His hands slid away from her face, snaking round to the back of her scalp, where he raked his fingers through her hair before gathering it together.

He broke away and tugged her hair back, angling her chin up. 'Are you sure you want this?'

In answer, she pulled out of his hold and took a step back. She yanked her T-shirt off and threw it on the floor. 'Does this answer your question?'

Witnessing the desire in his eyes sent a powerful bolt of need running through her. She closed the gap between them, deliberately pressing her naked breasts against his bare torso, and squeezed his bottom.

He moved to kiss her again, but she stopped him with a hand to his chest, brushing his nipple with her mouth before covering his entire chest with her lips and tongue, moving lower down to his flat navel, and further still to his low-slung shorts.

When she had first met Nico she had refused to acknowledge the raw masculinity that emanated off him in waves. Somehow she had blanked it out, pretended it didn't exist. Now, the testosterone that seemed to seep out of his pores merged with the feminine hormones *he* had conjured in her and she revelled in his virility, welcomed it as her due.

As his shorts were already unbuttoned, it was a simple matter of tugging the sides to make them drop to his ankles and release his erection, which stood to throbbing attention. Rosa had always considered the male member unsightly, but Nico's was glorious: long and thick and satin-smooth to the touch.

His heavy breathing became ragged when she dropped to her knees and took him inside her mouth, gently cupping his balls as she pleasured him. Or was the pleasure all her own? With every groan that came from his throat, with every dig of his fingers into her scalp, her own need grew.

'God, Rosa,' he said hoarsely, pulling away, although he kept a hand gripped firmly in her hair. 'You're going to make me come.'

'That *is* the point, isn't it?'

He emitted what she assumed to be a laugh before pulling her up onto her feet and stepping out of his shorts. The laughter left his face. 'I want to come in you.'

The moisture that had been bubbling gently at the apex of her thighs heated to an almost unbearable level. Wrapping her arms around his neck, she pressed herself against him, holding on tightly for fear her legs would give way.

Somehow he shuffled them to the bed and laid her down, his mouth reclaiming hers in a fury of passion, arms and legs entwined. Only her lacy knickers provided any barrier to relief. Nico dealt with them the best way: by ripping them off and throwing the scraps to one side. Immediately his hand was *there*, his palm rubbing gently against her bud.

'Spread your legs,' he demanded between kisses when she clamped her thighs together to trap his hand.

She obeyed, spreading her thighs, groaning when he dipped a finger into the hot moistness and increased the friction.

'Go with it,' he urged, then dipped his head to capture a puckered nipple in his mouth, his hand still moving at a steady tempo.

His mouth was everywhere, smothering her breasts, and then his tongue was trailing down to her rounded belly until he was there, replacing his hand with his tongue and burying himself in her heat.

It was too much. Already a burning mass, the pulsating pressure inside her spilt over. Crying out, she arched her back and came in waves of riotous colour.

There was no time for her to glory in the wonder of it. No sooner had the pulsations started to abate than Nico was sheathed—from where, she knew not, and cared even less—and inside her, filling her completely.

She moaned and ran her nails down his back.

He thrust into her, over and over, in a frenzied coupling of pure need. She grabbed his buttocks and drove him deeper, their tongues clashing ferociously as they kissed and nipped and pulled at each other's lips.

He stilled and breathed deeply into her ear. 'I don't want to come yet.' He hooked an arm around her waist and rolled onto his back. Somehow he manoeuvred her with him, without breaking the intimate connection between them, so she was straddling him. His hands rested on her hips. 'I want to watch you come on me.'

His words very nearly did it.

She took a ragged breath and closed her eyes.

Without even realising, she had allowed him to take control again.

Now all the power was back in *her* hands.

She leaned forward to cradle his head in her hands and began to move. She wanted to take her time. Like Nico, she wanted to savour it.

'That's it, my angel, let yourself go.' He captured a breast in his mouth and sucked, sending a bolt of pleasure through to her core.

She ground herself on him, almost flat against him, rubbing their groins together. With his hands at her waist, his tongue making such magic on her nipples and his erection filling her, she forgot herself completely.

How badly she wanted to hold on, to make the most of every thrilling second. But she could not. Nico bucked beneath her, a ring of perspiration breaking out on his brow. He flung his head back and with a cry that seemed to come from his very depths thrust upwards into her, the complete fulfilment and friction sending her over the edge and into the stars.

It took an age before the pulses zipping through every part of her lessened enough for sanity to break free.

She was slumped on him, her face buried in his neck. One of his arms was wrapped tightly around her waist, the other hand making circular motions up and down her back.

She did not want to move. She could happily stay there for ever, locked in his arms in the most intimate way imaginable.

But of course that was impossible.

'Where are you going?' he asked, his voice thick.

'You need to get rid of the condom.' She slid off him and slumped onto her back, taking great pains to keep her voice neutral. 'By the way, where did you get it from?'

'It was on the floor.'

She almost smiled as she recalled him ripping open a large box of them, half the contents spilling everywhere.

He turned onto his side and traced a finger down her stomach. 'I'll be back in a minute.'

Despite herself, she watched his retreating figure stride to the *en suite* bathroom and marvelled anew at the muscular perfection of his broad back, the tight buttocks and the powerful thighs. Oh, but he was perfect. How wonderful it would be to fall asleep wrapped in the security of his arms. It could not happen, though. Not now. It was too late for that.

She expelled a puff of air and wrapped herself in the blanket, closing her eyes when she heard the toilet flush.

When Nico had finished in the bathroom and returned to bed, he found himself confronted by the coldness of Rosa's back. 'Are you all right?'

'Sleepy. G'night.'

Resting on an elbow, he blinked in shock. 'Is that it?'

'It was just sex, Nico. Go to sleep.'

She had to be joking. Except, judging by her low rhythmic breathing, this was no joke.

Whilst disposing of the condom he had mentally braced himself for one more sleep with Rosa wrapped all over him. It had been the strangest feeling ever, sleeping with the warmth of another pressed against him. Instead of withdrawing, as every instinct had told him to do, he had told himself it would be too cruel. The few times he had shifted slightly Rosa had closed the gap in an instant. It was almost as if she had been afraid to lose the physical contact. This from a woman who had always shied away from human affection.

Tonight there was none of that. Her back was firmly placed towards him, cocooned in the blanket. The only thing she hugged was a pillow.

Relief should be coursing through his veins.

So how come the only emotion distinguishable through the rivers raging through him was disappointment?

Ending their marriage was the right decision. Of that he had no doubt. Rosa needed so much more than he could ever give.

As much as it twisted his guts and made his skin feel as if a nest of wasps were freely stinging him, he prayed with every fibre of his being that she would find it.

* * *

Rosa trained the powerful binoculars on Butterfly Island. Without them it was but a speck in the distance. With them she could see the mountainous backdrop and its verdant greenery darkening as the sun made its descent. It wouldn't be long now.

For once she had risen before Nico. She had deliberately left him sleeping. She'd had no wish for a post-mortem on her behaviour in the early hours of the morning. She still didn't know where that wantonness had come from, but she did not regret it.

Nico had hurt her. Really hurt her. It was as if he had reached a hand into her heart and ripped it out without anaesthetic. Making love on *her* terms had done little to mitigate the hurt, but it had allowed her to regain some control. Turning her back on him had felt like a fitting finale.

The more she played events in her head—over and over, as if on a loop—the higher her temperature rose. Whilst she felt desperately sorry for the pain he had gone through, and the experiences that had shaped him into the man he was today, she struggled to forgive him.

Her initial instincts had proven correct. Nico had played with her as if she were an unwanted toy another child had tried to steal. Before she had told him about Stephen and asked for a divorce his interest in her sexually had been zero. He'd liked their marriage because it suited *him*. He'd decided to have sex with her because it suited *him*.

Not once had he asked himself if it suited her too.

No, Mr Arrogant had not bothered to look beyond the surface. He had assumed she would be happy to continue in a loveless, emotionless marriage as long as he took care of her physical needs. As soon as he'd discovered she was more complicated than he had credited, he'd done a U-turn so swift her neck had almost cricked again.

He wasn't even prepared to try forging a proper relationship, and he had twisted this cowardice to make it sound s if he was doing her a favour.

Last night she had made love to him because it had suited *her.* For once she had put her own needs first. And now her hurt was gone. Other than what she considered to be justifiable anger she felt nothing. All that resided inside her was a black void.

Her anger abated slightly into concern a short while later, when Nico came into the saloon from their cabin, where he had been changing before they docked, his phone clutched in his hand. One look at his ashen face was enough for her to know something was wrong.

'What's the matter?' she asked, half rising from the table she was sitting at.

He slumped into the chair opposite her and dragged a hand down his face. 'My father's had a stroke. They don't think he's going to make it.'

Thank God for Rosa.

As Nico was driven from Moscow airport to the private hospital holding his father, the image of his wife's calm efficiency soothed him.

He had never before understood the saying *A burden shared is a burden halved.* Now he did. Rosa had immediately comprehended the urgency of the situation and, breaking him out of his stupor, had set up a plan of action. He'd had no hesitation in granting her Power of Attorney. The contracts with Robert King would go ahead with Rosa's signature on the documents.

Knowing his business could not be in better hands had freed him to concentrate on the minutiae of his travel arrangements. The doctor had told him in no uncertain terms they were talking *days*. At the most. It had been imperative to become airborne as soon as possible.

Now, as the car pulled up alongside the hospital entrance, he knew his debt to Rosa could never be repaid. His father was hanging on. Because of Rosa Nico would be given the opportunity to say goodbye to the man who had given him life and raised him.

An austere nurse was waiting for him at the main door. Her calm efficiency reminded him of Rosa. He followed her down wide corridors to a wing that was as silent as it was stark. He had spent the day-long journey mentally preparing himself for what he was about to see, but when the nurse opened the door to his father's private room he realised all the time in the world could not have prepared him.

His father, a person he always envisaged in his mind's eye as a giant of a man, had shrivelled. His skin—what could be seen of it behind all the tubes and the oxygen mask connected to him—had become translucent and had a powdery hue to it. When he pressed his fingers gently to the cool forehead he half expected a residue to adhere to the tips.

Mikhail Baranski opened his eyes.

Nico had to act quickly to smother his shock. All his father's vibrancy had gone. It looked as if someone had placed Clingfilm over his eyeballs.

Through the mask Nico could see his father trying to talk. As far as he was aware Mikhail had not uttered a word since the stroke occurred.

'I am going to take the mask off,' he said to the nurse who was hovering behind him.

'That is not advisable.'

He quelled her with a look. 'I wasn't asking permission.'

If she'd wanted to argue about it, whatever she saw in Nico's eyes warned her of the futility. Instead she turned on her heel and left the room—no doubt to find a doctor and report him.

Alone with his father, Nico pulled a chair as close as he could to the bed without knocking any of the equipment and took a seat. He lifted the mask, taking care not to remove it completely.

'Nicolai?' Only the right-hand side of Mikhail's mouth worked, and his words were a laborious slur.

'I'm here, Papa,' he said, clasping his fingers around Mikhail's withered hand.

The shrunken chest heaved. 'Your wife? Here?'

'Rosa?' Nico had to fight the instinct to squeeze his fingers at the mention of her. His father felt so fragile he feared he would snap the bones in his hand. 'No, she's not here.'

The filmy eyes blinked. Was that reproach he detected in them?

And then it came to him. The last time he had seen his father a few short months ago he had promised he would bring Rosa on his next visit. In one of his more sober moments Mikhail had confessed a longing to meet his daughter-in-law. Nico had thought it wise not to confide that his marriage was one of convenience. He'd had a gut feeling his father would not approve.

Mikhail took another deep breath. 'Picture?'

'You want to see a picture of Rosa?'

A blink.

'Let me check my wallet.' He knew the gesture was pointless. Why would he carry a picture of Rosa with him? But to say that would be cruel.

After replacing the oxygen mask securely, he dug into his back pocket and pulled out his wallet. He opened it and pretended to rummage through it, stopping short when his fingers brushed the creased edge of a photo he had not looked at properly for a decade.

With hands that were not quite steady he pulled it out and stared at the faded picture of his mother. The colour quality had dulled dramatically over the years, but nothing could diminish the vibrancy of her ebony hair or the sweetness of her smile.

'I'm sorry, Papa,' he said quietly. 'I don't seem to have a picture of Rosa on me.'

Mikhail's eyes fixed on the small photo in Nico's hands.

'It's a picture of Mama,' he explained, turning it over and bringing it close to his father's eyes.

For an age nothing was said. He was about to place it back in his wallet when a tear leaked down Mikhail's sunken cheek.

'Papa?'

The filmy eyes were fixed back on him, beseeching him.

Understanding his father was trying to talk, Nico removed the mask again.

'Katerina.' His mother's name came out like a long, rattly sigh.

His chest tight, unsure if he was doing the right thing, Nico held the picture inches from his father's face.

A light came into his father's eyes, and a look of contentment stole across the distorted face. Mikhail drew in another long whistling breath. 'My Katerina.'

Such was his father's stillness as he stared at the thirty-five-year-old picture that for the time it took his heart to leap into his mouth and begin to choke him Nico feared he had slipped away.

Only when the filmy eyes blinked and refocused on him did Nico start to breathe again. In his heart he knew it wouldn't be long. The time elapsing between each rattling, whistling breath was increasing. His father could not hold on much more.

Placing his mother's picture on the pillow, he leaned over

and, for the very first time, pressed his lips to his father's forehead. His senses were consumed with a scent that was both familiar and yet also wholly unknown—a scent that clutched at him and twisted his guts. 'I love you, Papa.'

But Mikhail was spent. As he struggled to form words with lips that no longer worked Nico placed a finger to them.

'It's all right. I know you love me. You've always loved me.'

And as he looked into the diminishing light of his father's eyes—eyes that contained such love and, strangely, such peace—he knew it to be true. He could feel it in every atom of his being.

Rosa's words came back to him. *'It took guts for him to keep you. He must love you very much.'*

His beautiful Rosa. A woman who had known such darkness, yet had thrown off the shackles of fear and reached for the light. A woman who had reached into his black heart and coloured it. The woman whose face was the very one he would want to see when the time came for *him* to leave this earth.

Mikhail's eyes were no longer seeing. Even so, Nico held his mother's picture before him and stroked the cooling forehead, the tears pouring down his cheeks falling like rain, soaking them both.

CHAPTER FOURTEEN

ROSA READ THE message one more time.

I'll be back in London early tomorrow evening. There are things we need to discuss. Appreciate you meeting me at the house. Regards, Nico.

'Tomorrow evening' had now arrived, and as she punched in the security code at the gate with clammy fingers she felt all *bitty*—as if the working parts of her body had fragmented and none of the connecting parts knew how to work together any more.

This would be the first time she had seen him since Butterfly Island. He had been in Moscow for the past ten days, dealing with his father's funeral and sorting out the legalities.

In all the conversations they'd had since he'd left, only one had driven into personal territory. Nico had called her shortly after his father had passed away. He had wanted to thank her. His voice had been so bereft that she had felt any residue of anger vanish on the spot. Well, most of it had. It had been hard to hold on to it after witnessing the sheer devastation in his eyes when he had told her of his father's stroke.

But she needed that tiny residue. Without it a black pit of despair beckoned, and she couldn't afford to fall into it.

Even so, she had been unable to hold back the tears. When

the call had ended she had sunk onto the floor and cried for them—for the future they would never have—and then she had cried for Nico and his father. The urge to get the soonest flight to Moscow so she could be there for him had at times overwhelmed her. The day of Mikhail Baranski's funeral had been especially hard to endure. Thinking of Nico grieving alone had cut her like ribbons. *She should have been with him.*

But he'd relied on her to see the deal with Robert King through, and she had been determined to see it through properly. In any case, he wouldn't have wanted her there—not his soon-to-be-ex-wife.

In the end, the contracts had been signed without any fuss. Robert had been as determined to see as smooth a progression as she was. Six days later she had returned to the UK to step into Nico's shoes at his London office. Since then all their conversations had been entirely work-related.

Intuition told her this meeting was *not* work-related. This was personal. This could only be about their divorce.

She drove through the gate and parked on the gravel at the front of the house.

The front door swung open before she could climb the steps.

'Hello, Rosa.'

Her heart tripped. She paused and gazed at him. 'Hello, Nico.'

As all her recent memories were of him wearing shorts and nothing else, it was startling to see him decked out in an impeccably ironed white shirt and grey trousers. They provided a stark contrast with the rumpled look of his face. With large bags under his bloodshot eyes, he looked as if he hadn't slept in months. His hair was as messy as ever, which she found strangely comforting.

'Why haven't you parked in the garage?'

'It seemed a bit pointless, seeing as I shan't be staying

long.' At least she *hoped* she wouldn't be staying too long. At that moment she was doing an admirable imitation of nonchalance, but it was hurting every sinew in her body to keep it up.

Work, as always, had been her salvation. Throwing herself into the contracts and then ensuring Nico's empire ran smoothly in his unexpected absence had enabled her to push aside all the pain. And if she'd lived on a diet of strong coffee, unable to stomach food in a belly that ached, then so be it. Anything had to better than having time to think.

Now, standing before him, she was overwhelmed with how badly she had missed him.

He inclined his head and stood aside to admit her.

'Where's Gloria?' she asked, automatically kicking her shoes off as she stepped into the reception room. For a split-second she searched for her slippers, before remembering they were at the hotel she would call home for the next few weeks, until she could move back into her old flat.

She hadn't been able to face returning to the empty house. Gloria had kindly brought all her possessions to the hotel for her. If she had an opinion on Rosa moving out, she had kept it to herself.

'I sent her home,' Nico said.

She followed him into the kitchen, blinking in disbelief. She hadn't expected them to be alone.

'It's all right,' Nico said, correctly reading her thoughts. 'I wanted some privacy for our talk. Coffee? Or something stronger?'

'Seeing as I'm driving, I'll have coffee, thank you. Instant will be fine.' She didn't want to hang around while he faffed with the percolator. She wanted to get this conversation over with and return to the privacy of her hotel room and lick her wounds.

While he made their drinks she could not help but gaze at him. He turned his head and caught her staring.

Something intangible yet very real passed between them—something that pulled and tugged inside her. He had lost weight. She was certain of it.

'How are you? I mean really?' she asked softly.

His lips curved into a rueful smile. 'Better now you're here.'

Before she could react to that answer, he'd turned back and poured the boiling water into cups, giving both a vigorous stir.

He picked them up and walked past her. 'Let's go and sit in the living room.'

Rosa took her usual seat on the far sofa and waited for Nico to take *his* usual seat opposite, with the coffee table dividing them. Instead, after setting their drinks down, he took the armchair closest to her.

'How did the funeral go?' It was something she had wanted to ask for days, but as he had led all the conversations between them since and kept them on a strict work footing, the moment had never felt right. She half expected him to dismiss the question now and dive straight into their divorce talks.

'It was very nice,' he said, before adding heavily, 'If a funeral can ever be described as *nice*. A lot of people came.' His eyes lightened at the reminiscence. 'The church was full of drunks. At one point I thought they would throw empty bottles instead of dirt onto the coffin.'

She snickered before she could stop herself, relieved he could still find some sunshine at such an awful time. 'I really am sorry.'

'I know you are. But he is happy now. He's where he's wanted to be for over three decades. With my mother.' He sighed heavily and reached for his coffee. 'When I was sorting through his stuff I discovered boxes he had kept that I did not know existed. They were full of love letters and mementoes, all between him and my mother.'

Resting his elbows on his knees, he took a sip of the scalding coffee.

'I also found the diary he kept for the first few years after she died. It made illuminating reading. All my life I assumed he drank out of boredom. I knew he was an alcoholic, but I always thought the root cause of it…' He shook his head. 'He never got over her death. He drank to numb the pain. Raising me was the only thing that got him out of bed in the morning.'

Rosa sat ramrod-straight, hardly daring to breathe, afraid to utter a word. Despite their impending divorce, Nico was sharing confidences out of choice. A huge part of her yearned to wrap her arms around him, hold him close and soothe all his pain away.

He fixed his beautiful, tired green eyes on her and smiled. 'Don't be sad for him, or for me. He is with her now, and there is no other place he would rather be. He left this world happy his only son had settled. His only regret—*my* only regret—was that he never got to meet you.'

He must have seen the shock she was not quick enough to hide. 'I told him all about you—about your intelligence and your sense of fair play and your refusal to judge people.' His lips quirked. 'Unless they look like supermodels.' His features straightened, his eyes penetrating. 'I never cared to think of the reasons why you shied away from women like that. I was so self-absorbed at the beginning of our marriage it never occurred to me there was an underlying reason for your insecurity.'

'Other than being an unremarkable frump?' she couldn't resist retorting, thrown completely off-balance at this turn in the conversation.

Her equilibrium was knocked further off-kilter when he reached over and pressed a warm hand to her neck. 'If it takes the rest of my life I swear one day you will look in the mirror and see the beauty *my* eyes see when they look at you.'

'You don't have to try and sweet-talk me,' she said, edging away from him. 'Not any more.'

'I'm not trying to sweet-talk you.'

'Then what *are* you doing?'

He closed his eyes, then placed his cup on the table and moved to the sofa next to her, his thigh brushing against hers. When he spoke, his voice was low. 'I need to ask you something and I want you to promise to tell me the truth.' He grabbed her hand and placed it on his lap. 'Promise me the truth, Rosa.'

It was the urgency in his voice that made her nod her agreement. She had not the faintest idea what could be so important. 'I promise.'

'Why did you really go out with Stephen on your birthday? And why did it end so badly?'

He might as well have stuck a pin in her. Slumping back, she closed her eyes.

'Look at me,' he commanded. 'I need to know. It matters a great deal to me.'

'Why?' she whispered, keeping her eyes shut.

'Because ever since you told me you slept with your ex it has felt as if my stomach has had acid thrown into it.'

She tried frantically to swallow away the brick that had lodged in her throat. Of all the things he could ask her, why this? And why now? And what the heck did he mean about acid?

'You promised.'

His deep voice rumbled in her ear.

'Please, Rosa. I need to know.'

'I went out with Stephen because I was hurt that you stood me up. Actually, scratch that. I was *devastated* that you stood me up.' There. She had dredged the words out.

She waited for him to respond, but after a few too many seconds of silence she opened her eyes. Nico, his face inches from her own, was staring at her with an intensity she had never seen before.

He slowly inclined his head. 'Go on.'

'It wasn't just about you,' she admitted with a sigh. 'Although that was a big factor in it. I'd been feeling low—I'd made contact with my brother…'

'You did what?'

'I contacted my brother.'

'You never told me.'

She shrugged helplessly. 'You weren't there to tell. And it was personal—not part of our deal, remember?'

It was Nico's turn to close his eyes. 'I remember.'

'I'd convinced myself that now he was an adult he might want to get to know his big sister. So I wrote to him asking to meet up.'

'What happened?'

'He texted me back. He said he was very busy, but if he ever found the time he would get in touch.' She expelled air through her nose and shook her head. 'He blew me out. He didn't want to know me any more than our mother did when she was alive.'

It was only when Rosa yelped that Nico realised he was squeezing her hand hard enough to cause her pain. 'I'm sorry,' he muttered, removing it and placing it very carefully on her thigh.

Every time he heard about the callous treatment meted out to her by her so-called family he wanted to punch something to ease the rage that screamed through his blood.

He knew how much it must have cost her to write to her brother in the first place and what a low place she must have been in even to go down that route. He could only imagine the torment she'd suffered when her brother rejected her too.

What was *wrong* with these people? How could they treat their own flesh and blood with such cruel indifference?

Very soon he would tell her something that should ease the suffering caused by those bastards, tell her that his Australian investigator had found her great-aunt Myra and that Myra wanted to meet her. But first, selfish as he knew he was being, he needed to hear the rest of it.

'How soon before your birthday did all this happen?' He traced his fingers lightly over her hand, his chest constricting when he realised she had removed her wedding ring.

Its absence felt like a punch in the gut.

'A week or so.'

A week. A whole week for it to fester before he had called on the day of her birthday and told her he wouldn't be able to make it home. His cowardice at a time when she'd needed him had driven her into the arms of another.

No wonder she had removed her ring. He was only surprised she hadn't removed it sooner. It would have been no more than he deserved.

'I'm sorry. I should have been there.'

'Why? How could you have known? It wasn't—'

'I know: it wasn't part of our pact,' he finished for her, before confessing, 'I could have made it back if I had wanted to. I already knew a couple of days before your birthday that I wouldn't be investing in the Moroccan site.'

'Oh.'

The feeling of her shriveling next to him splintered through him like shattered glass. Any guilt he had felt was magnified by a hundred. 'I kept dreaming of you.'

'Oh?'

Nico laughed mirthlessly. He had known this evening would be difficult. He had also known the only way they could forge a future together—a proper future—was to lay all their cards on the table. Reading through the letters exchanged between his parents, learning of the strength of their devotion to each other and seeing the sheer honesty in the emotions on the page had been a revelation. Nothing had been held back between them.

Now he and Rosa had to find that level of emotional honesty. As Rosa knew to her cost, the spoken word could cause irreparable damage. But, as he had come to realise over recent times, the unspoken word could cause just as much harm.

He drained his coffee and turned to face her. Unable to resist, he palmed her cheek, taking comfort from its softness. 'When you told me you'd slept with Stephen I felt sucker-punched.'

Her warm caramel eyes widened a fraction.

'Forget all the excuses I've made to you and myself. The truth is I've used Galina as an excuse to avoid proper relationships because I tasted failure and I did not like it. Until then I had never failed at anything I set my mind to. I assumed my coldness was a result of my childhood, and I accepted that and used it as weapon to prevent myself from tasting failure again. Looking back, I can see it never occurred to me my ambivalence towards Galina was because I was not in love with her.'

Rosa's forehead wrinkled in that adorable manner it always did when she tried to comprehend something.

'I spent months denying I felt any attraction for you. Your refusal to work for me permanently was, I admit, a blow to my ego, but with hindsight I can see it was more than that. I knew I had no proprietary rights over you, but I have never felt such anger and such pain as I did in those minutes when I thought you were leaving me for Stephen.'

'But—'

'Please, let me finish,' he said, brushing her lips with his thumb. 'We had agreed to what should be every red-blooded man's dream—an open marriage. It didn't even occur to me until you told me you wanted to leave that I'd never made use of that freedom.'

If her eyes widened any further he feared they might pop out.

'What? Never?'

He shook his head solemnly. 'Never. There were opportunities, but I never felt the slightest urge to act on them. Since we married you have been the only woman in my head. There is no room for anyone else. I can fight it all I want—and, believe me, I have been fighting it hard—but it doesn't change the facts. Somewhere over the past year you have crept under my skin and into my heart.'

It twisted that heart to watch her blink rapidly, trying her best to hold back the tears brimming in her eyes.

'Why are you telling me all this?' she asked, her chin wobbling.

'Because I love you. And I want you to come home. Not because of work, not because I want to make love to you every hour of the day—which I do—but because living without you is torture.' As the words rolled off his tongue a huge weight shifted in its vice-like hold on his chest.

A solitary tear rolled down her cheek. She wiped it away in a furious motion. 'You are a complete and utter bastard.'

'Yes.' He could not deny it.

'And a coward.'

'Yes.'

'You really hurt me.'

'I know.' Imagining what he had put her through cut him like ribbons. 'I swear I will spend the rest of my life making it up to you. If you will let me.'

He swallowed, waiting for her to speak.

He had known laying his heart on the line was a risk. He had known it could end in failure. But not trying was no longer an option. He needed Rosa. Without her by his side it had become impossible to function properly.

Time stretched beyond all measure. The only sound was their quickening breaths.

'I called him by your name,' she blurted out, her neck suffused with colour.

He stilled. 'Sorry?'

'It was horrible. I should never have gone back to his flat. I should never have…' Her voice tailed off and she swallowed. When she spoke again her voice was a whisper. 'We never finished what we started. I only endured what we *did* do by closing my eyes and pretending he was you. And then I called him by your name. And he got understandably angry and threw me out.'

Shock paralysed him. For long moments his brain struggled to understand what she had said. 'He threw you out? On the street? In London? In the middle of the night?'

She nodded and wiped away another tear with a scowl. 'I can't blame him. He assumed I was going back to him. When he realised I was in love with you…'

His pulse accelerated. 'You *love* me?'

'Of course I love you,' she whispered, her face white and pinched. 'I think I've been in love with you since we married.'

Now it was his brain struggling to comprehend. 'So why ask for a divorce?'

'Because I knew staying with you would destroy me. I knew I was nothing but a convenience. Going with Stephen that night, as horrible as it was, made me realise how much I felt for you. Every time you went abroad the loneliness became unbearable.' She shook her head wistfully. 'You had become so…ambivalent towards me. Thinking you felt nothing for me, imagining all the women you were sharing your bed with and thinking you would never look at me with the need I felt for you…' Her eyes closed. 'I couldn't bear it.'

He could hold on no more. Wrapping an arm around her, he pulled her to him and held her tightly, inhaling that sweet scent he had so missed. 'I love you, Rosa Baranski. You have no idea how much. You are everything to me.'

She expelled a sigh and tilted her face to look at him. 'I love you too. More than anything.'

'I'm scared,' he finally admitted, his chest heaving with the words.

'Of what?'

'Hurting you.

'You've already done that and I'm still standing. And, Nico, you can't put all the blame on your own shoulders. We're as bad as each other at keeping things internalised.'

'Not any more,' he vowed, clutching her hand and pressing it against his chest.

He had always needed his physical and mental space. And yet after spending three nights sharing a bed with Rosa sleeping alone had felt…well, *wrong* was the only way he could describe the strangeness of it all. And who else had he ever felt compelled to confide in? Who else's opinion did he value? No one. Just Rosa. Just his wife.

But what if he slipped back into his old, cold ways? He could not stomach the thought of causing her further pain. She had suffered enough in her life. They both had.

He'd closed his eyes when she palmed his cheek in turn. 'Nico, look at me,' she commanded in a tone she must have picked up from him.

When he opened them, he found her eyes full of such softness and love he feared his chest would burst from the pressure inside it.

'I am not expecting miracles and neither should you,' she said gently. 'You are who you are, and I wouldn't change anything about you—not even your bastard tendencies. Just as I am who *I* am, with all my insecurities. As long as we love each other, and are honest and committed to *us*, we can work anything out.'

His chest expanded at the faith and love reflecting from her eyes.

'It feels as if I have spent my entire life alone,' he said, keeping her hand tight against his chest, certain she could feel the hammering of his heart. 'But I never felt lonely. It wasn't until you left that I realised how empty and cold my life really was and how much I needed you. Without you, nothing is the same. Everything is wrong. You, *daragaya*, are everything to me.'

Her eyes didn't waver. 'And *you* are everything to me. You make me whole.'

He gripped her hand even tighter, his finger grazing the spot where her wedding ring should be. 'Marry me.'

Her brows furrowed into a question.

'Marry me—let's renew our wedding vows and do it properly this time. And this time the rings we exchange will mean everything they should have done when we first did it.'

Rosa's smile could have illuminated an entire city. 'I can't think of anything I want more. Yes. A hundred times yes.'

Hands snaking around each other's necks, they pulled together into a kiss full of such love and hope the last residue of self-doubt was dislodged and their hearts became complete.

* * * * *

MARRIAGE MADE OF SECRETS

BY
MAYA BLAKE

Maya Blake fell in love with the world of the alpha male and the strong, aspirational heroine when she borrowed her sister's Mills & Boon at age thirteen. Shortly thereafter the dream to plot a happy ending for her own characters was born. Writing for Mills & Boon is a dream come true. Maya lives in South East England with her husband and two kids. Reading is an absolute passion, but when she isn't lost in a book she likes to swim, cycle, travel and Tweet!

You can get in touch with her via e-mail at mayablake@ymail.com, or on Twitter: www.twitter.com/mayablake.

CHAPTER ONE

'SIGNORA?'

The voice, hesitant but insistent, jerked Ava from deep sleep. Momentarily disoriented, she pushed a swathe of Titian hair off her forehead but the nightmare…*that nightmare*…clung to the edges of her consciousness.

'I'm sorry to disturb you but *Signore* di Goia is on the phone. Again.' The stewardess, dressed in the emerald silk suit that displayed her employer's unique insignia, held out the sleek black phone. Ava eyed the phone, the same one she'd been presented with three times since the di Goia jet took off from Bali almost eight hours ago.

Different emotions replaced her irritation, dispersing the last of her dream-fuelled anxiety. The lingering sense of loss, which dogged her whenever she thought of Cesare, rose to mingle with the almost helpless excitement that thoughts of him elicited…

For a few seconds she forgot the heart-rending devastation she'd left behind. Her mind crowded with the forceful presence of the man at the end of the phone. A man who despite being thousands of miles away, had the power to make her breath catch. The man who she knew within the depths of her soul she was losing with every second that passed.

'Please tell him, again, that I'll speak to him when we land.' She needed to conserve every ounce of her strength for what lay ahead.

The stewardess looked bewildered. 'But…he insists.' No doubt she'd never encountered another living being who refused to fall at Cesare di Goia's feet. Especially when that being was currently ensconced in unspeakably sumptuous luxury that barely began to epitomise the mind-boggling scale of the di Goia experience.

All around her, from the deep burgundy leather club chairs, the shiny cream marble tables to the bespoke silk-trimmed cashmere throws that graced every seat on the jet that could easily have carried several dozen passengers, Cesare di Goia's wealth and influence made itself forcefully blatant.

'Signora?' the anxious stewardess pressed.

Guilt for her predicament made Ava reach for the phone.

'Cesare.' She held her breath.

'Now you deign to answer my calls,' came the deep, tight voice.

'Why should I take your call when you've been avoiding mine for over two weeks now? You told me you'd return to Bali last week.' The ease with which he'd put her off made her hand tighten on the phone. It was with much the same afterthought that he'd conducted their marriage for the last year.

'I was delayed in Abu Dhabi. Unavoidably,' he added tautly.

Unavoidably. How many times had she heard that before? 'Of course. Was that all?'

An exhalation of ire came down the line. 'No, that is *not* all. Explain yourself,' came the unyielding command.

'I take it you mean: why have I commandeered your plane?'

'Sì. This was not the plan.'

'I know, but my plans have changed too. *Unavoidably,*' she replied with a lightness she didn't feel.

'In what way have your plans changed?' he bit out.

'If you'd bothered to pick up the phone in the last two weeks, I would've told you.'

'We have spoken in the last two weeks—'

'No, Cesare, you called twice, both times to tell me you were postponing your return…' Her voice threatened to break as memories flooded her mind—her endless phone calls to Cesare's assistant to make sure his calendar was kept clear, shopping for the most enticing outfits and making sure the chef at the luxury rented villa in Bali prepared his favourite foods. She'd planned everything to the last detail…all in an effort to save her marriage. Only to have it backfire spectacularly. 'Anyway, I'm saving you the trouble of making the long trip, or of coming up with another excuse. Goodbye, Cesare.'

'Ava—'

She pressed the end button, cutting off the growled warning. She'd barely exhaled when the phone rang again. Carefully, she set it down on the table, unanswered.

The stunned look on the stewardess's face made Ava smile, despite the rush of her thundering pulse. 'Don't worry, his bark is worse than his bite.'

The woman coughed out an incoherent sound before hastily retreating to her station at the front of the plane.

With not quite steady hands, Ava poured a glass of water from the crystal-cut jug and took a tiny sip. Yes, Cesare ruled his world with unquestionable domination. But she'd never been one to ask *how high?* when told to jump, a fact which had, in the past, both intrigued and infuriated Cesare.

The past…before everything had settled into a passive indifference, before Cesare had slowly withdrawn from her, and chosen to stay in Rome more and more instead of at their home in Lake Como. Before the devastation of the South Pacific earthquake had shattered the last of her dreams of salvaging her family.

The decision she'd made so bravely in Bali yesterday

now caused a thread of anxiety to weave inside her. Despite her bravado, her legs shook as she pushed aside her throw and padded down the long cream-carpeted aisle of the plane towards the smaller of the two bedrooms.

She turned the door handle.

Annabelle lay fast asleep. Soft light from elegant lamps illuminated her daughter's raven hair and long limbs splayed on the bed.

Unable to resist, Ava raised the camera slung around her neck and took a few quick shots, grateful for the near-silent clicks of the digital device.

Retreating just as silently, Ava returned to her seat, desperately trying to calm the hordes of steel butterflies trying to beat their way out of her. The last thing she wanted was to return home an emotional wreck. Her grip tightened on the camera.

The past month had been tormenting enough but she needed to be stronger still. She would need to be to stop hiding and face the truth.

Marry in haste...

Her insides twisted in pain and anxiety. Their coming together had been fast and furious. Right from the beginning, things had careened out of control. She'd been swept away by a passion she'd been unable to stem or understand.

But even in that maelstrom of whirlwind dates and mind-bending sex, Cesare had *felt* like the home she craved, the very essence of the family she'd never really had.

For a time...

This insanity needs to end! Cesare's heated confession when he'd taken her without mercy one day in a closet during a benefit dinner slammed through her mind.

Ironically, she'd found out she was pregnant with Annabelle the very next day.

And Cesare had begun to withdraw from her.

Shaking her head, she slid up the window screen, let a sliver of morning light warm her cheek, wishing it would also thaw her through. But it was no use. Inside, she felt cold, hard pain.

No. She couldn't—*wouldn't*—let him do this to her. If for no other reason, Annabelle deserved a parent who wasn't bogged down with acrimony. She deserved a mother who was content, at the very least. The family she'd craved and thought she'd found with Cesare had been a mirage. The sexy, powerfully dynamic man she'd married had changed into a man as coldly indifferent to her as her father had been.

And in her desperate desire to hold onto the illusion of what she'd probably never had, she'd nearly lost her daughter.

Annabelle had been through enough and Ava had no intention of letting her daughter suffer any more rejection.

'What the hell do you think you're playing at?'

Cesare di Goia's deep, dark-as-sin voice had the power to arrest her in her tracks; as did his impressive, hard-packed six feet two frame. Dressed in a pristine white open-necked polo shirt and black designer jeans that hugged lean hips and disgustingly powerful thighs, he stood tall and proud like any of the hundreds of statues that graced his homeland's capital city.

His black hair, damp from a recent shower, sprang from his forehead, looking even thicker and longer than when she'd last seen him. And he still said exactly what he thought when he felt like it and to hell with whoever heard him.

Damn him.

'Frighten the living daylights out of my child, why don't you?' Ava invited with soft sarcasm, while trying to calm Annabelle's sleepy squirming.

Eyes the colour of burnished gold shifted to Annabelle and a small grimace crossed his face. 'She's asleep,' he stated.

'Not for long if you keep growling like that. She's been through enough, Cesare. I won't have her upset.'

Tension radiated off his darkly tanned skin, so palpable she fought not to withdraw from it. 'Don't speak as if she's a stranger to me, Ava. I know exactly what she's been through.' His tone was framed almost conversationally but, although his voice had lowered, the fury in his deep tawny eyes had escalated in direct proportion.

'Forgive me for having to remind you, only you seem to have forgotten. Just as you seem to have forgotten *us*. Annabelle's emotions are still fragile, so dial back the hulk-smash attitude if you please. As to what I'm playing at, I thought I'd made myself perfectly clear.'

'Do you mean that highly informative one-line text that read: *We will arrive at 2pm* you sent seconds before my plane took off from Bali or the equally cryptic *my plans have changed too?*' he accused, making no move to shift his imposing frame from the doorway.

'Both.'

'Ava…' His voice was pure warning.

'Seriously, are you going to move or do you intend to carry on this conversation on the doorstep? What are you doing here, anyway? You hardly come to the villa any more.' Another sign of Cesare's withdrawal she'd ignored for far too long. She stared into his eyes, ignoring the warning that glinted in his narrowed gaze.

'What I'm doing here doesn't matter. You were supposed to wait in Bali until Annabelle was given the all-clear. Then I would've come for you.'

'The doctor gave Annabelle the all-clear three days ago.'

Surprise lit his eyes, then he looked beyond her shoulder to the car, his gaze searching. 'And Rita?'

'She was having nightmares of the earthquake. Once she was discharged from hospital, I booked her a flight home to London. She's racked with guilt—she thinks she failed Annabelle because she let go of her when the tremors started…' Recalling the nanny's inconsolable distress, a lance of pain—one of many that seemed ever ready to cause damage—went through her. 'I thought it was easier this way.'

Despite his grim look, Cesare nodded. 'I'll make sure she receives the proper treatment and severance package. But *you* didn't have to make this journey yet—'

'No, Cesare. Rita wasn't the only one who needed the comfort of home. *You* were supposed to return to Bali two weeks ago, only you were in *Singapore,* then in *New York.*'

He shoved a hand through his hair. 'This isn't really a good time for us to be doing this.'

'There hasn't been a good time for a very long time, Cesare.' A wave of sadness threatened to drown her but she straightened her spine and stood tall.

Tendrils of hair clung to her neck. Against her bare shoulders, the late afternoon sun singed her skin. If she didn't get out of the northern Italian sun, she'd be as red as a lobster by morning. 'We're home now. You should thank me for saving you the trouble. Now, are you going to deal with it or has being under one roof with us become a problem for you?'

His nostrils flared and his gaze dropped to Annabelle. 'It isn't a problem.'

Ava's grip tightened around her precious bundle. 'That's a relief. I'd hate for you to be *inconvenienced.*'

With Annabelle getting heavier by the second, the weariness of trying to keep a nearly-four-year-old entertained on a twelve-hour plane journey dug bone-deep. But she struggled not to show any weakness as Cesare continued to glare at her, his impressive body blocking the massive oak doorway to the Villa di Goia.

'Ava, we should've discussed this properly—'

'It's a good thing I'm not paranoid, Cesare, or I'd think you were trying to avoid me more than usual,' she snapped. When he didn't refute the allegation, a shaft of ice pierced her heart. 'I think you're right, maybe this isn't the time to do this. I'll take Annabelle to my studio for a few hours. Let me know when you leave and we'll come home.'

She'd barely moved a step when a hand closed over her arm and jerked her back. She landed against hard, lean muscle. The scent that filled her nostrils was pure Cesare. A mixture of sandalwood aftershave and man, it attacked her senses with the force of a spinning hurricane.

'No. Annabelle stays here with me.' Tension shimmered from the body plastered against hers.

'If you think I'm letting her out of my sight after what she's been through, you're seriously deluded.' She tried to pull away. He held on.

Heat spiralled upward, surging through her blood like wildfire. The sensation, familiar yet unexpected, made her stumble. Cesare's hand tightened, one hand coming to rest gently on Annabelle's back as he steadied them both.

Pulse hammering, she glanced up. Dark emotion flashed through his eyes, quickly smothered but nevertheless sparking along her every nerve ending. The breath she sucked in felt as dry as the desert. Fresh tingles shot down her spine and she forced a swallow to ease the restriction in her throat as he continued to hold her prisoner.

'I'll give you ten minutes to tell me of these new plans of yours, then—'

'No, this is how it's going to work. First, I put Annabelle down for her nap. Then we can have a civilised conversation.'

He gave a low, deadly chuckle. *'Civilised?'* His warm breath brushed her ear, sending heat-filled tremors coursing through her body. 'Remember how we met, *cara*?'

Sensation drenched her. Instantly she was wrenched back to their first explosive meeting.

He'd almost run her down at a pedestrian crossing because she'd been distracted by the stunning architecture of a centuries-old building she'd been trying to capture on her camera. The combination of near-death experience and the impact of his stunning looks had made her slam her fists down hard on the sun-baked bonnet of his blood-red Maserati.

His fury as he'd stepped out of his car to examine the damage had swiftly morphed into something even more dangerous, forbiddingly thrilling. 'We barely exchanged names before we were tearing each other's clothes off. *Dio mio,* you lost your virginity to me on the bonnet of my car within hours of us meeting!'

Memory's flames burned from head to toe. 'Is there a point to this?' she rasped.

'I'm just reminding you that nothing of our time together could ever be described as civilised, so let's not hang that particular label on it.'

'Speak for yourself. You might wish to wallow in caveman-like behaviour but I don't have to stoop to your level.' Somehow, she *would* overcome the riotous emotions Cesare engendered in her. For her daughter's sake.

Again, she pulled away. This time he let her go.

'Throw a gloss over it if you wish, *cara.* We both know the truth. When we let it free, our passion is uncontrollable.'

Eyes tracking her like a pitiless bird of prey eyeing a juicy rabbit, he pushed the door open, stood to one side and folded his arms.

For a second she couldn't move as she was drawn to the play of muscles underneath his shirt. Was it her imagination or were the hairs that peeked through his unbuttoned polo shirt even silkier?

Forcing her gaze away, she crossed the threshold of Lake Como's most breathtaking palazzo, the place she'd called home for the past four years.

The terracotta exterior with its multi-fountained courtyard, tiered gardens and baking paving stones sharply contrasted with the cool cream interior. High, perfectly preserved stuccoed walls framed vaulted ceilings where discreetly placed conditioners circulated cool air through the rooms.

On either side of the exquisitely trellised archways that fed the hallways leading to the four wings of the villa, tall shuttered windows had been thrown wide open, drenching the room with dazzling light.

A quick glance around was all she allowed herself but it was enough to make her catch her breath all over again. From the exquisite pieces arranged in the hallway to the impressive Renaissance art and family portraits that hung on the walls, the palazzo was still reminiscent of the time when the Villa di Goia had been a renowned museum. The Venetian marble and parquet floors beneath her feet gleamed with the opulent gloss only the super rich could afford.

'Nothing has changed since you were last here, Ava. I suggest you spend less time admiring the architecture and more time on explaining yourself. You now have eight minutes.' Tension seethed beneath the veneer of calm he presented.

She breathed in a deep breath and faced him. 'I suggest *you* stop the clock watching and help me with Annabelle. Unless you want a cranky child on your hands?'

The faint widening of his eyes was barely distinguishable, but she saw it nonetheless. Had the situation not been fraught with tension, Ava would've laughed. As it was, her daughter's weight seemed to be doubling by the second.

His lips firmed, then he stepped forward and calmly relieved her of her burden.

Ava heard a faint intake of breath as he hitched her close to his chest.

'She looks well,' he rasped, his voice a shade deeper.

'She is. The doctor is happy with her progress,' she stressed, flexing her arm to relieve the painful stinging needles.

More emotion flashed across Cesare's face as he continued to gaze at his daughter. Ava didn't need a crystal ball to divine that he was thinking of the last time he'd held her like this. The indescribable emotions that had gripped them both when they'd finally found her after the earthquake…

He turned abruptly towards the majestic sweep of stairs that led to the upper floors. His long strides made short work of the grand trellised staircase and she had to move quickly to keep up with him.

When he turned towards the east wing, Ava couldn't hide her surprise. 'You've relocated her bedroom?' Annabelle's room had previously been in the west wing.

'*Sì,* I've rearranged a few things. I wanted her to be close to me when she returned.' His voice was gruff, irritated, as if he didn't wish to be questioned. Another dagger of ice pierced her heart. *Me,* not *us.*

Following him into the room, Ava bit back a gasp.

The room had been redecorated in Annabelle's favourite colours of pink and green, complete with canopied bed. Toys of every description a child could want dotted the room but she noticed that the long-maned horses which were Annabelle's favourite were especially plentiful.

She watched as he gently placed Annabelle on the wide bed and stepped back. He waved her away when she stepped forward to help, and took off Annabelle's shoes and socks.

Pulling a light sheet over her shoulders, he plucked a stuffed horse off a shelf and laid it in the crook of her arm.

Pain scythed through her. How many times had she wished Cesare would do this when Annabelle was a baby? How many times had she dreamed of him bending down to kiss his daughter's forehead, murmur *buono notte, bambina…?*

She managed the pain for a second before he turned from the bed, his gaze slamming into hers.

'Come. Our daughter's presence is no longer an issue.

Let's have that talk, shall we?' With purposeful strides, he headed for the door.

Tension emanated from the broad, set shoulders and, with every click of her heels on the marble floor, her own tension grew. She rubbed sweaty palms on the folds of her long skirt and suppressed the anxiety growing inside her.

She arrived in the living room to find him facing the large floor-to-ceiling windows overlooking the lush, perfectly manicured gardens and private mooring that abutted the world-famous lake. The view was so breathtaking, her fingers briefly itched for her camera before she forced herself to focus.

Cesare's gaze tracked a sleek speedboat skimming across the turquoise water but she knew his mind was locked in the room.

'You should've waited in Bali until I came to collect you, Ava.' He spoke without turning.

'I've never been good at taking orders without question, you know that. And you didn't seem to be in a particular hurry to bring us back home.'

'You had everything you needed.'

'Yes, the staff you hired for us were highly trained and extremely resourceful. I only had to lift a finger for my every wish to be catered for.'

'But?'

'But I'd had enough of being surrounded by complete strangers. It wasn't good for Annabelle. So here we are,' she said calmly.

'You should've told me!'

'What exactly is the problem here? Are you angry that I wanted to come home or annoyed that I dared to question your authority?'

He inhaled sharply. 'A lot has changed—'

'I'm very much aware of that. Staying away wasn't going to make it any better.'

'So why return earlier than we planned?' he enquired.

'Because this isn't just about you, Cesare. Life goes on and I need to make sure Annabelle returns to normal as quickly as possible. Besides, when I told you my plans had changed, I meant it. I've been contracted to cover the Marinello wedding.'

He frowned. 'You're an award-winning documentary photographer. When did you branch into covering celebrity weddings?'

'Annabelle needs to be around the familiar for the foreseeable future. I'm not taking her on assignment to the far reaches of the planet. She needs me to be here.'

His jaw tightened. 'The Marinello wedding is turning into a media circus. I won't have Annabelle exposed to that sort of environment.'

'I've never let my work disrupt her life in any way. It definitely won't this time round.'

'You didn't think to inform me of this Marinello thing before now?'

'Just take it as the side effect of my aversion to being abandoned.'

'You weren't abandoned. Annabelle needed medical care and she couldn't travel before then.'

'Yes, but that stay wasn't indefinite. Although I'm beginning to suspect maybe that's what you had in mind.'

'It wasn't. I agree that Annabelle needs to be home, but not…' He paused.

The cold grip on her spine intensified. 'Not your wife?' When he refused to reply, she let out a shaky breath. 'You don't have to say it, Cesare.' Her smile cracked around the edges. 'Annabelle's welfare is my priority right now. As long as she remains okay, you can go back to being indifferent to me. Or go back to Rome.'

A dangerous gleam flashed through his eyes. He balled his fists, his nostrils flaring. For a very long time he didn't speak. The air crackled with each charged heartbeat. Finally, he rasped, 'I'm staying here for the summer.'

Her heart skipped a beat, then immediately fell when she read the displeasure on his face. 'Then this is going to be *very* awkward for one of us.'

'I don't want you here. Not right now.'

The blunt words stung deep.

'Why not?'

'I'm in the middle of…' He stopped and shoved a hand through his hair. 'We both know things haven't been right between us for a while. But I can't be…distracted by anything right now.'

She pulled in a shaky breath and reminded herself why she was doing this. She set her bag down on the coffee table in the middle of the room. 'The state of your marriage is an inconvenient distraction?'

A nerve pulsed in his jaw. 'Especially the state of our marriage. If you'd stayed in Bali—'

'I didn't. You like to control people and things around you but I'm not one of them. This is your home as much as it is mine so I can't exactly throw you out. So you'll just have to tolerate my presence here, just like you have to tolerate your daughter.'

'Tolerate her? I'm her *father.*'

'Trust me, I know a thing or two about being *tolerated.* I don't think you'd want your performance as a father or husband to be rated. You wouldn't like the results.'

His colour receded a little beneath his vibrant tan and the room seemed to darken with turbulent forces. She watched him visibly swallow. 'If you want the civilised conversation you claim to want, I'd advise you to tread carefully, Ava. What is happening between us will *not* affect our daughter.'

She tried to stop the pain from biting deep. Selecting a seat as far away from his forceful presence as possible, she sat down.

'That's one thing we can agree on, at least. I suggest we set up a schedule. You spend time with her in the mornings while I meet with my clients; I'll take over in the afternoons. As long as she's happy, I need not interfere in… whatever it is you think I'm interrupting.'

He gave a harsh laugh. 'You're as non-interfering as a bull in a china shop.'

'Only when I need to be.' Like when confronted with an icily cold, angry, astoundingly gorgeous Italian male who threw out commands like they were sweets at a kids' party. Or when you grew up isolated in a house ruled by a distant father who treated you as if you were invisible and brothers who were more than happy to emulate their father. 'Sometimes it's the only way people take notice of you.'

'Is that why you've returned so suddenly? You want me to take notice of you?' he enquired with disquieting softness.

That voice, *that* precise, perfectly pitched cadence, bathed her skin in goose bumps that had nothing to do with pain and everything to do with unwanted memories. It threatened to dominate her senses. Forcing them away took much more effort than she was happy with. 'I'm here because my daughter needs to be home.'

Another dangerous gleam darkened his eyes. '*Our* daughter. She's as much mine as she is yours, Ava.'

She stormed to her feet. 'Really? You've barely seen her in the past year. You choose to stay in Rome and make one excuse after another as to why you don't come home any more. So what are you doing here, really? What's changed? What's prompted this sudden yearning to play *papà?*'

A peculiar look crossed his face, too quick for her to assess its meaning. 'She's my daughter. My blood. There was never any question that I'd resume my parental rights.'

'*Resume!* You can't press *pause* on parenting every time you feel like it. So what, now you've suddenly found time to slot her into your schedule? For how long? What if another deal suddenly crops up in Abu Dhabi or Doha or Outer Mongolia? You'll press *pause* again and fly off in pursuit of your next venture?'

A frown darkened his brow. 'You think I'll abandon Annabelle for a business deal?'

'Oh, don't act so annoyed. How many times did you leave me to jet off to parts unknown when another too-good-to-miss deal cropped up?'

He waved her away like a troublesome fly. 'That was different.'

The uncaring delivery of his words stole her breath. 'You expect me to think things will change because we're talking about your daughter now instead of your wife? When you didn't have any trouble choosing business over returning to bring her from Bali?'

Ava had spent far too much time torturing herself with the *whys.* What she needed was to concern herself less with the *why?* and more with the *why now?* Cesare never made a move without calculating at least a dozen steps ahead. Which made his sudden decision to summer at Lake Como and demand to have his daughter all the more suspect.

Dangerously suspect.

'Things have changed, Ava.'

'Enlighten me, then. How *exactly* have things changed?'

His gaze slid away. 'The earthquake was an eye-opener for us all, I won't deny it. I agree that Annabelle needs the safe and familiar around her right now. Both our jobs are very demanding. If something unavoidable comes up, she'll be adequately cared for. Lucia will step in for now until I can hire another nanny. Between them, she'll be cared for around the clock.'

She sucked in a breath. 'Lord, you have the nerve to say the earthquake was an eye-opener but in the next breath you admit you'd happily abandon your daughter when the lure of a business deal proves too much!'

His stare turned icier. 'I'll make time for her as much as possible, but my work doesn't stop just because it's the summer vacation. I can't just abandon it.'

'Of course you can't. I'm not even sure why I'm surprised. Cesare di Goia, venture capitalist with the Midas touch, hasn't changed one iota, has he—?'

'Annabelle turns four in a few weeks.'

Thrown by the sudden turn of the conversation, she frowned. 'Yes, I'm very much aware of that. I've made plans.'

He glanced at his sleek silver watch. 'But if you're covering the Marinello wedding, you'll need to be in Tuscany for the next three weeks.'

'I see you're well informed.'

He shrugged. 'For some reason, Agata Marinello seems to think I need updating on every detail of her son's wedding arrangements.'

'You're the guest of honour and your company is bankrolling Reynaldo Marinello's reality show. You don't need a crystal ball to suss why she wants to stay on your sweet side. Besides, I think all the guests receive email and social media updates.'

'Which is exactly why I've blocked her messages as of this morning.' A look of impatience crossed his face. 'I haven't even officially accepted the wedding invitation yet. Not with everything that's going on—' He stopped and shook his head. 'I'll ask for the jet to be refuelled. Paolo will deliver you to the airport within the hour to take you to Tuscany. Annabelle will remain here with me. When you're done with the wedding, we'll talk.' He started to cross the room towards the house intercom.

Feigning ease she didn't feel, she settled back in her chair and took her time to cross her legs. 'I see you're all about minimising your carbon footprint.'

He paused mid-stride. 'You know my line of work necessitates the use of a private jet. If I didn't, I'd suffer permanently from jet lag.'

'Yes, I'm sure all the environmental charities would love that explanation.' She'd aimed for spiky snark intended to win her further ground. Instead her reply faltered as her treacherous mind conjured up the very effective means by which Cesare conquered jetlag—the enormous king-size bed in the larger, chrome and grey bedroom of his Gulfstream. The silky satin sheets, the soft, decadent pillows… the en suite made-for-two shower…her intensely erotic initiation into the mile-high club…

She tried to stare him down, but heat slowly crawled up her neck, stung her cheeks. She knew her pale skin had given her away when a small *knowing* smile whispered over his lips.

'I'm sure they'll allow me this small concession given my support of their other eco-saving efforts. Now, if you've finished berating me, I'll instruct Lucia to provide you with some refreshments before you leave.' He walked towards the villa's intercom next to the extensive drinks cabinet and lifted the receiver.

Any lingering arousal fled as his statement sank in.

'The Marinellos changed their wedding venue three days ago—the official stance is a termite infestation at their Tuscany villa but I'm guessing *your* being here has something to do with the wedding's relocation to Lake Como.' She shrugged at his frown. 'I'm meeting with them tomorrow afternoon to discuss staging and the pre-wedding catalogue. But even that notwithstanding, I don't think you've quite grasped what I'm trying to tell you. Annabelle and I are a package deal, Cesare. Where I go, she goes.'

Slowly—excruciatingly slowly—he replaced the handset. Ava's heart thumped so hard against her ribs she feared the organ would expire from overuse.

'I warn you against rocking the boat, Ava. This isn't really the time to bring things to a head between us.' His voice was soft but edged in steel.

'And maybe you need to give up this false pretence of trying to play *papà,* return to Rome and just let us be.'

He lounged against the wall, sliding long fingers into his pockets in a display of utter calm. But she wasn't fooled.

The lazy way his gaze raked her from head to toe only served to raise her hackles, along with her pulse rate.

Warning shrieked in her head. Cesare was most dangerous at his calmest. He hadn't built a globally successful venture capitalist company without being extremely calculating and ruthless where he needed to be.

He shrugged amiably, as if they were discussing which entrée to have. 'No, you're right. On second thoughts, maybe this is just what we need.'

A thread of trepidation unfurled in the pit of her stomach. 'And what exactly is *this?*'

'To have this marriage brought under the scrutiny it deserves,' he delivered. 'For us to stop avoiding the fact that this marriage is anything but a sham. Maybe once we face facts, I can get round to discussing the more important issue of custody of my daughter.'

Her laughter was so strained it scraped her throat. 'And you think when that happens I'd allow you anywhere near Annabelle?' It didn't click that she'd surged to her feet, that she'd bridged the gap between them, until her forefinger jabbed his chest. 'You really think any judge on earth would grant custody to a less than part-time father who's abandoned his daughter for most of her life?'

CHAPTER TWO

CESARE FLINCHED, THE sting of her words like whips lacerating his skin; the stab of her finger pierced like a knife in his chest. Raw pain pounded with every heartbeat as Ava's words barrelled into him.

He'd abandoned her.

When his daughter had needed him most, he'd failed her. He'd been unable to protect Annabelle…

Dark torment crept in, threatening to drown him every time he thought of what he'd let happen. He'd been too quick to believe…too swift to embrace his destiny.

And in choosing that path, he'd done the unforgivable.

The heart he thought had withered to nothing clenched hard. But within that torment, within the potent swirl of guilt and recrimination, a different emotion crept in.

Excitement. The guilt and recrimination were ever present, but alongside it a flood of hot excitement stole over his senses, awakening that treacherous desire he thought he'd slain a long time ago.

With every ounce of control he possessed, he tried to push it away, but like a drowning victim accepting the inevitable, he let it close in on him, submerge him deeper in its relentless maelstrom.

Dio, he felt…alive; from her single touch, he felt more alive than he had in a very long time. More than he deserved to feel after what he'd done.

Ava's finger jabbed him again, but all he could think, could feel, was how much cleaner the air smelled—richer, bringing a clarity that had eluded him for a long time.

'From the moment she was born, you abandoned her.' Her rough, pain-racked whisper stabbed deeper than if she'd shouted. 'And the day of the earthquake, you were supposed to spend time with her; instead you were on a *conference call!* You palmed her off on Rita—'

He wrenched back control and sucked in a breath. 'The minute I knew what was happening, I went in search of her. We both did. We tore apart that Bali marketplace with our bare hands.' Until they'd bled both inside and out.

Her hand dropped and she shook her head. 'Do you know how it feels to know neither of us were with her when the earthquake hit?' she whispered in anguish.

The thought tortured him day and night. '*Sì*, I know. I've lived with that horror every day since. I know how very easily we could've lost her. But I also thank God she was found.' *Someone else* had dug his daughter out of the submerged marketplace. *Someone else* had cared for Annabelle, taken her to the hospital and taken the time to put her photograph on the missing person's wall. 'We may not have found her ourselves but she was found,' he repeated. 'She was all right. She was *alive*.' Somehow, *miraculously*, his daughter had survived the devastating earthquake that had killed tens of thousands.

And, for as long as he lived, he intended to make sure his daughter never came to harm again.

'She was all right,' she repeated numbly. 'So you just thought you'd carry on being emotionally unavailable to her again?' Her words were hushed, but the pain behind them ripped through the silence.

Icy calm slowly built inside him, pushing aside his pain. Cesare welcomed it. 'I was there, Ava.'

Her face hardened and she folded her arms around her

ribcage. 'You mean just like you're here now? In the same room but wishing you were somewhere else?'

His jaw tightened. Ava would never know how difficult it had been to keep from roaring his gut-ripping pain when he'd believed Annabelle was lost to him. She thought him cold. But he'd had to be, he'd had to shut off his emotions, to shut off any hint of yearning for what he couldn't have.

Except for Annabelle.

His daughter was the one thing he wasn't prepared to give up.

It'd taken him years to finally heed the warning he'd blindly ignored. To accept that he had no business taking a wife, never mind fathering a child.

He might be astute when it came to business but his personal relationships had always come at a price. A very steep price, he'd come to realise.

'And now you've decided you want your daughter you think you can just click your fingers to make it happen?'

'It was always going to happen. I'm sorry if you believed otherwise.' The horrendous events of the past few weeks had painfully brought home to him that Annabelle was the only child he'd ever have. And now she was here—albeit earlier than he'd anticipated—he had no intention of letting her go.

'Your arrogance is astounding, you know that?'

'Isn't it one of the things about me that turns you on?' He had the fleeting satisfaction of watching colour surge under her skin. Anger soon replaced her blush.

'Dream on. Your attraction level has dropped lower than the temperatures in the Antarctic.'

His fiery *moglie* had the tendency to lash out first and think about the consequences later. Wasn't that what had drawn him to her in the first place? Her vibrancy? Her blind, uncontrollable passion for life?

He sidestepped that reminder.

With a swish of her brightly coloured skirt, she stalked

to the window. Cesare caught himself following the sway of her hips and reined himself in. Things were fast getting out of hand.

Again.

Their first meeting had been a heady, mind-blowing experience. She'd been a potion to end all sweet potions, lighting up his days, blazing through his nights like a spectacular comet. Against his every instinct, he'd let his guard down.

Once again he'd let a woman get under his skin. Something he'd sworn to himself and to his brother, Roberto, he'd never let happen again.

Cesare had walked out of his last meeting in Abu Dhabi the minute he'd learned Ava had summoned his plane. He'd even contemplated ordering his pilot to return her to Bali. But he'd known she would've found another way of achieving her goal.

She turned, arms folded in battle stance. He suppressed a grim smile. His Ava hadn't changed. Corner her and the fierce lioness emerged.

Except she wasn't his. He never should've taken her in the first place—although the exhilaration of being her first lover still made his blood pump faster—never should've placed the di Goia emerald on her finger…

His gaze fell to her bare fingers. 'Where is your wedding ring?' The burning need to know erased every other thought from his head.

Surprise widened eyes the same colour as the famous di Goia family heirloom. 'My wedding ring?' she echoed.

'*Sì.* Where is it?'

'In a box…somewhere. What does it matter?' she challenged.

Cesare had the completely irrational urge to grab her arms and shake her, demand to know why the ring wasn't on her finger. Instead, he jammed his fists into his pockets and forced himself to stay put.

'Just checking that you hadn't donated it to the commune you were growing fond of in Bali.'

Her arms tightened. 'I'm glad to see you think so highly of me, Cesare. And I don't need to pawn your jewellery off to help the causes I believe in. I'm more than well compensated for my job to fund my charitable endeavours.'

Did she realise how gripping her arms so tightly pushed her breasts up, so they looked even fuller, more tempting? The faint outline of her areolas against the white of her cotton halter top and the faint freckles marching across her chest sent the pulse kicking in his groin.

'Do you have a lover?'

Dio, where the hell had that come from? He raked unsteady fingers through his hair, the sheer astonishment his question caused clearly reflected in the slack-jawed look on Ava's face. But then was it really that astonishing? They'd spent so much time apart in the past year, he didn't even know which circle of friends she moved in these days.

Whose fault is that?

Her hand fluttered to her neck, crept around to her nape and flipped her flaming hair over one shoulder. He followed the movement, his fascination with the ripple of sunlight through the long tresses causing him to tense further.

'Don't you dare go there with me, Cesare,' she snapped.

Her non-answer made jealousy sear his insides. He'd distanced himself from her. She should be free to take other lovers. So why did his gut clench in sharp rejection of the idea?

'Why? Did the commune make you sign an oath of secrecy?'

'It wasn't a commune. And the people there are—'

'Eat, pray, love advocates?'

'No, believe it or not, they're professionals who've given up their time to help better the lives of others, especially the victims of the earthquake.'

'In the hope of *finding* themselves in the process?'

Her lips firmed. 'We can't all find ourselves in the next multi-billion euro deal, Cesare. Why did you abandon your daughter?'

He gripped his nape, renewed tension clawing through him. 'I thought it was better that I stay away. If it makes you feel better, call it an error of judgement on my part and leave it be.'

The understatement of the millennia. Marriage to Ava, *Dio,* to any woman, had never been on the cards for him. Not after what he'd put Roberto through. Not after Valentina…

In some ways, while he regretted the devastation it had wrought on countless lives, the earthquake had been his wake up call. His head had been wrenched violently from the sand. And now he had the rest of his life to made amends to his daughter.

'An error of judgement?' Ava shot back immediately, like a damned terrier intent on ravaging its favourite toy. 'Does that include our marriage?' she demanded.

Ignoring her, he strode to the drinks cabinet, curbing the urge to pour something stiff and bracing. He'd drunk himself into a stupor more than once this past year. He couldn't afford to do so now. He needed to stay focused on the female who prowled restlessly behind him.

'Answer me, Cesare. This…whatever's going on between us…is it another woman?' she persisted in that damned husky tone.

Bitter laughter escaped before he could stop it. He poured a tall glass of water and handed it to her. 'Why do women always think it's another woman?'

She gazed straight at him. 'Because men are as predictable as the tide during a full moon.'

'Would it make it easier if I said it was another woman?'

He didn't miss the shaft of pain that flitted through her eyes. Her lips wobbled before she pursed them. But her gaze didn't waver from his. '*Is* it?'

In a way he wished it had been as easy as infidelity. Because infidelity would mean he'd stop caring. Or wanting what he couldn't have.

'Turn down the Marinello gig. Return to your commune in Bali. Or take another assignment abroad. Give me the summer with Annabelle. We'll talk when you return.'

Her eyes flashed rebellious fire at him. 'No. Annabelle needs me. Besides, too much has happened for me to just up and leave on an assignment. I think deep down you know that.'

He silently conceded the point. The earthquake had changed things between Ava and him just as much as it'd altered his relationship towards his daughter. As much as he didn't want to admit it, looking at Ava in battle mode he hadn't witnessed for a long time, he knew in that instant he was screwed.

He gritted his teeth. 'The foreign minister is a close friend. You didn't become an Italian citizen when we married. All it would take is a single phone call and I can have you thrown out of the country. Do you realise that?' He threw out the straw-clutching Hail Mary.

'Yes,' she stated simply, not in the least bit cowed. 'But if I leave I take Annabelle with me.'

Against his will, his eyes strayed to the soft curve of her mouth. It would be as soft and supple as he remembered. Along with the rest of her.

Having her close would drive him crazy.

But the need to have his daughter close—to begin to repair the damage he'd caused outweighed all else. His internal debate lasted milliseconds.

'Fine. We'll both stay here for the summer.'

Her mouth dropped open, then her eyes narrowed. 'That was a little *too* easy.'

'Don't delude yourself, Ava. This isn't going to be easy for either of us. I know what you want and I can assure you I am unable to give it to you. What I can do is ensure

Annabelle isn't caught in the crossfire of our…situation. You understand?'

She sucked in a ragged breath and Cesare knew he'd got through to her. The late afternoon sun slanting through the windows danced over her fiery hair as she nodded.

Grimly satisfied that his control was under firm guard, he headed for the door, ruthlessly suppressing the old sensations pulling at him, reminding him that his attraction to Ava had always held a fatalistic edge that had excited him.

Doomed him. He'd let it get out of hand the same way he'd let the situation with Roberto and Valentina unravel…

'So, does that mean you agree to a truce? That you won't try anything *double-crossy* somewhere down the line?'

He turned back from the door.

Her eyes reflected a defiance that reluctantly sparked his admiration. None of his family or subordinates would dare press home their advantage this way.

But a line needed to be drawn. 'That very much depends on you, *cara.* Your innate inability to not rush in where angels fear to tread could prove your undoing.'

Her lips tightened. 'Are you calling me a fool?'

'I'm inviting you to prove me wrong. Stay out of my way for the next six weeks and I'll have no need to declare war on you.'

Ava frowned at the closed door, her mind a whirlpool of jumbled thoughts.

She walked over to the French windows and gazed at the sparkling infinity pool. Something was wrong with the picture Cesare was presenting her with.

Even as a newly-wed, she'd realised very quickly that business came first with Cesare. She'd lost count of the times he'd upped and left on a business trip on the strength of a single phone call.

Now, all of a sudden, he'd taken weeks off to spend his summer here.

She wanted to believe that living through a devastating earthquake had changed him…but it was painfully obvious that Cesare was determined to keep her at arm's length.

Although his attitude towards Annabelle had changed…

Recalling his face when he'd laid their daughter down for her nap, a bittersweet emotion filled her.

If Cesare meant to spend time with Annabelle, Ava welcomed that, although she couldn't stop the tiniest well of jealousy from rising up.

Pushing the doors open, she stepped onto the terrace. The palazzo baked in the late afternoon sun. Perfumed scents of lemon trees and the specially reared roses the team of gardeners took immense pride in mingled in the air. She inhaled deeply, letting the fragrance suffuse her senses. But the clarity she sought never materialised.

The holiday in Bali had been her last-ditch attempt to reconnect with Cesare. She'd failed spectacularly right from the get-go. That first week, he'd shut himself away in the luxury villa's study and worked until the early hours of each morning.

On the first morning of their second week, desperate for a break from the overwhelming evidence of her failure, she'd left the villa armed with her camera. She'd been taking pictures of the beautiful local wildlife when the earthquake struck.

Her insides clenched anew at the heart-rending three days they'd searched for Annabelle and Rita.

She shuddered and blinked back the rush of tears. Ironically, she'd felt closer to Cesare in those bleak moments they'd spent ripping apart the marketplace where Rita had been strolling with Annabelle than she'd felt in a long time.

Well, Cesare had been right about one thing…she was a fool.

The staff had unpacked and folded away her clothes in the master suite on the other side of Annabelle's room by the time she went upstairs. It took moments to confirm Cesare's *I've rearranged a few things* didn't mean he'd moved back into the suite they once shared but rather the one on the other side of Annabelle's room.

Ava refused to acknowledge the knot in the pit of her stomach and undressed. The sheer gold-coloured muslin curtains that framed the queen-sized bed had been caught up with white velvet rope.

Approaching the bed, she picked up her coffee-coloured kimono-style silk gown and went into the bathroom. Bypassing the sunken marble bath, she entered the shower cubicle. After a refreshing shower, she donned an ankle-length green and white flower-patterned skirt and white top and checked on Annabelle. Finding her still comfortably asleep, Ava slipped her feet into a pair of white thongs, grabbed her laptop and went downstairs.

The aim had been to head to the *salone* that hugged the western side of the villa and overlooked the stunning gardens. She'd always found that room soothing. But in the hallway she slowed, lingered, unable to stem the flood of memories from washing over her.

Her first time to the Villa di Goia had been on her honeymoon. Two weeks of bliss when they'd only come out of the bedroom to swim in the pool or for Cesare to teach her to waterski on the lake.

He'd wanted to take her somewhere exotic, but for a girl brought up in a dysfunctional working class home, who'd never travelled beyond the shores of England, Lake Como at the end of a hot summer had been exotic enough. And after being carried over the threshold and falling as swiftly and deeply in love with the charming elegance of the Villa di Goia as she had with its owner, she'd had no wish to be anywhere else.

Besotted fool that she'd been.

With an irritated shake of her head, she banished her thoughts. Through the window she caught another glimpse of the sparkling swimming pool and smiled at the thought of Annabelle's delight when her water-loving child was re-united with her favourite pool.

'If that's a smile of victory, I'd caution against being too precipitate,' a deep drawl sounded from behind her.

Cesare lounged against a Louis XVI credenza that had been in his family for four generations. Above him a portrait of another di Goia, long dead but no less imposing, stared down at her with similar unnerving tawny eyes. How long had the living di Goia stood there, silently watching her take the stupid trip down memory lane?

'Poor Cesare. I can see my being home fills you with all sorts of unhappy feelings. I get it. But I'm not going into hiding just to please you and I'm certainly not going to stop smiling in case it offends you.'

His smile mocked her. 'I have no problem with you smiling, *cara,* I just don't want you deluding yourself that you've won an easy victory.'

'I wouldn't dare. But remember your rule goes both ways. I can't stay out of your way if you insist on straying into mine.'

He straightened and sauntered towards her. 'Is this where we indulge in the childish game of who was here first?' he asked.

She shrugged. 'It's not childish. *I* was here first. And, if you must know, I was smiling at the thought of Annabelle being safely home and being surrounded by familiar things.' Ava caught herself, realising she didn't owe Cesare any explanation. 'Anyway, I'll let you reclaim your domain—'

'You weren't just thinking about our daughter. You were reminiscing about *us*.' He said it so calmly, so matter-of-factly, Ava felt a shiver race up her spine.

'You're wrong.' The need for denial was visceral.

'Liar. We may have been apart more than together for

most of the past year, Ava, but you're still as easy to read as an open book.'

'Then it's a book whose language you don't quite fully understand. Because, from where I'm standing, you couldn't have got things more wrong if you'd tried.'

His jaw clenched, the mocking smile wiped clean. Part of Ava wanted to punch the air in triumph. The other just wanted to weep because if she'd been as open as Cesare claimed, then it meant he'd recognised her heart's one desire—the need for the comfort of the loving family she'd never had—and he'd still denied her.

'And, just so we're clear, my memories are my own. They're not a subject for your amusement or dissection.'

'Then learn to hide them better.'

'Why—do they make you uncomfortable? Would you rather I strip myself of every humanising emotion, like you?' she challenged and immediately bit her tongue when he tensed. The light pouring through the tall shuttered windows carved his face in taut, almost statue-like relief.

'You think I'm without emotion, *cara*?' he queried so softly the hairs on her arms rose in desperate foreboding.

'Not where I'm concerned. When it comes to me, you're as emotional as a plank of wood.'

His eyes narrowed. Almost in slow motion, she watched his hands leave his pockets, reach up and curl around her arms. One slid down, relieved her of her laptop and set it carelessly aside.

'What are you doing?' Her question squeaked out as he captured her nape.

He didn't answer, at least not verbally. The slow burn in his eyes and the steady pressure of his fingers on her skin told its own story. With effortless ease, he pulled her close. Ava actually heard her thonged feet screech across the floor in protest as he dragged her into stinging contact with his body. When he had her close enough, he boldly cupped her bottom.

'Cesare!'

Electric heat, wicked and powerful, snapped through her, zapping awake her senses with a force so potent she gasped. She should've wanted to move away from it. *Should've* worked harder to release herself from the powerful, chaotic destruction.

Instead, she found herself straining up to meet the havoc-causing mouth descending towards hers, pressing herself up against the heat of the rock-hard body.

His mouth slanted over hers, barely stopping to explore before his tongue slid through the parted welcome of her lips.

Somewhere in the outer regions of her mind, she knew she should feel shame for letting him kiss her thoroughly with so little resistance. But the pleasure racing unfettered through her was too heady, too blissful, to deny.

But she tried anyway. 'No…'

'Yes, most definitely, yes.' He tugged her closer.

With a soft moan, her hands settled on his chest. His polo shirt might as well have been non-existent as her hands stole over the hard contours of his muscled flesh.

When they slid around his neck, Cesare groaned. Heat erupted between them; the kiss grew fervent, rough. His tongue slid further inside her mouth, engaging hers in a rough play that made sweet fire rush to the apex of her thighs. Her nipples hardened into painful, rock-hard points. Boldly, she grabbed the hand at her nape and settled it over her breast.

He accepted her gift with a deep groan. One rough thumb grazed back and forth over her nipple, eliciting deep tremors of excitement within her.

If she'd thought distance and indifference would've lessened the power of Cesare's attraction, she was sadly mistaken. If anything, the deep chasm between them had only intensified her need.

She *yearned* for him with a hunger that deeply terrified

her. Knowing she would joyfully have given anything she owned to feel his potent arousal deep inside her should've shocked her. Knowing she wanted nothing more than to sink to her knees, free his erection from the confines of his jeans and take him in her mouth the way he'd once loved her to, dismayed her. Yet, even as the thought struck, her hand was moving lower, seeking the silver square of his belt buckle.

When her hand brushed his erection, he jerked, then plunged his tongue deeper into her mouth. His fingers closed around her nipples, squeezed and teased repeatedly until she wanted to die with pleasure.

She grappled harder with the buckle. The more she tried, the more her fingers fumbled. Using both hands, she managed to pull the belt through one hoop. Just then Cesare slid one hand between her legs. She lost the use of her fingers as unrelenting pleasure ricocheted through her. Unerringly, he found her nub of need through her cotton panties. Her breathing grew ragged as she parted her legs to accommodate him.

His buckle forgotten, she grasped his arms to steady herself and drowned in bliss. Reality fogged. Had she just thrown her head back? Was that his tongue sliding over the highly sensitised skin on her neck, drawing her closer to the edge of her endurance?

'*Dio*, you're so hot!' he rasped.

'Only because you set me on fire.' Deep down, she knew that fire would be her undoing. But, for now, she remained blinded to everything but the storm raging within.

The sensation of being lifted registered, then the cool wall touched her back. Cesare increased the pressure of his fingers as his mouth captured one aching nipple. Mercilessly he teased, then his mouth returned to hers to smother her cries as she shuddered and fell headlong into cataclysmic ecstasy.

Slowly, sounds began to impinge as the force of her

orgasm abated. Cesare's scent mingled with the smell of arousal coating the air. Another shudder raked her frame when he withdrew his fingers. As if he knew letting her go would cause her immediate collapse, he wedged one muscled leg firmly between her thighs.

Against her stomach, his arousal burned hot and heavy.

More sounds encroached. She stood, dishevelled, in the hallway of the villa, barely hidden behind a trellised arch. Any member of their household staff could walk past. But Ava didn't care. She'd just had a sizzling reminder of the potent lovemaking she'd experienced only with Cesare. Her senses had sprung to vivid life, her body readying itself for his fullest possession.

She looked into his face. Torrid heat blazed in eyes that held the look of barely leashed hunger. Her gaze dropped to his lips. The force of her kiss had bruised his lips and the sight of it made her melt with wanting. She reached for his button. 'Your turn.'

Ava was woefully unprepared for the swiftness with which he clamped strong hands over hers. 'No.'

CHAPTER THREE

A SHARD OF ice splintered her post-orgasmic haze.

'You want me. I know you do,' she blurted, slightly dazed by the thought that he would deny what he felt. The evidence was unmistakable, even through the layers of their clothes.

He stepped away from her, but not far enough, as if he wanted to be close when she collapsed. And certainly her legs were unsteady enough to make that a distinct possibility.

'This wasn't about me.'

She looked into his eyes. Slowly his meaning sank in, obliterating her desperate, humiliating desire. 'You bastard.'

He took another step back. Suddenly the scent of their lovemaking—if she could call it that—nauseated her. Because it was the smell of her weakness.

'You wanted to humiliate me,' she said.

'I merely wanted to prove a point. Passion is an emotion, *cara*, one I relish in the right circumstances. But I *choose* not to let it rule my life.'

She lowered her eyes, chagrin eating like acid through her at how easily she'd fallen for his ploy. 'You mean I let it rule mine?' She wanted to slink away in shame, but she was damned if she'd give him the satisfaction.

'I've just demonstrated that this is so.'

'Wow, so that display was all for me? Well, I hope you're proud of yourself.'

He stepped closer and slowly passed a finger over her swollen lip. '*Sì,* I am. And it's good to know I can still reduce you to putty.' His tone reeked smugness.

She didn't rise to the bait. They both knew he'd won this round. She straightened her clothes. 'Sure, you can dominate me with the sheer force of your sexual prowess. The orgasm you gave me just now? Out of this world. I'm a red-blooded female after all. But you've also proved that you're so cold-hearted you can control your life to the point where nothing touches you unless you want it to. So pardon me if I don't wholeheartedly buy your reasons for being here.'

He let go of her as if she'd suddenly developed a contagious disease. For a moment he looked almost...disarmed. But she didn't feel victory, just an emptiness that grew larger with each passing second.

'You're trying to rile me.' The face of the man who regarded her wasn't the Cesare who'd kissed her senseless moments ago, whose heart she'd felt beating unsteadily against her own. This was Cesare back in control, the master in complete command of his world.

'I'm speaking the truth. Deal with it.'

'It seriously terrifies me how prone to recklessness you can be.' With cool poise, he reached down and picked up her laptop. 'If you want to maintain that truce, I think we need to establish some ground rules. Come.'

Without waiting for her agreement, he strode off in the direction of his study.

By the time she found enough strength to straighten away from the wall and follow, he'd disappeared.

She found him seated behind his massive antique desk, his fingers steepled against his mouth. If he'd been any other man, she would've suspected he was hiding behind the desk to avoid her. But Cesare was no ordinary man.

He'd just proven catastrophically and conclusively that

he could turn her brainless with desire, ride through the storm of passion with her, and emerge unscathed.

'If you're going to dissect what just happened—'

'What happened just now doesn't need dissection,' he said, cutting across her. 'But I do want to discuss Annabelle and the impact our being together will have on her.'

She frowned. 'Why should it impact on her?'

He ignored her question. 'How did she take Rita leaving? I know they were close.' His gaze bored into her with the force of a laser drill.

'She was distressed, of course, but—'

'You also said she's a bit more sensitive than she used to be.'

Her hackles rose. 'And you think this is in some way my fault?'

He exhaled. 'I'm not laying blame, Ava. I'm just trying to find the best way to settle her without causing her any more upset.'

'She's back home where she belongs, and I'll be with her every day. A loving family is what she needs.'

Tawny eyes hardened a touch. 'You'll be working some of the time.' His gaze strayed to her laptop, which now sat on his desk. 'You cut back on your work when we got married. Why the sudden return to full-time work?'

'Because I found out that playing the role of neglected wife isn't all that challenging—I could do it with my eyes closed, in fact. I needed something more.'

'Is that supposed to be some sort of statement?' he asked.

'You're the genius. Work it out.'

'You're my wife, Ava, and therefore my responsibility—'

'Isn't that a mere technicality?' She ignored his icy glare. 'You can't have it both ways, Cesare. We've been drifting apart almost from the moment Annabelle was born. Hell, we've barely lived together for the last year. Calling me your wife when it suits you or as a means of salving your conscience—what there is of it—is disingenuous. Your career has always been your first priority so don't you dare question my dedication to mine. You can continue to provide for your daughter, but I can more than take care of myself financially.'

'Nice speech. Although I see you didn't hesitate to make use of my jet when you needed it. You can't have it both ways either, *cara*. While we live under the same roof you're my responsibility and we both do what's best for Annabelle. We share all meal times with our daughter. And at all times we present a united front.'

'To show her *Mummy* and *Papà* don't hate each other?' she threw at him.

His mocking smile displayed perfectly formed white teeth. 'Her Mummy and *Papà* don't hate each other. I think I proved that conclusively just now.'

A residual post-orgasmic shiver raked her insides at the reminder. 'Sexual desire without a solid foundation fizzles out eventually, Cesare.'

One dark eyebrow tilted upward. 'Is this another enlightened nugget you were fed in your commune or did you conduct a personal study?'

'I don't need a study to tell me that it won't be long before Annabelle starts asking probing questions. She's beginning to notice that her kindergarten friends have mummies and daddies who live together. Last month, before we left for Bali, she asked me why you don't live with us. Those are the easy questions, so prepare yourself for the tough questions because they're just around the corner.'

With the swiftness of a flash flood, the smile disappeared and a veil descended over his bronze features. Before her eyes, he withdrew behind a veneer of cool indifference. 'Many couples live apart. When the time is right, we will explain things to her.'

'I can't wait because I'd quite like some answers myself. For instance, why are you wearing your wedding ring again? You weren't last month.'

He glanced at the simple gold band on his finger, a peculiar look crossing his features. It dissipated so quickly she almost missed it. But its haunting quality lodged a stone in her chest.

Before she could question it, his desk phone rang. His gaze flicked over her as he reached for it. 'I've arranged for dinner to be served earlier tonight, at six-thirty, for Annabelle's sake. We'll decide then on the best routine for all of us going forward.'

For an insane second, she wanted to rip the phone out of his hands, chuck it through the window and demand he answer her questions. But he'd already swung his leather seat towards the window, shutting her out as if she'd ceased to exist for him.

She grabbed her laptop and marched from the room before the temptation to smash it over his head overcame her.

A headache niggled at her temples. Although tempted to blame it on the effects of travelling through several time zones, she knew Cesare was the reason for it.

From the start, he'd imprinted himself so indelibly on her psyche that it had seemed as if Fate herself had willed it so. Even now, she only had to see him to feel a part of her unravelling, for her insides to weaken.

She hated herself for those weak moments almost as much as she hated herself for what she'd let happen in the hallway. It'd only taken a handful of minutes for him to reduce her from a sane, rational woman to a heap of shuddering wantonness. And for him to gloat about it.

She entered the *salone*, walked past the sumptuous green and white overstuffed chairs and whitewashed tables and chose her favourite seat—an elegantly carved chaise longue facing the breathtaking view of the lake.

After switching on her laptop, she resolutely fished out her iPod and stuck the earphones on in the hope that the music would drown out the sinking realisation that she only had to think about Cesare for him to take a hold of her mind and, it seemed, her body.

Clicking on the application she needed, she read over the list of locations she needed to visit and typed up a suitable schedule and the cameras she would require.

Reynaldo Marinello and Tina Sanchez were the Posh and Becks of Italy. The renowned footballer's engagement to his pop-star girlfriend six months ago had sparked a media frenzy, which Ava normally tried to avoid.

Witnessing the post-earthquake devastation in Bali, however, had sparked a need to raise awareness and money for disaster-stricken areas through her photography—which meant she couldn't afford to turn down lucrative assignments like these.

The Marinello pre-wedding catalogue would entail photographing various members of the prestigious Marinello family around the Lake Como area, with special emphasis on the bride and groom. Mind-numbing work, but if it enabled her to stay close to Annabelle she didn't mind one little bit.

Almost an hour later, Ava removed her earphones as a maid entered with a tray that held a tall pitcher of homemade lemonade and pastries. On her heels, Cesare strode in, carrying a wide-awake Annabelle, who in turn clutched a bright red toy horse with flowing mane.

'Mummy, *Papà* woke me up,' her daughter said. 'I had a bad dream.'

Irrational guilt sparked as Cesare's cool gaze met hers.

'She tells me she has bad dreams sometimes. You didn't tell me about them,' he said almost conversationally, but she didn't miss the steely undertone.

'The doctor said it was to be expected, after her trauma.'

'Look, Mummy, I have a pretty horsey.' Annabelle's demand helped her tear her gaze from Cesare's accusatory stare.

'I can see that. It's gorgeous.' She tried to keep her voice light.

'*Papà* got it specially for me.' Her daughter's wary gaze darted to her father. At his smile, hers widened a touch.

'You're a lucky little girl,' said Ava. Her laptop trilled as it shut down.

Cesare's gaze zeroed in on it and she was mildly surprised the machine didn't incinerate under the laser beam of his disapproval.

Shoving it aside, she stood. Cesare's scent, coupled with the freshly washed smell from her daughter, caused an intense pang of pain to dart through her.

Hastily, she stepped back and busied herself with pouring drinks, refusing to let her mind flash back to the hallway incident. Annabelle gulped her drink down and immediately jumped down again, ready to reacquaint herself with her home.

'I asked if there was anything else I should know. You didn't think I needed to know about her nightmares?' he rasped fiercely.

Ava bit her lip. 'They started last week, after I sent Rita home. She calms down when she knows I'm nearby.'

Cesare swore fluently under his breath. 'I needed to know, Ava.'

She nodded. 'This was why I wanted to come back. She's always been happier here.'

His jaw clamped so tight a pulse kicked in his temple. 'You will tell me everything, no matter how small or insignificant. Agreed?'

The power behind his words rocked her to the core. From near total distance to this fierce protectiveness of Annabelle made her reel. That she had a destructive force of nature to thank tightened chaotic knots in her stomach. 'Agreed.'

After several seconds, he relaxed.

'So,' Cesare drawled, his gaze following Annabelle, who'd picked up Ava's iPod, inserted one earphone and was now dancing around the room, 'your commune didn't just teach you to eat, pray and love, did they also teach little girls how to dance like eccentric rock stars?'

Ava found herself taking her first easy breath since she'd arrived back home. 'Just because you can't dance to save your life doesn't mean you can look down your nose at others. Besides, she gets her dancing gene from me.'

'No doubt about that,' he drawled.

'Watch it!'

Annabelle danced over to them. 'Can I have a biscuit, please?'

Cesare picked up the plate and held it out to her. 'It's called *biscotti*. Try saying it, *piccolina*.' He smiled with undisguised pride when she pronounced it perfectly.

Ava swallowed but the solid lump wouldn't move from her throat. Blinking away sudden tears, she jumped up and picked up her laptop.

'If you don't mind watching her, I'll go and put this away.'

'Then we can swim, Mummy? You promised.' As a prize for being good on the plane, she'd promised her daughter the earth—and a long swim when they got home.

'Yes, we can, so don't have too much lemonade, okay?'

As she left the room, she felt Cesare's incisive gaze probing her back. Her steps quickened, defiantly trying to outrun the calm, completely rational voice asking if she knew what she was letting herself in for.

They weren't in the *salone* or at the pool when she returned five minutes later, dressed in an orange one-piece swimsuit and white shorts with a loose white shirt over the top. Ava was about to return indoors when she heard her daughter's voice.

Following the flower-lined pathway that curved round the villa, she stopped in her tracks. Cesare and Annabelle were bent over a rose bush, admiring a trio of butterflies fluttering from one bud to the other.

It wasn't the picture of wonderment on her daughter's face that stopped Ava's heart. It was the look of intense pain reflected in Cesare's face as he gazed at Annabelle. He looked so starkly distraught that she leaned her hand against the wall to steady herself.

And immediately pulled back with a gasp as the baking concrete singed her hand. Cesare glanced up. In an instant the look was gone. If it hadn't registered for more than a few seconds, Ava would've thought she'd imagined it. She held her breath as he straightened up and strode to her.

'Are you all right?' he questioned coolly.

'Hot wall, bare skin. Bad idea. Should remember that.'

He claimed her hand and examined the heated flesh. 'There's some ice on the table. I'll put some on it for you,' he said.

She glanced at Annabelle.

'She's enthralled with her butterflies for now. Come.' The word was more command than suggestion.

'Seriously, it's nothing.'

He cast her a grim smile and marched her to the poolside. 'Is that why you're grimacing? Because it's nothing?'

'Fine, it hurts like hell. Satisfied?'

Pushing her into one of the padded seats, he sat opposite her. 'Why do women always say *it's nothing,* when clearly it isn't?'

'I don't know. You've probably known more women than me. You tell me.'

He didn't deny it. Just smiled in that oh-so-smug way that made her yearn to kick him. Hard. 'Normally, it's just a way of attracting more attention.'

Irritation grew, along with her already heated temperature. He'd used the fully equipped pool house to change into swimming trunks in the time she'd gone upstairs and his bare muscular thighs almost imprisoning hers were covered in short silky hairs that taunted her with their luxuriant promise. The reaction it caused to her body was as unwelcome as it was unstoppable.

'You think I burned myself deliberately to get your attention? You really think I'm that pathetic?' Why did her voice sound so husky? And why, when he hadn't even administered the ice on her stinging palm, were her nipples peaking so painfully?

He smiled, wrapped several ice cubes in a linen napkin and placed it in her palm. 'No, *cara mia*. Because you're not most women.' His gaze captured hers, the tawny depths smoky, intense and way too captivating for her sanity.

'Thank you. I think.' Foolish pleasure stole through her, accelerating her already racing heartbeat.

'Prego.' The deep, softly muttered word flowed over her overheating senses.

Everything fell away. The sound of the water splashing against the side of the pool, the warm buzzing of bees in the afternoon air, the sound of boats on the lake. Everything, except the heat radiating from Cesare's eyes, the warmth of the fingers curled around hers and the emotions rippling through her. His gaze traced her face. When it lingered on her lips, it took all her willpower not to lick them in shameless anticipation.

Unavoidably, her own gaze fell to the sensual curve of his lips; lips she'd tasted mere hours ago.

Heat collected and oozed between her legs, stinging with a need that gripped with relentless force. Realising she hadn't taken a breath in a dizzyingly long time, she sucked in air through her mouth.

The sound ripped through their sensual cocoon, intensifying the tension arcing between them. Cesare swallowed, the movement of his strong neck making her pulse skitter and her fingers yearn to caress his skin.

His fingers convulsed around hers. Her gaze returned to his face and found his attention riveted on her breasts.

Desire wove a dangerous path through her as she remembered how much he'd once loved her breasts. How he'd used to mould them, shape them with his hands and worship them for what seemed like long, endless hours while he murmured heated Italian words in homage.

His gaze darted back to hers and she knew he was remembering too. Remembering how he'd loved them even more when they grew fuller with her pregnancy.

She couldn't take it any more. Her eyelids grew heavy, her blood thickening with unbearable yearning even as she tried to pull away.

He held her easily.

'Cesare…' She wasn't sure whether she was pleading or protesting.

His eyes darkened to a burnished gold. He wanted her too. *Desperately.* The thought sent delight racing through her veins at the exact moment he gave a strangled groan.

'Cesare, please.' She wasn't even certain that she wanted him to answer the sexual need clawing through her. All she knew was that she wanted *answers.*

She saw his withdrawal even before Annabelle's distressed voice reached them. '*Papà,* they flew away. I wanted them to stay but the butterflies flew away!'

'*Mi dispiace, piccolina*, but these things happen. It wasn't meant to be.'

She knew his words were directed at her. He continued to stare at her as he curled her fingers over the napkin and placed her hand on the table.

She closed her eyes, willing away the intense pain spiralling through her. *Breathe…just breathe. In. Out.* Over the sound of her fracturing emotions, she heard Cesare soothe his daughter's disappointment.

What about me? What about this gaping ache I carry inside because I don't know what's happened to us?

Questions crowded in her head as she sat there, the ice doing its job to soothe her palm while, inside, confusion congealed into a tight ball behind her breastbone. Slowly it dawned on her that she'd let it happen again; she'd let Cesare toy with her emotions, disrupt her thought patterns until she wasn't sure whether she was coming or going.

Dear Lord, she'd been in his presence less than half a day and already she'd let him weave his potent spell around her twice. *What was wrong with her?*

Intensely irritated with herself, she let Cesare take over entertaining Annabelle, listening to her delight as he swam up and down the pool with her on his back.

Dinner was brought out to the poolside just as the sun started to sink over the lake. Annabelle started to flag soon after with the effects of jet lag. By the time Cesare carried her upstairs, she was almost asleep.

Weariness sapped Ava as she lingered over Annabelle's bedtime story. For a moment she contemplated walking through to her own suite, crawling under the covers and letting the whole world fall away.

No. She straightened her spine.

Cesare had demonstrated in the last year that he could erase her comprehensively from his life. That he had every intention of continuing to do so.

But, for the sake of her sanity, Ava needed to know *why.*

Cesare picked up his wine glass and tried to marshal his thoughts. But even *thinking* had become a gut-wrenchingly difficult task. Unbidden, the scent of Ava's orgasm rose to torture him. *Dio*, he'd been close—so close—to experiencing that sweet heaven again. But he knew, as much as it killed him, he had to walk way. And continue walking away. Every single time.

For Roberto's sake, as some small, pitiful measure of penance for what he'd done to his brother, he couldn't give in to the craving.

Besides, the last thing he needed on top of the trauma and devastation life had thrown his way was the complication sex brought. Especially the uncontrollable kind that always felt a heartbeat away whenever he touched Ava.

This afternoon he'd boldly laid down his plan for ensuring he and Ava wouldn't run into each other more than necessary for the next few weeks. But already he saw the plan unravelling. The incident in the hallway and the few hours he'd spent with her by the pool had refuelled the sizzling attraction he'd tried and failed to bury. An attraction he had no right to rekindle. Or crave.

That only left him with one option.

Light female footsteps approached. Cradling his wine glass in one hand, he watched Ava emerge onto the terrace, child monitor in hand and a look of fierce determination in her eyes.

Although his heart sank a little, a part of him welcomed the situation.

Because, if nothing else, being caught in the middle of an earthquake had hammered home just how unpredictable life could be. He'd ruined his brother's life. He refused to remain in a situation where he could ruin another.

He'd tried to reason with Ava. Now it was time to be cruel to be kind.

She stopped in front of him and set down the monitor. 'I'm hoping being home will make them stop, but if she has another nightmare we'll hear her.'

He merely nodded. A flash caught and drew his attention to his wedding ring. He'd slipped it on when he'd lunched with his mother during his quick stopover in Rome. His parents had suffered enough in the last month; the last thing he'd wanted was to distress them further by exposing the state of his marriage.

Before him, Ava shifted from one foot to the other. Then she exhaled. 'What you said this afternoon…about things not meant to be. What did you mean?' she demanded, her arms once again crossed in battle stance.

He took his time to twirl his wine glass, allowed his

gaze to rise slowly from her bare, stunning legs, linger at her rounded hips, past her deliciously full breasts, to capture hers.

His grim smile felt as strained as the tightening in his groin. 'When we met, I was blown away by your beauty. You were sexy, vivacious, with a reckless streak that drew me like a moth to a flame. And the sex…' His breath stalled, his pulse kicking up another dangerous notch. 'The sex was unbelievable, better or quite possibly the best I'd ever had.' Her shocked gasp bounced over him and disappeared in the night breeze. 'Unfortunately, I let it blind me into making an unforgivable error.'

Her eyes darkened. 'What was that error?' she whispered.

He threw back his drink in one greedy, hopefully fortifying gulp and set the glass down. 'I think you'll agree that catastrophe has a way of bringing into sharp focus what's important.'

'Yes.'

'Two things became clear to me in the aftermath of the earthquake, *cara mia*. The first was that my daughter means more to me than my life itself and I would rip my heart out before I let anything remotely close to that devastation happen to her again.'

The fire in her eyes told him she felt the same. For a moment, he didn't want to utter the next words, but he knew he needed to. 'The second was that I…as deliciously tempting as you were…as mind-altering as the sex was, *bellissima*, I know now that I should never have married you.'

CHAPTER FOUR

I SHOULD NEVER *have married you.*

Ava stabbed the trowel deeper into the soil, oblivious to the heat and sweat cascading down her face. A grim smile stretched her lips as she recalled the horror on Lucia's face when she'd asked for the gardening supplies.

But it had been that or go mad from replaying that statement in her head over and over. Agata Marinello's endless text messages every two seconds hadn't helped to improve her disposition either.

Hard physical labour was what she needed. Bone tiredness meant she would collapse exhausted into bed at night and fall asleep without torturing herself with thoughts she had no business thinking.

For the past week, Cesare had stuck religiously to the schedule they'd set out on her return. He spent time with Annabelle in the morning while she met with the Marinellos; she took over in the afternoons and they had supper with their daughter before they took turns giving her a bath and putting her to bed.

Living under the same roof as Cesare was going smoothly. The truce was working. She should've been happy.

She wasn't. A very unladylike snort escaped her throat. How could she be when she was constantly in knots over Cesare's behaviour? The man had proved himself a champion at avoiding her, yet she could feel his presence as closely as the air on her skin. Could sense his gaze on her from his window when she played at the pool with Annabelle or when they went down the jetty to watch the luxury boats sail by. What was frustrating her most was the longing she could sense in his gaze.

Cesare yearned to spend more time with his daughter, but he was keeping away because of her. Had she really got it so wrong? Had her need for a family blinded her to the fact that she was setting up that family with a man who didn't want the full package?

Pain ripped through her and her fingers stilled as she tried to recall for what seemed like the millionth time, when things had started to change.

Cesare had been shocked by her pregnancy, even though he bounced back almost immediately. Hell, she was sure he'd been ecstatic.

He'd been a godsend during her pregnancy. Unbelievably, the sex had been her favourite part of being pregnant—the seemingly innocent back rubs that had often reached very pleasurable conclusions.

A flush suffused her face in recollection of the times he'd only had to whisper *back rub* in her ear to make her pulse race.

Then Annabelle had been born. Cesare had taken one of his rare trips to visit Roberto. And then, seemingly overnight, everything had changed.

She slammed the trowel into the soil.

'Careful there, *cara*, or you'll petrify the seeds before they get a chance to grow.'

'Careful there, Cesare, or you'll lose a foot if you annoy me.' She silently cursed him for his ability to move so quietly despite his impressive size. If it'd been one of her brothers, she'd have had no compunction in biting his head off. In fact, she'd done so many times with Nathan, the youngest of her three brothers.

But her emotions were too raw, too close to the surface to risk losing control in front of Cesare. She took a deep breath.

'*Bene poi,* since I value my foot way too much, I'll stay out of harm's way.' Droll amusement tinged his voice and she gritted her teeth not to react to it.

'What do you want?' Her surly voice matched her mood.

'You mean aside from checking that my land isn't being desecrated by your vicious digging?' he asked.

She sat back on her heels and glared at him. 'You own more than your fair share of land in Italy and the western world. I'm sure you won't miss a six by ten foot square piece.'

He shrugged, disgustingly unperturbed by her censure. 'Lucia tells me you're growing oranges. You do remember we have oranges delivered fresh every day from my orchard in Tuscany, don't you?'

'These are miniature oranges,' she replied, trying not to let her eyes wander over the stunning perfection of his lean, hard-packed frame.

From her disadvantaged kneeling position, he seemed even more devastating, more domineering in a way that made her struggle to hide a small shiver of desire.

'Ah,' he retorted. 'So you prefer your oranges small?'

'The oranges aren't small, only the trees—' She stopped when she saw the mocking smile that flashed across his face.

He was making fun of her. Disconcertingly, she wanted to grin in response. She bit her lip hard to hide its Judas twitch.

'What do you want?'

He held out her phone. 'It's been pinging text messages every few minutes. I thought they might be important.'

She took it and flung it on to the grass. 'Agata Marinello and her unending demands can go to hell. Was that all?'

He didn't answer immediately. In fact he remained silent for so long that she glanced up at him.

The trace of a smile had vanished. His gaze was disturbingly intent as he stared down at her. Her throat dried as she experienced a sudden, inexplicable feeling that he was about to tell her something she wouldn't welcome.

'We have a guest coming to dinner this evening.' The notice was delivered with little warmth and no pleasure.

She frowned. 'You seem unhappy about it.'

His lips pursed. 'I'd prefer not to have any company but it is what it is.'

'Tell them not to come then,' she said simply. 'What would be worse, begging off hosting a dinner or exposing the guest to an unwelcome reception?'

'It would be discourteous of me since I myself arranged it a…while ago.'

Her heart lurched unsteadily as it occurred to her that Cesare's displeasure didn't stem from having an unwelcome guest, but from Ava's presence at the dinner table. 'You mean before I decided to bring myself and my daughter back home unannounced?'

'Something like that.'

She cleared a sudden painful constriction in her throat. 'Is it a business dinner?'

'No, Celine is a friend of the family and is…important to me.'

'Celine?' Why had her insides suddenly gone cold despite the sun's intense heat?

Cesare had invited a woman to dinner. Big deal. But she couldn't stop the sudden tension making her fingers tighten around the trowel. Dull pain shot up her arm. Even then she couldn't let go of the tool.

Cesare had friends. Not that she knew many of them. Theirs had been a jealously guarded courtship, preferred by both of them because she didn't have to share Cesare with her disapproving family and he'd been based in London at the time with easily ignored business acquaintances.

She'd met his parents at the wedding, although not his younger brother, Roberto. She'd also been introduced to the smattering of uncles, aunts and cousins that Italian families abounded with—a family she'd been desperate to become a part of. A family that had on face value welcomed her—until Cesare's gradual distance had quickly become a family-wide phenomenon.

Her memory wasn't faulty enough to have forgotten a *Celine*. And certainly not one who was *important* to Cesare.

'Ava?'

She realised she'd missed his question.

'Sorry—what?' The words were forced through stiff lips.

'I asked if seven-thirty was okay with you,' he repeated slowly, as if making allowances for her sluggish brain.

Was seven-thirty okay with her? 'No.' It slipped out before courtesy or caution could stop it.

'Perdono?'

'You asked if the time was okay, I said no. It's obvious you don't want her here now I'm back. Use me as the excuse. Tell her not to come because the time is not okay with me.'

This way, she'd never have to meet the *important* Celine, never have to endure her gut twisting in knots the way it was now at the prospect of meeting the woman who might one day replace her and wear the famous di Goia wedding ring Cesare had presented to her with such dignified pride the day he'd proposed to *her*.

Cesare's clear disbelief at her response almost made her laugh out loud. *Almost*.

'As much as I appreciate your *selfless* efforts, unfortunately it doesn't work that way.'

'Well, can I be excused? She is *your* guest, after all.' Why did she have to break bread with the woman?

Anger laced his movements as he shoved his hands in his pockets. 'You will be dressed appropriately and ready to greet our guest at seven-thirty, Ava. Do I make myself clear?'

'Ooh, I love it when you go all domineering and masterful,' she purred, only to gasp as he sank down to her level, bringing six feet two of bristling masculinity up close and very personal.

'Did the consequences of last week teach you nothing about challenging me?' he asked in a deceptively soft tone.

Ava knew she was playing with fire, but she couldn't seem to stop herself from testing the depths of the flames. 'You mean pushing us both to the edge before withdrawing? I don't know, you tell me. I'm still digesting your *I should never have married you*. How long does blue balls last?' she taunted.

'*Che diavolo—*' His jaw actually slackened before he managed to clench it tight again. When he spoke again, it was between gritted teeth. 'Just be ready at seven-thirty. *Capito?*'

'If I must.' She raised the trowel in a mock salute and watched him stalk away, shoulders stiff with tension.

With renewed vigour, she dug into the earth. In a few hours she would meet Cesare's *important* guest.

Maybe the gods would be kind and make Celine short, fat and dumpy as all hell.

The gods granted her one wish.

Celine *was* short.

But fat and dumpy she was not. She was the original pocket Venus, with the kind of fragility that made men want to instinctively take care of her, in a way that made Ava, with her five foot seven frame and the three-inch heels she'd slipped into as an added confidence booster, feel like the *Leaning Tower of Pisa* as she reached out to shake Celine's proffered hand.

Celine di Montezuma reeked cute perfection from the top of her expensively styled gleaming black hair to the pointy toes of her designer heels. What grated the most were her open friendliness and genuine, pleasant smile she directed at Ava as she removed her silk wrap and handed it to Cesare.

'I've heard so much about you,' she said to Ava.

'Really? I hadn't heard so much as a peep about you until four hours ago.'

Ava ignored the warning glint in Cesare's eyes as he straightened from cheek-kissing Celine.

Their guest's warm laugh echoed in the vast hallway. 'He didn't just drop my visit on you, did he? Don't you hate that about men?'

'*Hate* is too mild a word.'

She laughed again and tucked her arm through Ava's. As much as Ava wanted to hate her, she grudgingly, painfully understood Cesare's attraction to the vivacious Celine.

The feeling increased all through Lucia's superbly prepared dinner of egg and salmon frittata starter, followed by slow-cooked lamb in herb sauce and diced potatoes. Which she hardly touched.

The lump that had lodged in her chest since Cesare announced her arrival grew with each second she watched the warm interplay between the two Italians.

For the first time since her return, Ava saw Cesare smile with genuine affection at another adult. The whites of his teeth gleamed in the subdued lights of the dining room as he responded to some joke Celine made.

Picking up her glass, she drained the last of the white wine she'd nursed throughout the meal.

Cesare slid her a narrow-eyed glance.

What? she wanted to blurt out. If he was callous enough to force her to watch him and his new paramour enjoy each other, then she could damn well get drunk doing it.

As if sensing the change in the air, Celine turned to her with a slightly wary look.

'How is Annabelle?' she asked.

Had Cesare tensed just then? Unfortunately Ava's head had started to swim from the sudden intake of alcohol and she couldn't be sure. Certainly, his fingers seemed to cup his wine glass a little tighter. Her gaze darted to his face, but his expression reflected arrogant calm.

Ava answered. 'She's fine, thank you for asking.'

'Is she adjusting well to being back home?'

'Sun, lake, swimming pool and all the toys a little girl could have, thanks to a suddenly attentive and over-indulgent father. What's not to like?' She couldn't quite curb the sarcasm that emerged with her answer.

Celine's smile slipped another notch.

Watch it, Cesare's gaze warned.

Drop dead, she threw back. He shouldn't have invited her if he expected her to play nice with his girlfriend.

'I was hoping to see her this evening,' Celine said, breaking into the tense silence.

Surprise and more than a little anger surged through Ava, until she remembered she wasn't supposed to have been here when Cesare invited Celine to dinner.

Was that what he'd planned all along? Had he made plans to get rid of her and spend the summer with Annabelle and Celine?

The sheer scale of Cesare's anger at her arrival suddenly fell into place.

Pain swiftly replaced surprise. Calmly she placed her wine glass on the table. She didn't think the crystal was safe in her hand any more because the sudden urge to throw it at Cesare's head had gained astronomical proportions.

How dared he arrange for Annabelle to meet his girlfriend…without consulting her?

She shot him a glance. His cool, composed expression told her the same story it had since she'd got to know him.

Cesare answered to no one. He did what he wanted when it suited him. And if he wanted to introduce his mistress to his daughter tonight, that was exactly what he would have done.

Except he hadn't. They'd put Annabelle to bed together with no mention of her meeting his guest.

'She's asleep. We put her to bed over an hour ago,' Ava responded since Cesare didn't seem inclined to.

'Oh.' Celine's disappointment made Ava experience a small fizz of gleeful satisfaction. 'Perhaps I can just look in on her?'

Glee and satisfaction evaporated. 'You want to look in on her?'

Again Cesare didn't seem surprised by the odd request. When Ava glanced at him, he merely shrugged and carried on twirling the stem of his glass between his fingers.

Ava swallowed down the heated *Over my dead body* that sprang to her lips. It was clear Celine was very much a fixture in Cesare's life. Whether it was tonight or another night in the very near future, Celine and her daughter would meet.

But it didn't have to be tonight, an irrational pain-filled voice whispered in her head. *It might happen, but it didn't have to be right now!*

'I don't think it's a good idea—'

Cesare pushed back his chair, and rising to his feet, halted her words. 'Come, Celine. I'll take you.'

'No you won't!'

His smile brushed the outer fringes of courtesy. 'Don't worry, Ava. She won't be disturbed. I'll make sure of it.'

He rose and beckoned Celine. The other woman's clear discomfort made Ava cringe inside but she forced her chin up and smiled despite the tide of acid anxiety that swallowed her whole.

'Make sure you don't. If she wakes up she'll be impossible to put back to sleep.'

Cesare didn't turn around as he escorted Celine out of the dining room, their footsteps echoing in tandem down the hallway.

Ava sat frozen in her seat, unable to stem the ever-increasing tidal wave of despair. A small part of her hadn't quite accepted it when Cesare told her Celine was important to him. Even through the ordeal of dinner, a small part of her had hoped that she was nothing more than a fond family friend.

But would a *family friend* insist on seeing Annabelle after being told she was asleep?

Of course not. Which meant, the woman whom her daughter might soon be calling stepmother was now upstairs, looking in on her precious daughter…

…while she sat here, clutching her figurative pearls like a tragic, overdramatic Victorian heroine.

Swift burning anger propelled her upright. She reached the sweeping staircase before she remembered she'd discarded her shoes under the dining table.

Whispered voices as she reached halfway up the marble stairs made her thankful for her bare, silent feet. Her hand curled over the smooth wood of the banister, her heart in her throat as she froze on the step.

'How long are you going to keep this from her?' Celine questioned passionately.

Cesare responded in Italian, his delivery too quick for Ava to follow, but she sensed it wasn't what the other woman had expected to hear.

Another burst of Italian, this time from Celine, resulted in Cesare's heavier footsteps heading towards the landing, and Ava.

'*No.* It's impossible,' he responded in an implacable voice.

Ava held her breath as they both came into view, Celine's short steps quickening to catch up with Cesare's longer strides.

'It's painful, I know, but you have to tell her. She deserves to know what's going on.'

Cesare reached the stairs, saw her and froze. A second later, Celine spotted Ava too. Her eyes widened with alarm before they shut in dismay.

Cesare's mouth opened but no words emerged. His hands balled into fists and his piercing eyes bored into hers with a mixture of anger and frustration.

Ava tried to swallow, but the throat muscles required wouldn't comply. Her fingers tightened around the banister and she prayed desperately that her legs would support her for just a little while longer.

'Ava…' Cesare finally rasped.

But her pain was too sharp, too decimating for her to stand there, listening to whatever explanation his astute brain had swiftly concocted for her.

'Save it, Cesare. I may be slow on the uptake, but I'm not stupid.'

His colour faded considerably beneath his tan. A look, curiously close to alarm skittered over his face as he braced a hand on the post next to him.

'So…you know?'

The depth of his reaction to her discovery only increased her despair. She glanced at Celine, who stood clutching the rail—as white as a sheet.

For a second Ava wondered whether she would go all out and add to the overly dramatic scene by performing a Victorian swoon, perhaps save herself the embarrassment of a confrontation by fainting. But Celine stayed on her feet, even though her hand managed to find Cesare's arm and grip it.

Tearing her gaze from that proprietorial display, she addressed Celine. 'I know you're sleeping with my husband, if that's what you're so anxious for him to tell me.'

Cesare sucked in a swift breath. '*Dio mio*—'

'But as long as we're still husband and wife, you'll stay

away from him and from our daughter. Do you understand?'

Celine shook her head. 'No! *Per favore,* Ava—'

Ava raised her chin. 'It's *Signora* di Goia to you. Now, get out of my house.'

CHAPTER FIVE

'*MADRE DI DIO,* Ava, there are no half measures with you, are there? You always have to jump in with both feet.' Cesare had just slammed the door behind a hastily departed Celine. The fury radiating from his body made her swallow nervously.

She flipped her hair over her shoulder in a show of bravado that was fast fading in the face of his anger. 'If you mean I don't tolerate being made a fool of in my own home, then the answer is yes.'

'Need I remind you that we're all but separated and this is *my* house?'

She shrugged. 'What's yours is supposed to be mine too, isn't it? I'm sure I've seen that tattooed on a body part somewhere.'

'*Porca miseria.* You insult our guest and all you can do is crack jokes?'

'You should've warned me you were sleeping with her. Maybe then I would've been on my best behaviour!'

His eyes narrowed, his fury intensifying by the second. 'I'm *not* sleeping with Celine,' he said through gritted teeth.

'Oh, don't take me for a fool. You two were making enough moon eyes at each other to keep this villa illuminated for a month!'

'I've known her for a very long time. There is a familiarity between us—'

'Yes, it's called *sex.*'

He took an unchecked step towards her, as if to physically restrain her from speaking. At the last moment he lurched away and stalked to the window. Shoving his fists into his pockets, he stared out into the softly lit garden.

'Celine is the daughter of one of my father's oldest friends. I've known her since she was born. We've always been friends but she was much closer to Roberto.'

Ava tensed at the mention of his brother's name.

For as long as they'd been married, Cesare had remained close-lipped about his reclusive younger brother. All she'd ever been able to find out was that he lived in a castle high up in the Swiss Alps and only permitted Cesare to visit him from time to time. Ava had never been told why Roberto di Goia had withdrawn from the world.

'So Celine is Roberto's friend, not your girlfriend?' Stupid hope flared to life.

He shrugged. 'I think our respective parents hoped Celine and Roberto would marry one day. I know Celine waited a long time for Roberto to propose.'

'You mean before he went to live in Switzerland?'

'Yes.' The word emerged with a poignancy that scraped her heart.

'Don't tell me. The proposal Celine wanted never arrived and now your parents want you to step in and do the right thing by her? Honour the agreement or something?'

He turned from the window, his tawny eyes gleaming with grim amusement in the half-light. 'You've watched too many vintage *mafioso* movies, Ava. No one *demands* honour marriages like those any more. There was never any agreement, just a wish.'

A pang of discomfort made her realise she was twisting her fingers into knots. 'So what happened between Roberto and Celine?'

The fleeting amusement faded, to be replaced by a pain

so deep and gut-wrenching she took a step towards him. 'Cesare?'

He didn't respond for a long while, his bleak gaze fixed in the middle distance. Finally, he heaved a heavy sigh.

'I should've told you… I'm sorry, there didn't seem to be the right time to announce that sort of thing.'

She frowned. 'Announce what? What didn't you tell me?'

'Roberto…' He stopped and another pain-filled sigh ripped from his chest. Fear clutched Ava's chest.

She bit her tongue, torn between screaming for an answer and the need to protect him from the obvious pain of what he fought to say.

The need to know won out. 'What about Roberto?'

He inhaled again. 'He…died two weeks ago.'

Shock ripped through her. '*What*?'

Cesare shot her a dark, tormented look. Then he glanced absently around the room. When his gaze returned to hers, his features were once again resolute.

'Roberto is dead. Celine never got the chance to marry him. The fact that she didn't doesn't mean I see her as anything more than a friend, so you can contain your hysteria about us having an affair. And I would appreciate you curbing any such future outbursts in front of our guests.'

This was the Cesare she knew—commanding, resolute, domineering.

He strode past her, ready to walk out.

She grabbed his arm. 'Wait! You can't just announce that Roberto is…you can't just drop something like that and walk away. Why didn't you tell me this earlier?'

Another flash of pain crossed his eyes. 'Think about what's happened between us lately—the earthquake, the trauma you and Annabelle have been through. When do you suggest I should've dropped this on you?'

'You could've found a way to tell me. He was my brother-in-law—'

'A brother-in-law you never met.'

'And why was that? You've always been reluctant to talk about Roberto, what happened to him or why you two weren't close.'

His eyes grew bleaker. 'Leave it, Ava.'

'Why should I? You accuse me of jumping to the wrong conclusions. How can I arrive at the right one when I seem to be operating in the dark? Tell me what happened between you and Roberto.'

For a long time she thought he wouldn't answer. 'Valentina happened,' he slid out.

Ava was almost too afraid to ask. 'Who's Valentina?'

'Celine's older sister. Seven years ago, I'd just opened my New York office when I met her at a party. She was thinking of relocating and she had a good head for numbers so when she asked me for a job, I offered her one.'

'Did you sleep with her?' The words shot out before she could stop herself.

His eyelids descended. 'Ava…'

'It's okay; it was before we met. I guess I have no right to ask you that.' Although the jealousy that seared her insides told a very different story.

'The answer is no, I didn't sleep with her. But Roberto thought I had. He turned up in New York a month later and accused me of poaching his woman. Turns out they'd been dating in Rome before she came to New York. I didn't know.'

'Hell. Surely you explained things to Roberto?'

He gave a bitter laugh. 'Until I was blue in the face. But he wasn't in a listening mood. We had the mother of all fights, right in the middle of a meeting in full view of my board members.' He paced to the window and turned back sharply. 'Unfortunately, that wasn't the worst of it. In the middle of all that carnage, Valentina announced she was pregnant with Roberto's child.'

Ava frowned. 'How was that worse?'

'Roberto got down on one knee there and then and asked her to marry him. She declined his proposal.'

'Oh no.'

'I got the blame for that too but I convinced him not to give up so he kept trying. She told him she wasn't ready to get married or settle down, even though she intended to keep the baby. Roberto begged her to return to Rome with him. I think he wore her out in the end…'

'But…?'

'Roberto never truly believed the child was his—Valentina liked to party hard and often. He talked her into having an amniocentesis. She nearly lost the baby.'

Ava gasped. 'Oh my God.'

'After that she flatly refused to stay with Roberto. She came back to New York…asked for her job back. She was carrying my brother's child. I could hardly say no.'

'And Roberto blamed you all over again?'

He shrugged. 'We'd never been particularly close growing up. He was ill more often than not, constantly in and out of hospital as a child, while I was away at boarding school ten months out of twelve. Valentina was his first and only serious relationship.'

Her heart clenched hard. 'So the big brother he thought had everything had swooped in and stolen the only woman he cared about.'

Cesare's jaw clenched hard. '*Si*. He refused to believe that I'd had no hand in Valentina's defection. Nothing I said made a difference. I tried to talk to Valentina but she refused to return to Rome.' He sighed. 'I gave her all the support I could. In hindsight, I think I may have given her too much support.'

'She never went back to Roberto?' The question slid from numb lips as it struck her just how very little she really knew about the man she'd married.

'No, she never got the chance.' His husky reply broke through her thoughts. 'She overdosed on sleeping pills midway through her second trimester. Turned out she was manic-depressive and her state had been heightened by her pregnancy. Roberto lost his mind with grief. He cut me off, he cut our parents off and moved to Switzerland.'

Ice drenched her soul and, for the first time in her life, Ava found herself struck dumb. Neither of them moved for what seemed like an eternity.

Then he exhaled a harsh breath. 'You wanted to know. Now you know.'

The words hit her like a slap in the face. 'You still should've told me. At the very least our child deserved to know she'd lost her uncle.'

His gaze slid away. 'Roberto died two weeks after the earthquake. I didn't think it was fair to burden you with that news.'

'And in the time since then? You could've texted, emailed…hell, you could've Tweeted me, for heaven's sake.'

A rough hand shoved through his hair. 'Yes, I could've done all of that. But I didn't. Let's just chalk it up to me being the heartless bastard you think I am and move on, shall we?'

Ava wanted to rail at him but, seeing the grief behind his words, she opted for peace. 'Will you at least tell Annabelle? She deserves to know.'

Cesare's gaze met hers and Ava's heart caught at the pain in the dark depths. '*Sì,* I'll tell her about Roberto when the time is right.'

A thought niggled, but danced away before Ava could fully grasp it. 'Was that what Celine meant when she insisted you tell me?'

'She thought you needed to know about Roberto, yes.' His tone implied he would very much prefer if she dropped the subject. Pain stung again.

The niggling persisted. 'But why did she insist on seeing Annabelle? It all seemed a bit OTT to me, to be honest.'

A grim smile crossed his mouth. 'Celine, like most women, doesn't know the meaning of subtle. She knows about the earthquake and has been asking to visit since you and Annabelle returned. She takes her role of honorary aunt very seriously.'

'As long as that's the only role she's banking on.'

'Drop it, Ava.' The warning was back in his voice, tension sizzling in that flattened line of his mouth. 'You insulted her and jumped to the wrong conclusions. You should thank your lucky stars I'm not rescinding our truce after that performance.'

Her heartbeat thundered. 'It's your fault. If you'd told me all of this *before* she arrived, we wouldn't be having this conversation!'

Cesare pinched the bridge of his nose. 'You push me… all the time you push. You never stop.'

The bone-deep weariness behind his words pulled her up short. 'What do you mean?'

Tawny eyes turned grave. 'From the very beginning you pinned high hopes on me—your need for a family, for *togetherness*. Don't think I didn't know what the Bali trip was all about. Did it occur to you that I wasn't in a position to provide you with all of that?'

Ice skated down her spine. 'Where is this coming from? If you felt like this, then why did you bother to come to Bali?'

He looked away. 'You rarely ask me for anything any more. You asked for that and I couldn't refuse you.'

'So you came anyway, knowing I was trying to save our marriage but knowing you had no intention of engaging with me?'

'I was hoping you'd see we were beyond help.'

'Well, silly me. That sailed right over my head.'

His jaw tightened. 'I was wrong, of course, to think things would go smoothly with you around; wrong to think I would be spared the reminder that I've failed you.'

'I'm just trying to understand—'

'Understand why I don't fit into your mould of a perfect husband and father? Because, above all else, it's what you want, isn't it?'

'*Above all else?* God, you make me sound like a needy, pathetic creature.' He remained silent and the ice unfurled. 'Is that what you really think of me?'

'I've never been good at the family thing, Ava. My parents had their hands full with Roberto. He was their number one priority for a very long time. Don't get me wrong, I wasn't neglected but I learned very quickly to be content with my own company. After a while, I preferred it.'

'Then why marry me?'

'You were carrying my child.'

The numbing ice encased her whole being. He stilled for a moment then jerked closer, the edges of regret on his face as he lifted his hand. She ducked out of reach before he could touch her.

'You don't need to soften the blow,' she forced out. 'In all things I would prefer brutal honesty.'

'Has it ever occurred to you that I keep you in the dark for your own protection?'

'I'm not a child, Cesare. And I especially don't want to be kept in the dark about things that affect our daughter. I want the truth. Always.'

A bleak look entered his eyes and his shoulders stiffened. 'In that case you need to know something else,' he said.

Her heart lurched. 'What?'

'Although he was sick on and off for months, we don't actually know what Roberto succumbed to in the end. That was part of the reason for Celine's visit.'

'Her…what *exactly* does Celine do?'

'She's a doctor.'

Her brain cogs slowly engaged until his meaning sank in. 'So asking about Annabelle…?'

'She also wanted to check on her *medically*. On all of us.'

Fear tightened her chest. 'What does she think could be wrong? And please don't sugar-coat the truth to protect me.'

'We honestly don't know. Roberto refused medical treatment in the weeks before his death. It could even be that he took his own life.' Raw pain drenched every word.

'Suicide?' she rasped. 'Dear God.' She sank into the chair. After several minutes, she raised her head. 'Is there anything else I should know?'

He visibly pulled in the reins of his control. 'No. The results of the cause of death should be available in the next few days. But tomorrow morning we'll call Celine and you'll apologise for your behaviour. *Si?*' The soft, dangerous tone sent sweet shudders chasing up her spine, melting the ice just a little.

'And if I refuse?'

'*Cristo,* why do you challenge me at every turn?'

'Because I'm not a doormat. You liked that about me once, remember?'

'I'm not in the mood to reminisce about us.'

She wanted to tear her gaze away, to stomp away in fury, but she was frozen, held captive by the magic of his voice, the seductive uniqueness of his scent that filled her senses, made her want to linger a while longer, breathing him in.

'If you meant what you just said about your…deficiencies, I think it's in all of our best interest that we tackle the subject of *us* sooner or later, don't you think?'

'Don't push me tonight, Ava. I'm at my limit.'

Something softened inside her. 'Not tonight.' She stepped closer, an invisible cord pulling her to him, his heat a craving she couldn't resist. Tentatively, she touched his firm cheek. 'I'm truly sorry about Roberto. Will you tell me if there's anything I can do?'

He muttered something low under his breath. Incoherent and pithy, but it caught and stopped her breath nevertheless. Mesmerised, she watched one hand come up slowly, building her anticipation as it touched and traced the skin underneath her ear.

She shuddered. The pad of one finger traced the vein pulsing heated, frantic blood through her body. Her breath grew shallow, causing her heart to accelerate even more from the lack of oxygen. When his finger came to rest on the pulse at her throat, it was all she could do not to moan.

He caught her to him, one strong arm snagging her waist and lifting her off her feet like a pirate claiming his bounty.

His mouth replaced his finger and she moaned at the relentless drum of desire beating in the swollen flesh between her legs, at the urgent tightening of her nipples. But he didn't relent. He lapped her flesh with his tongue, driving her nearly out of her mind before he sucked, deeply, mercilessly.

Oh dear God, she'd have a mark on there tomorrow, blatant evidence of Cesare's rough possession.

But right at that moment Ava didn't care about anything except prolonging the pleasure of Cesare's hot mouth on her. Eagerly, she tilted her head, offering the sensitive expanse of her neck to him.

With a groan he accepted her offer, kissing the length of her throat and back again, before biting hungrily on her soft lobe.

Her nails dug into his shoulders. Holding on tight, she lifted and threw her legs around his waist, anchoring herself against the pleasure of his lean frame. The hard rigid evidence of his arousal grazed her damp panties.

The shockingly intimate position made them both tense, then draw together as if unable to resist the magnetic force of the desire arcing between them.

When he started raining kisses along her jaw, she turned her head, met his mouth in a fierce kiss that rocked them both. She was hardly aware of him moving, barely aware of the firm sofa behind her back as he lowered her onto it.

All she knew and craved was Cesare, above her, around

her. Everywhere but inside her, where she desperately needed him to be.

Frustration bit deep. Tightening her thigh muscles, she tried to draw him closer to the centre of her, to the place that wept for his possession.

'You do this to me every time,' he said against her lips. 'You drench me in this…this *insanity*.'

'You make me sound like some witch, wielding a potent spell.'

The moment the words left her lips she regretted them. Because, just like the first afternoon of her return, her voice reacted like ice on his skin.

Tense muscles locked in fierce rejection as he disentangled her from his body. Face taut, he levered himself away and stared down at her. When he stumbled backwards, she clutched his arm.

'Please tell me this wasn't another stupid caveman demonstration?'

His pupils dilated and she glimpsed his turmoil before, with jerky movements, he removed himself to the other side of the room.

'It wasn't an intentional one, no,' he replied huskily.

'Then what exactly was it? God, Cesare, you're blowing so hot and cold, anyone would think you were a virgin.'

His face tightened. 'You don't know what you're asking, Ava.'

And she had a feeling she would regret the words, but her need to be with him, to experience the sheer bliss of Cesare's lovemaking had pushed her past shame. 'You're my husband. I'm your wife, albeit an unwanted one. What could be simpler?'

He whirled around. 'We haven't had sex in almost a year.'

A harsh laugh left her throat. 'Trust me, I *know*. And I'm not sure whether to be ashamed because I've let myself accept this preposterous situation between us or disgusted with myself because, despite everything, I still want you.'

His smile was tinged with an arrogance that made her palms itch to slap it off his face. Then kiss him like he was her last breath. 'Our chemistry defies reason and description. Always has. But you're chasing a dream, *cara*. One that can never become reality.'

She stopped and licked her lips. 'Then why are you still here?' Knowing he still wanted her, still desired her enough to shake his formidable control made her bolder.

Cesare had always prided himself on his control. It was only with her, on occasion, that she'd seen his formidable willpower slip. She'd suspected for a long time that he resented her for that loss of control.

She watched his hands unclench, and immediately clench again. 'Because it's becoming physically impossible to stay away from you.'

His gaze locked on hers, studying every movement like a predator tracking a doomed prey. 'Now it's your turn. You know I can't give you the wholesome family you want. What are you prepared to settle for?'

The white-hot gaze slid down to linger on her lips. She knew exactly what that look meant, and yes, she could have settled for wild, untamed, skin-melting sex. But she knew it would never make her happy. 'I'm not prepared to settle.'

Her heart thudded as he gathered himself together. His features hardened, closed off as completely as a solid steel door slamming in her face.

'Then we have nothing left to talk about.'

Pain rushed like an icy river through her veins. Gasping in air, she lowered her head to hide the effect of his words. With numb detachment, she noticed her neckline was gaping, showing the full upper curve of her breasts. Hastily, she rearranged her dress, thankful her hair had loosened enough to cover the heat rushing into her face.

She sensed him coming closer. For a second she thought

he would touch her, soothe away his harshly spoken words, but when she risked a glance she saw him veer towards the door.

Anger, gratefully received in place of fruitless hope, roiled through her. She surged to her feet and yanked her dress down.

'Why?'

He didn't turn around.

'Tell me why you still wear your wedding ring but are condemning our marriage?' She heard the strained bewilderment in her voice and would have given her eye teeth not to. 'Is it…is it because you don't love me any more?'

With one hand tensed on the doorknob, he turned. 'Any more?'

'Yes. Is that it?'

'Ava, I desired you. I craved you with a need and desperation that bordered on the unholy. But I never claimed to love you.'

Ava lay in darkness, sleep a thousand miles away as Cesare's words played an unrelenting refrain in her head. Words that had cut into her, devastated her so completely that she'd sunk into the sofa, incapable of speech.

Cesare, of course, had walked out after reminding her coolly of their call to Celine the next day. She'd clamped her lips together, begging whatever fates were within hearing distance to help her hold it together until he was out of earshot.

Then a long, hideous whimper had escaped her. The sound had reminded her of a wounded animal, alien and ugly, torn from the depths of her soul.

In that moment she'd hated herself. She'd always been weak when it came to Cesare. Minutes after meeting him, and agreeing to have a drink with him at a wine bar in London, she'd known in a deep, innate part of her being that he possessed the power to make her do things, *feel* things no other human being could. They'd never made it to the wine bar. He'd taken her to his country pad in Surrey and they'd ended up making love, right there on the bonnet of his car in the middle of his driveway. It had been the start of the most erotic, soul-shaking six weeks of her life.

Yes, he'd enthralled her from the very first look.

But the sex wasn't why she'd fallen for Cesare. During those six weeks, he'd taken care of her, treated her as if she was the most important thing in his life. And for someone who'd always felt like an afterthought in her family, it'd been like being handed a little piece of heaven.

Ava turned over, punched her frustration into her pillow. For Cesare to deny the man he'd been before their marriage and Annabelle's birth hurt her deeply. Because that man had been there—she hadn't dreamed him. Or had she?

She sucked in a shaky breath. Cesare's accusation that she was pushy, of foisting her dreams on him, cut through her muddled thoughts like deadly acid.

Falling pregnant with Annabelle so soon after meeting Cesare had merely accelerated the realisation of a lifelong desire, because nurturing a family she could call her own had always been her one and only dream. And when Cesare had proposed, she'd thought it'd been his dream too.

How wrong she'd been.

Because, she recalled, for a split second after she'd told him she was pregnant, Cesare had looked like a man who'd just glimpsed his worst nightmare.

'But we were so careful. How could this have happened?' he'd asked in shaken disbelief.

Since she'd asked herself that very same question, but with a burgeoning joy, she couldn't have summoned an answer to save her life.

Ava threw back the covers and padded to the window. Moonlight gleamed off the courtyard flagstones—the same flagstones she'd stood on when Cesare had proposed.

I never claimed to love you.

Foolish tears prickled her eyes. She wanted to hate Cesare for his callous words, but he was right. He'd never said the words. Oh, he'd demonstrated his desire exceptionally well; he'd provided for her every carnal and materialistic wish. But he'd never told her he loved her. She'd just...*assumed*...

Damn it. She wouldn't cry. Hell, at the back of her mind she'd accepted that at some point one of them would have to make a move to dissolve this empty marriage.

Except, of course, when the time had come she hadn't demanded a separation or divorce. She'd practically begged for him to take her back.

How pathetic was she? Furious with herself for wallowing in self-pity, she threw a shirt over her thigh-length nightgown, grabbed the monitor and left her suite.

Aimlessly wandering the house, she finally ended up in the kitchen. A wry smile twisted her lips. Her brother, Nathan, the only one of her three brothers who'd come remotely close to acknowledging her existence when they were growing up, would have mocked her mercilessly if he'd seen she'd reverted to her old habit of comfort-eating. Opening the fridge, she took out a half bottle of Soave and poured herself a glass.

A small platter of *stromboli* stood next to the large stove. She picked one and bit into it, then, on impulse, she tugged the phone off the wall, dialled her brother's number. Her disappointment was tinged with relief when she got his voicemail.

What would she have said to him anyway? That her husband had announced he'd never loved her and a part of her believed she'd caused her marriage breakdown by forcing a family? Grimacing, she left a short, nondescript message and hung up.

She turned and jumped at the shadow looming in the doorway. Her heart flipped several times more when Cesare stepped into the subdued kitchen light.

'*Mi dispiace.* I heard voices.' His narrowed glance went to the phone, then returned to her. 'Who were you calling at this time of the night?' he demanded.

'Nathan. I got his voicemail. I was leaving a message.'

'Have any of your family been in touch recently?'

'You mean have they developed a desperate need to get to know the sister they've rejected all their lives? That would be a no.' She refused to acknowledge the pain.

Cesare frowned. 'Do they know what's happened to you this past month?'

She swallowed the lump in her throat. 'They don't concern themselves with my well-being, Cesare. They never have.'

'I'm sorry—'

'I don't need you to be. And I don't need your pity. What I need you won't give me, so you can either leave me in peace, or we can change the subject.'

He stared at her for a full minute, then he leaned against the doorjamb. His gaze slid over her, lingering in places it had no right to linger. She wanted to scream at him to stop looking at her. But this was Cesare. Asking wouldn't mean getting.

Silence stretched as neither made a move to speak. The air in the open space closed off, growing thick until it felt as if they breathed the same pocket of oxygen.

Slowly, excitement licked through her belly, transmitting knee-weakening desire along her nerve endings. Ava forced herself to remember. Remembering how she'd humiliated herself a mere two hours ago fortified her resolve. She moved forward, then paused, realising that to walk out of the door she'd have to go past him.

Her glance fell to his hands and took in white padding and red specks where his knuckles bled. 'You've been in the gym?'

Cesare kept a fully equipped gym in all of his homes and kept ultra-fit by boxing.

He gave a grim nod. 'I was overwhelmed by the need to pummel something.' His eyes locked on hers, drilling into her until she feared he could see right through her.

'How did that work out for you?' Her voice emerged breathless, strained. She took a hasty sip of her wine.

'Not nearly as successful as I'd hoped it would. You?'

'I leave the pummelling to others.' She raised the items in her hand. 'I prefer to wage my war armed with carbs and wine. I'll let you know later if I'm winning.'

Half of her had hoped her answer would drive him away. The other half, the foolish half that never listened to reason where Cesare was concerned, leaped with joy when he came closer, slowly unwinding the padding from his bound fingers. Sweat glistened off his honed biceps, emphasising the play of superb muscle as he moved. Even more riveting was his half smile, more potent now he'd stopped beside her.

'Pour me a glass, would you?' He nodded at her glass.

'Do you think it's a good idea?'

He surveyed her with the sleepy regard of a jungle predator. The taut smile that barely curved his lips was acutely discerning. 'For me to drink wine, or for us to be in the same room at the same time?'

'Both.' She cursed her candid tongue and tried to address the less volatile issue. 'Also, isn't water the recommended drink after hectic exercise?'

Heat flared in her cheeks as his gaze turned even more intense. The torrid promise of sheet-burning sex pulsed between them. His nostrils flared for a second before he moved to the sink and ran his hands under the tap.

'I drank water after the workout. Now I need something…stronger.' His gaze dropped to her chest, his bold stare causing her breasts to grow heavier. 'I'll get the wine myself if you can't stand to be here.'

The clear challenge made her bolder. The red in her hair

and nature made backing down from a challenge an impossibility—or so she'd often been told.

She wouldn't slink away like a scared puppy just because Cesare was in a testy mood. Setting her drink on the vast centre island, she pulled out a stool and perched on it.

Cesare grabbed a glass, brought over the plate of *stromboli* and placed it down between them. She poured his wine as he took a bite of bread. After taking a sip, he sat back and looked at her.

'Sleep was eluding you also?'

'I think sleep would elude any woman whose husband announces he never loved her and regrets marrying her.'

He tensed immediately. 'Ava—'

'It's okay. No, actually, it's not okay but I'm not about to launch into another bout of hysteria if that's what you're worried about.'

He exhaled. 'You're the last woman I'd accuse of hysterics. But *grazie*.'

The piece of pastry she popped into her mouth to delay her response tasted like sawdust with a hint of garlic. Taking another sip of wine helped her force it down, but realising another bite wasn't a good idea because she risked choking, she put it down.

'Don't thank me just yet. I'm still reeling from the revelations about Roberto and about us. Just because I'm calm now doesn't mean we don't have a situation that doesn't need to be resolved.' Clearing her throat, she forced the words out. 'I think it's time we stop playing ostrich and take what's happening between us to the next…permanent level.'

The violent scrape of the stool as he pushed it back on the tiled floor raked across nerves already raw with her ravaged emotions.

Cesare planted both hands on the smooth surface and glared fire and brimstone at her. 'Di Goias do not divorce.'

Her mouth fell open. '*Excuse me?* Shouldn't you have

thought of that before you decided to enter a marriage you didn't want?'

'You were carrying my child. I had no choice.' His lips barely moved with his words.

She sucked in a stunned breath. 'Wow, you do know how to keep piling on the charm, don't you? I'm sure you would've made some damsel a perfect husband in the Dark Ages. Unfortunately for you, we're in the twenty-first century, so unless I signed on to this *Di Goias Do Not Divorce* without knowing about it, I don't see that you have a choice.'

His glare intensified. 'You knew we were only marrying because of Annabelle.'

'Wrong! I thought you were marrying me because you loved me, that you wanted to make a *family* with me.'

He stepped back abruptly as if she'd physically assaulted him. 'Again with the family!'

'What is so wrong with that?' she yelled, suddenly not feeling so calm any more.

'I never confessed such a feeling.'

'I know. Stupid me, mistranslating all those heated Italian endearments you whispered to me in bed as words of devotion and undying love.'

A dull flush washed across his taut cheekbones. 'I never lied to you about my feelings in or out of bed.'

'But you made me think you cared about me, that you wanted what I wanted. It was a lie by omission.'

As if frustrated with her logic, he whirled away from the island and started pacing in tight circles. She followed his prowl, helpless to avert her gaze because Cesare had always been a source of intense, almost worshipful fascination for her.

He finally returned and gripped the edge of the countertop. 'I never lied to you, Ava. And I did care.' His gaze speared hers, almost imploring, as if he willed her to believe him.

She swallowed. 'Obviously not enough. Ultimately, it was all about the sex for you. Shame I had to go and get pregnant, wasn't it?' The words were forced through a painful knot in her throat. 'Whatever you say next, even if you think and feel it, please do not tell me you regret having our daughter.'

Pain flitted over his face. In the next instant it was gone. 'I have not for a single moment regretted Annabelle. But you have to admit, things got very complicated very quickly with us.'

She released the breath locked in her throat and quickly swallowed down the threatening tears.

Enough.

Before she got sucked down into a quagmire of her own making, she stood. 'Well, it's time to *de-complicate* things. There's nothing to stop me seeking a divorce so whether you want one or not doesn't really matter. You said you shouldn't have married me, that I was too fixated on wanting a family with you to see that you didn't want one. I hate you for misleading me if that's the way you really felt. You still want me—do us both a favour and don't deny it, please. You want me but you don't want to be married to me, and yet you still wear your wedding ring.

'Frankly, I don't have a clue what's going on, but I'm done turning myself into a basket case trying to figure it out. So I don't really give a damn if it's the *di Goia thing* or not, Cesare. I want a divorce.'

CHAPTER SIX

CESARE DESCENDED THE stairs, his mood no less foul than when he'd gone upstairs three hours earlier under the pretext of going to bed.

Sleep had been non-existent. No surprise there. Irrational anger and frustration pulsed in equal measures through him. For the most part he was extremely disturbed by his reaction to Ava's announcement in the kitchen. Which in turn confused him. He was not a man who enjoyed being confused!

And yet, what had he expected when he announced they shouldn't have married? That she would dissolve in helpless tears and beg him to reconsider?

He gave a grim smile. Ava was not like that. No, his redheaded tigress reacted with claws, not tears. But there'd been no signs of claws last night…only a calm resignation after her hysterics-free announcement.

The disturbing hollowness inside him expanded.

Even if some masochistic part of him had wanted her to fight, what good would it have done? He wasn't wired to be a family man. He never would be.

Di Goias do not divorce. He snorted under his breath. For a man who prided himself on being ruthlessly straight in his business dealings, he was sure as hell making a pathetic ass of himself in his private life.

Ava only needed a competent Internet search engine to

verify his hot-headed statement as a pack of lies. Granted, divorce in his family was rare, but wasn't his Uncle Gianni neck-deep in a particularly messy one with his third wife right this very minute?

Cesare slammed the door to his study and paced the room. A dark part of him registered his anger was irrational. As irrational as the fear he'd felt when he'd had to leave Ava and Annabelle three weeks ago to rush to Roberto's side. Then, as now, he'd felt as if his life was ripping apart with the same deadly intent as the earthquake had.

He detested the hellish, out-of-control feeling.

The past weeks' events—the earthquake, Roberto's death, the soul-shaking despair of not being able to control anything in life had only cemented his belief that he shouldn't have married Ava.

So why should he be angry now that she wanted out?

'Basta!' he swore under his breath. Glancing at his watch, he stalked to the phone. It was still early on a Saturday morning, and it was about time his lawyers earned their fat monthly retainer.

'Ciao!'

Cesare pulled the phone from his ear, surprise spiking through him when he realised whose number he'd dialled.

'*Buon giorno,* Celine.'

'You sound surprised even though *you* called *me*.' Her bewilderment matched his.

'*Perdono*, I was calling someone else,' he said.

Celine's laugh was a little strained. 'Maybe it's Fate forcing us to finish last night's conversation.'

He sighed. 'I've told her. She knows everything.'

'Oh, I'm so glad, Cesare. I allowed Roberto to push me away and I'll never forgive myself for not being there for him until it was almost too late. We barely got a chance to say goodbye before he was gone. I'm glad you're not making the same mistake…' Her voice broke.

Pain tightened in his chest before he forcefully hardened

his emotions. He wasn't in the mood to enlighten Celine that he and wife couldn't be further apart if they tried. 'I appreciate what you did for Roberto, just as I appreciate what you're doing for my fam—for me. *Ciao*, Celine.' He quickly ended the call and threw the phone on his desk.

His jaw tightened against the helplessness that dogged him and he had the feeling Fate wasn't done with him yet.

Closing his eyes, he tried to clear his head but there was no erasing his mind's fixation on a particular woman. A woman with hair the colour of a glorious Tuscany sunset, peach-perfect skin dusted with freckles as countless as the stars. Emerald-green eyes that sucked him into seductive pools in which he wanted to happily drown.

The arousal that had plagued him since she returned throbbed to life, an insistent beat of desire that pounded through his system like a relentless drumbeat.

It would all go away. He just needed the right focus. One call on Monday to his lawyers to set divorce proceedings underway and this feeling would go away.

Satisfied that he'd regained some control, he left the study.

Lucia was laying out the breakfast things and turned at his approach. The usually stern face of the woman who'd been part of his household for longer than he could remember relaxed into a smile as she regaled him with Annabelle's antics of the day before.

Cesare had noted the change in his household since his daughter's return. The household staff who normally went out of their way to avoid him now smiled openly and even exchanged greetings instead of hurrying away when they saw him coming.

As he poured himself a coffee, he admitted to the lightness in his own heart since Annabelle's return. But there was also a stab of pain so acute his hand shook. He'd almost lost her once. He had no intention of doing so again.

She was the only child he would bear; she would one

day inherit the di Goia fortune. Which meant she had to be prepared. And, for starters, a daughter who spoke more English than Italian was simply unacceptable.

'You look like you're plotting world domination.'

Ava stood framed in the terrace doorway, dressed in a short white sundress. The sight of her long bare legs sent volcanic heat surging through his veins.

Sunlight flamed hair brightened by the Balinese sun. Her fair skin never browned enough to tan, but it glowed with a healthy hue and shimmered as if she'd smoothed a special lotion over it.

He watched her glide on bare feet towards him. In all the time he'd known Ava, he'd only seen her wear shoes when they went out and, even then, at the earliest opportunity she kicked them off. Instruments of torture, she called them. He'd never objected because he found her unadorned feet extremely sexy. He'd never have imagined he had a foot fetish before he met her.

But then he was equally fascinated with her fingers, with her lips, with the delicate bones of her clavicle and the sweet temptation of her round, supple breasts.

Madre di Dio! he cursed as his insane desire for her rose to torment him again.

Hips swaying beneath the soft, clingy material, she reached the table, chose the chair next to him and folded herself into it. Immediately the subtle scent of her perfume hit his nostrils, sending desire surging higher.

'Should I be afraid?' Her voice was a husky rasp in his ears. He had to concentrate hard to remember what she'd said.

He forced a smile. 'I am plotting, *cara*, but not world domination. What I desire is much smaller, but no less important.'

Unease entered her eyes but she tried to mask it. When she looked away and poured her tea, he couldn't resist the irrational urge to tease her, to pay her back for the suffering he endured. Hell, he knew it wasn't her fault that he found her so alluring, so damned beautiful that all he wanted to do was bury the stiff, pulsing part of himself inside her, but he felt rattled enough not to heed caution's voice.

'Don't you want to know what it is?' he asked softly.

The teapot shook and she set it down. That small betrayal was quickly masked because when she glanced at him the deep endless pools of her eyes were clear and calm. But they still drew him in like a siren's call.

'Not particularly, but I get the feeling you're in a sharing mood.'

He smiled. 'I am indeed. Annabelle doesn't speak any Italian.'

Her eyes widened. 'What?'

'My daughter does not speak Italian.'

Her eyes flashed. 'And whose fault is that? English is *my* first language, not Italian.'

'But you have a great handle on Italian. Or at least you did when we were together.'

She shrugged and he cursed himself for being distracted by the delicate movement of her shoulder. 'Since I seem to have misinterpreted so much of what you said to me in Italian, maybe I didn't have as great a handle on the language as I thought.'

He deserved that but it didn't make him seethe any less. 'I want her to learn my language.'

To his surprise, she nodded. 'I don't have any objection. Lucia is already teaching her. She's a very quick study. I'm sure she'll pick it up easily enough.'

Her easy capitulation unsettled him even further. Seeing his reaction, she shrugged again. 'I'm determined to be hysteria-free from now on, Cesare. Deal with it.'

'Deal with it?' He wasn't sure why that particular statement made him angrier.

'Do you mind taking care of Annabelle this morning? I know we're supposed to spend weekends with her but I need to check out the lighting for the blessing in the church and the caretaker can only make today.'

'Where is this church?' he bit out.

'The Duomo in Amalfi.'

'I'll drive you there.'

'There's no need.'

He set his coffee down. '*Sì*, there's every need. If we all go together then we don't break the agreement to spend time with our daughter. Where is she, by the way?'

'She took a detour to the kitchen to ask Lucia to put blueberries in her pancakes. But—'

Before she could protest further about his decision to drive into Amalfi with her, Annabelle flew onto the terrace, her hair streaming behind her like a fast-flowing river. His heart caught with joy, then sang with pride when she greeted him in halting Italian.

'*Buon giorno, piccolina,*' he responded, trying to keep his voice steady.

Ava watched the play of emotion on Cesare's face as he lifted Annabelle onto his lap for a kiss. Another sliver of unease darted through her. On the surface, Cesare's request that Annabelle learn Italian had seemed innocuous. But she couldn't dismiss the anxiety that settled in her stomach like a lead balloon.

Was she blowing everything out of proportion, just like she'd blown her importance to Cesare out of proportion? Maybe Cesare was being exactly what he claimed—an Italian father with the natural urge to speak his language with his child.

Her fingers stilled on the banana she was peeling for Annabelle and she watched father and daughter converse—one voice a deep, gravelly tone, the other a childish but attentive copying that filled her heart with equal measures of pride and pain.

As if sensing her gaze, Cesare glanced up.

The breath left her lungs and her heart careened around her ribcage like a crazed animal seeking freedom.

Even after Annabelle grabbed her banana and settled in her seat to munch on it, he continued to stare at her. Heat arced between them, just like it had from the very first time they'd met.

Once again the stinging betrayal of her need echoed between her legs. A helpless moan escaped her before she quickly disguised it as a cough.

His eyes darkened nevertheless.

'Stop it,' she muttered fiercely.

He raised an eyebrow and shrugged. 'Can't help it.'

'Try harder!' Or she was scared she'd spontaneously combust the way her pulse was skittering out of control.

Tawny eyes narrowed. 'Is that an order?'

'It's a friendly health warning.'

His smile was pure male arrogance, his gaze unwavering as he sipped his coffee.

'My parents wish to see Annabelle. I also have a few meetings in Rome, so it would be a good time to make it happen.'

'How are they coping with…' she paused, her glance sliding to Annabelle '…with what happened to Roberto?'

A flash of pain passed over Cesare's face, his eyes straying to Annabelle. 'As most parents would, I expect.' His gaze returned to Ava. 'They need not know about our… situation just yet. I don't want them upset.'

Ava abandoned the pretence of eating and tucked a strand of hair behind her ear. 'They know we've lived apart for a year, Cesare.'

'But my mother assumes since we're both here, living under the same roof that we've resolved our differences. Once the summer is over, we'll update them on what they need to know.'

Against her will, but because she didn't want to cause any further distress to newly bereaved parents, she nodded.

'When were you thinking of going to Rome?' Annabelle's grandparents doted on her and she'd never deny Orsini and Carmela di Goia the chance to see their granddaughter.

'Monday morning. I have meetings in the afternoon.'

'How long will you be gone?'

He drained his coffee. 'If you agree, Annabelle will spend the night with my parents on Monday. I'll pick her up on Tuesday and we'll return on Wednesday.'

'Two nights…' She would miss her child but the time away would help her put her feelings regarding Cesare into some sort of perspective.

Being constantly around him, waging a seemingly hopeless battle with her feelings had become draining. In a way, this was a blessing in disguise.

The time would also be useful for a drive down to Amalfi to scout out some more locations for the wedding catalogue.

She tried not to be distracted by the play of his hair-dusted bicep as he reached over and plucked a peach from the bowl. 'I suppose two nights isn't so bad. Is Lucia coming with you?'

'No, she isn't.'

She frowned. 'I don't think it's a good idea—'

'You think I'm incapable of taking care of our child?' A hard glint entered his eyes, chilling the skin on her arms.

'It's not that,' she answered truthfully.

'Then what is it?'

'Annabelle can be a handful, especially when she gets tired. I just think it's a good idea to have some help, that's all.'

'Which is why you're coming with us,' he said.

'*Me?* But I wasn't—I didn't…'

'Wasn't that the agreement? We spend every day with our daughter?'

'Yes, but what about my work? I have a meeting with Reynaldo and Tina on Monday morning.'

He frowned. 'What time will you be done?'

'About eleven.'

'*Bene*, we'll leave at midday.' He turned to his daughter. 'If you want a swim with *Papà* after breakfast, then go easy on those pancakes, *piccola mia*.'

'Will you swim too, Mummy?' her daughter asked.

'Yes, she will,' Cesare answered for her. 'Mummy is not in any danger because she's barely eaten a thing.' His disapproving gaze moved from her barely touched plate to her face, and challenged her to refute his words.

The discreet but extremely rude finger gesture she used in his direction produced an amused smile. Then his gaze released hers to travel at leisure down her face to the frantic pulse beating at her throat.

Unable to stand the sensual heat any more, she set back her chair and stood.

'I'll just go and change.' As she walked away, a saucy thought entered her head. Since she'd got here, Cesare had teased and taunted her sexually.

Well, two could play that game.

In her room, she quickly selected her skimpiest bikini, one bought for her trip to Bali when she'd been under the delusion that she could save her marriage.

She tried it on now and nearly lost her nerve. The bright green Lycra material—where there was any—clung to her skin in a blatantly provocative caress.

Flushing, she pulled a matching green shirt over it, grabbed a bottle of sun protection and hurried out of the room before she changed her mind. With each step towards the pool, she reiterated to herself the purpose of her actions.

She'd never been a pushover. On the contrary, she'd learned very early on in life to push back when pushed. Cesare had pushed her buttons enough.

The moment she shrugged off her shirt and caught his gaze, her heartbeat screamed out of control. Where sexual heat had burned lazily in his eyes before, this time they blazed with pure volcanic heat. The sheer power of it made her stumble to a halt. Heat rushed up and engulfed her whole body. Uncertain, she stood at the edge of the pool.

Cesare's face set into hardened lines. His nostrils were pinched and his jaw was clamped tight as if holding himself by a bare thread. He couldn't have made it plainer that she'd succeeded in pushing him to his very limit.

She wanted to run as fast as she could back to her room, tear the bikini off and burn the damned thing. But she couldn't move. Concrete-heavy limbs remained riveted to the tiles, her whole body drenched in a need so strong it took her breath away.

His gaze slid downward, his expression growing tighter as it travelled over her and back to her face.

Finally, he turned to his daughter, made sure her armbands were secured, then he swam to the side of the pool.

In one vault he was beside her. 'What the hell are you trying to do to me?'

She fought to hold a smile in place. 'Payback's a bitch, isn't it?'

He stared down at her, and then proceeded to circle her. When he reached her back, she heard a harshly drawn breath.

Despite her intentions, she cringed at the sound because she knew what he was seeing. Three fragile lines barely held the bikini together. It would take little more than a tug for it to disintegrate.

'*Santa Maria*. You've never played this dirty before,' he croaked.

'I'm…sorry?'

'You're *not* sorry. You're trying to punish me, make me want you so badly, I can't see straight.' His mouth was next to her ear, his breath hot against her skin.

Heat fired through her but she refused to back down. 'I'm merely playing your game, Cesare. Question is, what are you going to do about it?'

He gripped her arms and whirled her to face him. 'You want me to demonstrate the thousand different ways I want you? Now, in front of our daughter?'

'I—' Words failed her as shame racked through her. This wasn't the outcome she'd wished for when she'd brazenly flung on the costume. 'I didn't mean to—'

'You wanted to make me suffer, *sì*? Consider yourself successful. I'm burning for you, Ava. Make no mistake about that.'

Helplessly, she shook her head.

Without warning, his lips captured her lobe and he bit her less than gently. She barely managed to smother her gasp as hot darts of desire pelted her from head to toe. But, before she could completely melt under his assault, he'd released her.

By the time she'd opened her eyes, her shirt, warm from the sun, was once again around her shoulders. Cesare stood behind her until she'd folded her arms into them.

She started to move away but he grabbed her waist.

'Are you satisfied now? Are you pleased with your little *experiment*?' He pulled her back against him. The solid imprint of his arousal burned hot against her back. This time she couldn't suppress her moan. But it was a moan of frustration and regret because she knew, much as she'd wanted him to suffer, she'd only succeeded in prolonging her own suffering.

'Yes,' she managed to say.

'Good, because this is as far as you're ever going to get, Ava.'

Her heart cracked and her legs threatened to give way. 'Why? Have you developed a premature ejaculation problem?' she mocked, unwilling to concede defeat despite every atom in her body wanting to slink away in shame.

Cesare gave a husky laugh. 'Far from it, *bella,*' he taunted, even as he pressed himself closer. 'But you want a divorce, remember? So, technically, my hard-ons no longer belong to you. Think about that the next time you decide to test the fires so brazenly, *tesoro mio.*'

With supreme effort, she snatched herself from his arms. She stumbled a few steps before stopping to drag air into her lungs. When she was certain she could stand without collapsing, she tugged the folds of the shirt together. Her fingers shook too hard to button it, so she just held it with one hand.

When she risked a glance at Cesare, he'd wrapped a large towel around his waist and now sat on the edge of a sun lounger, his eyes tracking his daughter as she exhibited her newly learned crawl. His fists were bunched tight on his thighs and his breathing was shallow, as if he'd run a marathon.

Without a word, she turned and went inside as fast as her legs could carry her. The bikini ripped as she tugged it off. Staring at the garment in her shaking hands, she felt a huge lump wedge in her throat.

She'd pushed them both to the limit. And what had that proved? They were still as hot as hell for each other…and? *And nothing.*

Hot sex could never sustain a marriage that had been doomed from the beginning. Deep down, she knew that.

Ava sank onto the side of the bed and finally admitted to herself the reason why she'd felt the need to test his resolve.

Her marriage was well and truly dead. It was time to accept it.

CHAPTER SEVEN

ROME IN JULY was a seething, vibrant mass of sensible locals who sought shade and tourists who defiantly basked in the rapidly soaring temperatures. Ensconced in the limo heading towards the restaurant where they were meeting Cesare's parents, Ava was grateful for the air-conditioner. What she wasn't safe from were the thoughts reverberating in her head.

This is as far as you're ever going to get.

She tried to push the haunting words away. They pounded harder, bringing with them a dreadful sinking in her stomach. When her phone buzzed, she pounced on it, only to frown as she saw the text sender.

'It's Agata Marinello again. She's whining about your continued silence. Why don't you just tell her you won't be attending the wedding and be done with it so I can have a bit of peace? Or am I so far in the dog house you can't even be bothered to find the key and let me out?'

Cesare looked up from the electronic tablet he'd been working on since they'd transferred from helicopter to car.

'Why would you be in the dog house?' His voice was coolly neutral.

Her fingers tightened around her phone. 'Really, are we going to play this game?'

'No, there will be no more games, *cara*. I think we've reached an understanding on where we both stand. Finally.'

His cool demeanour was nothing like the held-together-by-a-thread aroused male he'd been at the pool.

He'd picked her up from her meeting dressed in a custom-made suit, polished shoes, sunglasses in place, looking intoxicatingly magnificent, as always.

After seeing him in casual clothes every day for almost two weeks, the sight of him dressed for business, his dynamic persona in place, only made her agitation worse.

The short drive down to the helipad and the flight into Rome been accomplished in near silence, save for Annabelle's chatter.

'You intend to freeze me out for the foreseeable future? That's fine. But can you find half a minute and text Agata and tell her you're not attending her precious son's wedding? Because her texts are seriously driving me insane. And I won't be accountable for my actions if she keeps it up,' she warned.

He shot her a hooded, speculative look before he nodded. 'I'll get in touch with her before the close of play today.'

'Thank you. You can go back to ignoring me now.'

After checking Annabelle still dozed in her car seat, she stared out of the window as the car edged around the Trevi Fountain and headed west towards Campo de Fiori.

His tablet pinged as he shut it off. She knew the moment he turned to stare at her, the weight of his gaze so heavy, anxiety ratcheted several notches higher.

'Ava—'

'I'm sorry, okay?'

He stiffened, his fingers tightening around the stylus he'd been working with.

Pain settled in her chest as she recalled how those hands had felt on her, once upon a time. How spell-bindingly erotic they could be.

A car horn blasted, making him turn momentarily to glance out of the window. Sunlight glinted off his black mane, casting it a glossy blue-black. His profile, stunning and powerful, hit her in the solar plexus, causing her breath to lodge in her lungs. She didn't know why she was surprised by her reaction.

Cesare, even with the slightly crooked nose sustained during a boxing match in his youth, was as close to physical perfection as any man could get. The urge to touch him made her fists clench until her nails bit into her palms. Sitting this close to him and stopping herself from touching was pure torture.

For a second, she regretted not insisting on staying in Lake Como. She glanced at him again and considered returning to the villa.

Wuss.

'I'm sorry,' she forced out again. 'I know I get rash at times. The pool incident…I don't know what I was thinking.'

His gaze flicked to Annabelle, and then back to her once he'd assured himself she still napped. 'I do, and I'm sorry too,' he said with a sigh. 'Sex—or the promise of it—has become our fall-back solution to what's happening between us. I used it to teach you a lesson the day you returned. You returned the favour yesterday and I deserved it. We've been pushing each other relentlessly. One of us was bound to reach boiling point eventually.'

'And of course it had to be me.'

'No. I haven't been fair to you, Ava. The earthquake shook all of us out of our complacency. And losing Roberto…' His jaw clenched.

Uncurling her hand, she placed it over his and felt momentary warmth flow between them. 'When will we find out what happened to Roberto?'

His eyes darkened. 'Soon…' He stopped when his phone rang but he ignored it and pinched the bridge of his nose. 'We're almost at the restaurant. After that, I have meetings. We'll talk some more tonight. Okay?'

Her heart climbed into her throat but she forced a nod. 'Okay.'

With a long deep breath, he pulled out his phone. *'Ciao.'* His smooth, husky voice echoed in the air-conditioned car.

She tensed when a female voice returned the greeting. The rapid flow of Italian was too much for her to follow, but her tension escalated as he spoke in low, intimate tones.

Ava's fists tightened further when he settled back and made himself more comfortable. The movement brought him closer, his powerful thigh brushing hers as he widened his legs. She was trying to shift away from the torturous contact when he turned and held out the phone.

'Celine wishes to speak to you.'

She drew in a quick breath. 'Why?'

He shrugged. 'We never got round to making that phone call. I tried to apologise on your behalf but she wants to make sure there are no bad feelings.'

She snatched the phone from him and placed her palm over the speaker. 'How dare you apologise on my behalf? I'm not some child whose behaviour has to be excused.'

He regarded her coolly. 'Well, this is your chance. You can hang up or you can speak to her. Your choice.'

Futile irritation welled up inside her. 'God, I really hate you sometimes.'

He merely smiled.

She cleared her throat and removed her hand. 'Celine, hello.'

'*Ciao*, Ava,' she answered. Her tone was warm, totally devoid of censure, which made Ava feel worse.

'Look, I'm sorry about the other night…' As she made her apologies, it occurred to her that she'd made a lot of them in the last hour.

'…being married to a man like Cesare would make any woman guard her place in his heart. He's very special.'

The arrogant upward curve of his mouth told her Cesare had heard Celine's words.

'He's also stubborn and extremely infuriating,' Ava muttered.

Celine laughed. 'You won't hear any arguments from me. But his heart is in the right place. Please remember that.'

The vehemence in Celine's tone made Ava frown. She watched Cesare put his tablet away and couldn't look away from the elegant hand he rested on his thighs. The memory of those hands on her skin hit her sideways. Her fingers clenched around the phone; Celine's words were lost in a jumble as heat surged through her.

She glanced up to find Cesare's eyes on her. Unable to pull her gaze away, she pressed her lips together to stop them tingling. After a few seconds his eyes flicked to the phone, his brow raised.

Celine was calling her name. Embarrassed, she apologized—again—then forced herself to conduct a somewhat coherent conversation. Minutes later, she gratefully disconnected the call.

Cesare laughed under his breath.

'Smugness is an unattractive trait,' she snapped, her voice disgustingly husky from the feelings rampaging through her.

His smile only widened. 'But it does my heart good to watch you eat humble pie,' he returned.

'Well, before I dig in, you should know I've accepted an invitation for Celine's birthday tonight.' She named the club. 'She's texting me the details shortly.'

His smile disappeared. Cesare hated nightclubs.

With a satisfied smile of her own, she held out his phone. 'Not so smug now, huh, *caro?*'

Cesare let himself into his apartment just before seven that evening and was immediately struck by the silence. It was different from this afternoon, when the sound of Annabelle's laughter coupled with Ava's huskier laugh had bounced off the walls. Realising how badly he missed it, he dropped his briefcase and loosened his tie.

Nothing was going according to plan. The business he'd thought he would have concluded by mid-afternoon today had stretched well into the evening. He knew his lack of concentration had been mostly to blame. He hadn't missed the surreptitious glances his board executives had exchanged when they'd thought he wasn't aware.

How could they know he was dreading the next few hours? This was the first time he'd be alone—truly alone—with Ava. And he didn't trust himself one iota.

Stalking to the cabinet, he plucked a glass from the shelf and contemplated the extensive array of drinks. He poured a shot of cognac, knocked it back and slammed the glass down.

Get a grip!

He eyed his briefcase. Part of the answer to his problems lay in there. All he had to do was sign the divorce papers his lawyers had drawn up and Ava would be out of his life.

He stepped forward and stopped when something soft gave way underfoot. Bending down, he picked up Annabelle's teddy. With a pang, he clutched the toy and clenched his gut against the pain shooting through him.

He loved his child beyond imagining, and yet he'd never been able to celebrate that love without a heavy dose of guilt. How could he when his actions had deprived Roberto of the same joy of being a father?

Cesare placed the teddy on the table. A sound behind him made him turn.

Ava stood at the entrance to the hallway, dressed in a long satin robe, her freshly washed and shining hair falling over one shoulder in an innocently seductive gesture that made his head swim. His chest tightened and he forced himself to remain still, to fight the urge to drag her close, imprison that trim waist and devour her lips with his.

'I thought I heard someone in here.' She moved into the

room. As hard as he fought, he couldn't stop his gaze straying to the sensual sway of her hips.

His whole body tautened so tight he was sure he'd snap in two.

Santa cielo! A year without sex was messing with his mind. Only monks took perpetual vows of celibacy. And his body was reminding him in the most elemental, primitive way possible that *he* was no monk.

He turned away to hide his growing hard-on.

'I just got in. Did my parents get away with Annabelle okay?'

Her robe whispered as she came closer. He closed his eyes. Before long her scent would reach him. Mingled dread and fierce anticipation scythed through him.

'Yes.' He heard the smile in her voice. 'I'm not sure which one of them was more excited. Their plans for tomorrow exhausted me and all I did was listen to them.'

'She left her teddy.' He needed to fill the silence or give in to the urge to touch her.

'Hmm, I know. I called Carmela and offered to take it over but she said no. I think I handed her the perfect excuse to take Annabelle shopping for another one.'

Unable to resist any longer, he turned. Her smile was breathtaking. *Dio mio, everything about her was breathtaking.* Shoving one hand through his hair, he pulled his tie away completely with the other.

'What time is Celine's thing?' Getting out of here might help with this unrelenting obsession to keep checking out his future ex-wife.

'Eight o'clock for drinks and dinner, then on to the club.'

He grimaced. The last thing he wanted was to socialise to the beat of thumping music. But anywhere else was preferable to being cooped up in this apartment, alone with Ava and his shockingly impure thoughts.

'Give me twenty minutes to shower and change.'

Her fingers toyed with the knot in her robe belt. He directed his gaze elsewhere.

'I'd hoped you'd return earlier. You said we needed to talk?' she ventured.

'I'm sorry, I was delayed. Unavoid—' He stopped when her smile dimmed. 'We don't have to stay long at Celine's party. We'll talk when we get back, *sì*?'

Her lips firmed. 'We'd better. The suspense is killing me.'

Twenty minutes later, he was seriously contemplating calling off the evening. But he knew he'd never hear the end of it if he disappointed Celine.

Grimly, he slid silver cufflinks into his black silk shirt, shrugged on his dinner jacket and emerged from his room just as Ava shut the door to the guest room.

His couldn't describe the miasma of emotions that fizzed through him.

The emerald-green thigh-length sheath she wore had no back. He knew this because her skin was exhibited in soft, gleaming peach-perfect invitation.

'Are you missing something?' His voice sounded strained even to his own ears.

She performed a perfect pirouette and then stared wide-eyed at him. The tingle of satisfaction he felt that she still found him attractive disappeared underneath the seething idea of other men seeing her in that piece of nothing.

She made a show of touching her fingers to the diamond studs in her lobes and the stylish pendant around her throat before checking the silver open-toed heels on her feet.

'No, I think I'm all set.' Her hair gleamed in the light as she raised her gaze to his.

'Are you sure, because you look stunning, but I think you're missing several yards of material at the back of your dress.'

Despite the surge of blood reddening her cheeks, she

raised an eyebrow. 'Oh, and suddenly you care how I look, Cesare?'

His gut tightened at the blow. '*Sì*, I care. We aren't divorced…yet. I don't want other men to get ideas about you.'

'Just be a gentleman and stick to compliments. I spent a small fortune on my dress.'

'Ava, you look breathtaking. That is always a given. But the caveman in me would love to see you in something…else.' A shroud-like *something* that wouldn't make any red-blooded male wonder if her skin felt as soft and velvety as it looked.

She planted a hand on her hip, a pulse-heating smile playing on her glossy lips. 'What exactly is wrong with it?' she challenged, her eyes sparking fire at him.

His frustration escalated. 'Aside from the fact that it barely covers your backside and is missing a back, you mean?' It was just too damn *shimmery.*

'But I look hot?' she pressed with a smile that now dripped pure mischief.

'You look hot. You look like a pure, sinfully tempting fantasy. Is that *gentlemanly* enough for you?' The material caressed her thighs, brought attention to legs that seemed to go on for ever. And she'd done something to her toes. 'What's that?' he rasped, barely able to take a full breath.

She followed his gaze. 'It's a toe ring,' she replied. 'Cesare, we have twenty-five minutes to get there. Will you be able to handle me looking like this or are we going to be late because you've suddenly developed a dislike for any other man seeing me in a short dress?'

He swallowed, tried to speak and ended up just shaking his head as her gaze wandered over him.

'Oh, and for the record, you look hot too. I could tell you to button your shirt all the way up so no woman can see your manly, mouth-watering chest, but see, I'm a grown-up, so I'll just suck it up. Now, shall we go?' Her eyes had grown dark when she raised her gaze to his.

Their expression and the knowledge that she felt an iota of the feelings rampaging through him made him feel marginally better.

'Celine will be made aware in no uncertain terms that she owes me big for this.' He strolled over to her and held out his arm.

'Behave yourself, Cesare.' At his snarled, pithy response, she laughed. 'This is going to be a long, trying evening, isn't it?'

He took in the thrust of her chin, the hectic race of the pulse in her throat and an all too familiar spike of lust raced to his groin. '*Sì,* it is.'

Cesare knew he was being ridiculous. Jealousy had no place in his feelings because he knew by rights he had no hold on her. Besides, he would bet his sizable fortune that most of the women at the club tonight would be similarly dressed.

But most women weren't his wife!

Another growl emerged before he could stifle it. Cursing the possessiveness that had sprung from nowhere, he grabbed her arm and stalked down the hall. 'I don't begrudge you the dress, *cara*. My only wish is that you'd received *more* of it for your efforts.'

She bared her teeth in a fake smile. 'Well, keep wishing, *tesoro*. Who knows, Santa might come early.'

Ava was only half-listening to the guest whose name she'd forgotten. That he didn't speak more than a dozen words of English made it easy. Her eyes tracked Cesare, who she'd smugly believed hated nightclubs and would hate this evening.

No. Far from smouldering arrogantly the way she remembered him to, he was on the dance floor, enjoying the attentions of the blonde who'd attached herself to him the moment they'd walked in the door.

She glanced down at her dress, and again wondered if

she'd been wise to listen to the saleslady at the shop on the Via Condotti who'd insisted the green dress was perfect for her.

Compared to Cesare's dance-partner's dress, Ava's was downright demure. The woman could easily be mistaken for a runway model. Her bone structure alone was enough to make the men here salivate with lust. The fact that she was currently breathing the same air as Cesare didn't seem to deter other men from watching her.

A fist of jealousy lodged in her chest, squeezing until she couldn't breathe.

It didn't help that all day she'd felt on tenterhooks.

She couldn't help but feel her life would unravel even further once she and Cesare finally had their talk.

'You mustn't worry, *il mio amico*. Giuliana is a man-eater, but trust Cesare.'

She turned to find Celine watching her with an expression sickeningly close to pity.

Ava forced out a laugh. 'I'm not worried.'

'I hope it's because you trust him.' Celine's brown eyes narrowed. 'You know he will not deliberately hurt you?'

Anxiety and confusion warred through her. 'Unfortunately, I know nothing of the sort.' Cesare's withdrawal from her had shattered the foundations of her belief.

'Hang in there. Di Goia men don't give their love easily.' Sadness clouded Celine's eyes.

Ava touched her arm. 'Cesare told me about you and Roberto...and Valentina.'

Celine's eyes widened. 'Really?'

She gave a slight grimace. 'I demanded to know his connection to you.'

Celine's smile wobbled. 'I'm glad he told you. Even though *he* loved my sister, Roberto was the love of my life. A part of me is angry he died before I got my chance with him. But it's not too late for you two. Whatever happens, hang on with everything you've got.'

Several minutes after she'd left, Ava remained rooted to the spot, Celine's words echoing through her mind.

She didn't deny Cesare held tremendous sway over her emotions. One smile was enough to light up her whole day. The occasional glimpses of pain she saw flash through his eyes caused her heart to echo his pain over losing his brother.

But, no matter how she felt about him, she couldn't dismiss the fact that he'd only married her because she'd been pregnant; that he'd tolerated her because she was the mother of his child. Despair rose like a riptide, threatening to suck her down.

The music ended and she watched Cesare and the stunning Giuliana head for the bar. As he plucked two champagne flutes from the counter, his eyes met Ava's. His gaze raked over her, sending her pulse into overdrive.

Suddenly annoyed with his effortless power over her emotions, she lifted her glass in mock salute.

There was no future to hang on to. At least not where she and Cesare were concerned. She didn't doubt his love for Annabelle and therefore didn't doubt his capacity to love. But that love didn't stretch to her.

The distress the thought produced made her glass tremble in her hand.

Setting it down, she found the guest she'd spoken to earlier next to her. Before she could excuse herself, he smiled. Racking her brain, she remembered Celine had introduced him as her second cousin. He was charmingly good-looking, with light brown hair and attractively boyish brown eyes. Not wishing to appear rude, she smiled in return.

He moved closer. 'Drink?' A champagne-serving waiter lingered nearby.

Hastily, she shook her head. She'd barely eaten more than a few mouthfuls at dinner. Drinking on an empty stomach was a bad idea.

Her admirer set his glass down with a decisive click.

'Balliamo?' He gestured to the dance floor. When she hesitated, he clasped a dramatic hand over his heart. *'Per favore?'*

On a sudden whim, she nodded. She'd never been one to slink away to lick her wounds. As much as she wanted to shut herself off, preferably somewhere quiet, and indulge in a monster ice cream-fuelled pity party, she wouldn't.

She was here because of Celine. The least she could do was pretend to enjoy herself.

'Wait.' She laughed when he tried to steer her towards the dance floor.

His face fell but when he saw her shucking off her shoes, his grin widened. The blaring hip-hop was the perfect antidote to her melancholy.

Mario—she remembered his name now—led her to the middle of the dance floor and proceeded to prove himself an energetic dance partner.

The next few songs flew by. Somewhere, during a twirl, her hair clasp slid off and disappeared. Feeling freer, she let go.

When the songs slowed, she stopped dancing, grateful for the chance to cool down. 'Thank you, that was—' She stuttered to a stop when his arms slid around her waist.

Just as quickly she was disengaged from him. She almost lost her balance as rough hands grabbed her from behind. The tingle along her nerve endings announced who held her before she heard his voice.

'It's time to leave.'

Without waiting for her agreement, he tucked her behind him, then murmured low, heated words to Mario. In the strobe light, Ava saw the younger man pale.

Cesare's jaw was set as he straightened and manacled her wrist with one hand.

Before she could draw breath, he was tugging her off the dance floor.

'Cesare, wait!'

He ignored her and headed towards the exit.

'For goodness' sake, stop! I need to get my shoes.'

He stopped so suddenly she careened into him. His hard body easily absorbed the impact, but she was left with a vivid imprint of his broad, bristling masculine form. With his fingers still imprisoning her wrist, his gaze dropped to her feet.

'You danced barefoot?' he grazed out.

'Yes. Now I need to get my shoes.'

'Why? You'll only discard them at the earliest opportunity.'

'That doesn't mean I want to leave them behind. They cost me a bomb.'

His eyes glinted with danger. 'Do *not* move from here.'

The crowd parted for him as he headed for the bar. He returned seconds later, her silver shoes dangling from his fingers. Wordlessly he thrust them at her. When she didn't immediately put them on, his eyebrow shot up.

'What? My feet are killing me.'

His gaze dropped again to her bare feet. For some reason, the sight of them seemed to annoy him further. When he glanced at her, his eyes were ablaze with a look that made her swallow and step back.

He advanced until she was backed into a corner. 'What do you think you were playing at back there?' he asked through clenched teeth.

'I could ask you the same thing.'

He bared his teeth, but nothing about his expression showed he was in a merry mood. 'How long are we going to keep doing this? We've tested the theory a few times these past weeks. *Per favore*, Ava, you need to *stop* pushing my buttons because I'm hanging by a thread here, and I'm seriously scared of what the consequences will mean for us if I snap.'

CHAPTER EIGHT

THE INTENSITY BEHIND his words sent a wave of panic through Ava.

She swallowed, cleared her throat and shook her head. She couldn't show him how his behaviour had affected her. 'You were too busy renewing your various acquaintances to be bothered with me, so I decided to make my own friends.'

Tawny eyes darkened into stormy pools. 'And you thought the best way to enjoy yourself is to let another man put his hands all over you?' His fists were clenched and his pallor had faded a little underneath his tan. The tic beating a wild tattoo in his cheek made her belly swan dive.

'We were just dancing. No big deal.'

His disbelieving laugh grated on her ears. *'No big deal?'*

'What did you expect? That I'd sulk in a corner pining for you?'

He released a harsh breath. 'Ava…'

'You want to leave, so let's go.' Unable to withstand the pressure, she pushed past him and threw open the heavy oak doors that led outside.

The cool breeze after the nightclub's cloying atmosphere was a refreshing welcome. Heaving lungfuls of air into her oxygen-starved body, she stopped beside the bronze and gold column that fronted the club. She sensed Cesare behind her but thought it safer not to turn around.

'We can't keep doing this to one another,' he finally rasped in a fierce undertone.

'I agree. We can't. You've withdrawn from me completely, and yet you can't stand it when another man comes within touching distance of me. Whatever is wrong with us, it's driving me insane and I can't stand this any more.' Feelings she didn't know how to deal with ricocheted through her at lightning speed.

She seethed with anger, she wanted to cry and she wanted to scream.

Plunging shaking hands into her hair, she lifted the suddenly heavy tresses off her heated shoulders. Tears prickled at her eyes but she furiously blinked them away.

Divorce, it seemed, was her only escape. And yet the thought of that final severing from the man she'd dreamed she would spend the rest of her life with brought a hard lump to her chest.

Her frenzied fingers twisted her hair into a rope at her nape.

Cesare drew closer, bringing a renewed rush of awareness. His relentless, all encompassing heat bored down on her. She sucked in a breath and held it in, afraid to let it out lest it somehow transmitted her turmoil.

Firm hands brushed hers away and his strong fingers replaced hers. Her breath grew laboured as his fingers glided through her hair. 'It's time we have that talk, *carissima*.' His breath fanned her sensitive lobe.

A shiver went through her. She'd started to turn when a loud wolf-whistle shattered the air from a trio of men who'd just emerged from the club.

The sight of her—arms raised, bare feet and naked, seductively curved back—garnered very male interest that made Cesare growl low in his throat.

With jerky movements, he shrugged out of his jacket. '*Basta!* I don't care if it offends your female sensibilities.

Put this on, *now*,' he hissed. Pulling her arms down, he draped the jacket around her shoulders.

His limo, which had pulled up while she'd been lost in thought, stood with Paolo holding the door open. Cesare ushered her into the back seat, climbed in beside her and yanked the door shut.

Rough fists clenched and unclenched on his thigh, but it wasn't until the car was moving that he spoke.

'It seems you've turned into quite the exhibitionist, *cara mia*.' The cold endearment emerged more as a reproach than an affectionate term.

She flinched and tried to move away. Immediately he trapped her arms, stopping her sideways escape.

'A lot of things have happened while you've been busy pretending I don't exist, Cesare.'

His lips firmed. 'I can see that. And I'm wondering how all this impacts on my daughter.'

She turned sharply. 'Stop right there! You'd better erase that whiff of *you're a bad mother* I hear in your voice, PDQ! And stop referring to her as *your* daughter. Up until very recently, your part in all this has merely been the biology. *You chose to live away from us!* You lost the right to be a father when you withdrew so far physically and emotionally from *our* daughter, she may as well have been dead to you!'

In the darkened interior of the car, his head went back as if she'd struck him. What little colour had remained left his face. She couldn't have struck a deeper blow if she'd shot a bullet into his heart.

Immediately contrite, she reached out and grabbed his hand. It remained cold and unmoving beneath hers.

'Cesare, I didn't mean that—'

'I deserved that. But I had good reason. Or I thought I had for a long time, well before the earthquake. What happened with Roberto and Valentina…I didn't think I deserved a child when Roberto had lost his.'

'Do you really think Roberto begrudged you a family?'

'I didn't think—I knew. He told me many times that I didn't deserve a family—' a tight edge of pain roughened his voice '—that I deserved to be alone the way he was.'

Her insides fractured at his torment. But she couldn't stop her own pain from welling up alongside it. She sank deeper into the warm jacket that had so recently draped Cesare's body. Curiously, she drew strength from it to fight him. 'I'm sorry he said that to you. But did you really think Annabelle deserved to suffer because your brother was fighting his own monsters?'

'It was my duty to protect him—'

'You also had a duty to your wife and child. I know you married me because I was pregnant,' she forced out painfully, 'but you shouldn't have left me alone to bring up our daughter alone.'

A small, taut silence reigned before, 'You were never alone,' he said, almost under his breath. 'You had nannies, household staff and a security detail.'

Rage smashed her burgeoning hope to smithereens. '*Security detail*? Oh, that's all right then. You know I've never been part of a family. I told you how my father and brothers treated me. God, Cesare, I had no idea what I was doing when I had a baby. I expected you to stick around and help me, be with me. Instead you jumped on your jet at the first opportunity, and chased deal after deal. I didn't marry your household staff or your security detail. I married you! *You* should have been there, not them!'

His hand tightened painfully on hers and his head dipped in solemn acknowledgement. 'I should've been. No matter my inadequacies as a husband, I should've tried harder as a father. Trust me, Ava, I know my failings where my daughter is concerned.' He spread his fingers in a purely Latin gesture. 'It's why I'm here now, trying to right that wrong. I intend not to lose sight of the fact that she is the most important thing in all of this.'

Hearing the words—so resolute and promising where

their daughter was concerned, and so excluding where she was—made Ava's heart catch so painfully she couldn't speak for several seconds. But she didn't need to. Cesare was in the mood to unburden himself. '*Dio mio*, Ava, you must remember we barely knew each other before you got pregnant and yet you so quickly put me front and centre of everything you wanted in a family. I couldn't think straight. You say you had no idea what you were doing but to me you seemed the epitome of calm and composure. When, after a while, you didn't seem to need me, I left.'

Ava reeled, fiercely glad she wasn't standing up, for surely she'd have lost the power of her legs. Her spine turned liquid and she collapsed into the soft leather seat. 'I had no idea…'

The rest of her words dried up as he shook his head, raised a silencing hand before clenching it into a fist mid-air. The action, so wrought with despair, made her inhale sharply. She glanced at his profile.

The corresponding look of wrenching pain on his face made her reach out.

'Cesare—'

Cesare couldn't stop the hiss of pain that slipped through his lips. 'Enough! Do not say another word.'

Regret, self-condemnation, jealousy and anger all coalesced into a seething ball of emotion in his chest. Emotions he'd been fighting what felt like forever sank their steely talons deeper into him. He was exhausted… *Dio*, *was* he exhausted.

'I'm tired of trading verbal blows with you, Ava.'

He needed a distraction, and he reached for the only thing that had ever been potent enough to melt his control.

Ava's gasp echoed in the car as he yanked her against him.

Soft contours moulded against his hardness, her eyes widening as she encountered a particularly stiff part of him. His gaze dropped to her lips, his focus hazing at the thought of possessing her, of washing away the tide of blackness that threatened to consume him in the most effective way he knew how.

He slanted his lips over hers, and nearly groaned. Heady, seductive, infinitely dangerous to him. But, right at that moment, he didn't care about the danger. He wanted a reprieve from the demons clamouring for his soul.

With a feathery sigh, she melted into him and he exhaled in satisfaction. He'd expected bristle and bite, for her to fight the way she always did. Instead she sank further into him.

His tongue, eager to taste, captured hers. Another gasp echoed in the silent interior as his fingers explored what he'd been itching to explore for far too long.

No woman had ever tasted like Ava. Innocent and bewitching, bold and insecure—one minute she kissed him as if she wanted to devour him, the next she whimpered with a touch of timidity.

The heady mix made him harder, torturing him with the need to pull up the short hemline that had been taunting him all evening and just *take, take, take*.

But, as much as he wanted to rip her panties off, spread her open on the wide limo seat and pleasure them both until one of them passed out, he couldn't.

There's nothing wrong with kissing, his insistent body clamoured. He deepened the kiss, letting his mouth perform the task his body couldn't be allowed to. Ava's mouth opened wider, her tongue growing bolder in its own exploration.

A dark thought seeped into his mind. Fighting the blackness, he wrenched his lips from hers.

'You never answered me when I asked if there'd been anyone else. I need to know.'

'Why, so you can go growl at them the way you did with Mario tonight?'

Irrational jealousy he'd experienced earlier returned. He planted a hard kiss on her lips, determined to wipe the feeling away with the smooth sweep of his tongue.

'Mario has been left in no doubt as to the consequences should he ever dare to come within three feet of you again.' He hesitated a beat. 'Ava?'

Mesmerising green eyes held his. 'I'm still a married woman. I take my vows very seriously.' She sniffed, and her eyes darkened. 'Has there been for you?'

He shook his head. 'We're still married, *mia amante.* I would never dishonour you in that way.'

Her eyes darkened and her swollen lower lip trembled. 'How can you say things like that to me and expect me not to have hope for us?'

His insides clenched. 'Ava…'

'For God's sake, shut up, Cesare. Just…shut up and kiss me.'

He didn't need to be told twice.

Lust thundering forcefully through him, he went deeper. She was all fire now, voracious and demanding, her hands frantic as they grasped his nape, grabbed his hair and twisted it between her fingers. His heart tore around his chest like a crazed animal. When her full breasts pressed against his chest, he nearly lost his mind.

His hand moved to her back, encountered sleek, smooth flesh. He pulled back, sucked in a deep breath and watched her fight for breath too. The sight of her moistened, kiss-swollen lips made him groan.

'What?' she asked huskily. Her fingers still worked through his hair, scraped his scalp. He'd never have imagined such a simple gesture could be erotic, but the fierce throb of his erection indicated otherwise.

'We've arrived at the apartment.'

It took a few seconds for his words to register. In that suspended time, he basked in her warm supple body plastered against him.

Eyes widening, she sprang away from him. The loss was a fist in his gut. She reached for his jacket and settled it around her shoulders and, oddly, Cesare felt comforted that she had a part of him on her. He toyed with asking Paolo to take them on a long drive out of the city but already the door was opening.

She stepped out, exhibiting an obscene amount of leg, and her bare feet made him want to growl some more.

He carried her shoes and trailed her into the building. He'd chosen to lead a separate life away from his wife and child because he hadn't thought he had what it took to be a husband and father. He'd drifted through each day, doing what needed to be done—making deals, making more money, taking financial care of his parents.

Now he was hyperaware of every passing minute, of every atom of his being poised on a knife-edge of sharp focus. Focus on the woman in front of him, her stunning body and shapely backside swaying underneath his jacket as she strode towards the lift on the balls of her bare feet.

Inside the lift, he caught her to him but didn't kiss her. If he started he wouldn't be able to stop.

Once they were inside the apartment, he kicked the door shut with his foot and reached for her. What he grabbed instead was his jacket, held out by Ava with a determined look on her face.

'Come here,' he commanded, every muscle tight with need.

She raised her chin, exposing the satin neck that sent his pulse sky-high. 'No.'

Shock froze him in place. *'Che?'*

She remained defiant and out of reach. 'I won't sleep with you just because you've decided that you want me again.'

He prowled towards her. She backed away, making him want to pounce on her. He cautioned himself not to. 'Again? Hell, haven't we proved conclusively that I've never stopped wanting you? *Dio*, you only have to walk into a room to make me rock-hard for you.'

Heat bloomed in her cheeks, appeasing him somewhat. As did her soft lips parting on a breath. The fierce shake of her head, however, plunged him back towards supreme frustration. Again he tried to reach for her. Again she danced out of his reach. Irritation sizzled through him.

'As hot as that was intended to make me—'

'Did I succeed?'

The rapid rise and fall of her breasts gave him his answer. 'I'm not going to fall into bed with you, Cesare.'

She shook out his jacket like a matador trying to distract a raging bull. He ignored it and focused on his prize. Another step brought him closer to her. He breathed in her scent and acknowledged that his need for her was beyond his own understanding.

And he was infinitely weary of twisting himself into knots about it.

'Tell me you don't want me, *mia sposa*.'

'You know I do, but I won't let you toy with me. What happened to—*this is as far as you're ever going to get?*'

Unwelcome heat crawled up his neck. For a man who had a superb command of words, he couldn't compose a suitable answer aside from the pure, unadulterated truth. 'We both know that bikini should've come with a skull and crossbones warning. I was angry with you for killing me with temptation and wasn't quite myself when I uttered those words.' Having Ava taunt him with her body when he'd been fighting his desire had been the last straw. He hadn't liked being held on the knife-edge of control, as he'd been right from the beginning with her.

'And now you've just decided *to hell with it*?'

Stalking away from her, he tore off his constricting tie and tossed it away. 'I haven't decided anything! What I do know is that you're driving me crazy and…' His fist clenched. 'Dammit, Ava, you flaunted yourself so blatantly.'

'Well, you're in luck. I'm not flaunting anything any more. Goodnight, Cesare.'

At first he couldn't comprehend what was happening. By the time the shock wore off, Ava's deliciously tempting back had disappeared down the hall and into the guest bedroom.

Unclenching his fist, he raked his decidedly unsteady fingers through his hair. *Bravo, Cesare.* He'd finally succeeded at what he'd been trying to do since Ava returned—he'd pushed her away.

Except satisfaction tasted like ashes and thwarted lust sucked. He swore and paced the room. It was no use asking himself what he'd been thinking.

When it came to Ava, she only had to touch him and he lost his mind. She only had to look at him with those smoky emerald eyes and his senses flamed with the promise of pleasure.

He spotted his briefcase and his jaw tightened. He strode to it and pulled out the papers. The cold, stark words taunted him. With a simple stroke of his name along the dotted line, he could be free of this madness.

But was that his only option?

Ava's words in the car struck him. From the beginning, he'd known she had a strained relationship with her own family. To all intents and purposes, he and Annabelle were the only family she had. He'd married her, only to leave her to her own devices because he'd been too caught up in his own angst to see clearly.

Was he man enough to start now?

His fist tightened around the papers. On a decisive thought, he ripped them in two. He'd been too long locked in his own pain for his part in Roberto's seclusion, he hadn't stopped to think about Ava's needs when she married him.

A grim smile crossed his mouth. Had Ava asked for a

divorce two months ago, hell, even the day before the earthquake, he probably would have granted it. But not now. He ripped the papers until they were indecipherable pieces.

He still didn't have it in him to offer her what she wanted, but he, if nothing else, was a damned good negotiator. There would be no divorce.

So what now?

Hell if he knew. He would just have to work it out later.

CHAPTER NINE

AVA PACED THE length of the guest room, unable to calm her frenzied pulse or her mind's racing.

First Cesare pushed her away, then he wanted her to fall into his arms. She squeezed her eyes shut and tried to quell her body's clamouring for what she'd stubbornly denied it. But her pulse wouldn't quieten. The thought that she'd come within a hair's breadth of making love to Cesare again after so long sent her pacing faster. She should be thankful she'd resisted him.

Yeah, right.

Truth was, she wanted to jump her husband so badly, she could barely think straight. The heat of his body, the intoxicating scent of his hard-packed muscles rose in her mind like the promise of a delectable feast after an endless famine.

Would that be so wrong?

She felt herself sway towards the door and dug her toes hard into the luxurious carpet. What was she thinking? Sure, he'd been shocked when she walked away from him. *But he hadn't followed. And he's not exactly breaking down your door, is he?*

While she was in here torturing herself, he was probably enjoying the view, nightcap in hand, or halfway to securing another multi-million euro deal.

Whirling, she stalked to the window.

The stunning vista of night time Rome lay before her. Cesare's penthouse apartment sat atop a converted luxury villa off *Campo de Fiori* and commanded views as far as the Vatican and St Peter's Dome.

Was he staring at the same view? Raising a hand to the window, she watched her skin heat the cool glass. The view outside faded when she caught a glimpse of herself in the reflection.

Wild, fiery hair, tangled into shameless disarray by Cesare's seeking hands. Her eyes were wide pools of confusion and hurt she wanted to hide away from and her lips were swollen and bruised with Cesare's kisses. She wasn't surprised to see her chest rise and fall as if she'd run a marathon.

And all because of the man whose presence impacted her life and emotions as effortlessly as if she were a puppet on his string.

Her breath rushed out, frosted the glass, distorting her view as she remembered… In the fevered chaos of the kiss and the argument that had followed, they'd never got round to talking about the solution to their problems.

She eyed the door, then almost in a trance, her hand went to the button securing her dress at her nape. With one short fumble, it pooled at her feet. She contemplated taking a shower, but feared her resolve would desert her if she delayed for too long.

Padding to the dresser, she picked up her hairbrush. The rhythmic strokes reinforced her strength, which in turn abated the haunted look in her eyes. She hadn't needed a bra with her dress, but she still wore her thong. The thought of going to Cesare naked heated up her blood, but she quickly abandoned the idea.

Crossing to the wardrobe, she selected a short forest-green silk night slip and matching gown of hers she'd found when she'd unpacked earlier. Shrugging them on, she tied the gown and quickly left the room before she lost her nerve.

The hallway was as quiet as when she'd walked down it a short while ago. The dimmed light in the living room revealed it as empty as the kitchen and terrace.

The idea of confronting Cesare in his bedroom sent a confidence-shaking shiver of alarm through her. Slowly, she walked towards his door and paused outside. Catching her lower lip between her teeth, she listened for sound within. What if he was asleep?

Or, worse, he'd reverted to the cool, distant man she'd grown to hate this past year? Fear of rejection dried her mouth but she didn't back down. Inhaling deeply, she turned the knob.

He was lounging against the king-size bed's intricately designed headboard, a glass of cognac in one hand and an electronic tablet in the other.

His gaze snapped and locked on hers. Slowly he placed the glass on the nightstand.

Ava's eyes landed on his bare chest and hot air seared her lungs. She'd seen his naked torso many times but the sheer magnitude of his potent masculinity never ceased to raise her temperature.

'To what do I owe the pleasure, *cara*?'

Her tongue darted out to moisten dry lips. 'Our talk…I want to have it…now.'

He turned away from her, shielding his expression from her as he laid the tablet down. 'Are you sure that's what you come for? To *talk?*' His eyes narrowed and he linked his hands together over his hard, ridged stomach. Despite his stance, he reminded her of a hunt-mode predator, ready to pounce with merciless precision.

Her fingers clenched on the doorknob. 'Yes.'

He nodded, grabbed the corner of the sheet and drew it back. 'Then, by all means, make yourself comfortable and let's…talk.'

She didn't need to look to know he was naked. Cesare slept in the nude. 'Are you…are you going to put any clothes on?'

'No.'

'Cesare…'

'I don't know what that would achieve. I told you what happens to me when you enter my presence. Clothed or *in flagrante*, the effect is the same.'

Desire punched a hole in her belly. Dangerous, treacherous desire. She needed to leave, only she couldn't move. 'But…'

He sighed. 'I don't want to have this talk with you all the way across the room, Ava. Come here, it's much more comfortable, I promise,' he murmured silkily.

She shook her head and pulled the door open, her bravado deserting her. 'You know what? Maybe this wasn't a great idea. It's way past midnight and…I can't deal with you this way. We…we both need to get some sleep. We'll talk in the morn—'

Quicker than she'd ever imagined it possible for him to move, he sprang off the bed, shot across the room and slammed his hand against the door. Her gasp was strangled in her throat as he pressed his hot, bristling *naked* length against her back.

'Oh no, Ava *mia*. You do not get to flounce off for a second time,' he breathed hotly in her ear.

'I don't *flounce!*'

'No. You sway. You mesmerise. You capture and hold my attention until I feel like I'm drowning in your seductive beauty.'

'I don't know what on earth you're talking about…'

'Oh *sì,* you do. Or you wouldn't be here now. I'll give you what you want, *tesoro mio.* We will have that talk. But there's a very high possibility that you'll hate me when we do.'

She gasped and turned within the circle of his arms.

'Why would I hate you? You said there'd been no one else!' A sickening feeling invaded her at the thought that he'd lied about that.

His eyes burned into hers. 'I meant it.'

Relief poured through her. 'Then what else could there possibly be? Unless you're about to confess you're some psycho serial killer?'

Her comment didn't lighten the mood as she'd expected. Instead his jaw tightened, then released. 'I did have homicidal thoughts about Mario tonight. In fact, I had unholy thoughts about every man at the party who dared to look at you.'

'I'm surprised you had a chance to notice, seeing how you were so enamoured of Giuliana's bosom.'

He shifted even closer until his granite-hard arousal pressed against her pelvis. He gave a low, deep laugh. 'It seems we've both been clawed by the sharp talons of the green-eyed monster.'

Pain stabbed through her desire. 'Jealousy would imply that we care for each other, Cesare.'

His smile slowly faded, replaced by a growing hunger as his gaze slowly raked her face as if imprinting it on his brain. '*Sì,* it would. I never denied that I care about you, Ava.'

'But only sexually?'

'Don't underestimate the power of sex, *mia cara.* It has brought down kingdoms and ruined powerful men.' As if to emphasise its power, he leaned into her.

'So far you've managed to remain untouched by it,' she croaked.

His thick arousal registered boldly against her belly at the same time as his mouth settled heavily over hers.

The power of thought instantly deserted her. This kiss was nothing like they'd shared in the car. This was a full, unapologetic assault on her senses, a bold display of Cesare's power and the firm intent of what he meant to happen between them. His tongue stroked boldly against hers, performing a dangerous dance that had only one destination.

Heat swelled and rocketed straight to her core. The shock of how quickly her body reacted to him made her head spin, but even that reaction was ruthlessly swept aside under the torrent of need building inside her.

Her fingers encountered Cesare's naked torso. Her nails bit deep and she revelled in the groan that shuddered through him.

He raised his head, his breathing harsh in the darkened room. With a quick dip, he licked her tingling lips. 'I'm far from untouched, *cara.* Hasn't it always been this way between us?' he demanded thickly. 'One touch and the whole world burns up?' As if to demonstrate, he ran a lazy finger down the side of her neck.

'Yes.' Her moan brought a satisfied smile to his face.

Bringing his hands onto her shoulders, he eased the robe from her. The gown followed, but she barely felt it slither off her arms to fall to the floor, entranced as she was by the molten heat in his eyes.

With unsteady fingers, he traced a path from her neck, down between her breasts to her belly until he grazed the top of her thong.

Words, murmured in Italian appreciation, tumbled from his lips.

'English, please. I need to understand what you're saying.'

He repeated the raw, explicit words. When her face flamed, he laughed and reverted to Italian. Every syllable touched her skin like a kiss, making her limbs lust-heavy until all she could do was sag against the door as his touch drummed a beat of desire through her.

'Cesare,' she sighed, unable to form a more coherent sentence past the sweet benediction of his name on her lips. Gathering every last ounce of strength, she pulled back. 'We…we still need to talk.'

He dropped another hungry kiss at the corner of her mouth. 'We will. But I need…we both need this before we do. And, whatever happens, Ava, please know this now. I'm very sorry I hurt you.'

Tears gathered in her eyes and clogged her throat. When they spilled onto her cheeks, he wiped them away with his thumbs.

With a sigh, he scooped her in his arms and carried her to the bed.

Sheets warmed by his body immediately engulfed her in his scent. When he stepped back and she saw, really saw him—naked, magnificent and needy—desire dragged through her belly, amplifying the power of her own need, propelling her to reach for him, to make sure he was real and not a figment of her fevered imagination.

'Come closer.'

He complied. She reached up and traced the sculpted lines of his face, from hollowed cheek, over smooth lips to the rough shadow of his stubble. When she made another pass over his lips, he snagged her fingers in his teeth. Boldly, he sucked on her forefinger.

Fresh fires of desire licked through her. Her nipples, long puckered into nubs of excruciating need, hardened further. Without releasing her fingers, Cesare settled down beside her and placed one hand below her breast. Her temperature shot up another notch.

'Touch me, please,' she pleaded. But he just rested his hand there, under the curve of her breast, while he leisurely sucked on her finger.

Liquid heat oozed between her thighs. Her lids grew heavy as the motion of his mouth tugged her closer to the edge of ecstasy.

His hand edged closer to her breast.

Moaning with desperation, she tried to move closer to his touch. With a final, hot lick he released her finger. His gaze blazed down at her, dissecting her every reaction. 'Not yet.'

Pressure built in her nipples, almost as painful as the relentless heat pulsing between her legs. Just when she thought she couldn't stand the pressure any longer, his hand traced the underside of her breast. She jerked in protest and moaned as he started to perform slow, excruciating circles on her flesh. With every rotation bringing him close but not close enough to the aching pinnacle, Ava feared she would die from need.

Finally, at the point of begging, he slanted his mouth over hers, and closed his thumb and forefinger over her nipple.

Her cry was swallowed up into his mouth. Her orgasm slammed into her with the force of a tornado, twisting and tossing her high, leaving her no room to breathe.

Firelight exploded behind her lids as ecstasy awakened and tore through her. Through it all, Cesare kept his mouth on hers, lapping up her cries of bliss.

The intensity of his kiss lessened as she slowly floated back to earth. When she could bring herself to open her eyes, he was gazing down at her, his eyes full of heat and something close to wonder.

'You're still so responsive, *tesoro mio,*' he rasped. 'I thought my fevered imagination had conjured it up in the hallway two weeks ago, but I know different now. You've never lost it.'

'Does that please you?' she asked in a husky voice.

'That sex between us has always been raw and intensely special? I'm a red-blooded Latin man, am I not?' came the smug response.

Her fingers closed over his rock-hard bicep, renewed need clawing through her. 'Maybe you should demonstrate, before I die of anticipation?'

A curious expression flitted over his face, gone quickly before she could decipher it. She started to ask him what was wrong, but lost her train of thought when he chose that moment to kiss her again.

By the time he raised his head to rasp, 'Are you still on the Pill?' she could barely string coherent words together to answer.

'Yes,' she croaked.

He recaptured her mouth, then rolled them over so she was on top of him. The first touch of his bare chest against her breasts sent her fevered pulse rocketing once more. Unable to resist, she rubbed herself against him. His deep groan only fed her hunger.

Against her thigh, Cesare's erection pulsed, hot and insistent. She rolled her hips against him, the friction driving her quickly to distraction. His hands clasped her bottom, impatient fingers diving beneath the elastic to brand her flesh.

Another moan filled the room, her heart's frenzied beats echoing in her ears until she could hear nothing but the promise of bliss, feel nothing but the equally intoxicating pounding of Cesare's heart.

One hand fisted in her hair and drew her back. Tawny heat-filled eyes caressed her face. '*Perdono, cara,* but I have to do this.'

Before she could ask what he meant, the sound of tearing fabric ripped through the room. 'God, that is so macho,' she teased on a pant.

He grinned. 'I don't have time to ease it from your hips.'

'What do you have time for?'

'This,' he whispered, raised his head and rolled his tongue over one nipple before sucking it into his mouth.

Her cry was loud, desperate and tinged with pain as pleasure arrowed forcefully through her. Her back arched under the intensity of her delight. Cesare suckled harder, then relented to lick her burning flesh. Before she could draw breath, he repeated the action. Her fingers convulsed in his hair as pleasure consumed her.

Once again bliss beckoned and she rushed blindly towards it. But, just as she was about to dive into the abyss, he pulled back.

With a quick motion, he flipped her underneath him and knelt between her thighs. He pulled open a drawer and extracted a condom.

Watching him rip open the contraception sent a bold thought through her head. Rising to face him, she placed her hands on his. 'Let me.'

Cesare's eyes widened. 'You've never done that before.'

'I've had a long time to think about us, like this. Will you let me?'

He nodded and handed it over. That her offer pleased him and intensified the fire of arousal in his eyes only spurred her on.

She crawled on the bed until she was behind him. With an open-mouthed kiss between his shoulder blades that sent a fevered shudder through him, she took over the task. The powerful breadth of his shoulders meant she couldn't see what she was doing, but her touch was enough.

Slowly, glorying in his potent, silky arousal, she slid the condom over his erection. Smooth, velvety skin veined with his thick blood surged underneath her fingers.

She bit the flesh she'd kissed moments before and felt her own fever rise as he trembled.

'*Tesoro,* I fear your disappointment if you don't cease this torture.' His voice was pained, tinged with a desperation that matched her own.

Equally desperate for him, she completed her task quickly, but couldn't resist a last caress of his hard flesh.

'*Per favore,* I need you,' he pleaded hoarsely.

Twisting around, he grabbed her and returned her to her original position.

Sure hands grasped her thighs and spread them wide. Her scent rose between them like a potent aphrodisiac. Cesare's gaze dropped to her open sex and his eyes darkened to a burnished bronze.

Swallowing hard, he murmured, 'I had forgotten how exquisitely beautiful you are down there.'

Sweet pleasure stole through her. Reaching up, she curled her hand into his smooth, hard chest. 'I never forgot, for a single moment, how beautiful *you* are.'

To her he would always be a god among men, the powerful, captivating figure who had gripped her attention from the moment they'd met and had never let go, despite everything that had happened between them since.

He glided his fingers down her inner thighs, trailing a path of fire that threatened to ignite her very core. She bit her lip, fighting the haze that encroached, the promise of heaven suspended just out of reach. But this time she wanted more, wanted the power of Cesare deep inside her to be the only thing that triggered her ecstasy.

Which was why she wasn't prepared for the skilled finger that slid inside her sensitive opening.

Her spine arched clear off the bed. 'Cesare!' His name was a cry ripped from her throat, a cry that sounded again when his thumb swiftly found her nub of desire. Blood pounded through her veins, crashed through her head until it was the only thing she could hear.

He groaned as her fingers bit into his shoulders. Her head thrashed against the pillows, fighting but knowing she was losing the headlong flight into rapture. The brief reprieve she experienced when he gently removed his fingers was easily lost again when the blunt head of his powerful erection replaced his fingers.

'Open your eyes, Ava.'

Weakly, she obeyed.

Curling her legs around his hips, he plucked her hands from his shoulders and placed them both above her head. 'Now don't move.'

His gaze stayed on hers as he rocked forward. At the

first thrust, every instinct urged her hips to move. 'I can't not…it's too much…'

'You can. Just do it.' He fed more of himself into her, stretching unused muscles and sending her senses into near freefall. Her heart hammered, her lungs begged for air and the sheer pressure of being filled by Cesare threatened her sanity.

Finally, he was deep inside her. His gaze fixed on hers, he held still, allowing her to savour the full force of his possession. Time suspended between them, the only sound their shared breath as the power of being joined held them in thrall.

At last, he breathed, 'Now.'

They moved at the same time, slamming together with a force that rocked worlds. His grunt of pleasure triggered her shuddering moan. Pleasure like she'd never known surged through her. Clamping her legs tighter around him, she met him thrust for thrust, falling into a long-forgotten rhythm like a song to a lark. The world fell away.

Nothing else mattered but Cesare, his sounds of ecstasy filled her ears as he thrust over and over inside her.

Her flesh welcomed him, enclosing him in a tight, silken embrace that gradually milked his pleasure. His face contorted in a mask of pained pleasure as he crept closer to the edge.

In the single moment before all became lost, Ava glimpsed a connection, an unspoken bond that drew at her heartstrings and made her catch her breath. Before she could analyse it, she was swept away. Holding back was not an option so she flew towards ecstasy and a release that annihilated every single thought. Unable to bear the assault, she clamped her eyes shut. Firelight rained again, showering her in pleasure so profound, tears prickled the back of her lids.

Above her, triggered by her relentless convulsions, Cesare hurtled towards his own release. For a split second, he stilled, his whole being gripped tight in indescribable sensation. Her legs around his back strained to keep him locked against her. With a final desperate groan, he gave up control, managing just in time to adjust his position before he collapsed on top of her.

Ava drew her arms around him, her fingers slowly caressing his sweat-slicked flesh as shudders chased through him. Somewhere in the lost minutes, he turned his head and planted kisses along her jaw, but no words were uttered. None were needed.

She couldn't recall when he finally disengaged from her but she had a vague sense of being settled against him. But something different tripped her senses. It wasn't until she was drifting off to sleep, his strong arms coming around to anchor her to him and soft words gently ushering her into sleep, that she realised what it was.

In the moments before his climax, Cesare had pulled out of her.

CHAPTER TEN

CESARE STOOD AT the foot of the bed, gazing down at his sleeping wife. Guilt bit hard into him. Although a careful inspection of the condom had set his mind at ease somewhat, he didn't delude himself into thinking that would be the case every time.

Their passion hadn't abated in their time apart. If anything, the opposite was true. He'd had to stop himself from taking her in the raw and earthy way his senses had clamoured for him to, and he didn't fool himself into believing he would always remain in control. Ava needed only to be within touching distance to erode his willpower.

His senses sprang to life again as she shifted and stretched on the bed, baring a little more of her body.

He locked his knees to stop himself from crawling back beside her. When his feet disobeyed, he clung to the bedpost, gritting his teeth as arousal fired deep inside. For a split second he resented the unrelenting need Ava had always elicited in him.

From the first moment he'd laid eyes on her at that busy intersection in London, something vital had shifted inside him, knocked him sideways. He'd labelled it as lust back then, but now he wasn't so sure it was mere lust. Lust faded. But the thought of Ava walking out of his life permanently made his chest tighten in fierce rejection.

She murmured in her sleep. Every sinew in his body

protested at the idea but he forced himself to take a step towards the door.

'Cesare?' Her soft voice stopped him in his tracks.

She was sitting up, the sheets slipping to her waist. Her lush curves gleamed in the ambient light. Her nipples, half hidden by the heavy fall of her fiery hair, crested breasts he longed to mould and caress again. His body's instant reaction made him swallow hard. It was that or risk choking. He hadn't had sex in a year. His need was more than great, but staying would mean pushing his luck way above acceptable levels.

'What are you doing out of bed?' she asked.

'Letting you get some sleep, *amante.*'

Slowly she sagged back against the pillows. Her hair parted, revealing the full allure of her breasts. In a slow, seductive sweep designed to drive him insane, her gaze left his and caressed its way down his nude body.

His heart hammered as she boldly stared at his erection. When she moistened her lips, a rough tremor coursed through him.

'I'm wide awake now,' she stated in a husky murmur.

Heat rushed through him, propelling him forward before he could form a single thought. When he reached the side of the bed, he paused. 'I don't want to make you sore.' She'd been tight when they'd made love. There'd been no one else. The thought sent a powerful surge of primitive possession through him. If he got his way, and he would once he dedicated enough strategic thinking to the issue, his wife would know no other man but him.

'It wasn't that bad.'

Unable to help himself, he traced his finger along the warm colour that crept up her neck into her cheeks. 'Are we rating my performance or your soreness? My delicate ego seeks clarification.'

Her gaze dropped to his engorged male flesh, one brow

raised as her sinful mouth curved. 'There's nothing delicate about you, *caro*.'

His breath fractured. Somewhere inside it registered that this was the first genuine smile he'd witnessed from her in a long time.

The thought that he'd missed it without realising his loss hit him squarely in the chest. Before he could assess his actions, he lifted the sheet and slid in next to her.

'On the contrary, I'm as delicate as a baby when you look at me like that.'

'Like what?'

'Like I'm the sole focus of your world.'

Her smile slowly faded. 'You were my only focus, Cesare. For a very long time. Then you took yourself away.' Her voice caught and his heart caught with it.

Leaning down, he kissed her, his chest tightening with the need to offer reassurance he had no right to give.

'I'm here now,' he offered instead.

It was inadequate, and her darkening eyes told him so. But he had no solution. Not yet. So he did the next best thing. He deepened the kiss, infusing her with his crazy desire for her, savouring her immediate and complete response. Pleasure, hot and fervid, rose inside when her hands moved around his back and held him tight.

Ava's thigh slid between his, creating mind-altering sensations that washed away his troubled thoughts.

When her hand closed over him, a groan erupted from his very soul. Feeling himself slide closer to the edge, he quickly reached for another condom.

'Not yet,' she rasped in between planting hot open-mouthed kisses on his chest. With a firm hand, she propelled him onto his back and rose onto her knees. Her nails scraped along his torso. His dark curse brought another smile.

'You're enjoying your power?'

'I'm enjoying…something.' Her eyes danced with delight, then she leaned down and boldly tongued his nipple.

His heartfelt groan earned him another flick of her tongue. He clenched his fingers in her silky Titian hair, holding her close as he lost himself in the pleasure that filled his every cell. With every breath, every inch lower she went, he skated closer to the edge of madness. She sank her teeth into the skin below his navel and his heart stopped.

'Ava…' He wasn't sure whether he warned or pleaded.

In response, she closed both hands on him, caressed him up and down.

'*Dio mio.* Again.' A definite plea this time.

She complied, her gaze rising to snag his as she moved her firm grip over him. She maintained eye contact as she caressed him, a boldness in her actions he'd never witnessed before. The look, coupled with the mind-bending effect of her hands, scattered his thoughts. She leaned in closer, parted her lips and took him in her mouth and it was in that moment Cesare knew the true meaning of insanity.

He barely remembered passing her the condom when she demanded it. He was so consumed with her, he couldn't see straight. He welcomed her when she positioned herself over him, her beautiful body poised to take him inside her heat.

Her gasp of pleasure triggered his own, and just like before they found their own unique rhythm, the sheer bliss of their coming together so mind-blowing he was at the point of no return before he knew it.

Cesare forced himself to hang on despite the teeth-grinding need to let go. The effort it took was monumental, especially in the moment when Ava slammed down onto him one final time before losing herself in her blistering orgasm.

'Oh God,' she rasped as she collapsed onto him, her spasms causing him to see stars as he waited…waited… 'God, Cesare, I've missed you so much.'

The heartbreak in her voice made his gut tighten painfully.

'I've missed you too,' he responded gruffly. Her spasms gentled. He gripped her hips and pushed his hard length inside her, finally permitting himself to take his own pleasure. It didn't take long. With one final thrust, he pulled out of her. Ava jerked in surprise. He kissed her and she melted into him. He groaned in pleasure, unwilling to entertain the tinge of regret permeating his pleasure as he lost himself in his climax.

Several minutes later, their breaths calmed. Against his chest, Ava murmured sleepily. As he caressed his fingers through her hair, Cesare knew without a shadow of a doubt that he would fight Fate herself for a solution if he had to.

Ava walked into the large sunlit kitchen and immediately saw the note pinned to the fridge door. She'd woken to an empty bed, an empty apartment and troubled thoughts.

Her intention last night had been to find a definitive solution to the state of her marriage. Instead she'd fallen under her husband's spell. Again. Pulling her robe around her, she padded further into the kitchen. Plucking the note from the magnet, she read Cesare's sprawled, bold writing.

Gone to get breakfast. Present for you on coffee table. C.

She studied the complicated-looking coffee machine for several minutes before pressing the least harmful-looking button. Crossing her fingers that it wouldn't end in disaster, she trod on cool wooden floors to the all-white, stunningly decorated living room that boasted floor-to-ceiling windows.

Her heart skipped a beat as she eyed the large, exquisitely packaged box. Raising the lid, she gasped at its contents.

The camera was one she'd coveted for a long time but had never thought she'd own because of its astronomical price. State-of-the-art, with a zoom lens and sharpness beyond anything she'd ever seen, it was the crème-de-la-crème of cameras.

Her fingers tingled as she lifted its heavy but comfortable weight. It had already been assembled and a gleeful smile curved her lips when she turned it on.

Rushing out onto the terrace, she focused and snapped a series of panoramic pictures, making sure to catch the iconic St Peter's Dome in the frame. She took a few closer still—Campo de Fiori a few hundred metres away, the ever-present fountains that could be found all over the city, and the awe-inspiring statues that Rome was famous for.

Leaning over, she focused her camera on the street below. Several residents enjoyed breakfast at outside cafés that shot off from the square. She zoomed in with her finger poised to click, only to pause when a familiar figure swung into view.

Ava lowered the camera and stared.

In the morning sunlight, the sight of Cesare in a torso-hugging T-shirt and jeans stole her breath. He held a container bearing her favourite breakfast *trattoria*'s logo in one hand, a newspaper tucked under his arm and his phone to his ear. A slight breeze ruffled his hair, and several women seated outside a smart café turned to ogle his long-legged body as he passed.

He seemed oblivious to the looks. In fact he seemed far away. Slowly, she lifted the camera and zoomed in on the man she'd shared her body with last night.

She clicked several times, the professional in her adjusting the camera to make the most of every single frame. But with each picture she took, her heart lurched.

Without warning, he stopped. The newspaper fell from his arm and Ava saw his face whiten. For several minutes he stared into space, until a scooter backfired in the distance, galvanising him into motion, the newspaper discarded.

When he disappeared from view to enter the apartment

building, Ava slowly lowered the camera. With dread, she glanced down at the pictures she'd captured.

Ice clutched her heart as she reviewed each frame. Far from looking like a man who'd just left his wife's bed sated and happy, Cesare looked as if he was caught in the middle of a living nightmare.

The sun disappeared behind a cloud, momentarily casting the terrace in shadow. The portentous effect wasn't lost on her.

She'd risked her heart again by sleeping with Cesare last night. A heart that had never completely healed from being battered once. Now she knew she'd placed it in harm's way again.

Her fingers clenched around the camera when she heard Cesare's key in the lock. Taking a deep breath, she walked into the living room just as he entered.

He saw her and paused. Wordlessly, his gaze raked over her, sending her pulse on a roller coaster dive.

'Thank you for this—' she indicated the camera '—it's very kind of you.'

'*Prego.*' His gaze stopped at her bare feet, then climbed back up. 'I wasn't sure what I'd hope for more on my return—to find you still in my bed or to have the temptation of making love to you again taken away from me by you being out of it. Not that a bed is necessarily a means to an end.' The grim delivery of his words made her heart drop further into despair.

'You don't sound like you would've preferred the former option.'

His ragged laugh as he veered towards the kitchen caught at her insides. 'Trust me, *cara,* I would've enjoyed it. I would take sweet oblivion with you over reality any day.'

She trailed behind him. 'So, you don't regret last night?'

The carton containing their breakfast landed on the countertop none too gently, followed by his phone. He came at her, stopping a bare inch shy of touching distance.

'I explored your body so thoroughly that every inch, every kissable freckle is imprinted on my memory. I should be sated but my hunger for you burns with a force that almost hurts. Right this minute I would love nothing more than to spread you over this counter, bury my mouth between your legs, lap my tongue over your sweet spot until you come for me, again and again. Does that sound like regret to you?' he breathed, his eyes fixed on hers in studied concentration.

Ava wasn't sure how it was possible to feel hot and cold at the same time. But she did. Somehow, she managed to croak, 'No.'

His body tight with tension, he stepped back and strode over to the coffee machine. 'I'll make another cup for you. This one's cold.'

'Cesare, what's wrong?' she asked because something was wrong. Desperately wrong. Despite her bold words, she quaked inside.

His shoulders stiffened, but he carried on pushing buttons. Only when the familiar sound of coffee percolating echoed through the kitchen did he face her.

'You know that bit in a movie when you know the good guy has done something really bad and is going to get it in the neck but you keep rooting for him anyway?'

Ava set her camera down before she dropped it. 'Yes?' Her voice emerged shaky.

'That's not me, Ava. I'm the bad guy, who selfishly took what he shouldn't have, then compounded his situation by making things a million times worse.'

'How have you made things worse?'

He shook his head as if words failed him. She moved towards him, her feet hardly making a sound across the hardwood floor.

Cesare heaved a breath, struggled to calm the riotous feelings rampaging through him. He raked a hand through his hair, unable to bear the thought of telling her what he'd woken to—what the future held for them.

When he lowered his hand, Ava reached for it. He focused on her, his heart thumping now to a different beat, the hard pounding of want, of the selfish need to forget the last ten minutes. To go back and suspend time at the exact moment he'd woken up in Ava's arms.

But questions flooded her eyes—questions she'd grown so tired of asking but had never diminished nonetheless. What had she asked him? What was wrong? As if he'd spoken aloud, she nodded. 'Tell me,' she demanded firmly.

He tried to speak but the words wouldn't form. To speak would be to condemn him to hell for ever. But he'd known as he'd torn himself from Ava's warmth this morning and seen the missed call from Celine that he'd run out of time.

His hand tightened around hers and he led her to the living room and urged her down onto the sofa. He paced, yearning with everything inside him not to have to shatter her peace. She watched him, her expectant gaze gradually turning into a frown.

'For God's sake, whatever it is, just spit it out. Please,' she added, her plump lips trembling before she firmed them. 'You're scaring me with that bringer-of-the-Apocalypse look.'

Sucking in a breath, he sank down next to her. Immediately her evocative scent filled his nostrils. The urge to remain silent, to breathe it in and just drown in her heady essence almost overcame him. He suppressed a grimace.

He clasped his hands to stop their shaking. 'Celine called this morning but I missed it. I called her back ten minutes ago.'

The fear that entered her eyes chilled his heart. 'And?'

'She had the results. Roberto died from Late Onset Tay-Sachs syndrome.'

A shake of her head. 'I've never heard of it.'

'It's not a common condition. According to Celine, it

is almost always misdiagnosed. Most people only know about it when it affects them.'

'Is it…did Roberto suffer?' she asked in a pained whisper.

His breath shuddered through his chest. '*Sì*. It's a horrible disease.'

When she put her hand on his cheek, he nearly lost it. He greedily absorbed the touch because he knew it would be gone soon, once she knew the whole truth.

'I'm so sorry, Cesare. For you and for what Roberto went through.'

'Save your sympathy, *cara*. I don't deserve it.'

Her fingers trembled against his cheek. 'Why would you say that?'

'Because the condition…it doesn't begin and end with Roberto. It's a genetic defect that is passed down from parent to child.'

Her eyes remained blank, then slowly widened, filling with horror as the implications of his words finally sank in. Her hand dropped like a stone and she paled, the freckles dusted along her cheeks standing out against milk-white skin.

With everything inside, he wanted to take the pain away.

Ava fought to breathe. Moments ago, she'd been harbouring hope that they were about to discuss how to find their way back to each other.

Instead, he'd dropped this…this…

'Are you saying…that…you and Annabelle both have this gene?' The words scoured her throat.

Pain ripped across his face. 'Yes. I passed it to her. You called me bringer-of-the-Apocalypse. You were right.'

'But…she's perfectly healthy. Other than the odd cold, and what she suffered with the earthquake, she's never been sick a day in her life. And you're not sick either.'

'No, I'm…not.'

Something in his response caught her attention. 'Cesare, what aren't you telling me?'

His glance held a wealth of pain that made her heart lurch. 'Because both my parents carry the gene, what happened to Roberto could happen to me.'

'Did your parents know?'

'I'd like to think they wouldn't deliberately keep something like this from Roberto and me. I saw what losing him did to my mother. I'm guessing they don't know. Like I said, most people don't know they have it until they fall ill.'

For one blazing second she was fiercely glad his parents had been ignorant because they'd not only brought Cesare into her life, they'd also given her Annabelle. Then a thought trickled through, further chilling her blood.

'So what are the repercussions for Annabelle?'

His eyes took on a haunted look that stilled her heart. 'It could remain dormant all her life, or…the gene could mutate and she could develop complications,' he replied starkly.

A dark sound tore from her throat. Horror built, overcoming every other emotion as her insides screamed with disbelief at what he was telling her. Her daughter, her lovely daughter who had survived an earthquake, susceptible to a potentially life-threatening disease…

'Did you suspect something like this? Is that why you kept Roberto's illness from me?' The thought made her heart crack with pain. 'How long had he been seriously sick?'

'He'd been deteriorating for a year. It worsened in the last six months.'

Shock made her draw back, tears swiftly following as emotions tumbled through her. 'You knew all that, knew that something was very wrong and you kept it from me?'

He tried to reach for her. 'These were all second-hand reports. I didn't know just how bad he was. And I wanted to protect you—'

'Don't you dare say you were trying to protect me! You had no right to keep such a thing from me. What if Annabelle had fallen sick and I didn't know what was wrong?' Terror clutched her heart. 'Dear God, Cesare, what if she'd…' She couldn't voice the words. When he gripped her arms, she didn't move because she couldn't find the strength. Her insides felt numb and the horrific reality gripped her.

'Don't think like that.'

Slowly she raised her head. 'Why not? It's what you've been doing. At least now I understand the look you get when you look at Annabelle. You've been expecting the worst, haven't you?'

Cesare paled even more and the lines around his mouth compressed. 'I needed to be sure. It was why I postponed coming back to Bali. Roberto refused my attempts to see him. But six weeks ago, just before we left for Bali, he asked for me.' He sucked in a shuddering breath. 'He'd taken a turn for the worse. I think deep down he knew he wasn't going to make it. When I found out the extent of his illness, I contacted Celine. She tried to make him see a specialist but he refused. It was almost as if he'd given up…which was why we suspected suicide.'

'Oh God…' A strangled sob emerged.

His hands tightened on her arms. '*Cara,* I'm sorry—'

She wrenched away from him. 'You shouldn't have kept all this from me, Cesare.'

He gave a grim nod. 'I regret that. But I wanted to spare you the pain.'

'You had no right to shoulder this alone. We were thousands of miles away. What if something had happened to you?' The thought brought a fresh bolt of horror.

'Nothing did. You had enough to deal with after the earthquake. I was not going to add to your distress.'

'That should've been *my* choice to make.'

Regret bit into his features. 'I told you, when it comes to you I seem to specialize in making bad situations worse.'

Her daughter—her precious baby girl—had a condition she'd never even known about. A deep shudder wracked her body. She tried to still her trembling but it got worse. A quick glance showed Cesare was caught in his own personal hell.

'Umm…the Apocalypse thing…I didn't mean it,' she muttered through stiff lips.

He gave a raw, pained laugh. 'But you were right.' He lifted a hand as if to touch her, then dropped it back down. 'Roberto shut himself off in Switzerland because of me. He suffered…alone for a long time because I didn't know how to reach him.'

Ava sucked in a breath. 'No. He shut himself off because he lost the love of his life, and decided to deal with it his way,' she said but Cesare wasn't listening.

'I keep thinking if I hadn't met Valentina in New York, hadn't given her a job, Roberto would've known some happiness…had the family he wanted.'

'Unless you have a direct dial to Fate, I think you can let go of that one. Some things you can control but sometimes things *just happen*.'

'The earthquake—'

'Just happened.'

'*Dio,* Ava, our daughter shouldn't have been there in the first place. You *saw* that marketplace in Bali. How could I *not* think she had been taken from us as payback for what I did to my brother?'

'You can choose to live in guilt for the rest of your life or you can choose to believe that ultimately you weren't responsible for Roberto. Even though you weren't close, you tried to look out for him. You took the woman he loved under your wing and tried to help, even when he blamed you for what happened in New York. I think you need to give yourself a break for that.'

He digested that for a while but, even though the pain in his face abated a little, his eyes remained haunted.

'As for Annabelle, she wasn't taken from us. We found her,' she added.

Another harsh laugh. 'Yeah, we did. And look what I've delivered to her fragile life. You have to face the fact that I'm bad for you, I have been since the moment we met. But…' He shoved a hand through his hair.

'But…? You're going to walk away again?'

'No!' He lifted his gaze, and Ava's heart stopped at the gut-wrenching bleakness in his eyes. 'I can't. Annabelle is my flesh and blood, the most important thing in my life.'

Ava's gut tightened until she couldn't breathe. 'And since I've made us a package deal you're stuck with me too, right?'

'I didn't say that—' He surged up beside her as she stood. 'Where are you going?'

She shoved a hand through her hair, unable to stop the terror churning through her belly. 'I can't stay here—'

'You can't leave!' He grabbed her arms. 'We haven't finished talking.'

'Why? Is there another bombshell you're going to hit me with?'

'No, but we need to discuss what happens next and I—'

'I…need some air. I have to think.' His grip tightened. 'Let me go.'

'Ava, please. Stay.'

Her breath snagged in her lungs. 'Why?' Her question was soft because of the tears clogging her throat and because she didn't dare to give life to the vain hope flaring inside. 'Why do you want me to stay?'

Silence greeted her question. Then, 'Because you are my wife. I made a vow to protect you and I believed I was doing the right thing by not burdening you with Roberto's news.'

Pain ignited inside her. She barely managed to remain standing, so strong was the grief that wracked her. 'You took other vows, too, Cesare. Or have you forgotten?' The words scraped her throat.

'They weren't as important as your protection.' An unfamiliar note altered his tone. Her heart hammered as she tried to read his expression. But his face remained inscrutable, his eyes a cool, impenetrable wall as he returned her stare.

'No. I suppose to you they weren't.' Unable to withstand his gaze, she turned away. He didn't stop her walking away.

All through her shower she felt numb. A part of her wanted to get into the first taxi, go and grab her daughter and hug her close. The other, more rational part of her knew she had to get her emotions under control before Annabelle returned. For her daughter's sake, she knew the latter decision was best.

Dressed in white linen trousers and an aqua silk-trimmed cotton top, she caught her hair up in a bun and slipped the camera strap over her head.

When she entered the living room, Cesare stood exactly where she'd left him, but the tiny espresso cup in his hand showed he'd busied himself with other things. His face was devoid of expression as he gulped it in one smooth swallow, set the cup down and came towards her.

Ava backed away. 'I…what time are your parents bringing Annabelle back?'

'After lunch, but we can make it sooner or later. Just say the word.'

She shook her head. 'After lunch is fine. I…I'll make sure I'm back by then.' She headed for the door, and stopped when he fell into step beside her.

'What are you doing?' she demanded.

'I'm coming with you.'

'No, you're not. I told you, I need some air.'

'There's enough air out there for both of us, I'm sure.'

'I meant alone.'

'Out of the question. You're reeling from the news I've

laid at your feet. I recognize that, as the person who's caused you pain, I'm the last person you want around you, but you're my responsibility nonetheless.'

'What? Suddenly your *security detail* isn't up to the job?'

'Why delegate when I'm in the position to do a better job?'

'*Now* you choose to play the attentive husband?'

His jaw tightened. 'I married you. I brought this chaos to your doorstep. And I'm damned if I'm going to abandon you now to deal with it alone. We deal with it together. And call me selfish, Ava, but I'm hoping staying with you will earn me your forgiveness quicker. And, who knows, if I manage to save you from being hit on by a mercenary local, then I may even gain some Brownie points.'

Her hand tightened around the camera. Looking at him, at the visible distress in his face, made the tightness in her chest loosen a little. 'It's not going to be that easy, Cesare. To be honest, I don't even know what I'm feeling right now.'

He nodded. 'Then we won't talk. Just walk, *sì*?' He moved past her and held the door open.

With a sigh, she went through it and waited while he called up the lift.

They walked for an hour without speaking, heading west instead of east where most of the popular Roman landmarks were located. Ava concentrated on documenting the local life.

But, even lost in the one thing she loved to do most aside from being a mother, she was hyper-aware of Cesare's pain-ravaged presence beside her. The part of her that acknowledged he must be reeling wanted to offer comfort. But her own shock was too great to process.

He might have suggested they wouldn't talk but she soon realised he had no intention of keeping his hands to himself—a hand in the small of her back to guide her across the street; around her waist to steer her clear of a group of excited tourists or a careless scooter, or a touch on her shoulder to draw her attention to a statue or a fresco he thought she might be interested in.

When the sun rose higher, he led her to a small local shop and bought her a wide straw hat, sun cream and a bottle of water.

Her breath caught as he squeezed a dollop of cream onto his fingers and applied it to her arms and face. When she lifted questioning eyes to his, his merely responded—*I don't want you to burn.*

Ava could've told him it was too late. She was already burning in hell. His every gesture demonstrated his regret for having kept Roberto's deterioration and death from her. Aside from that damning decision, everything else he'd done since had been to protect both her and Annabelle. Quietly, Ava had to concede that if she *had* been told so soon after nearly losing Annabelle in the earthquake, she wasn't sure she would've withstood the blow.

Her thoughts scattered when Cesare's arm slid around her shoulders. When she glanced at him, he nodded at a *trattoria* across the square overlooking the Tiber.

'We skipped breakfast. And also I think it's time to get out of the heat.'

Although she suspected she wouldn't be able to hold down a single mouthful, she reluctantly nodded.

The owner broke into a smile and ushered them in the moment he recognized Cesare. After they were seated in a far corner of the cool *trattoria,* Cesare ordered *cornetti,* fruit and coffee, along with a selection of sliced Parma ham.

Once they were alone, he sat back and watched her with narrowed eyes.

'I…haven't forgotten that in all this you've also received a horrible shock,' she said in a low voice. 'I'm sorry.'

'Does that mean I'm not in Hades any more?' he murmured.

She plucked the hat from her head and set it down on the

spare chair along with her camera. 'First of all, I want to know everything about this condition, and I mean everything. No protecting me from the unsavoury facts.'

'I don't want you to worry about—'

'No, Cesare. I want to know *everything!*'

His lips firmed but he nodded. 'Celine emailed me a report. I'll forward it to you.'

'Also, we have to tell Annabelle—'

'No, she's too young to understand.'

After a second she nodded. 'Okay, but as soon as she's old enough, we'll tell her. I don't want her kept in the dark.'

'*Sì,* I agree.' He met her surprised gaze with a mocking smile. 'You see, I'm learning the error of my ways. Which brings me to another subject.'

'What subject?'

'Us,' he stated baldly.

'Did we not agree only a few nights ago that there was no *us*?'

'I think in light of recent developments, we need to revise that view.'

'Recent developments…you mean us having sex? That changes anything, how?'

His hands fisted until his knuckles turned white. 'Are you saying it doesn't?'

A dart of pain arrowed through her. 'You said it yourself, Cesare—the sex has always been mind-blowing between us, but it doesn't form the basis of a sound relationship, let alone marriage. I need more.'

His normally golden features paled. He opened his mouth but, before he could speak, their waiter approached, platters held high. Cesare's gaze remained fixed on hers the whole time the owner fluttered around them in effusive Italian. After a minute, he fell into silence when he realised neither of them paid attention.

The second he left, Cesare rasped, 'And if I'm unable to give you more?'

She shrugged. 'I'll do anything and everything to ensure Annabelle remains healthy and safe. Between us we can plan for one of us to always be with her. I'll make sure that works for any future assignments. But when it comes to you and I, Cesare, unless something changes drastically between us other than the mind-blowing sex, I don't see why we need to stay married. Do you?'

CHAPTER ELEVEN

THEIR SECOND ATTEMPT at breakfast failed. Miserably. Neither of them could summon the words to reassure the *trattoria* owner that it wasn't the food.

When Cesare grimly collected her things and marched her out into the sunlight, Ava was more than ready to leave. Paolo was parked on the kerb, a fact which didn't surprise her one little bit. Cesare was worth billions, after all, which meant he could probably summon his car with a mere thought.

He slid in beside her on the limo's back seat and sent up the partition.

'Ava…'

'Please, can we go and get Annabelle? I want to see my baby.'

His lips compressed for a second. Then he nodded. Pulling his phone from his pocket, he made a call, presumably to his parents. Minutes later he ended the call.

'They've taken her to the zoo. We can collect her from there once we get our things from the apartment.'

'I don't want—'

'Don't worry, I won't force you to have this conversation now. But it will be discussed.'

'What is there to discuss? I won't subject myself to a marriage based on sex.'

'Last night's events suggested differently. Are you sure

you're not refusing to consider us because of another reason?' A shadow of vulnerability echoed through his words.

It took a couple of seconds for her to grasp his meaning. 'You think just because we've discovered you carry a defective gene, I'm taking the opportunity to bail out of a marriage *you* didn't want in the first place? You're unbelievable, Cesare.'

He had the decency to redden. 'So you still maintain your need for a family above everything else?'

'Yes. I want a family, and that's not what you've offered. You've offered distance, secrets and the occasional sex marathon. I want to be needed; I want to be loved. I want you to come to me when you have a problem, not turn to your childhood friend or deal with it alone. God, you don't trust me, not even when it comes to sex.'

He frowned. 'What are you talking about?'

'Last night, in bed…you…you pulled out before you… The first time I thought I'd imagined it. Then you did it again. I don't have to be a genius to work out that the last thing you want is to get me pregnant again!'

He cursed under his breath. 'Why does that surprise you? You got pregnant with Annabelle despite my use of condoms and you being on the Pill.'

'Can't you see what's wrong? Once again, *you've* decided, without asking me how I feel about it.'

'And if we'd had the talk you so desperately craved last night, if I'd laid all my cards on the table, would you still have come to my bed?'

'I guess we'll never know now, because you didn't.'

'*Santa cielo,* I can't believe you're condemning our marriage based on the fact that I won't come inside you!'

Heat engulfed her face and neck. 'You're vile! I'm condemning our marriage because you've never trusted me enough to tell me the things that matter!'

'I've told you everything!'

'How do I know? You didn't even tell me Roberto had

died. I have to drag everything out of you. Well, guess what? That *machismo* thing may be sexy for a while, but it wears thin eventually, especially when you know I'm not a wallflower who's scared of my own shadow. Face it, Cesare. Even though you claim not to, you're still trying to protect me. And it hurts.'

Relief shot through her when she realised they'd reached the apartment. She lunged for the door and was halfway to the lift before Cesare caught up with her.

'Ava, stop—'

Her phone pinged and she pounced on it. Seeing the message, her fury grew. 'For the love of sweet baby meerkats, please tell Agata Marinello you're not going to her son's wedding *before I kill her!*'

In silence, he withdrew his phone from his pocket and tapped in a few keys. 'It is done.' The lift came and he stepped in after her.

Just before the lift shut, her phone pinged again. Her mouth dropped open at the effusive message displayed on her screen.

'*You're going to the wedding?*'

He eyed her with a mixture of triumph and determination.

'*Sì.* I've messed up big time where we're concerned. But I'm owning it now.'

Her heart hammered. 'What does that mean—you're owning it?'

'It means you're not going to get rid of me that easily, *mia bella moglie.*'

When they picked Annabelle up an hour later, Ava had to restrain herself from smothering her child in hugs while Cesare stood a distance away talking to his parents. Her heart tightened when she saw the stricken look on their faces.

As he hugged his mother and shook his father's hand,

she contented herself with holding Annabelle's hand as she was regaled with tales from the giraffe pen and the varied animals she'd become best friends with at the zoo.

In the car, she fought back tears, especially when she caught Cesare's bleak stare.

'How are your parents?'

His haunted gaze connected with hers. 'They didn't know and they'll need time to process it. I've arranged for the specialist to speak to them and I plan to speak to them myself in a few days.'

She nodded and glanced at Annabelle, then blinked back more tears as emotion welled up.

'Mummy! You're not listening.'

'Yes, I am, sweetie. You're telling me how tall the giraffes were.'

'No, I *said* the leopard had *millions and millions* of spots.'

'Oh yes, of course, the leopard…' Her gaze caught Cesare's and her heart tripped at the sheen of tears in his eyes. Pushing aside her own pain, she grasped his hand and felt it tighten around hers.

Her life might have fallen down a rabbit hole, but her reason for living—her daughter—was also Cesare's reason for living. She had no doubt about that now.

They got to Lake Como by mid-afternoon. Although she protested long and hard, Annabelle eventually went down for a nap after a quick swim with Cesare.

Ava immersed herself in the last preparations for the wedding. She chose three of her best cameras, then, after a short contemplation, added the newest camera.

She reached for it and, almost on automatic, clicked onto the pictures of Cesare she'd taken that morning. Pain tightened in her chest as she read the meaning behind his anguish. Without warning, the tears she'd held at bay prickled her eyes. The faster she dashed the tears away, the quicker they fell.

'Ava?'

She stiffened. 'Not now, Cesare. I'm going to need a bit more time to deal with this.'

He came closer. Of course he did. 'You're crying.' His observation sounded hugely pained.

'I suppose you're going to order me to stop.'

'I learned a long time ago that I can't order you to do anything, *cara.* But I would like you to tell me why you're crying.'

'So you can add it to the list of things to protect me from?'

'So we can work through it.'

A bitter laugh scratched her throat. 'Do the words *too little too late* mean anything to you?'

He sat down next to her and every cell in her body reacted to his heat and proximity.

'We haven't reached there yet.' Without warning, he reached out and took the camera from her. Tense silence permeated the living room as he clicked through the pictures. When he'd finished, he turned off the camera and placed it on the large antique table where she'd been working. 'If those pictures moved you to tears, then we're not as irredeemable as you make out.'

Her lips firmed. 'Maybe they were cathartic tears, the *I'm-moving-on* type.'

He reached out and pulled her close, one hand capturing her nape to hold her steady. Tilting her chin with his thumb, he looked deep into her eyes. 'You're hurting for me, for us. And, as much as I would like to take your pain away, I'm learning that it's *your* pain; you have to deal with it. I don't like to see you cry, of course, but don't tell me to walk away when you're hurting.'

She tried to swallow past the huge lump lodged in her throat. 'Stop it, Cesare.'

'Stop what?'

'Stop teasing me with the promise of the man I thought I married. I can't take it.'

A grim smile curved his lips. 'We'll get through this, *cara.*'

Tears surged again. 'I really don't see how.'

'We agreed on a truce on your first day back. I know the past few days have rocked that a little.'

She gave another laugh. 'That's the understatement of the millennia.'

He leaned in and pressed his lips against hers. Heat surged through her, desire drenching her in a heady rush. When he pulled away, she nearly moaned in protest. 'It's strong enough to hold for a little while longer, at least until after the Marinello wedding on Saturday. We'll get away from here, go to the vineyard in Tuscany for a few days, yes?'

The promise of a reprieve, of not having to make a decision one way or the other about the state of her marriage, was one she welcomed, despite the full knowledge that it was only temporary. At Cesare's insistent look, she nodded. 'Yes.'

'*Bene.* I've told Lucia to serve dinner early. She's making your favourite—*fettucine ai funghi.* I'm hoping this time we'll make it past the seeing-but-not-eating stage.'

On cue, her stomach growled. Cesare gave a low laugh and released her. 'You finish up here, I'll go and wake up Annabelle.'

'Okay...wait!'

He turned at the door.

'You were going to give me the information on Tay-Sachs.'

A wary gleam entered his eyes but he nodded. 'We'll look at it together after dinner.'

Her heart hammered as she watched him walk away, his powerful shoulders and tall, streamlined body reminding her just what she stood to lose if she decided to walk away from him.

Confusion crowded her senses, along with the undeniable knowledge that the reason why she was in so much pain was because she'd never really stopped loving Cesare. If anything, the rare glimpses into the man underneath all that control—the man who, despite his brother's rejection, had done everything he could for Roberto—made her love him even more.

Far from what he led her to believe, family meant a lot to Cesare. His brother had meant a lot to him despite their rocky relationship, and she'd seen him remain strong for his parents.

Which meant it was *her* he didn't feel the ultimate connection to.

Would that ever be enough without his love? *What of the alternative?* The thought of never being with Cesare intensified her pain until she couldn't sit still any longer.

Jumping up, she grabbed her oldest camera, a gift from her mother the year before she died. The camera Cesare had given her was worth thousands of euros, but this one was priceless. Every time she used it, she felt closer to the mother who'd believed and championed her desire to be a photographer when her father had scoffed at the idea.

Her mother had protected her against her father's bullying right up until the moment she'd lost her battle against cancer. Ava's devastation had been all the more acute, because with her mother gone, she'd lost not only a parent but an ally and protector. Her father had barely acknowledged her existence, and her brothers had soon followed suit.

For a long time, her camera had been her only companion…until Cesare.

Could she bring herself to let him go? Or would staying to fight, to push for what she wanted only drive him further away?

Shaking her head, she went out onto the terrace and

walked down the jetty. The setting sun hung between the hills, its orange-gold rays a perfect backdrop for the yachts on the lake. The rich vibrancy of Lake Como in summer was a beauty to behold and, even though it didn't soothe her troubled soul, she took several pictures, her fingers clicking automatically.

Hearing voices behind her, she turned. Cesare stood on the edge of the terrace, Annabelle in his arms. Something she said made him laugh and Ava's heart caught at the love she glimpsed in his face. Acting quickly, she snapped a few shots of them. Cesare glanced up, straight into the camera, and the want, the need as his gaze connected with the lens stopped her breath.

She wanted to believe, yearned to trust what she saw in his face. But how could she, when her heart felt ripped to pieces?

'Be warned—our daughter has tasked us to bring back the perfect princess gown. Apparently it has to be purple. With pictures of giraffes on it.'

Ava summoned a smile as she buckled her seat belt. 'At least it's not pink.' She shuddered.

Cesare slammed the door and turned the ignition to the luxury SUV. '*Sì,* that *is* a small mercy. However, I'm at a loss as to where to acquire such a dress.'

'Ah, welcome to the challenges of parenthood.'

He looked worried. 'Seriously, you didn't see the look on her face when she told me what she wanted. I don't think I'll survive if I don't bring her exactly what she wants.'

Despite the despair ravaging her soul, she laughed. 'We'll find something that will please her, I promise. But you didn't have to come shopping with me. I could've sorted this out on my own.'

So far the truce was going well. It had gone slightly wobbly when Cesare had presented her with the dossier containing information on the genetic condition two nights ago. Seeing the stark words in black and white had sent her into another crying jag, one which Cesare had withstood with silent, unwavering support.

Tay-Sachs was a horrible disease, and her heart bled for what Roberto had gone through; what Cesare *could* still go through. Annabelle was less likely to suffer the same fate as Ava wasn't a carrier but she would need monitoring all of her life, a fact that had struck fear anew in Ava's heart.

'What makes you think only women have the right to the *I don't have a thing to wear* line?' His query brought her back to the present.

'Yeah, right. You hate shopping with such a passion that you instruct top designers to send you their collection at the start of the season so you don't have to lift a finger. Which makes me think you're only coming along because…' She paused.

He shot her a heat-filled look. 'You would be right. I'll take any moment I can with you, even if I have to endure a few brain cells committing *hara-kiri* while you shop.'

He joined in when she laughed. 'That is *not* the way to make a girl feel special. But thank you.'

His right hand left the steering wheel, caught hers and brought it to his lips. Heat drenched her and although her heart surged with foolish delight, a part of her clenched in distress. This was the part of the truce that wasn't going so well. By mutually unspoken agreement, they hadn't discussed sex. Or the distinct lack of it. At night, they went to their separate beds, where Ava endured either tortured yearning-for-Cesare dreams or hours of wide-awake craving-Cesare tossing and turning.

Another kiss on the back of her hand recaptured her attention. His darkened eyes told her he was struggling with this part of their truce too.

Unable to dispel the atmosphere, she plucked her shades off the top of her head and slid them on. Not that it helped one iota. 'Let's go.'

She found her dress in an exclusive designer shop in Amalfi. And, despite thinking it impossible, they found the perfect purple gown for Annabelle.

'Those aren't giraffes, *cara,*' Cesare muttered, the worry back in his eyes.

'No, but she loves purple horses just as much. We just have to manage her expectations a little bit.'

His lips firmed as he handed over his platinum card. 'If she threatens to annihilate me with those adorable green eyes, I *will* use you as a human shield.'

'Wow, I never thought I'd see the day when you'd be slayed by a three-year-old.'

'She's almost *four.* And you haven't been watching, *tesorio mio.* I was slayed a long time ago.'

Every single breath whooshed out of her lungs as she stared into Cesare's golden eyes. He stared right back, a vulnerability lingering in his eyes she'd never seen before.

In that single moment, Ava knew she owed it to herself and Annabelle to find a way to make this work—even if it meant accepting less from Cesare.

The Marinello wedding took place in another stunning palazzo on the shores of Lake Como after the official blessing at the Duomo in Amalfi.

Cesare watched his wife, who, in a stunning cream silk gown that bared her arms and back, and hugged her perfect backside, could've been mistaken for the bride, save for the camera slung around her neck. Despite that clunky accessory, she was a bombshell whose figure made his breath catch and his body burn with hunger every time he looked at her.

She was also scarily talented. Her work with the Marinello couple was displayed on a giant screen on the side of the ballroom where the reception was being held, and Cesare watched with pride as the guests effused over the stunning sepia and black and white pictures. Also, despite her threats to cause her bodily harm, Ava had managed Agata Marinello with a skill that left him awestruck. In the same circumstances, he wouldn't have been so kind to the shrill, demanding woman.

Lifting her camera now, she captured another image of the happy couple, then glanced down at the image. Raising her head, her gaze caught his. She tried to smile but he saw her distress. His insides churned.

They'd agreed to talk after the wedding but the back of Cesare's neck tingled with the premonition that time was running out. He had a toast to give—something Agata had sprung on him as they'd left the church—and several acquaintances and the Marinello family to acknowledge before he could reasonably get away.

He glanced Ava's way again. She was crouched, camera poised, as Annabelle and a newly made friend posed in front of her. This time her smile held a joy that made his own lips curve upward.

In the next moment, the alien feeling attacked him again. Sudden hunger clawed at his insides that had nothing to do with sex and everything to do with the unwavering feeling that he needed to act now or lose his wife.

Surging to his feet, he picked up a dainty sterling silver spoon and tapped it against his crystal champagne flute. His speech was a few minutes early but, what the hell. He had more important things to do. When he had everyone's attention, he racked his brain for appropriate words and made a reasonably coherent toast to the happy couple.

Duty done, he stepped from the VIP table and made a beeline for his wife.

'Your first dance is mine, I believe.' He caught her around the waist as the string quartet struck up.

'Cesare, I'm working!'

'I'm the guest of honour. If I choose to dance with the super-talented photographer of this wedding, then this is what I shall do.'

He drew her close, a deep satisfaction welling up as she leaned into him. His body sprang to life, the unique scent of her making him ache.

Pulling her closer still, he teased his lips over her earlobe. 'I can't wait for this thing to be over.'

'It won't be for an hour or so yet. And then there's the evening reception—'

He frowned. 'That is unacceptable.'

She laughed. 'I was going to say I've got most of the pictures I need. Once the bride changes into her evening gown, I'll need a few more shots but, apart from that, I'm done. Agata wants to be the one to take the last picture of them leaving on their honeymoon. I didn't see the harm, so I don't have to stay till the end.'

He exhaled in relief. She heard it and pulled back to stare at him. His breath caught at how beautiful she looked.

'Why the urgency?'

'Other than the fact that you look breathtaking and I'm insanely jealous of any man who looks at you?'

One elegant brow arched. 'Try again.'

He sighed. 'I know we were going to wait until after the wedding to talk but…I've been going crazy not to be able to be with you. I've missed you in my bed.'

Her lips parted on a sigh and his blood rushed forcefully south. She felt his body's reaction and stumbled. He used the excuse to bring her closer and watched her face bloom in a delicate blush.

'I…I thought we were putting everything on hold until Tuscany, including sex.'

'A foolish addendum. The moment we leave here I aim to resolve that.'

A look crossed her face that brought the feeling he'd experienced earlier back.

'And would sex come with strings?'

He frowned. 'What does that mean—*strings?*'

'I mean will you make love to me completely or will you…do what you did in Rome?'

Mild shock went through his body. 'Surely it can't mean that much to you?'

Her face flamed with the heat of a thousand candles, but she held his gaze. 'What if I said it did? What if I told you that when we were married—'

'We're *still* married.' He caught her left hand and, despite his displeasure at her bare fingers, he kissed the knuckle where her wedding ring should be.

She licked her lower lip and fire shot into his groin. 'I meant what if I told you that it's important to me because in that moment, when you lose control in my arms, I feel closest to you? That when you took that away from me I felt as if I've lost you completely? Would that change your mind then?'

Cesare froze. After several seconds, she pulled away. He couldn't find the strength to stop her.

'I thought not.' She left him on the dance floor, walking quickly away.

He didn't get a chance to talk to her again, not for another hour and not until Ava had taken her last picture and it was time to leave.

With Annabelle buzzing from making new friends and chatting incessantly, Cesare was forced to wait until they were back home. The chatter lessened as they drew closer to the villa and, by the time they were home, their daughter's head was lolling to the side.

'She's worn out,' Ava said.

'All day talking about horses and giraffes will do that to a girl. I'll put her to bed.'

'No, let me.'

'Ava…'

She avoided eye contact. 'I'll come and find you when I'm done with her.'

Cesare stood at the bottom of the staircase watching her

walk away. The sinking sensation in his stomach intensified and for a wild second he wanted to rush after them, crush them in his arms and never let go.

Stemming the need, he turned towards his study. He needed to put the decision he'd made in the small hours of this morning into effect. It was the only way to ensure his family's safety. Once he was in possession of all the facts, he'd tell Ava. She would probably argue with him but at least they would talk it through together.

Ten minutes later, he was regretting not having left this phone call till morning.

'I've given you all the pertinent facts.'

He listened and blew out an exasperated breath. 'Yes, I've thought this through. Are you able to make it happen straight away or not?'

The stuttered protests echoing down the line sent a wave of irritation through him. Surging from his desk, he strode to the window, the phone clamped to his ear. 'No, I don't need my head shrunk. I *am* thinking straight. I know exactly what I want and I'm counting on you to make it happen… No, my decision is final…I definitely do not want any more children.'

The pained gasp that sounded behind him was the deadliest sound he'd ever heard. And even before he caught sight of Ava in the doorway, her face paler than he'd ever seen it, he knew he'd lost her.

CHAPTER TWELVE

UNCONTROLLABLE SHUDDERS RAKED through Ava. She couldn't catch her breath and the lack of oxygen made her head swim crazily. She squeezed her eyes, hoping to stem the relentless tide of hopelessness that threatened to drown her.

Even when she heard footsteps in the *salone,* where she'd retreated to, she couldn't move. For several minutes, Cesare stood behind her in silence, his breathing unsteady. Then firm hands settled on her shoulders. She flinched but when she tried to move away, he held on.

'Ava, listen to me.'

'No…' A weak, drained breath puffed out. His fingers tightened momentarily before he let go. She sensed him move away but she was too numb to lift her head.

Seconds later, he returned and held a glass against her lips. 'Drink this,' he commanded.

She caught a whiff of the cognac and jerked away from him. 'Getting drunk, as tempting as it sounds, isn't going to solve what's wrong with us, Cesare.'

'No, but it will help.' Contrition tinged his voice as he sat down beside her. 'It will also calm you long enough to let me explain.'

'What's there to explain? You spoke in English so I don't need anything interpreted—' She stopped as her phone buzzed. She was almost afraid to check the message; afraid that yet another blow would flatten her completely.

He caught her chin between his fingers and swung her to face him. Golden eyes narrowed immediately. 'You've been crying again,' he rasped.

'And this surprises you, why?' she shot back.

'We may drive each other completely insane at the best of times but I've only ever seen you cry once. Your natural reaction tends to be to claw my eyes out.'

'I must be getting soft in my old age.' Her phone let off another ping.

'Come on, Ava. You're clutching your phone. Has something happened? Something other than what you *think* you overheard just now? Tell me,' he demanded.

She tried to free herself. 'Why should I? You want me to share, and yet you don't reciprocate.' She jerked when her phone vibrated for the third time.

He glanced from her phone to her face. 'Who's calling you?'

A terrified breath whooshed out of her. Before she could stop them, her eyes filled with fresh tears. 'I feel as if my life's unravelling,' she murmured, more to herself than to him. From the moment she'd woken up in Rome, she'd felt as if the unstoppable avalanche of heartache she'd been running from was catching up with her—fast. 'Every time I think I have a handle on it, something else slips out of my grasp.'

'Nothing's slipped. *I* haven't slipped. I'm still here.'

'No, you're not. You like to think you're changing but you're still the same—'

'I'm here, Ava, and I'm not going anywhere. Tell me what's going on. Now.'

She shook her head and finally glanced down at her phone. 'The texts are from Nathan. He called me five minutes ago. My father's ill. He's asking for me.'

* * *

Cesare stared down at her bent head, the feeling he'd experienced on and off back in full force. Something wasn't right. It took a moment before he placed his finger on it. His feisty wife was sitting before him with her shoulders bowed, her beautiful skin paler than porcelain. Her fingers fretted with her phone.

The fire seemed to have gone out of her. And it scared the hell out of him.

Setting down the glass containing the amber liquor, he crouched before her. 'What did Nathan say? How bad is your father?'

Her lips tightened for a moment before she spoke. 'The doctors say it's his lungs…it started off as acute bronchitis but it's been complicated by pneumonia. His forty-a-day smoking habit hasn't helped. They don't know if he's going to make it.'

He slid his hands down her arms, thankful that she wasn't pushing him away. The thought that she didn't care enough to do so plagued him. 'Give me the full details and I'll get the best team of doctors to—'

'No. I won't be doing what *you* want, Cesare. Not this time.'

Alarm gripped the back of his neck. 'What do you mean? We're in this together. I'm only trying to help, *tesoro mio.*'

She finally lifted her gaze to his and the cool resignation in their depths stopped his heart. 'No, thanks. I've asked Nathan to find me a flight. There's a taxi coming to take me to the airport in fifteen minutes.'

Shock made him rock back on his heels but he quickly regrouped. 'Cancel the taxi. First of all, you're exhausted from running around at the wedding. We'll have an early night and take the jet tomorrow—'

She pulled away from him and jumped to her feet. 'You're still not listening to me, Cesare. I came downstairs to discuss what was happening between us, but also to say that I'm sorry for putting the burden of my wanting a family on you. It's what I've wanted for longer than I can remember but it wasn't fair to put it all at your feet. I want to be with you and Annabelle more than anything, so I hoped we could find some sort of compromise, but I can see now there's no hope for us, not if you're not willing to let me in even a little bit.'

The rise of hope and its subsequent swift death left him reeling. 'I…*sì,* we can—'

'Do you know why I've always yearned for a family?'

He nodded. 'Because you lost your mother when you were very young.'

'It wasn't just that. After she died, my father stopped seeing me—not that he'd paid me much attention to start with. But it was almost as if I'd ceased to exist in his eyes. When I dared to make myself heard, he would shut me down. Do you know how that feels? Being made to feel invisible? As if nothing I have to say or do matters?'

The icy stream that had drenched his veins solidified. 'Ava, please listen—'

'No, I'm done with controlling men.'

Her fire was back, and for that he was thankful. But he felt the distance between them widening with every second. 'I wasn't trying to control you—'

'Of course you were! *You* decided that Annabelle and I were better off without you, so you withdrew from us. *You* decided that I wasn't strong enough or was too upset to be told that Roberto was sick, and when he died you kept that to yourself, too. And…just now…' She sucked in a deep breath as her voice broke.

Desperate, he reached for her but she pulled away. He shoved his hands into his pockets. 'You didn't hear the full story just now. Let me explain.'

'I'm exhausted, Cesare. My father isn't an easy man to deal with at the best of times, and I seriously doubt he's had a sudden personality transplant, which means my visit is going to be a difficult one. I'd rather not use what little strength I have arguing with you.'

He pushed his fingers through his hair, anxiety and a previously unplumbed depth of fear coursing through him. If he let her walk out of here, would he ever see her again?

She's leaving Annabelle in your care. That counts for something.

With everything in him screaming to do otherwise, Cesare stepped back. 'Cancel the taxi, *cara.* Rest for a few hours before you make the trip. Paolo will drive you and the jet will be at your disposal. I'm sorry, but I'll have to insist on that. I won't let you travel while you're exhausted.'

His heart sank even lower when she merely shrugged and looked away.

He prowled the hallway, his eyes darting to the stairs, even though Ava had long gone to bed. He gave a short bark of laughter at the irony. Had it been only two weeks ago that he'd tried to stop her from returning? And now he wanted to do the reverse because everything inside him rebelled against letting her go.

He stopped in his tracks, stunned all over again by the feelings coursing through him. He could storm upstairs, articulate them to her, but he risked her thinking it was another controlling ploy.

He had to let her go and hope he would get her back. Barring that…

Clamping down on the roiling emotions tearing through him, he strode into the living room. The discarded glass containing the cognac stood on the coffee table.

Picking it up, he knocked it back and sank onto the sofa. Fire and fear coursed a jagged path through his chest. The bottom of the glass mocked him.

Hell, he deserved more than mockery. To think that when he finally recognized his feelings, knew just what the woman he'd married meant to him, he couldn't tell her because he was too damned scared of losing her…

He tossed the glass onto the wooden table, saw it crack in two and barely gave a damn. Resting his head against the chair, he gritted his teeth against the need to do *something.*

It took the better part of an hour to accept that he could do nothing. Nothing but wait until Ava was ready to listen.

Cesare jerked awake and surged to his feet. The room was in semi-darkness. At some point someone—most likely Lucia—had drawn the curtains and left a couple of table lamps burning. Without consulting his watch, he knew it was very late.

Probably too late...

He wasn't sure exactly what had woken him but a feeling in the pit of his stomach sent him rushing from the room.

How arrogant of him to believe he could secure Ava's forgiveness just by telling her he'd been trying to protect her. *Dio,* how stupid was he?

He'd wounded his wife badly; he knew that now. But the thought of her walking away from him made him want to grab her and hold on as tight as ever.

He took the stairs three at a time. When his knock went unanswered, he pushed open her bedroom door. Her suite was empty. Fear clutching his soul, he rushed down the stairs, bellowing Lucia's name. He nearly collided with her as she emerged from the kitchen with one of the other maids in tow.

'Where is she?' he demanded.

The look she shot him was a cross between worry and disapproval. 'Signora di Goia? The taxi came for her an hour ago.'

A rush of blackness momentarily blinded him. 'What exactly did she say?'

The young maid answered. 'Nothing. She went to check on the *piccolina,* then come downstairs with her bag.'

He told himself to calm down, to think rationally. His inner voice just mocked him.

Returning to his study, he threw himself into his chair and clutched his head.

Cesare tried a mere half minute to talk himself out of it before he reached for his phone. His call went straight to voicemail. One minute later he tried again. After half a dozen tries, he left his first message.

Two hours later, doing everything to stem his terror, Cesare tried again. When Ava's husky tone instructed him to leave a message, he said the only thing he could think of.

An eternity later he ended the call and curled himself into the sofa, clutching his phone. Over and over, he told himself weeping was for the weak.

The good thing about travelling with one small bag was that she managed to clear Customs within minutes. The bad thing was that the temperature in London, even in early August, was rainy and damp enough to warrant a sweater. Shivering, she contemplated stopping to get one but quickly discarded the idea and headed for the exit.

Her hired car was ready and waiting. Twenty minutes later, she was driving down the familiar route towards the home she'd grown up in.

It was late, long past midnight, when she drew up in front of the semi-detached house on the outskirts of Southampton. The light in the upstairs window in what had been Nathan's room reassured her somewhat.

Quaking inside, she walked up the short pathway and pressed the bell.

Silence echoed after the jangling of the bell faded away, and then she heard feet thudding on the stairs.

Nathan's eyes lit on her. 'Ava, you came.' He stepped forward and enveloped her in a bear hug.

Surprised by the gesture, she drew in a shaky breath. 'Did you think I wouldn't?'

'I wasn't sure. You just said you'd think about it and then ignored my calls.'

'Is he awake? I need to speak to him.' Before she lost what little courage she had.

Nathan's eyebrows shot up and he checked his watch. 'Now?'

'Please, Nathan, it's important.'

He frowned, his brown eyes studying her face. 'What's happened, Ava?'

I think my marriage may be over and I want to know if I have any family left at all.

A hacking cough came from above and continued for a full minute. When it ended, Ava heard painful heaving as her father tried to catch his breath.

Nathan's expression was pained. 'He's been having a hard time of it. It's worst at night—' He stopped when the phone rang.

Curious as to who would be calling so late, she stared questioningly at Nathan.

'It's your husband. He's been calling every ten minutes for the last two hours. Should I?' He indicated the phone.

She nodded, waited for Nathan to answer, then held out her hand. 'Hello, Cesare.'

'Ava, are you all right?' His voice was strained but the solid sound of his voice soothed a wounded, devastated place in her heart.

'Yes.'

'*Dio grazie.*' The mingled relief and pain in his voice made her heart clench. 'I'm glad you're safe but if you disappear on me like this again, I swear I won't be responsible for my actions,' he tagged on in a fierce undertone.

'I needed to do this, Cesare.'

'Just…' He stopped and inhaled audibly. 'I understand why you need to do this. I was the same with Roberto, even though he pushed me away. I told myself it didn't matter but every time…it hurt.'

'But you never gave up. You never stopped fighting for your family.'

The small silence made her heart stutter.

'No, I didn't. And I never will. I'll never stop fighting for us, Ava.'

This time her heart stilled. 'What are you saying?'

'Have you seen your father?'

'No, not yet. I just got here.'

'Before you do, I want you to know that, no matter what happens, I'll be here. Annabelle and I, we will be your family from now on. You never have to feel invisible or unwanted. And you don't have to settle for less than you want.'

Her grip tightened on the handset. 'Are you…do you know what you're saying, Cesare, because if this is just about protecting me—'

'Protecting you from pain and rejection will always be non-negotiable and, yes, I know I've caused a lot of it. But this is also about a lot more, *tesoro.*' He breathed a sigh of impatience. 'I don't want to do this over the phone, Ava. I want to see you. Are you coming back?'

'Do you want me to come back, Cesare?'

A disbelieving huff echoed down the phone. '*Sì,* of course I do! You are my wife, the mother of my child. I would be with you right now if you hadn't asked to do this alone. See? I'm learning.'

Her heart tripped at the fervent possessiveness and need in his voice. Foolish hope bloomed in her chest. 'You have to do a whole lot more if we're to get through this, Cesare.'

'I know. But…but don't give up on us…*per favore…*'

Her heart tightened along with her grip on the phone. 'I…I…'

'Don't say anything just yet. Did you listen to my messages?' She heard the touch of vulnerability in his voice and wondered at it.

'No, not yet.' She hadn't had time to turn her mobile back on.

'Okay. I've sent the jet for you. It will be at your disposal when you're ready to return but it would help if the pilot knew when that would be so he can file a flight plan.'

She smiled at the tactic, but the smile slowly faded when the enormity of what she had to do settled on her shoulders. 'Give me a day with my father.'

'Of course. I'll call tomorrow.'

She didn't miss the implacable nature of that promise. Hanging up, she turned to find Nathan hovering in the kitchen doorway.

'I'm going up,' she said.

He nodded.

Ava entered her father's room and found him propped up against pillows, his face coated in sweat despite the coolness of the night. His eyes were shut, but she knew he was awake because he clutched an oxygen mask over his nose and mouth.

'Hello, Dad.'

His eyes slowly opened. For a moment, a light, reminiscent of the stern figure he'd been, blazed in his eyes. Then slowly it faded. He pulled the mask from his face.

'Caroline…' he said weakly.

One hand attempted to lift off the bed, but feebly fell back down. Going to him, Ava took his hand, tears clogging her throat as she saw how withered, how frail he'd become.

The ogre who'd terrorised her childhood was now nothing more than a shadow of his former self. A shadow who'd mistaken Ava for his dead wife.

His watery eyes dimmed then another round of coughing interrupted whatever he'd been about to say. When it was over, he could do nothing more than inhale the oxygen and try to get his breath back.

'Don't try to speak, Dad. It's all right.'

Tears clouded her eyes and the pain she'd carried with her for so long slowly disappeared.

What her father had done in the past didn't matter any

more. Hope flared in her heart. She and Cesare had a lot to work through but Ava had hope—a hope that grew stronger with each passing moment.

Leaning down, she kissed her father's leathery cheek. 'I love you, Dad. I'm here for you. Sleep now.'

A laboured sigh escaped him and his eyes shut.

As she went downstairs and entered the kitchen, she activated her phone and saw twenty-six missed calls from Cesare. Before she could replay any of them, Nathan appeared with a cup of tea.

'Is everything all right?'

She nodded. 'Dad's sleeping.'

'I meant with you and your husband.'

Surprised, she looked up and caught Nathan's uncomfortable look. 'I know we weren't here for you when you were young. I guess that's why you didn't invite any of us to your wedding…'

'I didn't think any of you would come.'

He nodded. 'For what it's worth, I've missed you. I think Cameron and Matthew have too.' He looked away, shamefaced. 'Growing up, it was just easier to take Dad's lead, you know? It's no excuse, I know, but…heck, Ava, I'm sorry.'

Setting her cup down, she placed her hand over his. 'It's okay, Nathan.' At his sceptical look, she pressed on. 'It really is. I've made my peace with the past, and with Dad. At some point in the future, I'll try and reconnect with Cameron and Matthew too. I'd like Annabelle to meet her grandfather and uncles eventually.'

Nathan nodded, rose and touched her shoulder on his way out. 'I'm glad you're here,' he said gruffly. 'Goodnight.'

With tears clogging her throat, Ava abandoned her tea and went upstairs. After undressing, she slipped into her childhood bed. She felt comfort at being surrounded by the things she'd grown up with. Acting on a faint memory, she pulled open her bedside drawer. There it was, an old picture of her mother she'd kept even though her father had got rid of every last trace of her after her death.

Caroline Hunter had the same red hair as Ava and, despite her frail appearance, there was strength in her eyes that resonated within Ava.

She hadn't been able to beat cancer but, while she'd been alive, her mother had fiercely protected her daughter. Ava knew deep in her heart her mother would've done *anything* for her, protected her from any harm.

In his own high-handed way, wasn't that what Cesare had been trying to do? She might not agree with the way he chose to do it, but could she really condemn him for it? If their roles were reversed, what would she have done?

Ava gasped in the darkness as clarity shone beacon-bright. Pulling back the covers, she rushed out of her room and hammered on her brother's door.

'Nathan, do you have a computer I can use?'

'Now?'

She spent the rest of the night researching and by morning her decision was made.

Taking a deep breath, she took her phone out of her bag. Ignoring the countless messages that beeped at her, she searched until she found the right number.

It was answered on the third ring. *'Ciao?'*

'Celine, it's Ava. I'm sorry to disturb you so early.'

'Don't worry, life's too short for sleep anyway, right?' Her voice was light but Ava sensed the question behind her flippancy.

She cleared her throat and glanced out of the window overlooking the small, overgrown garden. 'I need your help.'

'Sure, anything you want,' Celine said.

With another deep breath, she outlined what she wanted.

'Ava, this is a huge step. Have you talked to Cesare about this?'

Guilt momentarily assailed her. She bit her lip and forged on. 'I need to do this. For us.'

'But…'

'Celine, please. Just help me.'

The other woman sighed. 'If your mind is made up—'

Ava rang off after she'd scribbled down the phone numbers of two reputable Harley Street practices. She rang the first one at nine. The doctor she requested was on holiday. She rang the second number, shamelessly name-dropped and was immediately put through.

After she explained what she wanted, the doctor made an appointment to see her the next day.

She spent the rest of the day with her father. He looked much better and even recognized her this time. In halting words often interrupted by acute coughing fits, he tried to explain why he'd treated her so badly.

Her mother had fallen sick almost immediately after Ava had been born. Irrational as he knew it to be, her father had secretly blamed her for losing his wife.

'It's not an excuse, but every time I saw you I was reminded of Caroline.'

Tears clogged Ava's throat. 'I'm sorry.'

'Don't apologise. What I did was wrong. I pushed you away. I have no right to be, but I'm glad you're here.'

She left in a less sad mood than she'd arrived in.

Cesare might not love her but he cared about her enough to want her to return. Her heart tightened in pain at the thought that he might never love her as much as she loved him but whatever he felt for her…it was enough.

The drive to London took just over two hours and, all through the consultation, Ava told herself she was doing the right thing.

When the doctor finished talking through the procedure, she took a deep breath and signed the papers.

'How long will it be before I can go home?'

'If everything goes according to plan, you should be able to leave us in the morning.'

She could be back in Italy by nightfall tomorrow. The thought of seeing Cesare and Annabelle again sent a soft sigh of happiness through her.

Her phone pinged and she realised she'd never got round to listening to Cesare's messages the night before.

She scrolled through and pressed the first one.

When the nurse appeared to prep her for her procedure, she was stunned by the look on her patient's face.

Cesare cursed the traffic leading up into Regent Street, and resisted the urge to lean on his horn. Instead he made do with a string of coarse expletives as his heart lurched at what lay ahead of him.

What had she done? *Santa Maria,* what had his Ava done?

He'd already been on his way to the airport when Celine had rung in a panic. When he'd learnt exactly what his fiery, reckless, exceedingly breathtaking wife was planning, Cesare's blood ran cold.

Even as he sat here, uselessly inching his way forward in the godforsaken traffic, he could barely fathom it.

He gave into the urge and leaned on the horn. Rude gestures greeted his action, but he kept his hand in place until the driver in front crept forward enough for him to squeeze through.

Ten excruciatingly long minutes later, he slammed on the brakes and sprinted into the reception of the Harley Street practice.

When he announced himself, the receptionist's eyes widened.

'What room is my wife in?' he barked.

With a shaky finger, she pointed down the hall.

Cesare had never known such fear in his life as he skidded towards the door.

Dio, please let him not be too late.

Inside, Ava sat on the bed, her lovely hair tucked under a gruesomely ugly surgical hat. Her face was pale, but she wore the widest smile he'd ever seen as she pressed the button on her phone.

She hadn't seen him yet, her focus firmly on the phone. Cesare's breath caught as his voice echoed around the sterile room.

Ava, I know I've wronged you in the most hurtful way. But I am only mortal, cara, and this mortal loves you more than the fates will ever give me time on this earth to express. I promise to spend the rest of my life making amends, to giving you the family you've never had, if you let me. I will also let you go if that is what you ask of me. But please let me know you are safe, amore mio. I beg you.

'I can say it again in person, if you prefer.'

Her head jerked towards him, her stunningly gorgeous green eyes locking on his. Her smile slammed into his heart and he stopped breathing.

'*Cesare,* what are you doing here?'

Dio, he loved this woman. Loved her with a power that made his world tilt on its axis every time he looked at her.

'What am I doing here? Shouldn't *I* be asking you that? *What the hell are you thinking, doing this to me?*'

Despite her smile, her eyes rolled. 'I knew it was only a matter of time before it all became about you.'

She held out a hand to him. He swallowed and sent a silent prayer of thanks.

On seriously shaky legs, he approached the bed and took her hand. Warmth flowed from her. With another sigh of relief, he raised her hand to his mouth.

'Tell me you haven't gone through with the procedure—?'

'Not yet—'

'Not ever!' Several emotions coursed through him. He tried to keep it under control but they continued to shake right through him. 'Ava, why in God's name would you do this?'

'For the same reason you've been trying to find a way for us to be together. Last week in Rome before Celine called, what were you really going to talk to me about?'

'I was going to tell you there would be no divorce. I had no immediate solution but I was willing to do whatever it took to keep you and Annabelle in my life.'

'So you were ready to find a way to give me what I wanted.' He nodded. 'Well, I'm ready to do what it takes too. This is an equal opportunities marriage.'

'Yes, but this isn't your problem, *cara*. The Tays-Sachs aside, I let what happened with Roberto and Valentina shame me into suppressing what I wanted until it was almost too late. You and Annabelle are the most precious things in my life and I nearly lost you both.' He stopped, his breath shuddering out. 'I've accepted that I didn't handle things with Roberto very well and that I couldn't help him when he was in pain. It's something I have to live with.'

'Wherever he is, I'm sure he's at peace now,' she said.

He nodded. 'And I'll make peace with it some day. But not at the cost of my family. And not at the cost of this condition. I cannot…I won't let you take the burden on your shoulders.'

Although her heart lifted, a hint of shame stung her. 'I'm not without fault myself. What you said, about me putting you front and centre of everything I wanted in a family… you were right. After my mother died, dreaming of a perfect family was what kept me together. I was like one of those women you see sitting alone in a coffee shop, watching couples go past and doodling her imaginary husband and children's names on a napkin, only I used my camera. Then you appeared and I didn't stop to think of what *you* wanted…my whole focus was on making my dream come true. When you didn't immediately fall in line with my plans, I began to despise you for it.' She looked deep into his eyes, her heart laid bare. 'I'm sorry.'

With a deep groan, he pulled her tighter, kissed her until they were both out of breath. 'I'll forgive you if you give me a lifetime to make amends to you and to Annabelle for all the time I've lost with you.'

Her heart began to race. 'A lifetime?'

'*Sì,* non-negotiable.' He looked around the sterile room. 'And, speaking of non-negotiable, you accept that this is out of the question, don't you?'

'No. You've sacrificed enough for this family—'

'By walking away? By leaving you to care for our child on your own? How is that caring?'

'I was so hung up on finding a perfect family that I refused to see you were battling serious demons. I wanted you to be perfect for me and I had no right to do that. And the conversation I overheard on the phone, that was you arranging to have a medical procedure, wasn't it? You were willing to deny yourself a chance to become a father again just so you could hang onto us. What's that if not sacrifice?'

He clutched her hand tighter. 'I was going to discuss it with you first. I wasn't ready to give you up. Despite what I said in that message, I'm not and I never will be. But I don't want to risk passing this gene on to another child.'

She leaned forward and kissed him, and Cesare felt his heart stutter crazily.

'So let me do this. For us. It's time for me to lighten your load.'

'Absolutely not. You're not getting your tubes tied and I don't even want to hear the word hysterectomy.'

'Cesare—'

'It's out of the question!'

'You know, I'm sure there's a rule that says you can't yell at the patient.'

He didn't know whether to kiss her or shake the living

daylights out of her. He contented himself with pulling the ugly cap off her head and stroking his fingers through her gorgeous fiery hair. 'Then you need to be nice to me.'

She frowned. 'What do you mean—be nice to you?'

'When Celine called and told me what you were planning, I called the doctor and altered the arrangement a little bit. No, don't death-stare me. We will discuss this first like a normal married couple. And then we will agree to do things my way.'

'You're having a vasectomy.' She didn't frame it in a question because she saw the resolution in his eyes.

'*Mio bella moglie,* this is something I have thought long and hard about.'

'I'll think about it, too, if you repeat the message you left on my phone.'

'Which one?'

'The one that says how you feel about me.'

'They all say how I feel about you. Each and every one of them ends with me telling you how much I love you.'

Her mouth dropped open. Unable to resist, he kissed her.

'Oh God, please say that again,' she whispered against his lips when they parted.

Her helpless plea stopped his heart. In fact, Cesare was sure he hadn't taken a complete breath since he'd walked into the room. The enormity of the sacrifice she'd almost made swept him away.

Tears prickled his eyes and he squeezed his jaw tight to stem the flow. But he knew he'd failed when he felt wetness on their entwined fingers.

'I love you, Ava *mia*. I'll spend the rest of my life proving how much I love you.'

'I love you too, so much my heart bursts with it.'

Ava felt her heart lift at the complete adoration in her husband's eyes. Tears fell freely from her eyes as she basked in Cesare's love. When he leaned over and brushed them away more fell.

Gently, he cupped her face and smoothed his thumbs over her cheeks. Then, leaning forward, he kissed her eyes closed. '*Amore,* don't cry. I hate seeing you cry.'

'Get used to it. I intend to cry very often.'

'But only tears of happiness, *sì?*' he asked desperately.

'Maybe. I can't promise that any more than I can promise not to turn into a scream-with-happiness girl.'

'Whichever you decide to be, I'll be by your side, loving you.'

Ava's heart leapt and basically did crazy things that would've scared the doctors had they known about it. Cesare kissed her again and kept on kissing her until the nurse found the courage to knock on the door. The almost indecent scene she found made her hesitate before giving a delicate cough.

'The doctor's ready for you now, Mr di Goia. If you'd like to come with me, please?'

Ava grabbed him when he started to move away. 'Sorry, change of plan. We're both leaving.'

Cesare frowned. 'Ava?'

'If I'm not having the procedure, neither are you. We'll find another way. Together. Yes?'

His eyes shone with love as he nodded. 'Together.'

EPILOGUE

'ARE YOU ALL right?' Cesare whispered in her ear as they watched the old, gaily painted SUV travel slowly up the driveway.

'No,' Ava whispered back.

A deep masculine laugh caressed her lobe. 'Why can't you be like other women and say, *Yes, I'm fine, thanks*?'

She grinned and faced him. 'Where's the fun in that?'

'For a start, it would cause me less heartache.' He caught her fingers in his hand and kissed the di Goia wedding emerald he'd placed back on her finger the day he'd come for her in London.

She placed her hand over his heart and delighted in his hitched breath as it skipped a beat. 'I see what you mean.' When she went to remove it, he placed his hand over hers. He looked over her head at the advancing car.

'Do you think they'll like us?' His voice was tinged with anxiety.

Ava marvelled at the change in the strong, self-possessed man she'd renewed vows with six months ago. Cesare hadn't lost any of his endless self-assurance, but he'd become more open, more in touch with his feelings in a way that made her love him even more than she'd ever dreamed possible.

They'd agreed to go ahead with Cesare's vasectomy—he'd been too tortured by the idea of passing on his Tay-

Sachs gene to any future children—but only after Ava had insisted on gene therapy and a rather large sperm bank deposit. The idea of a vasectomy reversal had also remained firmly on the table.

So, whatever the future held, they had options.

For now, though, one decision they'd made together had come to fruition.

She leaned up and planted a swift adoring kiss on his lips. 'Cesare, the babies are six months old. The likelihood that they'll fall in love with you at first sight is very, very strong. Trust me.'

The vehicle stopped and two women alighted. Cesare, with his arm still around her, stepped forward to greet them. The moment he smiled, they melted.

Dear heaven, even nuns weren't immune to her husband's charm.

Smiling too, she descended the stairs and greeted the two nuns who ran the orphanage in Amalfi. After introductions were made, Ava led them into the *salone* before, heart thumping wildly, she brought herself to glance into the twin car seats.

There, lying sweetly beneath their blankets, were their son and daughter. Their approval for adoption had gone through two weeks ago. Her heart skipped in joy as *Suor* Rosa pushed the first seat gently towards her.

'Here is Maria. Her afternoon naps are very precious to her, so be warned.'

Suor Chiara smiled and handed the second seat to Cesare. 'And this is Antonio.'

Cesare glanced into the car seat and his eyes misted. She knew he was remembering Roberto.

'He's the quieter of the two, but he has a very strong will,' *Suor* Chiara said.

Cesare gazed down silently at his son, then lifted a hand to brush the baby's cheek. 'He will grow into a handsome man, just like his uncle.'

'No. Just like his father,' Ava murmured to him.

He smiled at her, a smile so filled with love her heart turned over.

An hour later, the nuns left. Ava stared at Cesare and he returned her look with an equally bewildered expression. 'Three children. Are we mad?' he asked.

'Quite possibly,' she said, laughing. 'So, shall we show them to their room?'

Inhaling audibly, he nodded. They picked up the seats and were barely in the hallway when an exclamation of delight sounded behind them. They turned as Annabelle flew towards them. 'The babies are here!'

Cesare stopped and introduced his daughter to her siblings.

Annabelle lifted wide eyes to her. 'Mummy, can I go show them my room? I'll share my toys with them, I promise. So can I? Can I?'

'That's a brilliant idea, sweetheart. I'm sure they'll love that.'

Annabelle whooped. Over the top of her head, Cesare's eyes met hers. His smile blew her clean away.

'I love you,' he murmured.

'Right back at you, *caro*,' she echoed.

* * * * *